It's You

D.Bunyan

Chapter One

At the question he looked up from his pint and wondered for a moment, only a fleeting whisper of a moment, what he was doing there. They were his people of course, his crowd, tethered together from university by little unflattering stories, little histories that got more irrelevant and agonizing as the years went by. To be fair, he suffered the least from these small ritual humiliations as, over the years, (eight was it now?) he'd been cautious, even when drunk. However it left them unsatisfied and when the opportunity presented itself they dug in further.

'Yes,' he replied, successfully removing any apology from his voice, 'it's costing a bloody fortune.' Why deny it, they would all be there, totting it all up as they filled themselves with his champagne. He gave a few details hoping to let himself off the hook.

'Yes, round the world tickets, no, can't remember exactly how much. We can just hop on and hop off as the fancy takes us. We'll probably be away for a year. I, *we*, have some savings but it won't be five stars all the way.' All eyes were on him now; he saw the questions lining up.

'Well I'd prefer to steer clear of the main tourist haunts, my Taj Mahal is a rainstorm in Kerala but I'm sure we'll be ticking a few boxes from, you know, '100 places to see before you die." It did the trick, who could resist? And there was a burst of opinion on the world and what to have seen before taking leaving of it. He sat back from his tense crouch and finished his pint in a long slow swig. There was a puddle of beer on the table in front of him and he concentrated on drawing it into shapes noticing with relief that the conversation seemed to be moving on. When he looked up he saw James looking at him, but the man's eyes flicked away instantly and again that quiver of uncertainty ran through him.

'Your round Dave.'

They were wedged into a nook, cosy but hard to negotiate out of and the table had to be bumped a few inches forward and knees twisted sideways but eventually he was at the bar, staring blankly at the optics, not really minding how long it took to serve him.

Tennis was his racquet game of choice, the chance of a breeze and a breather between shots but squash was edgier, more business than pleasure. He wondered if the boy had come into school just for their game as by this time of the year most of his year would have summer jobs. If he had it would have been decent of him, though unnecessary.

That Thursday David lost badly, floundering for the ball, gasping for air. He was dripping as they left the court and glancing in the mirror was embarrassed how red his face was. So far he and Mark had been pretty equally matched, they'd been playing together for six months but today was different, he was exhausted. It was almost the end of June and an exhausted expression on a member of staff's face was by now a mark of their commitment over the year. This, however, was the real thing and he quickly splashed cold water onto his face to reduce the colour. There should be no question that the games should not continue next year, the boy's availability for a weekly game was useful. It would be difficult finding a replacement, he certainly didn't want to play any of the fit PE staff, but a succession of defeats might be humiliating.

'Had the edge on me there,' he said cheerfully, showing

his defeat was no big deal was suddenly important.

'I'll go easier if you like sir.'

'No, no keep the pace, I'll just have to become less of a stranger to the gym, I'm not taking to my bath chair yet. Carry on in the autumn term eh?'

'Course.'

'I need to get a move on now though, DIY stuff to do at home, d'you want a lift?'

David turned to smile at him. Of course he wanted a lift with sir; door to door service, decent music.

'Yeah, thanks.'

The warm evening air they stepped into caused an unexpected rush of pleasure and almost resulted in him giving the boy a friendly, no hard feelings pat on the shoulder in lieu of his defeat. As they walked side by side down the path from the gym to the school car park David eyed the boy up out of the corner of his eye. He seemed a little bigger than he recalled, a little wider across the shoulders. And taller: had he had a sudden growth spurt? 'Get real Ashbourne' he chided himself, 'he's bigger, fitter and younger than you.' As if to highlight the age gap further, the sound and image of a wallpaper scraper, tearing into beige and brown swirls broke in and he pleaded with himself for one small goddam *break* to enjoy the walk, the air, the quiet, undemanding company before his second job started.

They hit the usual build up of traffic on the slip road to the bypass and David looked at the boy for a couple of seconds as they crawled along, expecting the usual eager smile but he stared ahead, slumped in his seat.

'Tired?'

'Mmmm.'

David turned off the chattering radio, 'a bit of hush OK?'

'Yeah, course.'

He slowed back down to a crawl after the bypass which had required a bit of concentration and he wondered where the usual schoolboy chat had gone. 'C'mon, c'mon', he thought, 'entertain me', anything to stop the cacophony of

5

today's lessons still churning round his head and the scraper, scraping off that paper he'd managed to live with quite happily until she had pointed out how awful it was.

'Can't remember if I've ever asked you, who do you support?' God, how many times had he asked that, his standard entrée before a pep talk? He was so tired he couldn't even add the slight show of interest he usually managed.

'No one.'

'Me neither. Cricket?' He winced inwardly, must have asked that him before.

'I'm not interested in following sport.'

Neither was he but he managed some faux enthusiasm for sport in the pub after a few pints. The boy clearly hadn't yet found the need to be phoney in order to fit in. 'What are you doing this summer?' David battled on, these lifts were usually far more amusing.

'Working in the garden centre, the one I work in on Saturday.'

'Saving up for driving lessons I remember.'

'Yup.'

'Started them yet?'

'Yes.'

'Enjoying them?'

'Yup.'

'Getting a car when you pass?'

'Dunno.'

'Cheap to buy but not to run, the insurance, for your age group, it's incredibly expensive.' Fuck, why did he say that? For once couldn't he stop being Mr Wordly Wise and widening the gap even further between them; it hadn't been long since his own insurance cost the earth. He glanced sideways again and his eyes caught the deep concertinaed white folds of the boy's shirt disappearing into sharp creases at his waistband as he sat slumped in the seat. It brought an unexpected image of thick icing sugar to mind. Get the light just right and it could make an enigmatic photo; what was underneath, a body or a cake? Cake, Christ, he had cake on the brain. There had been a small contretemps over the ridiculous prices of the wedding cakes Clare had shown him last night. Luckily he'd pulled back before he got too annoyed and insisted the decision was entirely hers. Then on cue The White Horse came into view, another error of judgement on the road to matrimony. He taught two of the manager's kids and he had been offered a substantial discount on the hall hire rate, not that he could take it in his position. It would have been fine though, a really nice recent refurb but Clare had scoffed; 'It's a *pub*!' He gave his victorious opponent another sideways glance, a smooth forearm emerged from the loose rolls of his shirt sleeve, his hand tightly grasping the handle at the top of his rucksack. He certainly didn't seem his usual relaxed self and unable to stop himself he took another glance. Was the boy's face getting thinner or was it the contrast with his neck which seemed to be filling out his collar more than David remembered; was he using weights? A lot of the others certainly were. Today the boy's hair was sticking up in casual chunks; he had watched him scrunching it up in the mirror before they left the changing rooms. Hadn't it been a bit longer and floppier last week? He couldn't quite remember. Did he like it? Yes, it was OK. Would something like that suit him? It might but the initial ridicule wouldn't be worth it. The boy continued to stare fixedly ahead but was clearly conscious of David's look, taking his lower lip in his top teeth, fiddling with his rucksack zip. After a further five minutes, the silence hung less easily. Why, here he was in the car with a bright, young thing; what's happening? What are they talking about these days? What music are they listening to? What do they do at the weekends? He could start by mentioning what *he* was doing that weekend; DIY mainly and then make a bit of a deprecatory joke about it being arguably the chief leisure pursuit for his age group and how tired he was of it. The boy would say 'why do it then?' disdainfully, and he would be obliged to explain it was all

7

about adding to the value of his house so he could move up the property ladder while all the time desperate to portray himself as youthful, free spirited and unconventional. You are a schoolteacher, driving a small hatchback home to scrape wallpaper of the walls of your three bed executive you pathetic fool, he explained to himself. OK, ask a couple of family type questions and leave it there. Come to think of it he knew very little about him apart from where he lived, but that was enough to know that there wasn't much money coming into the house. He remembered him mentioning that his father had died when he was small, he had a sister and a dog. It would be fun to see the dog, he loved dogs but he always held back, there was this invisible pupil teacher line, the boundary, he was quite unable to step over it, even to ask to see a dog. They were nearing Mark's estate and his silence was now unnerving and frankly disappointing. Give up; just stick to teacher questions to fill in the last five minutes.

'So, chosen your urban metropolis for the summer assignment?'

'Sao Paulo, the contrast between life in the favelas and the rich neighbourhoods, water, sewage, electricity, how the city is trying to improve conditions in the favelas.'

'Great! South America makes a change, everyone usually chooses India. I look forward to reading it.' Blimey, not even the end of term and he'd worked out what he was doing. A couple of potential conversation topics came to mind but he rejected them as an increasingly depressing sensation of being staff, old, past it and dull took a grip. He rehearsed his goodbye, something about next term, about how he'd see him then and how he'd keep himself in trim over the summer in anticipation of continuing with the squash, then ending with his best wishes for a good summer. But it stank. He swung the car off the tree-lined road of large Victorian semis onto Mark's estate and slowed for the speed bumps, great hunks of battered concrete yet to be replaced with the more comfortable rubber affairs. He hit one too fast and it caught his exhaust.

'Shit.'

The typical wide pavements and verges of the 60's estate bemused him. Why so much space? Why so much grass? Rich people had lots of grass, they must have grass. Then his favourite bit; the bold and brassy right to buy properties. Huge gateposts supported lions' heads guarding four by fours parked on paved-over gardens. Plastic Corinthian columns held up tiny porches sheltering front doors with bright plastic stained-glass panels. It was Regency living from the local DIY superstore. These splendid exemplars of Thatcher's legacy were often attached to, and holding their own beside, the dead façades of houses set in car graveyards and occupied by failure. It was the latter, and their occupants, that made him inexplicably just the tiniest bit guilty about leaving the boy there and driving away to his very nice, safe executive estate. The city's shanty, he mused, with extra grass. *You snob*, he rebuked himself quickly, it was easy to knock now, it must have seemed luxurious when it was built, everyone would have wanted to live there.

A few months ago after dropping Mark off, he'd stopped to take some photos from his car and then driven off smartly. The more spivved up and therefore photogenic the dwelling the more daunting he assumed its occupants would be and at heart he was a coward. None of Year 10 had been to the town which illustrated their text book so David had taken it upon himself to photograph the diverse housing mix of the city they lived in. His photos matched the book's examples but the class had buzzed as they recognised the places they knew. Their opinions had amused him, a few lived on 60s estates and they were divided on its attributes. David reminded them; room for children to play and cycle around safely, big gardens and generous room sizes. The builders of his own eighties house had not been so generous; nowhere to store anything, one of the bedrooms was almost impossible to get into now and the car never saw the inside of the junk-filled garage. There was a lot less room to play outside as well, not that they would be bringing up a family there. Photos of the of the eight bedroom 'monsters' at the end of his road impressed them though no one lived in one. 'They all go private' the children explained. The terraced houses around the station were deemed both pokey and sweet but they loved the new flats behind the shopping centre with cute semicircular glass balconies, turquoise railings, a gym and pool.

'No garage! No front lawn! Rip off!' was their judgment of a Georgian townhouse.

'It's on the market for well over a million,' he'd advised them, without adding that the details were currently lying on his kitchen table. 'Not worth it!' they jeered. Most of them lived in a semi which, he begrudgingly admitted to them, met most needs and had been his childhood home too. A couple more turns and he'd be there. They passed a parade of six shops, four were shuttered and unimaginatively grafittied, only a chip shop and corner store still bravely trading. He had taken some photos here too, conscious that someone one day might appreciate his forethought and they would appear in a 'days gone by' series in the local paper, if local papers still existed. A group of teenagers idled outside, none of them were from his school. He imagined they'd bunked off and he thanked some vague deity that he didn't have to teach them. He couldn't imagine Mark having anything to do with them, a bright, sensitive boy, he probably kept himself to himself though he was bound to come across them even if it was only on the bus to school. He saw him sitting at the front, near the driver, maybe getting off a stop too soon or too late, preferring a long walk to taunts and bullying, was that why he always liked a lift? He wanted very much to know that Mark appreciated these lifts for that reason. How could he possibly ask? He glanced sideways at him again, one last attempt before they reached his house. Possibly he was imagining the bullying and whatever novelty a lift home with a member of staff might once have had, it was now well burnt out.

'You've lost a bit of weight haven't you? It shows on your face.' It might at the very least prompt a final short exchange about what he was having for dinner. It didn't. 'A leaner machine eh?' he ploughed on hopelessly, only a few more minutes and they'd be there, 'must be all that heaving compost bags around at the weekend.'

'It's probably because I'm in love,' so soft David barely heard it.

'Ha!' David negotiated a mini roundabout breezily; amused at his confession, flattered that he had told him. So that was it, the poor blighter was lovesick, somewhere, thankfully, he couldn't say he'd been.

'Who is it then, *la belle* Suzanne?' It sounded too teasing, patronising even and he continued with more gravitas, 'I promise, seriously, not to tell, it's safe with me.' I want to be in his confidence, he realised, the slight feelings of rejection during the drive had oddly got to him. There was a pause before Mark spoke, again softly but firmly.

'It's a bloke actually.'

'Oh, *right*,' the merest hesitation he hoped, but it took him completely by surprise.

'*Right*,' he said again, this time hoping his tone conveyed both acceptance and indifference. Why hadn't he guessed? What did it matter anyway? They were silent for the length of Mark's road and David found himself completely at a loss, did he ask who? Is that what you did? Would it sound casual enough? Did his silence infer disapproval?

'It's you actually.'

Thinking back, as he would forever, he realised he must have gone smoothly down through the gears as they approached his house, must have drawn neatly up to the curb, gone into neutral and put the handbrake on but his recollection was always of virtually losing control of the car.

'Thanks,' Mark had flung himself out and disappeared.

There was an open bottle of red on the kitchen table when he got home and he swiftly threw back a large glassful behind Clare's back as she cooked. He stood very still as the wine numbed the bewilderment of the previous half hour and instead of heading for the dining table to make a start on his marking he poured another glass and leaned on the work surface fiddling with the cutlery until she pushed him out of the way into a chair. He pulled out his newspaper, but the print turned to gibberish, his mind had been high jacked. He finished the second glass as speedily as the first.

'You'll never guess what some daft 6th former said to me today', she liked to hear stories from school; this was a story from school wasn't it?

'Male or female?'

'Male.'

'Well?'

'He said,' and with one heart beat's hesitation between thought and execution, in one snap of a synapse he knew he no longer wanted to share this information with her. It was his. 'He said that an orgasm before an exam gave you an extra grade'. He retreated behind his newspaper, closing his eyes with relief at recalling this previous sixth former's unconvincing suggestion.

'And what did you say?'

'Nothing really.'

Their exams over, year twelve were free for the summer and he did not see the boy for the remainder of the term. A cheery hello in the corridor, a long, tedious technical answer to his question in class, they would all have brought the lad to his senses. But he'd gone and there was no chance to demonstrate his familiarity and understanding of these little school crushes and place it firmly where it belonged. Irritatingly Mark's confession stopped him short throughout the following days; the precise moment, the every beat of his reaction, the memory looping over and over unresolved seeking somewhere comfortable to be stored and forgotten about. As he drove to and from school in those final days of term, he tried to apply some logic to the situation. Had Mark planned to say it or had he pried too much and was it simply his way of getting him off his case that evening? Was it a wind up, a dare even, was he laughing now with his mates? Had he done it before, was it some sort of test, would he give him a knowing wink in class next term 'gotchya!' He simply could not find it in himself to find it funny. And what if it was true? A silly crush, and over the summer break he'd move on to someone else and it would be forgotten. And dominating it all, the humiliating knowledge that he had not had the wit to instantly joke back, that he had, for a moment, believed him. So the summer break began with him feeling confused and empty as though something terribly important had touched down and taken off again, instantly and forever.

Chapter Two

David and Clare had met in a pub, squashed together on either side of a mutual friend who introduced them, though David later learnt that she was already very well aware of him. They drank their way to conversation and when the mutual friend moved to get a round had filled the gap by sitting side by side. He thought he had seen her around, had she been someone else's girlfriend? He was single, someone else may have claimed ownership but as far as he was concerned he was single.

At closing time they had emerged into the sharp cold air with the bored, sober sacrificial drivers offering lifts to the barely upright. He was having a lift with Jenny, efficiently gathering her flock of passengers together and they had squeezed together in the back. He had taken her hand (or had she taken his?), anyway at some point her mobile number had been passed over and that was that. He did a little research the following day, curious about where she had come from and why she had been there and a suspicion surfaced that it had been pre arranged. They had fallen into coupledom almost immediately, the right person and the right time. She was petite and pretty with lozenge-shaped green eyes whose lashes met her eyebrows in an intriguing elfish way. He liked her self confidence and she surprised him with her drive and work ethic which meant his own did not have to be constantly justified. Judging by the frequent texts and phone messages she received, she had a complex network of friends who made considerable social demands and since he wasn't great at keeping girlfriends entertained, it was a blessing. Her dry observations on her colleagues made him smile: 'usual morning asthma attack from Judith's perfume.' And 'Liam poisoned by his local take away for the fourth Monday in a row so I insisted we get trading standards to close it down.' But as time passed he saw how quickly she fell apart at a work crisis and carried it home.

'You're a sly one.' An acquaintance had cornered him a few weeks after they met as he stood at the bar, 'thought you were with Elly.'

'No?'

'Not what she thought.'

'Oh really?'

'Yeah, took her by surprise.'

'I'm sorry if she felt that.'

'We all thought that too.'

David turned away, furious; there was the smallest element of truth. He threw back his pint, left the pub and standing in the car park rang Clare, 'I'm outside, let's go.' He watched as she appeared in the doorway and at that moment he made up his mind that from then on he would put his energy into their partnership.

He had left the parental home with enormous relief and if university itself wasn't everything he hoped, as a paid up member of the geography intake his social life was pretty much taken care of. Not that everyone was impressed with the way he hung around on the margins, waiting, as they suggested, for better offers, dipping in as it suited and for some reason he wasn't let off lightly; maybe someone with less good looks might have been. It was more a case of privacy as far as he was concerned, he'd been on his own since ten and adapted to enjoying his inner world. Girls either hovered or kept away according to how they viewed their chances with one of the best lookers on campus and he liked to have a girlfriend. Relationships usually just faded out through lack of fuel to fire them onwards, yet he liked them all.

After the accident when he was ten the house screamed its loss so he spent hours away from it with his dog and then camping trips from the age of fifteen and an interest in survival and outdoor living developed. At first he considered becoming an outdoor pursuits instructor but he got a good degree and a favoured tutor had opened his eyes to other professions in which his interests in the environment might not mean being stuck in front of a computer all day. He had taken his post graduate teaching certificate almost as a breather but enjoyed his teaching practice far more than he had expected and thought it might be a good start but never imagined it to be his final destination. As the years passed it fitted well with his interests and he discovered to his surprise that the students seemed to genuinely like him.

Clare proceeded to fit effortlessly into his university crowd, a good communicator she knew how to find something in common with everyone. Best of all she rode easily over his taciturn moments, able to move quickly on to light distractions and disagreements were managed as minor affairs. Her background was Home Counties, Hampshire, from a baking dynasty he'd never heard of who were the biggest local employer. Her elder brother had gone to Australia after university and had returned once, displaying not the slightest quality that her father could want in an heir to the business. 'Quite deliberate,' said Clare.

When they met she had a very central flat, owned outright, with a luxury kitchen that, although barely able to cook, he could still admire. She moved in with him because he had refused to move in with her, his case was simple; his house was near his school, you could park two cars in the driveway and it had three bedrooms. They had moved in together after six months with an inevitability that occasionally caught him by surprise, there had simply been no reason not to.

That summer Clare could only negotiate two weeks leave

and it had been assumed they would take off somewhere; the Greek islands or Italy but David fancied a rail trip around Austria and Switzerland, neither of them had ever been there in the summer. But for once David did not start trawling the internet for last minute deals, unusually he felt no strong desire to leave the UK, the appeal of booking flights and hotels had curiously faded. Clare was tired from a series of long days at work and her mind, he knew, was focused on selling the house, not holidays. At first he was content with the situation but as the weeks ticked by and it got closer and closer to the start of the new school year he wanted something to blame his inertia on and blamed the boy. So what if he was spending the summer working in a local garden centre and probably not having a holiday, what in gods name did it have to do with him? One throwaway comment from a foolish boy from an underprivileged home, and even that was an assumption, and he had landed himself some ridiculous burden of responsibility and it was preventing him from having a decent holiday himself. It was absurd and he would make sure the matter was thoroughly kicked into touch right at the beginning of the new school year. At the end of August he went into school to get the results and to his immense relief and pleasure the geography results at all levels were excellent, but his eyes were drawn magnetically to all Mark's AS results and felt a personal pleasure at his As and Bs.

September, without the unrealistic expectations of August, usually delivered; days still long, sometimes even baking and the hopes and expectation of a new start in the air. He was happy to be back, the staff had started a few days earlier but now the school buzzed with children. At lunchtime he watched a team start a warm up on the pitches from his office window and instinctively touched his stomach. Not quite the six pack, but not too far off that modern acme, not too bad for nearly 30. He left the main school and walked across the road to the 6th form building, once a rambling private house. Most of them were lounging in the sun in the garden, the boys' legs stretched out, the girls perched more coyly. Their final year, nearly men and women, mature and silly, smart and dippy, generous and arsy. He was easy in their company, often amused by their chat, he would remain just long enough, he decided, to welcome them back but not to outstay his welcome. He moved over to a group of four and they greeted him with jovial acceptance. With a contented sigh he sat on a bench, leaned back and folded his hands over his stomach tipping his head back to receive the warm rays.

'Good summers? Pleased with your AS results? They weren't bad, some could have been better, there was room for improvement' he said predictably. 'Been busy? Kept yourselves fit? Not spent too much time at the computer?'

'Nah, but I've done a bit of weights.'

'Don't give me *weights*.'

'I've been *waiting* at table for 6 weeks, ha ha.'

'Waiting and putting weight on looks like'

'I barely left the computer, except to eat of course'

'Shows.'

'Suzanne, can we expect to see you on the running machines again this term?' David asked politely.

'Last year she was rated *hot* I was lead to believe, you've got some work to do there *darlin'*.'

'My god, look who's talking!'

'My beautiful mind suffices.'

Stretching an arm across the back of the bench David waited for his moment. 'Going to give me a run for my money again? That's if you're still up for it?' It sounded fine; nice and casual.

'Course,' the boy smiled directly at him, 'No question, Thursday?'

'Yup. Right, I'm off, see you all in class.' He jumped up quickly and headed back to the main school and his shared office where the banter was not so easy on the ear. Spotting the head of art ahead of him he strode to catch up with her, 'hi,' he grinned.

'You look happy, that glad to be back?'

'Yeah, I am actually,' he heard himself sound so happy he felt an explanation was necessary. 'I must have been a bit bored over the summer. We didn't get round to doing much, a few weekends away, that sort of thing, I wasted it a bit I suppose.'

'Fancy a cuppa?' Sarah asked. No question, Mike would be in their office, the mere sight of him would wipe out this little high he'd been waiting for all summer. They walked round the perimeter of the main school building to the art block and he took the spare chair in her compact office. As she made tea he took his paper out of his case and they fell into a comfortable silence, she knew why he was there.

Over the summer he'd read the paper from cover to cover but today's copy failed to engage him, he gave up, folded it away and concentrated on dunking his biscuit. Sarah settled down to her computer and he watched her fingers fly over the keyboard, was she overhanging her swivel chair more than usual? Like a pile of rubber rings, one of top of the other, she bounced softly as she shifted her weight in the sprung chair, dressed as usual in a long loose black dress set off by a dramatic necklace. She would be surprised how much he understood the reasoning behind it all. The black dress to disguise her body and hide behind while the necklace emphasised her lovely porcelain face and neck and demonstrated her bold creative personality. She never touched the biscuits, in fact he rarely saw her eat, so why was she so, well, fat? How did she maintain it? She probably ate in secret, that's what Clare suggested after they'd met. Would he be there if she was very slim? He liked to think so; he couldn't for instance imagine regularly sitting drinking tea in Jane Kenyon's office, a nervy woman, very pretty but nervy. He opened his paper again; he was reluctant to leave until the last moment when he would rush to his office and grab his books for the afternoon.

His paper functioning as a screen he sank into thought about women. 'What a perfect couple you make,' Clare's aunt had said, probably meaning no more than they ranked equally in attractiveness but in fact it extended far further. Religion (none); so ditto, education, the same; so ditto, background; that's where they did differ, their body mass index probably matched though. One day, he mused, people would be matched by DNA so no one would say 'what did she see in him? And what did he see in her? And fancy those two getting together and who'd have thought it?' Their DNA profiles would be pasted to the wedding invitation and marriage certificate like proof.

Suddenly Thursday thunked him like an elbow in the stomach, *Thursday*, god, why had he agreed? What had he been *thinking*? A gremlin had requisitioned his senses for a minute, he should have laid a few ground rules with the boy about staff/student limitations before they embarked on squash again. He blinked anxiously behind his newspaper until he felt ready to emerge.

'I've bought a new camera,' he put down his paper briskly and turned his full attention on Sarah.

'How many's that now?'

'About six, I think. A compact but it's got a big screen.'

'At least you use them; I keep forgetting to carry mine. Any inspiration over summer?'

'I spent a lot of time on my back, so to speak. I got the perfect mackerel sky and the ultimate shot of a line of cartoon cumulus nimbus with black bases and huge soaring heads.'

'Only you would enjoy the crap summer we've had, are they for your book?'

'For my *portfolio*, I'm still in negotiations over the text book. Are you holding your photo competition again this term? I'll give you a hand. I've thought I may lend out a few of my older cameras to encourage entries and include some photography tips in lessons. How about portraits this time?'

Effort had been made in the jumble of mismatched buildings that made up the school to give staff offices, rather than a communal room and this had resulted in some very restricted spaces. David shared a room with Mike, one of three small offices for the geography staff and as office arrangements had been fixed before he arrived he was stuck with it. Everyone grumbled about workloads and colleagues who didn't pull their weight but Mike had lost the lightness and self awareness along the way that stopped everyone else becoming a bore. He had become a bore.

'Out the gate, three thirty on the dot every day and, *so I've been led to believe*, marking external exam scripts in lessons last week, lazy shit.' No one was spared and after a few weeks David had abandoned his clumsy attempts to connect with him and typed noisily until Mike drifted off to a lesson. Mocking drollery tipped with sarcasm was another talent and when it was directed at pupils their puzzled expressions allowed David a little smugness, he may have a reputation for being a bit nerdy but he did get the impression that he was not approached with such reluctance. It was the scrutiny of the daily paper out loud he dreaded the most, they read the same one yet they didn't. David skimmed over the politics but Mike headed there first. Even in these vanilla days where edges were blurred and New Labour had long since passed 'only getting better' Mike hung onto his dad's working man's values. He picked ruthlessly over the action in Westminster and to David's relief by the end of the summer term he appeared to have given up expecting any worthwhile response from him. 'I let him think I'm a bit politically naïve', David told Clare, 'I really don't care as long as he leaves me alone'. Surreptitiously they soon had each others timetables firmly committed to memory; any overlap in the office was now cut to the minimum. So he would sit, early in the morning, a blissful hour before Mike stumbled in and then made himself scarce after school when Mike stayed until the caretaker threw him out.

His desk faced the wall with a window to the right looking out over the playing fields, his bookshelves in front of him and a pin board covering most of the rest of the wall. Here he displayed his photos, something his young visitors liked to linger over so he changed them frequently, unsure of his own entertainment value. Over the summer he had printed off a set from his trip to India and Asia, it was good to bring them all back to life again, too much remained on his computer. A while ago now, in fact eight years ago, travelling light with a few university friends, utterly unprepared for the culture shock he'd struggled with the toilets and the begging until the colours and light gripped him. Peeling paint at home was to be rigorously nitromorsed, sanded, primed, undercoated and top coated but in India it was a feast of chalky softness flaking off in parched layers offering endless glorious dusky combinations to be admired and photographed. He lost himself for a while in the hot, dry dustiness spread across his pin board and it struck that he would probably never go there again if he was brutally honest, it was Europe now and a nice hotel preferably with a pool, Clare loved a pool.

'Here's my summer project, sir,' Oliver Sellers was a regular visitor with a variety of excuses and David took the folder without suggesting he could have waited for class like everyone else. Once inside Oliver would hover near the spare chair and, if David looked like he might have a moment for him, sink slowly onto the edge, ready to stay, ready to go. Today David put down his pen and his smile gave Oliver the confidence to fully occupy the chair. His shirt straining a little at his plump neck and expanding waist Oliver looked earnestly at the photo display.

'You've travelled a lot sir.'

'Yes, I've done a fair bit and would like to do some more.'

'I want to travel too, what's the best job for travelling sir?'

'How about a teacher, lots of time to travel.'

'I dunno know about that sir, seems like hard work.'

'There're a lot worse jobs. How's mum?'

'Someone comes now, in the afternoon, and she cooks our tea.' His voice trailed off and David turned quickly away from him to place his project in the corner of his desk, he knew Oliver would be blinking a lot, holding himself very upright.

'That's good eh? Let me know if anything changes eh?'

'Yes sir. Sir, you know Mark Derby?'

The adrenalin surge was intense; it took him a moment to deal with it. 'Yes, of course.'

"Well, yes I know you know him, he said you play squash together, well *his* sister, Abi, and *my* sister are friends and he came over last night and *he* cooked our tea. It was really nice and then he helped me a bit with my maths. He's got this dog, he brought it round cos he was taking it for a walk.'

'What did you have?'

'Chops, onions, peas and mash and gravy.'

'Good?'

'Yeah, really good, really creamy mash.'

'That was nice of him, was he helpful, with the maths?'

'Yeah. My sister likes him. You know, *likes* him.'

'Yes, I'm sure she does. Listen, I've a bit of marking to do. Let me know how things go, OK?'

Sometimes he would struggle with his role, he could see no point in doing the job unless there was some connection but it didn't always come easily. Oliver came because he was a little sad, even if it was only to sit for a few companionable moments with a teacher who he possibly recognised as a little sad himself. David peered out of the window and watched some of the middle school, never still, texting and chatting, swinging bags, throwing punches, doubling with laughter, grabbing, throwing. Further on he saw a group of sixth, stiller, assured, on their way to becoming like him.

After school that afternoon he drove to the local country park where he knew he could always find a parking space which allowed an unrestricted view across private farm land to a row of mature willow, drooping over the river, a view guaranteed to include nothing moving except cows. He would walk to the café and buy a coffee then return to settle with the radio on and do a little marking and finish his newspaper. Sometimes he would even have a short sleep, his paper propped against the steering wheel, to recharge his batteries before his evening with Clare started. Most staff would spend the remaining hour until the school closed in their offices and sometimes he forced himself to sit with Mike but today he longed more than ever for his own company.

A noisy flapping made him look up and three ducks struggled to get airborne and he watched them flail clumsily down river and wondered what had set them off and where they were heading. Feeling dozy he eased the seat back and looking at the familiar shapes of the willows let Oliver's information wash pleasantly round his head. He knew Mark lived on the same housing estate as Oliver, decent of him to cook for them, didn't know he could cook. He inserted himself into the scene, at first leaning against the work surface, pouring some wine, no maybe just Coke in the circumstances, stirring the onions, helping him dish out and then sitting beside him to eat.

They had not seen each other for nearly two months, a lifetime when you were that age. He might even have forgotten, you did when you were young, a fresh amour each week, not that *he* had done but that's how he understood it was for some and this boy was clearly one of that sort. The following day would be their first lesson of the school year and that morning his eyes had met his reflection while shaving and he had had that sickening stab of self recognition, his self facing his self and turned quickly away. The lesson was after lunch, it was obviously going to be a challenge but he practiced an easy relaxed manner in the preceding classes in preparation. By two however he had succeeded in winding himself up enough to be both seriously anxious and very annoyed. Instead of gradually bringing order to the first lesson of the A2 geography class he launched straight into a sermon on attitude, discipline and the academic rigours that lay before them but the class, used to his easy manner, would not let him get away with it, asking pointless questions to wind him up. As the lesson progressed he desperately attempted to ease up, even managing a few jests but left immediately the lesson ended, furious with his performance. Nonsense like this was so time wasting and it wasn't even as if it was the first time a pupil had had a crush on him. A lovesick girl at his previous school had lain prostrate on the floor in his classroom as he walked in in a desperate attempt to gain his attention after weeks of following him and silly notes. He'd had the presence of mind to back out immediately and call one of the female staff and there had been no further incidents to his intense relief. But this was somehow different, seismically different and continuing to feel troubled and uneasy he turned on his way to the car park after school to watch the sixth form troop in groups to the bus stop, looking for him.

'Let's just see what they say.' she'd said on the Friday and three estate agents were at the door the following morning. It was a sought-after road, one of the bigger properties, but certain improvements would increase the chance of getting the asking price. They were, of course, the improvements he'd resisted; replacing the patterned carpet in the lounge with a wooden floor, changing the rustic pine doors on the kitchen cabinets, emptying the garage of junk to show that it could actually accommodate a car. Basic obvious stuff that Clare had suggested and that you read about endlessly in magazines and he now realised, with a number of similar properties for sale on the road, he would have to give in to. Not yet though, he hauled his bike out of the garage as soon as they'd gone so there were no gaps she could fill with a trip to the DIY store and spent an hour tinkering before launching himself onto the by-pass cycle path. He pushed himself hard, resting his elbows on the handlebars so he could get his head right down, pumping the peddles so his thighs would ache the next day. The squash trouncing still troubled him. Soon he was sweating hard, the balmy

September weather was continuing and he mused, meteorologically, on the sources of an Indian summer. He eased himself upright as he settled into the long stretch home and a stab of intense happiness, rare and precious, caught him. He passed the garden centre but he didn't go there, not on his bike anyway.

By Monday morning, the matter having remained unresolved during the previous week, David again worked himself up into a fury. He really didn't have the time for such ridiculous nonsense, it must be dealt with once and for all, he would call Mark in and make his position clear. What he would say exactly he wasn't sure, the boy wasn't bothering him, in fact quite the opposite, but he felt the need to reassure him that as his teacher he understood and could put impulsive youthful behaviour into perspective. Today, he decided, was the day; they didn't have a class so he started to look for him round the school at lunchtime. After an hour, drawing a blank in all the obvious places, he started to actively search. He took the long way round after each class, each corridor and staircase a possibility, looking out of windows onto the paths and courtyards as he progressed round the rambling school. Eventually there he was, walking toward the sixth form house, laughing with his friends and in his relief at seeing him again he forgot his pact with himself.

Whereas before he might have engaged him and his friends in a cheerful conversation at lunch it now seemed fraught with meaning he didn't understand. And when, alone together for a moment in a classroom the opportunity for turning the joke back on himself arrived the right words, carefully prepared, failed him. Shaken he reworked the script over and over in his mind until it turned into a contrived and pitiable plea. And so it continued, day after day; avoiding, seeking, finding and ignoring. From his window he caught long views of him strolling by the pitches between classes, clocking who he was with, his gestures, how he touched his friends, comfortable and casual.

Gradually his view of Mark began to distort, he saw him at the hub of a charmed circle, moving in slow motion, admired and desired by everyone, his every relaxed gesture, the way he threw his head back to laugh was now a taunt he took personally, increasing David's bewilderment. What extraordinary confidence he thought, he could barely comprehend it, where did it come from in one so young and returned constantly to his own tense, inhibited teenage years where he had viewed the teaching staff as barely human. Their eyes met occasionally but David was a past master at the deadpan distant look, it had become second nature. Mark too appeared not to registered the moment, en passant to something probably infinitely more youthful, fun and important, his admission of love forgotten, *so* last week.

Thursday, he couldn't do the first Thursday, it would have to be the following week and he resorted to leaving a note in Mark's pigeon hole he was so wound up. There was no response to the note and Mark's 'OK for squash tomorrow?' the following week was delivered as they crossed in the corridor for lunch and sounded cool and indifferent. 'Yes' David replied instantly and let himself be carried along in the flow of hungry youth as Mark disappeared into the scrum. No chit chat, David resolved, straight into the game and any recurrence of Mark's joke would be dealt with smartly this time, certainly any further attempt to mock him and he'd call it a day on the squash. He sat down alone to his lunch in the canteen and after a few minutes found himself drawn into the usual search. Mark was sitting alone too and with his back to David and without his friends around him for once he seemed a more solitary figure, less capable of mocking him and the possibility that he did indeed have a crush on him seemed a vague possibility.

The game did not go well. Mark's words, even with the two month gap hung between them like a sullen child neither of them had any idea how to deal with. This time David had the upper hand, Mark's assured confidence seemed to have left him, he missed shots, stumbled, appeared to make less effort and they barely spoke. It was clearly a blessed relief to both of them when the 45 minutes were up. This time they showered, choosing cubicles far apart and as they dressed David's frustration with the matter came to a head, they had a year of work ahead of them, his unblemished record of A's must continue. That would mean one to one tuition for all of them as and when necessary, this crush nonsense was getting in the way, the squash would have to stop.

As they gathered their belongings together David bent down and picked Mark's racquet off the floor and handed it over and for one micro moment they both held it but David's 'd'you want a lift home?' that accompanied the gesture sounded snappy.

'No, its OK, I'll take the bus.'

The game had been a disaster, David knew neither of them would suggest a repeat, this could be his only opportunity to straighten things out, 'I'm *taking* you,' he instructed and walked out without waiting for a response.

They left the building, out into the same temperate evening that had followed their last game but this time the warm companionability of three months ago was replaced with mistrust. They walked side by side along the path from the gym until they reached the short cut to the car park between the science block and the fence. David made the slightest move to take the longer route past the front of the school but Mark turned for the shortcut, a narrow path. At this point, both carrying sports bags, single file would have made sense but Mark remained at David's side, and David at Mark's, their shoulders bumping. They both let it happen, almost defiantly, neither stepping back, right to the end of the path. The rear of the science block met the side of the art block, a rear door but no windows, a place for bins and discarded furniture, here Mark paused and in that heartbeat David knew, he knew.

Putting his bag down, the boy turned and slowly placed

the tips of his right hand on David's jacket and without meeting his eyes slid his fingers inside the jacket and spread the flat of his hand onto David's shirt. Finally he glanced up to look at him. It was the first time a man exactly David's height had been so close, it was powerful and he recoiled slightly, love had always come from smaller people and the effect of being slightly dominated was astonishing. Last time a male had been this close he remembered it had been a prelude to a schoolboy scuffle. Mesmerised he allowed himself to be gently pushed back a few feet into the gloom of a doorway and gradually Mark sank against him, his large warm hand pressed firmly and wonderfully against David's stomach. Now their mouths were centimetres apart, they were breathing each other's air, and finally he felt his mouth, a man's mouth.

I have let this happen, I have allowed myself to get into this situation, I am entirely to blame, I have led him on. He grasped Mark's wrists, flinging them away, '*Jesus*, get *off*,' he hissed.

Mark sprang back as if punched, his eyes downcast he searched for his abandoned sports bag and turned back to the path. Picking up his bag David followed him and they strode towards the car as if it alone could hide their confusion and embarrassment. David glanced behind him, had anyone seen them? It had been too quick; thankfully he'd seen it coming and dealt with it smartly. They stood in the car park, the car between them, avoiding each others eyes. He won't get in, surely, David thought but Mark did and he couldn't bring himself to ask him to take the bus. Shakily he drove off and when they were some distance from the school he pulled up.

'Listen, I'm really sorry, I've obviously given the wrong signals.' Should he put his hand on his shoulder, give it a couple of fatherly pats? No, best not and he clutched the steering wheel tightly.

'Doesn't matter.'

'It does, it *does* matter, we have to work together this year

29

to get you an A, that's my priority, my priority for *all* of you. I'm sorry, I didn't realise I was encouraging you, the squash, I've been naïve, really naïve, I thought you were…'

'I'll get over it.'

'You're a *great* bloke Mark, *so* much potential. You know, these things happen, you know, when you're young. Probably best if you, we, keep out of each others way, apart from lessons obviously.'

'Of course.'

David drove on, his face burned, his seatbelt cut into his neck, he wanted to open all the windows and scream into the cold draught as it filled the car. It was all over, whatever it was, something that for a summer had made everything in his life a little sharper and a little brighter than ever before had now gone forever. He drove too fast, catching his exhaust as he bumped hard over the speed humps on the estate and they parted company at his house with barely audible goodbyes. Nearing home he pulled up once more and sat for half an hour staring bleakly at the road and houses around him. He had dealt with it well, hadn't he? He hadn't hurt him or humiliated him, no one knew, things would be fine in class, he would pretend it had never happened. Big changes were ahead, he was getting married and taking over the family bakery business, things that a young lad like Mark would have little understanding of.

There was a soft knock at Mark's door. She came in, followed by the dog and sat resting her chin on her knuckles on the back of his chair looking at him with concern.

'Well?'

'I think you can guess.'

'You thought it would…'

'Yeah, but I was *wrong*.' He rolled onto his side and twisted Fletcher's silky ear round and round his fingers. 'He was nice about it, but nothing doing.'

'You thought…'

'Yeah I know, but I was obviously reading too much into

it.'

'What are you going to do?'

'Nothing, nothing *to* do. Keep out of his way as much as possible but that's not going to be easy. I've a suspicion he'll want to carry on with squash, just to make it seem like it never happened. I was going to let him win today but I was so fucking nervous I just kept missing and then I fell over and oh Jesus it was just a *mess*. Anyway I'm *definitely* not fucking playing squash with him again.'

'I found something out today.'

He looked at her sharply, 'it doesn't sound like something I want to hear.'

'I found out from Oliver's sister. He's getting married to his girlfriend next year.'

'I kind of guessed,' he said quickly but he hadn't. He had no idea. 'Leave me alone now yeah?'

She left and he stared dully at the cacophony that was his bedroom. To think he had imagined him here and his toes curled in embarrassment at the thought. Lying in the gloom he relived every moment that had led to such a mistake. Little things had given him hope; the commitment to the squash games, looping his scarf round his neck a bit too slowly, always time for him in the corridor, his attentiveness and interest in his life during the lifts home.

'Put one of your CDs on,' David would say,' and he'd deliberately have something urgent and sexy in his rucksack for that very moment. He flicked open his photos on his mobile. It had taken ages to get a good one, finally in the queue in the canteen with his appealingly lost and distracted expression that made Mark feel David was missing something, something maybe he could give. It had all seemed so possible; so far his instincts had always been right. He had never hidden his sexual preferences and if anyone was interested, well they found their way to him. But this man was very different, he was seriously smitten with him and he was ready for something more serious. Abi's words lay like a carcass on top of him, he knew he wasn't married

---

31

but the possibility of him *getting* married had never entered his head and tears rolled down his cheeks at the humiliation.

Chapter Three

So consumed was he, with the hash he felt he was making over dealing with one idiot pupil, that one morning in class David lost his thread entirely. He returned like a time traveller to no time having passed to find the first years, still slightly overawed, silently waiting for him to continue. That afternoon as he set off for his year ten class he slipped back to his teaching practice days when the thought of keeping the attention of twenty five hormonal teenagers kept him awake at night. As he rounded the corner of the corridor he could hear the sound that these days he easily managed to quash for forty minutes, even the brisk clip of his footsteps usually quietened them. But today was different; his stride was shorter and less authoritative, the previous class had left him drained, the department head had filled his break with talk of the new syllabus and he desperately wanted ten minutes alone to regain composure. He felt unsteady and flushed as he walked down the corridor, he must be coming down with flu he decided, there was a bit of it about. As he appeared the class looked at him, anticipating the amusing orders, the confident jests and the way he held the door open for them over their heads, making eye contact with each one, allowing them in one by one like sheep at a sheep gate. Today he hesitated at the door and the burst of energy that always effortlessly stamped his authority on the lesson from the start, failed to ignite. He stepped back and almost felt this quiet power he took for granted transfer to the fifteen year olds. They barged in ahead of him, swarming around and between the desks, only a few taking their seats. Last in he closed the door on his fate, his heart racing and he blinked frantically to pick out the troublemakers, his focus dancing a wild jig. He called for order repeatedly but his voice was weak, his lungs dampened by the pounding of his heart. They milled around, shouting, arguing and throwing punches, glancing repeatedly at him, waiting for the show of strength that would allow them to calm, but he was standing rigid and silent, a strange unrecognisable look of astonishment on his pink face. All he could see was a flashing blur and he was unable to pick out individuals; they were rebelling like a single unrestrained beast in front of him. Dizzy with the power of the mob, their actions grew more extreme; books flew across the room, then chairs and a fight broke out. A raging heat flooded his face and neck, surging down his arms and spread across his torso and the sweat prickling in his hair began to run down his face, stinging his eyes. The pounding in his ears made his mouth fall open, his knees buckled and he sank forward and clung onto the edge of his desk to stop himself falling. Everything was a frightening, stabbing pink and red blur. He was dying, this is what it felt like to die, he was dying in front of twenty five children, they were watching him die.

He felt his grip loosening on the desk and leaned forward to take his weight on his forearms as his head fell and heard himself say 'stop!' or was it 'help!' or was it both? Afterwards he was never quite sure. The riot at the far back continued but the rest of the class now watched in astonishment as he sagged over his desk, the ones closest seeing him shaking. To him hours, but in reality a second passed, the heat slowly drained away, he lifted his head and heard himself tell them to sit down and when they didn't he barked out detentions, it was all he could think of to do save run from the room, which was unthinkable. First for the two standing on desks at the back then another and another as they all refused to settle down until the entire class was staying late on

Thursday, a whole class punishment, a last and frowned upon resort. The few innocents, girls, were now fuming and expressed the unfairness as volubly and disruptively as the troublemakers.

'If we all shut up now will you cancel the detention?' Lucy had come round to his side of the desk and as his focus returned he saw her staring at him curiously, interested in what she had witnessed and what power she may have in the situation. He met her eyes; she was worth having on his side. He let go of the desk and managed to stand upright. The heat had entirely gone and he now felt very, very cold. Quietly he ordered them to sit down and get out their books in a voice he recognised, he would review the detention at the end of class dependant on their behaviour for the rest of the lesson he said and the familiarity of the text book calmed him and took him like an old friend to the end of the lesson.

At the end of the class he sat quietly in the empty room for a while, unable to face the mêlée in the corridors. Flu, it could only be flu.

The nights of waking started immediately; 2 o'clock, 3 o'clock, he would finally drop off and wake up to the alarm feeling exhausted and headachy. Beer didn't help, he was coming home early so he could start drinking early. It killed off his already diminished appetite and eating was becoming a trial, there were only so many excuses for not being hungry he could give to Clare. Was this *misunderstanding* really causing such anxiety? How could something so trivial *destabilise* him so much? By not dealing with it instantly the boy had taken advantage, he had exploited the sometimes unclear student/teacher boundary.

Finally, one evening, in a state of blissful intoxication, David resolved to remove all opportunity for contact; no canteen meals, straight back to his office and avoid all communal spaces as far as was possible. A couple of weeks and it would all be forgotten. Easy.

It was quite impossible, he saw him everywhere because he *looked* for him everywhere as though his eyes had a mind of their own and to add to the muddle, in attempting to avoid him all the places he was likely to see him now took on a nervous significance. The canteen, previously a place to simply refuel, made him tremble with anticipation and expectation. There were two entrances, one from inside the school and one from outside and you took the most convenient, it was quite straightforward. But no longer because from the outside entrance a better view of the hall was afforded, a better view of who was there without the inconvenience of having to step over the threshold. He took to strolling past the outside entrance and glancing in, at first to confirm he was not there and then, to confirm that he was. He soon learnt Mark's preferred eating times so in avoiding those times those times became intolerable. He brought sandwiches at break to eat at his desk and they turned into cardboard in his mouth. Arriving early at school as he always did enabled him to take a parking space that looked out across the road outside the school and sitting in his car, partly hidden by the wall he could just see the bus stop as bus after bus dropped off pupils, one of whom would inevitably be him.

Soon David was unable to leave his car until he had seen him through the school entrance, a condition to which everyday he added more and these self made traps turned his day into a battleground, every failure to meet an obligation made his heart pound with anxiety.

A busy weekend brought some calm and distance. On the Monday he unsteadily reclaimed the school, bracing himself for the inevitable encounter, his words and demeanour meticulously planned. But the boy was blanking him, doubling back to avoid passing him, leaving the classroom first or chatting animatedly to his friends with his back turned. So he sought him out, checking corridors, pausing outside doors but the prospect of dredging up light throwaway remarks and brisk teacher chat left him fretful and humiliated. What, he asked himself, was he frightened of? Had he not been entirely professional? Why had he said they should keep out of each others way, what had he to hide? All he wanted was to return to the way it had been yet he had completely lost sight of what that was.

Nervy and desperate to avoid company David took refuge in his car at breaks and lunchtime, driving it to the country park or a quiet street to avoid the quizzical taps on the window he got from fellow staff in the school car park. One thing he had always prided himself on and yes, it had been irritating he knew, was that he was a very rational man. Past lives, star signs, conspiracy theories, hippy claptrap; insufferable rubbish and he said so. But the logic that had always guided him was now failing him and to blame the pupil whose youthful confusion had simply unleashed his own pent up anxieties was unreasonable.

How often were problems too simple to see? Car won't start? Only a dirty spark plug. No power? Only a blown fuse. Could the culprit be no more than the amount of coffee and sugar he was putting into his system, driving up already high levels of anxiety. His intake of coffee had definitely been increasing and he decided to keep a detailed record until loosing track he excluded it completely for a few days resulting in lethargic afternoons and dull headaches. He tried Clare's blood pressure monitor; normal, a cholesterol test; slightly above average, took a diabetes test; negative. Was he deficient in iron and minerals, did he have a food allergy? The small controls and deprivations that resulted in this research were, if nothing else, distracting for a few days but who was he kidding, he knew what was causing it.

It was stress. The staffroom was heavy with stress, they were all stressed, all the time. If you weren't stressed you clearly weren't doing your job properly and to claim not to be stressed was almost an insult to the stressed. He Wiki'd it; signs of stress may be cognitive, emotional, physical or behavioural, he had the lot and it was hardly surprising. That was the thing about teaching, your adrenalin river in full spate, head just about visible above the raging torrent until the end of term when you're washed up exhausted onto an empty shore for a few weeks recovery time and then wham, it's next term and another inundation sweeps you off again. And he was getting married, wasn't that another event high on the stress scale? His body was pumping out endorphins as a response to it all and the high level of arousal necessary to cope with it was, in his case, causing him to bolt down the easy escape route of sexual lust. Except he was so *exceptionally* stressed he wasn't looking at a girl, he was looking at a *boy, for chrissakes.*

Stress suited nicely, he was comfortable with that explanation, stress could wrought all sorts of havoc. Clinging to this explanation the suburban view through his windscreen took on a new charm and he drove through the school gates with a new lightness of spirit. Go ahead, he challenged, face it head on, drive the obsession into a wall of boredom and indifference. Go ahead and walk down to the newsagent instead of getting the paper from the petrol station on the way to work if it was a chance of bumping into him. Choose to stroll across the courtyard for fresh air and to avoid the congested stairs if it increased the possibility of seeing him. As he strode confidently into his office his phone rang. A text from Clare reminded him she was out that evening and of an invitation for Friday, and would he buy some coffee. That's how things were between them; they were a solid team, but he replied, nevertheless, with more care than he normally did.

Yet despite all the satisfactory conclusions he felt he had reached about the source of his difficulties Mark's interest disturbed him. He now recalled the attention he himself had attracted in the past. The attentive neighbour helping him mend his bike and inviting him on cycle rides, the bloke following him home on a dark evening after school, catching up with him, touching him, until he ran towards a crowded bus stop. Later the fine limbed boy he couldn't seem to take his eyes off in hall one term and the almost violent jealous shock when he saw him one night, pressed against a wall by another man. He didn't avert his eyes when he saw an attractive face, he checked out shorts slung suggestively low, he could be intrigued if a glance his way lingered. It was only curiosity, checking out the competition or even wondering what it would be like if he was inclined that way. No harm in a little sexual frisson in his twenties but it looked like it resurfaced inconveniently in stressful situations.

The calm interregnum was short lived and fretful thoughts soon began to intrude again. The neighbour had taken advantage of his teenage loneliness and innocent friendliness. Was he now that adult, chasing a lonely schoolboy? In those relatively tranquil moments in class while diagrams were being laboriously copied into workbooks and set questions struggled over his impassive face did not give the slightest hint to the turmoil in his head. Should he be teaching if he couldn't share a sporting interest with a senior pupil without it giving the wrong messages? Should he be teaching at all if he could be so easily manipulated by a pupil? He was ten years older, he was dealing with young people and their hormonal swings all day, he didn't just know about staff/student boundaries, he'd had training, he'd led a staff tutorial on the subject, he had a handbook.

But in the peaceful half hour or so in the morning alone in his office, in a bubble of contentment broken smartly when Mike barged in, he wove fantasies into his day; how he could please and delight the boy from the information that he had picked up about his likes and dislikes during lessons and squash games and the drives home. From companionable bike rides and a lunchtime pizza his thoughts always drifted into areas of intimacy and the day dreams became more complex, with beginnings and middles and ends. Sometimes, if he was lucky, these pleasurable feelings butted into his day and he was slow to move off from lights, gave kerbs glancing blows, took two, three goes to park, left his mobile in the staff room, took the wrong text book to lessons and forgot names. One day Mark's workbook appeared halfway through the little pile he was marking, he had been waiting for it, now it had a charm and significance that none of the others had. How would he mark his work now? Would he feel obliged to be tougher than usual? He was very aware that he should not be marking it, his feelings compromised his position. The work was no better or worse than usual but he held the book for a while and turning it slowly in his hands noticed that a small tear had started at the corner and he mended it with some clear tape. How sad was that he thought, suddenly amused, would he notice?

Clare's current work anxiety proved useful, at home it was a relief to switch off from his own distractions and let her offload. One evening, as he began his evening retreat to alcoholic forgetfulness she arrived home particularly troubled. She wasn't hungry and they sat together cuddling on the sofa for the first time in months. He turned the TV off so he could concentrate on her words and she relaxed quickly which pleased him. It brought home to him how much he cared about her, how calming her company was and that she was the person he wanted to confide in as he was to her. For a moment he wondered if he told her, so if wasn't a secret any more it would die more quickly. She would obviously be upset and confused but so was he, and he would ask for her advice, she liked that, she liked to advise him. It would be like the confessional, how extraordinary to be able to walk away from that little wooden box with a clear conscience. Fess up, he thought, make it sound funny, take a little criticism for being so silly, suggest a weekend away. Wait till the adverts he decided, no there wouldn't be enough time. Wait till they'd settled down with their evening cup of tea but when that arrived she was still too distracted by her own problems. Maybe it would be sensible to tell her once things had improved at work for her. After a reassuring hug they settled down to sleep, it never occurred to him how infrequently they made love.
        Returning to his office at break one morning, David came suddenly face to face with Mark in the corridor.

'Alright?' The quick rearrangement of his vocal cords to achieve a casual tone failed, the sound emerged high pitched and Mark's reply, in contrast, a model of coolness. He headed quickly to his thankfully empty office and leaned heavily over his desk, paralysed with unhappiness and indecision.

'Dear god, get me out of this,' he murmured softly out loud, wanting to hear his ultimate plea for help. He shut his eyes and asked for the strength to break the deadlock from a god he had abandoned since childhood. After a few minutes he felt the crisis fade and a new clarity emerged. He would speak to him tomorrow after class, organise the one to one tutorial he had been avoiding, chat like they used to and be reassuring, sympathetic and professional. Surely then Mark would recognise that what had happened between them was forgotten and that whatever mutual respect they had clearly had for each other once could resume.

This resolution was no more long lived than any of the others, how could he possibly get this message across in the mêlée of a corridor? As for calling him into his office, his stomach lurched at the possibility not only of Mark's indifference but his trustworthiness. Frustration and bewilderment overwhelmed him again and he slumped into his chair. Logical, scientific explanations didn't interest him anymore and self pity moved effortlessly in. He wasn't coping with the pressures of working in a large state secondary school, an early mid life crisis, he was afraid of the increasing responsibilities he wasn't made for, the accident returning to haunt him, depression from excessive alcohol consumption. Then the boy burst through his despair, his narrow scarf knotted round his neck, his hands deep in his trouser pockets, pausing to look over his shoulder at him to smile, enchantingly.

No, he was, quite simply, in love.

Chapter Four

The Friday before half term Sarah stuck her head round his door at the end of the lunch break.

'No school for a whole, complete, blissful week,' and she shut her eyes for a dramatic moment, 'hardly seen you this week, going anywhere nice?'

Going anywhere? Where could he possibly want to go? He didn't even want half term, he wanted to carry on, to follow the rigid timetable, to know that on Tuesday at 2pm, Wednesday at 9.30 and Thursday at 11.15 he would teach him and for forty five minutes he would know exactly where he was and in between he would know he would not be far away. To go away was to crash land in a cold barren wasteland, to set off with what he could salvage from the wrecked plane, alone and hopeless and lost. The image was so instant and startling he wondered at his state of mind and it took a moment to compose his answer.

'No, a quiet week at home, masses to catch up on, and we have to make a start on the improvements ready to get it on the market, half term hasn't come too soon. By the way,' he stretched his legs out slowly and casually and twirled a biro, 'you're a bit of a reader aren't you, Clare's birthday's coming up and she wants a book, any recommendations?'

'What does she like?'

'Stuff about people, you know, love, relationships, but not trashy romance stuff.'

'Try the new publications table at the bookshop, I always

start there, and avoid anything with a pastel cover. Or the classics; Madame Bovary, Death in Venice, Anna Karenina, Austin, you can always re read the classics. Anyway as you're around give me a call over the week, if you want a chat.'

'What are you doing?'

'Nothing much, maybe finding religion.'

'Got any particular one in mind?'

'Umm... nothing that requires too much abstinence, one where any sinning is easily absolved with a few apologies and chants, lots of colourful festivals and feasts that are compulsory to attend and opportunities for contemplation in peaceful surroundings.

'Sound like a mix of Catholicism, Buddhism, Hinduism and Church of England, you might have to start your own, it could prove very popular.'

'Will you join? I'll let you pick and mix.'

'If it fits into my timetable, I've marking and prep to do you know, it all sounds very time consuming.'

'I've some of that on my hands.' She had taken her top lip and her big eyes widened. He didn't want to hear she was lonely and half term stretched ahead, empty. 'Oh, and choice of who I come back as.'

'For example?'

'A cat, owned by me or....' she paused and he looked up expectantly, 'someone like you.'

'Me?'

'You seem so sorted, you know where you're going and who you're going with. It must be amazing to be you.'

'I'm a duck, serene on the top, paddling frantically underneath.' At that moment he wanted to tell her so incredibly much. It was the perfect moment to confess that nothing was as it seemed, she had it completely wrong, he envied her her openness, it must be so liberating. Her mouth would fall open slightly and her big brown eyes hold his in disbelief and she would come into the office and slump heavily into Mike's chair and her earrings would tremble and all the inevitable warnings would pour out and he would say he didn't care, he didn't fucking care and have you ever felt so alive like you only had a day to live?

As he listened to the sound of her soft shuffle and jingling earrings disappear down the corridor he ran his eyes over his well stocked bookshelves. He enjoyed pulling a volume down, its smell as he opened it, its weight and the comfort of searching for that elusive fact. For relaxation though his choice was a travel book, a staple for birthdays and Christmas. Reading was a good distraction but he hadn't read much fiction beyond exam texts, something contemporary as Sarah had suggested was worth a go; see how authors today tangled and untangled feelings. His were now overpowering him, almost unmanageable, he'd even cut down on drinking because it interfered with wallowing in his predicament.

There was a slam of text books on the opposite desk.

'*Wa*key, *wa*key! Two minutes to the bell, it's not half term yet.'

The large bookshop in town was a regular haunt for travel books but as travel was the last thing on his mind these days David wandered around the front table as directed by Sarah and read the backs of a few just published volumes. He had never actually read a love story apart from Madame Bovary and that only an enforced set exam text at seventeen which he remembered as tedious and with no sex. In fact even the word love had been pretty much off limits for most of his life; girls read love stories. He looked at the political biographies in a special display but they reminded him of Mike and then wandered over to the classics, might another century and perspective calm his nerves and give him away time to get over his dilemma? Jane Austen sprang to mind but recalling the films he'd been forced to watch he decided they really were a century too far. Small suggestion cards from staff were pinned on the shelves under certain books and there was one for Thomas Mann's Death in Venice, one of Sarah's suggestions and he remembered seeing and enjoying the film. 'The obsessive love of an older man for a beautiful boy, he dreads disenchantment as the intoxication becomes so precious to him. I enjoyed it immensely.' said the label. He flicked through, hardly comparable with the silly muddle he was in but it wasn't long and the writing style would be a challenge. He took it, and another labelled book; Graham Green's The End of the Affair but changed it for The Quiet American.

Attempting to be amused by his nerves, which if anyone was watching looked like a silly smirk; he glanced around to see if there was a lesbian and gay section. He checked the shop with his lateral vision, everyone seemed absorbed and he walked purposefully toward a part of the shop as foreign to him as cookery. There was the faintest hint of a tremble in his hands as he took out a few volumes and read the back covers. Time passed, he felt people move behind him but no one joined him in this unexplored country. He became absorbed in a genre that now had some, well, academic interest and he chose two books, it looked better, as though he was researching the topic which, of course, he was. Queuing to pay he noted that the assistant was very pleasing to the eye and the fact that he noticed he was, was disconcerting.

He read the gay non fiction he had bought in the seclusion of his car, a lot of pride and diseases and comings out and identity. Useless, they offered no guidance at all on how to fight off love-struck doe eyed schoolboys. Before starting the Mann, like a good student he looked up the course notes on the internet but it didn't dispel the disconcerting ache and finally he lay on the sofa and read it in one go. Some paragraphs he read again and again, engrossed with Achenbach's passion and confusion, struggling to decode the author's meaning, was it love or lust or just the worship of beauty? Hardly comparable of course, the man had no other distractions whereas he hardly had a minute to himself, it would quietly fade next term, of that he was sure, but he remained for the rest of the afternoon on the sofa and made love to the boy.

Chapter Five

Jack, Clare's father, immediately booked David in for a visit to the bakery when he learnt they weren't going anywhere for half term, making it clear the visit was for David alone so he wouldn't be able to trail silently behind Clare like the consort. The possibility that as Jack's son in law he may play some part in the business had become apparent very slowly. Nothing had been specifically said but 'opportunities could arise' and 'it may fit with your long term career plans' and the slightly more worrying 'Jack is keen for it to stay in the family,' from Shirley, Clare's mother.

'Just go along with an open mind, look politely interested, keep dad happy, that's all you have to do,' said Clare lightly.

Jack's next email put paid to any possibility of a casual visit, there would be a meeting with the management and he would be shown every part of the production process. If *only* it was a brewery.

'I want you to meet all my team,' Jack said, 'they'll fill you in on the directions I want the business to go and we'll have the full product range and our samples out for you. I'm better at explaining the manufacturing process, the machinery we have and the machinery we'll need for new lines and further automation. I'm sure you'll find it fascinating.'

A perfunctory trawl of the Internet indicated the industry could be divided into small-scale high-end luxury special occasion cakes or automation on an industrial scale. He read of takeovers by conglomerates and businesses in receivership, of high overheads and companies sinking under the burden of business rates and bank loans. For the first time he stopped at the cake section in the supermarket, looked for the traditional tea time favourites he remembered as a child and studied the in store bakeries and continental imports. The rising costs of raw materials, the availability of skilled staff, the capital costs of new machinery, changing tastes and the burden of debt, he presumed he would find answers to all these questions in the management meeting and began to almost look forward to it.

To his embarrassment all the staff knew exactly who he was and were clearly expecting him, mainly women they greeted him by name and congratulated him on his engagement. To his surprise he found that many of them had in fact already been invited to the wedding along, in some cases, with their families. Their chatter reminded him that many of them had been working for the company almost all their working lives and how much it was part of the town, daughters had joined their mothers and in one case both parents and two daughters were working side by side. The company was very flexible to school hours and holidays and they said Shirley had been responsible for initiating that. The machinery was clever but it was the decorating that was so fascinating; the women's hands flashing between boxes of characters, flowers and letters and as he hovered, they moved over to make a space for him and invited him to decorate a cake himself. He sat between two women and cheerfully stuck an assortment of decorations round the edge of a cake and taking an icing bag scribbled in the middle. By now he was impatient with questions, and assumed the afternoon management meeting would pretty much cover them.

At the door of Jack's office he pursed his lips to stop himself laughing. Furnished like an Edwardian gentlemen's club Jack's high backed leather button chair dominated the space and a monster desk was just visible under redundant computer hardware, trailing cabling and piles of tottering files and catalogues. The accumulated junk of possibly decades contrasted with the orderly rows of framed black and white photos on the office walls of the factory and its workers since it opened in 1925. David walked round examining them keenly. There were formal photos of the staff in groups for what looked like the annual factory photo but it was the photos of the factory at work that were the most interesting, the women in long white dresses and starched caps, he searched them for detail noting the fruit slabs and Madeiras he had just watched being made. Jack talked him through some of the photos, 'by the way,' he said conspiratorially as there was a knock at the door, 'I think of you as family now.'

Three people joined them; the production manager, a middle aged female accountant, and the marketing manager, very overweight, and they all squeezed round a small table at the end of the room. Apart from the marketing manager nodding when Jack looked to him for agreement they remained silent. Jack painted an upbeat picture of continuing success and future expansion; he talked of his loyal employees, quoted consumer's praise for the quality of the products, interest from the big chains and partnership opportunities with a German company. As for any financial information, a children's birthday party would have had more economic insight. David glanced round the impassive faces, there was no agenda, minutes, questions, debate and actions, is this how family companies were run, or had the meeting been stage managed for his benefit? It occurred to him as they all shook hands that keeping the finances out of it had been a pre arranged agreement and decided to tackle Jack at a later date if he could be bothered. He wasn't insensitive to the possibility they saw him as a rival but as the day had now fully confirmed his total disinterest in the company, he didn't much care if they did. By this time the factory had shut for the day and as he wandered back past the now silent machinery he saw how most of it was in fact very old and without the bustle of the employees how tatty and dilapidated the building looked. He slipped his smallest camera from his pocket and took some shots.

Despite his disinterest in the company Jack's confidence in him was still a boost and he didn't get many of them. He felt a surge of confidence in his future, his lust would fade, there was no need for any derailments. He spent the weekend marking and cycling, and by Monday morning decided matters were coming off the boil and he was ready to take back control. Achenbach might have lost a bit of interest in Tadzio after a few hours of inane teenage chatter and Mark could certainly come up with his share of drivel in class.

'Mark, we need to go through your work, you're the last one.' He glanced up sharply at the end of the lesson, caught Mark's eye briefly then continued to shuffle busily through his course notes. Stupidly he'd left him till last; he had considered holding the tutorial as a pair but decided that might draw attention to his confusion. Finally alone together there was a chance that enough time had lapsed that they could even have a laugh over it and chat about feelings, he could put himself down a bit, mention his impending house move and how he dreaded it and mention Clare of course.

'Yes sir.'

'I'm free now so lets get it done OK?' he didn't look up, Mike was teaching all afternoon, he would have the room to himself.

'Yes sir.'

This time he looked at the boy steadily, but still kindly. Mark continued to sit at his desk, the rest of the class having disappeared. He was looking tired and didn't meet David's eyes and David suddenly felt less confident; go easy on him, maybe forget the tutorial and start with a friendly chat to ease the tension, something neutral, the weather maybe.

'Come on then,' his voice softened.

They walked through the school, Mark a few feet behind.

Pupils stopped David to speak, the staircases seemed interminable and an icy blast of air that almost made his teeth chatter hit him as they walked across a courtyard, or was it nerves? The journey seemed further than it ever had before, David rehearsed the meeting as he walked; his university applications would be a good starting point and he could bore him with a few anecdotes from his own university days. Turning into his office, off an empty corridor he realised that they would be alone together and asked Mark to leave the door open. He sat down at his desk and briskly indicated the seat beside him but Mark remained in the doorway and David tried summoning an expression that conveyed kindness but that he also meant business. But, finally completely alone with him, no need to keep his eyes moving so they didn't rest too long or significantly on the boy he allowed himself to look properly at the person who had haunted his every waking moment and disturbed his every night for the past three weeks or was it a whole year? And what he saw was someone who was utterly miserable, clearly dreading this encounter, full of regret at his impulsive behaviour, his confidence battered, his hair pushed up off his forehead as if in despair. He was also quite the most beautiful thing he'd ever seen in his life, and he stood up and took two shaky strides towards him to close the door with one hand and to place the other on his chest to keep him away but to feel him hot under his palm, his heart hammering and smell his scent, heavy from nerves.

'I'm so sorry. I'm so *sorry*,' his knees wobbled, he pressed the door hard into the frame and his other hand pressed the boy against the door.

'Sorry for what?' The boy grasped David's wrist holding the hand in place on his chest and they stood braced against one another as if caught in a brawl.

'It's OK, its all OK,' David murmured desperately over and over, paralysed by the deadlock, this wasn't what he'd intended, it had all gone wrong. If he moved his fingers, even slightly, it might feel like a caress but the boy suddenly

51

relaxed his grip and let his hand slip slowly up David's forearm holding David's gaze and David eased the pressure against Mark's chest, sliding his hand slowly up to rest his fingertips on his collar bone and up further to touch his neck just under his ear and then run his thumb gently along his jaw. He heard a sound in the corridor.

'Take you home, 5 o' clock?'

'What happened?' Abi called through his door.

'Nothing.'

'It did, I know it did.'

'Just take the bloody dog for a walk.'

Lying fully clothed under the duvet Mark recalled in the comforting darkness the events of the last hour in every puzzling detail. It had been weird, nothing David had said had given him the slightest hope but everything else had. He had been held as if he was the most divine and precious thing, his face and lips and hair touched and tasted as if he had been away a hundred years. But finally, dizzy with passion and held in his arms across the gap between the front seats of the car David had punched the life out if it. He had a partner, he could not deceive her, his social life was complex and full, outside work he had barely a moment to spare, he was working long hours to keep up with the marking and lesson prep, there was no room for him and there was very little likelihood of the situation changing. And then, with finality, 'anyway you're seventeen, you're underage, it's illegal.'

'I'm eighteen on December the fourth.'

'I know, but you're still *under my care*, it's a breach of trust.'

'There's nothing doing then?'

At this, David sank back against the headrest and sighed as if he'd driven it satisfactorily to ground but as Mark sat struggling to make sense of it all a story unfolded. David told him a tale of unnecessary trips to the garden centre for climbers and bags of bark chippings and, while Clare looked at the displays, wandering off down the aisles to the greenhouses at the back, searching for him, and on seeing him a weight lifting and going home calmed and putting it down to missing the routine of school and the mistake of not going away. And then in the school garden at the start of the school year, unable to settle till he'd seen him and putting that down to start of term nerves. And then, as if it might all sound too positive, more back peddling.

'This is all a shock you realise, it's not something I make a habit of, it's quite out of character, quite apart from the legality of it I'm not a free man, there's a great deal at stake.'

'I'm not asking for anything much.'

'I haven't anything to give.'

'Keep out of each other's way then?'

'No, I don't mean that,' and finding Mark's fingers he wondered where the dose of optimism was coming from, was he catching it from the boy?

'What's your dog's name?'

'Fletcher.'

'Let's take Fletcher for a walk tomorrow.'

It was the middle of October, still warm, still OK for shirt sleeves and all terrain sandals and leaving the back door open in the evening. When the clocks went back it signalled a closing in, an order to get home quick but David resented living his life around the TV for the winter, especially since Clare, despite protestations to the contrary, hung her activities around it. A certain dog and his owner could easily replace the evening run or the gym. He liked dogs, the dog needed walking, it was a reasonable and healthy way of winding down after a day of teaching he reasoned.

The next day there he was, waiting on the corner with a fluffy black creature at his feet and after a day tortured with misgivings seeing his smile as he drew up alongside, and the relief in the boy's face that he'd turned up, he was overwhelmed by a longing to make it OK for him and to never let him down.

Over the following week, as the evening sun slowly turned

everything warm and burnt and orangey in the country park they walked the dog, teasing and touching and finding each other irresistible. The dog busily trailed interesting smells into undergrowth where only dogs, or people looking for dogs went and they followed him, away from the eyes of stray schoolchildren lingering for a smoke on their way home. He was an inventive kisser, barely kisses, like picking raspberries off a bush and deep kisses that were to leave David, evening after evening, hard and anxious as he drove home. The teaching day and his equally demanding home life usually blocked the brooding thoughts but alone in his office and the car he wound himself to a standstill over how to keep the boy's interest in a chaste relationship, because that is all it could ever be. Refusing to go any further, hearing the boy's frustration and disappointment, he drove the relationship to the brink day after day. 'Listen,' he argued with some alter ego that sat curmudgeonly beside him on the drive to pick him up, 'it's just friendship, I've found someone I really enjoy being with, OK he's younger, the kissing, it's what he wants and it's harmless.' And his alter ego would remind him how meticulously he was in fact applying himself to keeping their cautious courtship alive and how closely Mark was watching.

The precise where and how and when it had all begun for both of them occupied David deeply, he wanted a defining moment, a big bang creationist rather than evolutionary explanation, what had the boy done to trigger the unthinkable?

'How did it all start, you know the very *start*?

'I can't remember, why does it matter?'

'It matters.'

'OK. You see you never encouraged me exactly, but you never *rejected* me either. It would have been pretty easy, just a word or a look and I would have left you well alone but you never *did*, there was always a thread to hang onto, just enough, and as I got to know you better I kinda got to know what you wanted, like game rules, and every time I got it right, a word or a gesture, even the way I chucked a ball at you, I got a reward, which was more of being with you. You must have *known*.'

'Um, sort of,' he lied, he'd been flirting and he'd hardly even flirted with women.

'Sometimes it wasn't that subtle, like at the end of last term you picked up my squash racket in the changing room and handed it to me, I was standing right next to it, it didn't need handing over. It was so friggin' sexy. And a few weeks ago you mended the corner of my workbook. That was so *hot*. And then Lewis made some stupid remark in class and I laughed out loud and it stopped you mid sentence and you said nothing, nothing at all and just watched me like you sometimes do, sort of intently and distant all at the same time.'

David turned to him quickly and slipped his finger inside Mark's collar so he squirmed. 'Oh *my, my*, when you laughed like that in class, your head back, your mouth open, your shirt pulled slightly out of your trousers.'

'Meaning?'

'*Guess*.' Guess that I was thinking does he look like that when he comes; will he ever come with me? 'It all sounds very subliminal, I didn't know I was capable of it.'

'Fancy a fuck might have been quicker. Not that there's been any of that of course, but if you really want to know *when*, for me, when you walked into class for the very first time, you know the beginning of my year eleven, that was a 7 on the Richter scale. And you?'

'It's been a series of minor seismic tremors that have frightened this particular native to death.'

'C'mon, I'm not the first bloke?'

'Basically.'

Was it basically yes or basically no but Mark couldn't bring himself to ask and gripped the front of David's shirt, 'come home with me, now, for a few minutes, Mum's out.'

'It's just *wrong*. What time do you have to be home, for

dinner?'

'Dinner's when I cook it.'

'For everyone?'

'Yeah, for my sister and for my mum when she gets home, she works shifts.'

'How long have you done that for?'

'Seems like for always, it just worked out that way, I've looked after my sister for years. I don't mind, Mum says I won't starve when I'm at university and I'll be very popular.'

'What d'you cook?'

'Anything, pasta, roasts, stews, curries.'

'And all the clearing up?'

'With my sister, she's persuaded after little light torturing.'

'You two seem to get on.'

'Yeah it's the way it panned out, it's not been straightforward.'

'Tell me?'

'Sometime.'

'Talking of food,' he leaned over to the passenger side and pulled a squashed cardboard box out of the glove compartment and lifted the lid. 'It's not going to be in top condition, it's been sitting in here a while. I decorated myself by the way' Telling him about the bakery during their first few days together to emphasise that he wasn't just getting married, he was expected to enter the family business failed hopelessly. 'It shouldn't have got this far he'd confessed,' quite unable to explain how it had.

'What's that squiggle in the middle?'

'It's an *M*, I made it for you.' He scrabbled around in the glove compartment again and cut a thin slice with the plastic knife he found.

Mark took a bite, 'it's a bit dry and sweet, it needs more butter and eggs.'

'It should have been you there not me, I know nothing about baking, you could have given them a bit of advice. But I can remember the stats: 282 employees, 2,000 gallons of fresh cream a day, the new depositor machine cost four grand.'

'What does it deposit, dog shit?'

'Meringues, sponges, éclairs, that sort of thing if I remember correctly. They showed me pictures of how it works but it wasn't actually working, it was sitting all new and shiny in the corner. The best bit was definitely the hand decorating line, really fast. One of the managers acts mustard keen, he can promote him; I'm certainly not going to stand in anyone's way. He's got all these plans for fancy new products and I felt I should at least show some interest in the finances but he kind of sidestepped my question and I felt it sounded like I was being critical. Only basic questions like who they're supplying and how big the orders are.'

'Did they look like they had orders, were all the production lines busy?'

'No, they weren't, precisely what was bothering me, and when I was decorating your cake one of the women whispered that she'd been put on short time and was looking for another job. It was the silence in the meeting that got me. Anyway I said I'd go and I have, and if I'd asked too many questions it would have flagged up my interest so I think he's got the message.'

The following evening was a parent's evening. Not a favourite with most of his colleagues but David squeezed a perverse enjoyment out of it, his deadpan comments demonstrating that, despite his sometime geeky manner, he was watching their offspring like monkeys in a research lab. Usually the parents that really needed to be advised of the truth didn't show, as much in denial as the pupil and this was always a disappointment, particularly when he had a little revelation up his sleeve. It was a strange few minutes of power as miscreants were outed and strugglers were recognised and encouraged. Settling himself into his chair in the hall a flutter of nerves caught him by surprise. His eyes strafed the room, had any of these people seen them together? He didn't appear to be attracting anyone's attention apart from the smiling parents standing in front of his desk but the rush of paranoia accompanied by a queasy stomach confirmed that things would have to cool. Year thirteen was hosting and during the evening he caught glimpses of Mark directing parents and supplying refreshments, he looked very happy and that made his heart lurch. He appeared halfway through the evening at David's desk with a cup of tea and a Kitkat, not a standard issue school biscuit and David acknowledged the gift with a swift nod and by eating it immediately.

This particular evening he toned his witticisms down, he felt wary and less inclined to smite specks from other's eyes when he was, what exactly was he doing? Consorting with a pupil? His thoughts went through the usual loop which now took seconds until another parent with a trailing daughter arrived at his table. Oliver was next with his aunt. It would have been kind to give him an easy time, what in god's name was he droning on about concentrating in class and neater work when the boy's mother was dying. As they moved off to another member of staff his body rose and fell in a huge sigh, he wanted the evening over and although on the one hand he wanted him to be waiting at the car he wanted to find he wasn't and for that to be the signal that it was all over and, thankfully, the boy's decision. Walking out into cold drizzle at the end of the evening he squabbled with himself over what he really wanted but there he was, leaning back against the car which David now parked at the furthest corner of the car park. His jacket collar was turned up, his bare hands jammed under his armpits, David could almost hear his teeth chattering as he approached.

'Coat?'

'It wasn't cold this morning when I left, anyway its too fucking tight for me.'

David put down his bag, shrugged off his own coat and thrust it at him, 'it's yours, I've got another.' He expected a rebuff but the coat was pulled on without hesitation.

'Button it up before I do,' he said softly, taken aback at his gesture.

Clare appeared in the hall as he came through the door, 'no coat? It's freezing out there.'

'Left it at school.'

'Well don't leave it hanging around, it's a wool cashmere blend, things can disappear. I lost a really nice coat once, it was just lifted off a peg at a conference, someone recognised the quality, anyway you have that other one, though it's a bit frayed at the cuffs, use it for school, keep the other one for best. Or you could wear your old ski jacket, you know the one I suggested you took to the charity shop, I mean there's nothing wrong with it. How did parents' evening go?'

'Usual. Oliver was there, with his aunt.'

'Is she still, alive?'

'I think so, we stuck to geography.'

'Poor lad, is he still coming into your office for little chats?'

'Yes, he finds excuses and I don't mind.'

'Quite the father figure!' she gave him what he assumed was a doting look and he responded with a sardonic smile. 'At least it's a boy, any moony girls?'

'None. Don't forget I have a pastoral role in the school, I'm supposed to be available to listen to troubles. Anyway I'm knackered I'm going to hit the hay soon.'

'Diaries, can we have a quick diaries session?'

They sat opposite each other at the kitchen table and she poured two glasses of red wine and smoothed open her diary. 'Someone at work said it was about time I joined the twenty first century and went e but I *like* the feel of paper, I *like* to use a pencil and to see a week at a time. Right, yoga on Mondays but I may do pilates on Tuesday instead, depending on how tired I am on Monday and this Friday it's Lucy's birthday and she likes a good session so don't stay up and didn't we agree to see a film on Saturday and I've *masses* of bits and bobs to do on Sunday oh and Dad sent another cheque, he said its for the lounge floor but I *know* how you feel so don't *worry*, I'm putting it straight in the bank. Right, what are you up to?'

As soon as he could he ran up the stairs and sifted though the wardrobe in the spare room for the other coat. Stupid and impulsive gesture but on the other hand it was fatherly and protective and not in the least sexy; it might douse the whole crackpot mess in icy water. One of his mates was bound to recognise it though. Ask for it back, buy him something else on Saturday, give him the old ski jacket instead, stop these nightly lifts home, just go without him or stand talking to someone else for ages, he'd get the message. He cleaned his teeth and sank under the duvet, there would be a text, that must stop and fumbling for his phone he read it, 'love coat' and deleted it. They'd driven in silence, Mark's head buried deep and contentedly into the collar, listening to music and before getting out of the car he had leaned over, arms pined to his sides like a tin soldier, to be hugged, childlike, in his new coat.

After a few minutes in bed Clare rolled over and wrapped her arm round him, cuddling him for a moment then slipped her hand down. He usually managed to respond but guilt's grip was taking an increasingly stronger hold, gradually shutting down the pleasure pathways and so they remained; him, rigid everywhere except where expected and her, unsure how to proceed.

'Tired?'

'Mmm, parent's evening, always knocks it out of me.'

She moved her hand instantly to his back and started to stroke him, exactly what she would have wanted him to do to her he thought.

'How old were you?'

'Can't really remember, 'bout twelve. You know messing around, wrestling and stuff.'

'No.'

'Never messed around, wrestled?'

'Can't say I did.'

'Missed out there!'

'Clearly, tell me more.'

'Well that's how it started, you know, friends coming back, play fighting, you know wrestling on your bed and the floor with your best mate?'

'No I never did that.'

'It just started to get a bit more er… interesting when I was fourteen, an older boy at school suggested he come home to play video games. You never did any of that, with guys?'

'No. What about girls?'

'Once, sort of, a disaster. But they seem to like me.'

I bet they do, he thought, 'What about more recently?'

'He was in the swimming team, it started when I was sixteen. I did training at the city pool every Saturday morning and a couple of evenings. He was in the county team, a much better swimmer than me; I never took it that seriously, it was for keeping fit really. Anyway we got sort of friendly and he invited me back to his place to play video games after training one Saturday. He didn't actually mean play video games of course.'

'Of course, and did you mind?'

'Mind? Are you joking? I fucking loved it, I wanted him.'

'How did it end, if it has?' the faintest wobble.

'His mum guessed, he was at uni but he lived at home then. I was under age, he got into a bit of trouble, I don't really know, they kept me out of it. Anyway I never went back to training. I saw him in town this summer, he followed me but I was with some friends.'

David thought long and hard about the messing around, friends never went into his bedroom when he was a boy at home, they stayed in the kitchen or lounge or they went out, his parents were omnipresent.

Chapter Six

After two weeks it was going nowhere, it could go nowhere. 'No,' he whispered one evening as Mark sought his mouth, 'it's so powerful,' and took the boy's wrists to keep distance between them yet hung onto them to keep him close. He could see no way forward, it must stay platonic, they must build their relationship on shared interests, respect and affection, but Mark would lose interest very soon judging by the speed of previous conquests. The sexual tension was already bringing in tiny resentments and they could only grow. He could feel Mark slipping away from him and hard as he tried he found it impossible sometimes not to ask about what he did when they weren't together. His life with his peers that had once merely intrigued him now troubled him. What did they talk about? Was he up to date enough on music and new technology? Was Mark being honest about not noticing the age gap? He had nothing to give yet desperately he wanted commitment but to what exactly? He was *his*, and the thought of him with anyone else was unbearable. Was Mark capable of using another lover as a bargaining tool and if he did would that be the permission David was waiting for? Clare had his heart; the boy was only feeding some primitive masculine urge that would splutter out.

Arriving home from meeting Mark that night he headed as usual for the wine bottle and threw back two glasses in quick succession, resolving in the instant kick of bravado to change the relationship with a few simple rules. There would be no parking the car in isolated spots, they would walk on well used paths, they would stop touching and if this was not acceptable it was a kind way of driving it into touch. The following day, after an uncomfortable ten minute silence, at the end of the wide shingle path that circled the country park Mark took his hand and pulled him under the trees, pulling and pulling until they were stumbling and tripping on the dense undergrowth.

'Please,' he said, 'I'll never, ever, tell, *please*, we're both so fucking *hard*, *all* the time.'

David held him tightly in a desperate bear hug which was all that was possible through the layers of winter clothing and Mark calmed against him.

'I like your new coat,' David whispered into an icy ear.

'My sugar daddy gave it to me.'

'He must be very rich.'

'He's extremely rich; he drives a four year old Golf and has a subsidised lunch in the school canteen every day.'

'How lucky you are to have bagged such a prize.'

'He's trying to push me away and I'm pretending I care but he doesn't realise I have a waiting list of admirers.'

'He is clearly out of his depth with such an Adonis but a door has opened into a very deep hole and he's fallen right into it and he's grabbing desperately at anything on the way down to stop himself.'

'Sounds like Alice in Fucking Wonderland. We haven't begun though, you're stopping us and we haven't begun.'

'Give me a break, only my bloody job and career are at stake.' Please god by December the fourth a stray asteroid would be heading toward the planet and a little light shagging of a pupil would be neither here nor there.

That evening, after dropping Mark home, distracted by the worry of losing him, a pile of marking and DIY awaiting him at home, it was his night to meet the young man with three pints inside him from an early evening drinking session to celebrate his twenty first, the stereo cranked up and his mate in the passenger seat urging him on to beat the lights. It happened at a junction he was as familiar negotiating as his own driveway, a right turn with a filter, not far from home. They were standard driving conditions for a rainy November night, the oncoming headlights dancing a light show on the wet road and his wipers a crazy blur across the windscreen.

They hit his passenger side, bouncing off to the right to smash into the central reservation and he was shunted and spun, rocking from left to right twice, finally settling to face the opposite direction. All six air bags went off. The emergency services arrived quickly, blaring lights and sirens, paramedics helped him out and found a few cuts and checked him for concussion. He called Clare and she was with him within minutes and took him home. He was told that it would take a while for the crews to get the two occupants of the other car out.

During the night he woke up and shouted out. Clare put her arm round his shoulders, thankfully, she said comfortingly, his car was modern and built to withstand collisions and luckily it was the passenger side that had taken the brunt of the impact.

The passenger side. In the tranquil moment of silence after the screeching of brakes, the bang like a bomb that instantly emptied his lungs leaving him gasping for air and before a stranger's face appeared at his window, it was his first and only thought. The seat beside him was empty, blissfully empty. He could so easily have been sitting beside him; he had been only fifteen minutes earlier. The airbags had gone off but he would still have been hurt because the door had caved in and his leg might have been trapped and he might have had to be cut out like in the other car and his leg might have been broken and maybe his arm as well and his head could have been knocked or there could have been an internal injury because that's what happened, internal injuries caused by the shock waves that aren't obvious straight away and they would have taken him in the

---

64

ambulance and he would have gone with him and Clare would have come too and it would have all come out because he wouldn't have been able to hide his distress and he would have had to explain where they were going and where they had been and Mark might have clung to him and said things he shouldn't say in his shock and he started to shake, it was delayed reaction she said but it was relief, profound, profound, relief.

She kept her arm round him for a while then slipped down under the duvet and dropped asleep, leaving him staring into the darkness, dealing with the sickening, metal crunching thunk of the crash playing over and over by holding onto the image of him tucked up asleep in bed and Fletcher curled up in his dog basket in the kitchen.

He took the following day off; his neck hurt from whiplash, the air bags had hit him in the face and Clare, full of concern, insisted on staying with him as he felt dizzy every time he turned his head, though only if he turned it quickly he insisted. By mid morning the fate of the occupants of the other car preyed on his mind and he rang the police. They had both suffered broken limbs and cuts but nothing life threatening and although they could have killed him he felt considerable relief at this news. He slept fitfully most of the day, curled up on the sofa at first then retreating to bed. He woke around three feeling better and looked at his phone, there were texts from the head; don't return until you are OK and Sarah; so sorry to hear about the accident, get better soon and Mandy on reception and John and even bloody Mike. Even if the news hadn't reached him by bush telegraph in the morning he had a geography class with him after lunch so why no reply to the text he'd sent when he woke? He got up and wandered fretfully around the house, for christ's sake the boy was always bloody texting him; was this it? Had he chosen this day of all days to decide he'd had enough? When Clare found him on his knees in the hall, measuring a laminate board to fit round the radiator pipe she pulled him to his feet and taking his elbows steered him from behind like a buggy to the sofa. 'Sit,' she ordered and put the TV remote in his hand.

At four thirty as he was going through the motions of making yet another cup of tea there was a knock at the door and he froze.

'How nice of you to call round,' he heard her say, and call into the house, 'David, it's one of the boys from school.'

Aghast he moved quickly to the door and, feigning surprise and pleasure at receiving a personal call stepped out onto the front path, placing himself between them. He felt Clare hovering behind him, 'I'll walk with him to the end of the road, I need some air,' and he turned to give her a conspiratorial 'better spend a few minutes with him as he's cycled all this way' look before she invited him in. He turned quickly back into the house to lift his jacket off the peg and smartly closed the front door. They walked in silence, Mark wheeling his bike between them until they got out of sight of the house then, holding the seat, swung himself behind the bike so they were side by side.

'That was such a stupid thing to do.'

'Your face is all cut.'

'Why? It wasn't necessary, I texted you to say I was OK'

'I wanted to see you.'

'She's bloody seen *you* now!'

'So what, I'm just one of the boys from school. She's pretty.'

'You wanted to see her, didn't you?'

'I heard first thing this morning, the head told us in weekly assembly, I've been desperate to see you all day, to see that you're OK. I didn't want to text; I promise I won't come again.'

What could he say? Rant about the minute by minute effort that was required to keep the whole madness going? He felt dizzy and stopped, steadying himself on the handlebars of the bike, 'you could so easily have been with me,' which was all that actually mattered. They continued to the end of the road and stood quietly.

'Babe, thanks for coming, I'm glad you did.' He put his hand inside Mark's jacket and stroked his stomach.

'Never called me that before,' Mark leaned into the caress and looked incredibly young and uncertain, that was all Clare would have seen David convinced himself.

'It's the accident; it's made me go all soft in the head. D'you mind?'

'I love it. I'll go.' Without taking his eyes off David, he lifted his leg slowly over the bike and pushing off cycled very very slowly around him, just keeping his balance and, having achieved the effect on David that he wanted, cycled off.

The visit gave David permission to shut down, he dozed placidly for two days returning to school to a mention in assembly and beams from staff who usually ignored him. That evening Fletcher had to make do with a quick circuit of the park before being bundled back to Abi. Heavy cloud cover kept the temperature just about high enough for sitting without the heater on in the car and they pulled into a lay-by that David had scouted a few weeks before. His car had been classified a right off, its frame compromised and getting into this courtesy car after the accident had been surprisingly nerve-racking. They sat muffled in their coats like an elderly couple he'd once seen in a car park overlooking the sea, thermos and sandwiches on the dashboard, maybe when he was eighty but not now, not with this stunning companion. The small encounter Mark had had with his home made him ache to take him there.

The next day he drove into town at lunchtime and on his return sat at his desk holding a plump envelope and stared pensively out across the pitches. It was a generous present, possibly too generous but it had a specific goal which justified the amount and would further define their relative positions. It was the sort of thing a parent or a generous relative might give. It was the sort of gift Mark could never match; practical and utterly unromantic it demonstrated only fondness and the thoughts of someone older and wiser with his future in mind. He pushed the envelope back into his case with satisfaction and mused enjoyably on how it would be received. It was all getting out of hand, this could be the clincher to restoring those affectionate but platonic feelings that had started this friendship over a year ago, and free Mark's time up for a bit of serious cycling together which was what the whole thing was really all about. And so, having satisfied himself that he had laid down the ground rules, set up the necessary barriers, identified the limited lines of engagement he made his way at break to the art department armed with a packet of Rich Tea and his paper.

'Happy?' Sarah asked after a while, not taking her eyes off her screen.

'Sitting with a hot mug of tea, a biscuit to dunk, my paper and surrounded by the work of the next Brit Artists? How could I not be? Why?'

'Just wondered, I'm reading one of those selfy helpy books, you know, how to be happy and find your inner peace.'

'I find it by filling my inner piece with good food and drink. I bet that's not one of the selfy helpy answers in your book.' It could have been something she was asking everyone but anything personal brought him out in a sweat these days.

'You've been very jittery recently but seem to have found some inner tranquility this afternoon. Something nice happened?" She'd noticed that the snapping of his paper sharply into readable folds and then into more readable folds and the constant shifting in his chair which had been going on for weeks, had stopped this afternoon.

'You want to be careful with those self help books, anyway I think you have plenty of inner peace, you don't want them to go and disturb it with too much thinking malarkey.' He took a long swig of tea and raised his paper to close the matter. Christ, was his anxiety that obvious, he couldn't let that happen again, who else had noticed?

'It's Mike isn't it?'

'Mike? I never see the fuckwit because I'm round here, chilling.' Now his heart was pounding as if he'd been caught with his hand in the petty cash. If she had noticed who else had? Clare?

'I get a bit of down time round here, you don't mind do you?' He gave her a big warm, uncomplicated, that's all there is to it, smile. The canary had sung her warning, he must get a grip.

'Course I don't.'

He took a deep breath and let it out slowly, like he'd told a weepy year seven to do last week, handing her a tissue. She'd recovered quickly as he continued to type; she'd only needed sympathy and a quiet moment. Pretty much what he was doing except he didn't need the tissue. Sarah heard his slow release of breath, he was a tough nut to crack, don't treat it like a challenge she warned herself or he'll be off.

At home the DIY schedule continued relentlessly. Test squares of neutral emulsions covered the living room walls and dust sheets covered everything else, they put the TV in the kitchen while they ate and decorated until midnight. Clare's single mindedness to complete the task was useful, she knew his heart wasn't in it so she made sure hers was and a touch of guilt about hating the place stopped her asking as often as she wanted about David's frequent late homecomings.

Chapter Seven

The birthday deadline was now three weeks away, he froze at the thought of how he'd set himself up. The location increased the trauma, they would have to find somewhere private, a hotel, and for some inexplicable reason a 1950's scene of pink candlewick bedspreads came to mind with an ice cold bathroom along a narrow corridor. Films were his only experience of illicit sex. These days it would be one of those hotels marooned on out of town slip roads, cheap, anonymous and basic. The prospect, now so close, made him nervous and anxious like an interview or exam results, one word of doubt from Mark and he would have ended it, there and then, driven him home and out of his life, apart from three geography lessons a week. During a long silence one evening Mark leant forward and rummaged in his rucksack at his feet producing a pack of cigarettes, pulled one out, lit it and took a long slow draw, David raised his eyebrows.

'What?' Mark said coolly.

'I've never seen you smoke before.'

'I do after sex.'

'I'm no expert but I don't believe we've *had* sex.'

'Just practicing for when we do. Anyway I do smoke occasionally, when I get a chance, aren't too many places you can these days. Suppose you're going to say I can't smoke in your car.'

'Not mine, go ahead.'

A spot of challenging behaviour, he was up to it and leaning over took the cigarette from Mark's fingers, put it in his own mouth and took a long pull himself.

'Haven't done that for a while.' They shared the cigarette, passing it softly between fingers and lips.

'That was sexy,' Mark whispered onto his mouth and laced his fingers with David's. 'How much fucking longer, I mean who's to know and when I *am* eighteen are you going to go all fuzzy on me because I'm still under your bloody care? It's driving me crazy; you're denying me my basic human rights. And that fucking car crash, Jesus why don't you just go and *die* on me before we do anything.' He turned his head away sharply and stared through the windscreen into the night.

David wished he could sum his own predicament up so neatly and they sat on in a brooding silence. Suddenly it was all too much; he threw himself out and slammed the door hard, leaning against it, his breath steaming into the cold night air. It was impossible, Mark wasn't teasing, he meant it; he was saying please, we have to move on or give up. God, he was behaving like some girl, not wanting to go the whole way yet arousing him, he had got this far, it was deceitful and wrong enough already. He dragged one hand hard across his face, letting his teeth dig into his palm, then scraped his fingernails hard down his face for the distraction of pain. He had gone over the facts a thousand thousand times, the breach of trust, the inappropriate relationship, cheating and deceiving Clare who had done nothing but love him and he looked ahead into the darkness, almost pleading for a solution. If he stopped thinking about it and fanaticising about it and *did it*, if it was a disaster then at least he'd know and could move on. The dilemma was no longer the way he felt, he absolutely no longer denied how he felt. End it, end it, end it *now* he ordered kicking back viciously with the heel of his shoe, digging a hole in the muddy ground till it was stupid and missing him he opened the rear door and climbed back in.

'Dave, I didn't mean….' Mark's anxious face stared between the seats and David took the shoulders of his coat and pulled.

'Come 'ere,' he said stubbornly and started tugging the boy's not inconsiderable frame between the front seats. Laughing with surprise Mark resisted but David tugged harder,

'Now, *now*,' he said almost angrily as they grappled. 'Didn't you ever wrestle? You missed out there,' he mocked. Then Mark understood and kicked his way between the seats and they rolled around on the back seat, falling into the seat well and pulling each other out, giggling until they gave up and lay quietly in each others arms.

'Let's take it slowly eh? No hurry.'

First ties, freeing their necks, then shirt buttons, a muddle of fingers as they skipped undecided between their own and each others. Then buckles and zips, David's hands now shaking but his mouth reassuring and convinced on Mark's. Clothed, yet not, pressing their bodies together from face to crotch they slipped their hands behind the layers to feel each others backs and shoulders and buttocks. Oh the hours indulged in lovemaking while he drove and marked and stared out of his office window, now here he was, dizzy with lust, but still acutely aware of the occasional headlights as cars swept past the lay-by, ready to spring apart if disturbed. He kissed him deeply, leave it at this? This could be enough, by far the longest and most ardent courtship of his life. Go on, whoever you are, send a sign; a torch flashing across the windscreen, another car pulling up behind them in the lay-by, a good old fashioned thunderbolt. But the cars sped past and save for the soft touch of a half moon on their faces they were secure in the pitch dark of the country lane. And so, finally sure of himself, he sank down onto the boy's penis, holding him when he came, watching intently his every gasp and shudder.

Lying with Mark's face against his chest and his fingers

entwined in his hair he silently promised them both that if there was a next time it wouldn't be in a car. They met each other's eyes and smiled almost shyly. Taking his mobile out of his pocket David noted the time and slowly buttoned his buttons, then Mark's.

'Sorry it's a bit cramped in here. I asked the garage for a bigger car.'

'Big enough for two guys to make out on the back seat?'

'I mentioned that requirement *specifically* but they said they didn't have that size available this week.'

'We managed. By the way, bit late now but it's still over two weeks away, December the fourth.'

David sat up dramatically, 'My god is it? I will offer my resignation first thing tomorrow, there's no other way forward.'

'Shut up.'

'I shall pack a small hold all and fly standby to Rio where I will proceed to wander lonely and penitent across the South American continent with nothing but the memory of this heavenly evening to sustain me till I die friendless in some squalid lodgings.'

'Don't talk crap.'

Don't use mockery to blank the guilt because it was surely on its way. 'Hey, *hey*, I'm staying right here.' He cradled his anxious face, kissing him over and over.

When he got home he showered immediately and put every item of his clothing in the wash basket, every centimetre of exposed skin had been kissed, there was semen on his clothes. He stood under the water for a long time, would he feel guilty like this every time, would he get used to it, would there *be* another time. He pressed the flats of his hands against the tiles and looked down the length of his body recalling over and over the soft wetness of the boy's mouth as the hot water pounded on his back.

Everything changed, everything looked different. He was different. He had done, and intended to continue to do, the unthinkable. Over the next few days he imagined his guilt seeping out into his speech like slime, every inflection, every nuance corrupted. It was his first experience of real guilt, it sat heavy on his lungs and stomach and he broke into sweat when his name was called or at glances in the corridor. How did the truly guilty cope? Murderers? Fraudsters, shoplifters even?

He felt anxious about Mark, he had handed someone the power to break him. When he thought about them together it was always as equals but this was a fantasy. Could he shift the power balance outside school so the boy felt more in control and would it make him more loyal? Nothing major, just small decisions like when and where, which pub and which seats and what to order. It wouldn't be hard, in some ways he was more of a follower than leader but often through laziness. Yet as he planned these strategies he knew the affair would expire quickly. After a few days he felt calmer than for a long time, almost liberated. Mark clearly understood the need for total discretion and in those first few heady days anything seemed possible. David kept his regular social engagements and one Friday evening he found himself unexpectedly curious about his male companions in the pub; how they sat with knees and elbows spread, voices loud and suitably sardonic. How the evening lurched along with a little light bragging, some competitive sarcasm and a lot of current affairs one-upmanship, they struck him as coarse and as sexually undesirable as they ever had. He also thought a great deal about Clare, how these days she chose a comfortable chair with the girls, absorbed in conversation with her friends she would barely glance at him, he was there, that was all she needed. It was only at the end of the evening, as they milled around saying their goodbyes that she confirmed her possession, slipping her arm through his.

'Happy birthday.' He took the plump envelope out of his inside coat pocket and put it in the boy's hands. 'It's boring but practical.' Mark squeezed it tentatively and opened it cautiously. 'Twenty lessons, on top of what you've already done it should get you through.'

Mark pushed the vouchers back into the envelope and looked away, 'you know I work at the garden centre to pay for them, I can't accept this, it's *so* much money.'

'Listen, most people buy presents that benefit *them* more than the recipient and I'm afraid this is a text book example. It's the only way I can see you, its dark and cold after school now, I want to see you on Saturday but you're working. This way we can be together for part of Saturday at least and do things together, we can go to the sports centre, go cycling. Please accept them, for us, please.'

'It's the most expensive present I've ever had, its really hard for me. How will I explain to Mum that I'm having driving lessons and not working? And it's like you're…'

'Buying you? Yeah, OK I am, I'm buying your time. And I'm also risking *everything* for you. Its only money.'

His careless generosity had scuppered his attempt at equality between them and he thought quickly.

'I thought it was romantic,' he said meekly. It worked.

'Thanks a million.'

He had dropped him off outside countless times over the past year, mildly curious about what it was like inside but now he was going to find out his imagination couldn't see beyond an interior equivalent to the dirty stark grey cement exterior. It was in its original state, including the crumbling awning, built around the early 60s to Parker Morris standards and still rented from the council. As he got out of the car the gloom of the early December evening and the sulpha yellow tinge of the sodium street light did not improve its appearance. The privet hedge, unevenly cut for years now billowed in obese bulges round the front garden but was, nevertheless, neatly trimmed up to the boundary with the adjoining semi whose own hedge sprang up in giant spikes.

Mark had explained his mother's shift pattern but David nevertheless prepared for her to be in with a detailed explanation ready of the extra work that Mark required to reach the grades Manchester would want. At first he'd protested that he couldn't possibly visit without meeting her, it was rude; it was out of the question. They argued, he reluctantly reminded Mark of his position, Mark reminded David that he wanted to be alone with him but had ruled out the car and David gave in.

Conspicuously clutching a pile of textbooks under his arm he strode purposefully up the path and checked his watch impatiently as Mark fumbled with the key. He glanced at the house on the right; a brick paved front garden, a PVC porch and glass door, right to buyed. Once inside he braced himself for signs of deprivation; ugly furniture, threadbare carpets, the smell of stale food and a filthy chip pan. Or maybe sage green throughout, in his opinion the interior design choice of indecision, in fact his parents' own colour scheme which he now loathed. Instead he saw large saggy sofas with coloured throws, walls covered in framed art and stuffed bookshelves, bohemian academic chic he decided, like a cuckoo in the wrong nest and he was hugely relieved.

'I have to start dinner.'

Still anticipating Mrs Derby's appearance David flinched as a figure appeared in the doorway but it was a girl of about twelve who sidled in and sat opposite him, her elbows on the table her head cupped in her hands. David smiled at her and took in the lighter hair, the same narrow face and her eyes, bigger and quite different. He recognised the uniform of an all girl's school in town.

'My sister Abigail, or Abi.' Abi had presented yet another dilemma, she would most definitely be in this evening and David refused to believe that a twelve year old would keep his visit a secret from her mother which caused another tiff, this time leaving Mark silent, his capacity for salvage finally drying up, 'don't come round then,' he'd said sullenly, 'I'm coming round,' David had replied instantly.

Fletcher, delighted to see David, pressed his head on his knees and he praised his obedience and ball catching skills and admired his heavy silky ears. Abi watched him silently and assuming shyness and disguising his own nerves he moved onto school, his high opinion of the one she attended and a few teachers he knew from local teacher get togethers. She listened patiently.

'Thank you for coming, we like having visitors.'

'Well it's very nice to be invited.'

'We used to live in a very nice house, you know, not like this one.' She fiddled with the plates on the table. 'We had bone china tea things and a breakfast room and a conservatory. That was when we had a father but when he died we had to move here because of the expense but we're going to move back into the same sort of house quite soon.'

Taking David's startled silence as encouragement she took a pencil and began to draw on the margin of his newspaper he had laid on the table. 'For *example*, we'll live in a cul de sac with paddocks and swag curtains. It will have manicured lawns, a big staircase, attic rooms full of ancestors' toys and a wing. And a stable block.' She paused as she drew the ties for the swag curtains, as if to summon more extravagance to mind. 'The gardener will grow pineapples in cold frames, there will be peaches on the south facing garden wall and the cook will make ice cream with the strawberries.' David glanced at Mark who paused in his potato peeling, widened his eyes dramatically, raised his eyebrows and looked hugely impressed.

'It all sounds lovely,' said David, latching on. A melange of Pride and Prejudice films, the cover of a thick historical romance and some TV programme about restoring historic gardens, no harm in her dreaming her way out of this grim estate.

He stood up and looked through the kitchen window, 'I think you have a very nice house here though, it's very comfy and you have a much bigger garden than I do.' He moved over to Mark, laying his hand on his back, if he didn't mind her being there then he couldn't object to some touching. He felt her watching closely.

77

'He's going to work at an American summer camp after his exams, he's applied already, and then he's going travelling, to South America.'

'Really?' He didn't look at Mark, had she been primed to give this information?

She left the kitchen but returned quickly with an atlas opening it to the double page spread of the world, indicating for him to sit in the chair beside her. 'I'm going to go travelling one day, I'm going to the Taj Mahal, *then* to the Grand Canyon, *then* Venice, *then* the pyramids, then Australia' Her finger zig zagged confidently across the world.

'In that order?'

'I don't think the order matters, does the order matter? I've seen this book about the places you must see before you die, if you were going to die then you might have to see the most famous first in case you died before you got to the end. But of course I would have to keep coming home to check on mum and Fletcher. That would change the order.'

'That's not what I meant,' but he stopped himself. 'I've probably only seen a fraction of these places it tells you to see. How about Mark, is he coming home to check on everyone?' He addressed it to his back, so lightly said, so heavily laden.

'It's a long way off, 'Mark replied without looking round. Finally with the potatoes and vegetables in pans on the stove, the sausages under the grill and the onions sweating over a low heat in the frying pan Mark turned away from the cooker.

'Let me show you my new video game,' he jerked his head in the direction of upstairs. 'Keep an eye on the dinner Abi, yeah?'

Anywhere downstairs was perfectly OK but he hesitated at the foot the stairs and looked up at Mark waiting for him at the top. He would stay a minute, just a quick look round his room to put him in context and straight back down again. Smiling reassuringly at Mark he ran up the stairs and froze in the bedroom's doorway.

It was a child's bedroom, for some inexplicable reason he'd expected a bachelor pad with neutral colours and contemporary fittings, Tony's place maybe. Mark watched, stony faced as David's eyes swept the room, taking in the fads and crazes of a late twentieth century boyhood, some of which he'd shared; Pokémon, Lego, Darth Vader, Ninja Turtles and what was that higher up? Chunky plastic diggers, My First Computer and rows of tiny figures from cereal boxes. The curtains were Bob the Builder, the duvet cover sported Toy story, Spongebob Squarepants hung, grinning manically, from the light fitting and faded animal posters sagged off the walls; there hadn't been a clearout since he was three, he was in a child's bedroom. All the smart talk, the narrow ties and slick shoes were packaging, he was with a child and his legs wobbled in fright, he must extricate himself as quickly and painlessly as possible.

'I know, it desperately needs a makeover.'

'Yes, yes it does. Box everything up and give it a lick of paint, trouble is you don't know what to do with the boxes you feel some of it might all be worth something one day,' he gabbled. DIY; practical, sexless, no nonsense DIY, talk DIY and then head off home for more DIY.

'They need to be pristine, still in their original packing is best.'

'That would have required far too much self control when I was young, not something I have much of now.'

'I disagree, you've been hard work.' Mark took a step towards him.

'Listen, I don't think I should be here.' He let his voice take on the timbre of the classroom, firm and no nonsense. 'Let's go back downstairs and help Abi and then I'd better be off.'

Mark's launch was so unexpected that the boy's thirteen stone punched all the air out of his lungs as he landed on the bed. As he gasped, trying to fill his lungs again Mark took his wrists and forced his hands over his head and though he fought hard to push him off, the spring of the bed did not give enough resistance. They struggled, tears of anger and frustration dampening the corners of David's eyes, he simply couldn't move him but at all costs he had to get out of the house. Finally Mark forced his knees up onto David's chest and he stopped struggling instantly, seriously afraid his ribs would crack.

'You're really hurting me,' he said coldly and the tear that escaped was of misery at the mess.

Mark rolled off instantly and sat on the edge of his bed. 'I meant to.'

'OK, you've proved you're stronger than me.'

'You know it's not *that*, this is my home and I want you here.'

David lay quietly; he would get off the bed slowly and deliberately and leave in a dignified manner in his own time. He took in the room again; a poster of an attractive, shirtless young man on the opposite wall, a computer and textbooks on the table and the solid frame of a man who had just physically overpowered him beside him. He relaxed as he regained his breath, the tussle had broken the tension and he was even lying on the boy's bed, for god's sake. Mark's head suddenly sank into his hands, and without hesitation David rested his hand on the boy's back, they had moved on he reminded himself. Gripping his waist and with a pull he rolled him into his arms, burying his face in his hair and they lay still.

'Sorry,' he whispered. Sorry he was embarrassed by the grotty room and grotty housing estate, sorry he was struggling so hard to be the uncomplicated lover that the boy wanted him to be.

'I like your sister.'

'Yeah, she's OK.'

'She obviously knows, about us?'

'She knows, I don't hide things from her. What's the point, I have to look after her, I have done for years. By the way, she never knew that lifestyle she described, she was a baby, she looks at old photos we have and then she makes up some stupid future from those magazines where they photograph rich people's houses and stuff she sees on TV.'

'No harm in her having those dreams.' Puberty would put paid to them.

He flipped Mark over onto his back and, looking steadily into his eyes, cupped the boy's head in his hands, lifting it off the bed and took its weight. 'Relax.' Mark's breath slowed, his eyes closed.

'S'nice.'

'I do it to all my boys. And their *mummies* like it too.'

'And their little sisters?'

'*Especially* their little sisters.'

Eventually they heard Abi call that the potatoes were done and David rolled off the bed onto his feet pulling Mark into his arms for a slow kiss. As they left the room David glanced round again, it wouldn't take much, new curtains and duvet cover, some decent shelving and track lighting. He noticed a large pin board on the wall of family photos, photos of Mark and friends and a photo of swimmers at the pool, their arms slung over each others shoulders.

Chapter Eight

Mark was pressed against the corridor wall as a stream of pupils poured into the canteen and he caught David's eye, holding his mobile up briefly before quickly disappearing. The anxiety on the boy's face made David abandon the queue and leave the building. Tucking himself into a doorway, hands thrust deep into his pockets, he cradled his phone in the crook of his neck, waiting for it to ring.

'You're not going to believe this, we've had a run through of the play, there's this running gag; have you seen Mr Ashbourne, yes, he's playing squash with Mark Derby. Five fucking times! Ralf and Suzanne didn't look at me but a couple of others picked it up and asked, you know, what's that all about? I mean it's not remotely *funny*, it's deliberate, you know? I didn't know what to say, I mean what could I say?'

David headed for his car, luckily parked facing a brick wall, only a brick wall was going to see his expression.

'It's Mike Thompson, yup, it's quite deliberate, it's not unexpected.' How ingenious, Mike outs him through the school play; 'I only meant it as a joke! If people want to read something into it then let them.' Why, he could ask Mike to write an ending for the affair while he was at it and save him the trouble.

'Let's finish, now, you'll get the sack, you'll have to leave, I couldn't bear it...' The words and tone were at odds, there was a 'you sort this out' challenge in Mark's delivery and thus cornered David did not feel cooperative.

'OK, fair dos; let's call it a day, we've had a decent run.'
There was a wail.

'Chill, I'll *deal* with it.'

Ralf was reading a magazine in the sixth form lounge
when Mark arrived, breathless from running and anxiety,
'Hey,' he swung his head toward the main door and jabbed a
finger into his mouth a few times. They pulled on overcoats,
Mark eager to leave quickly in case someone else showed
interest in joining them.

'Café.'

'Its too *cold*, lets go to the canteen.'

'No, the café, *please*, crisis,' and with a little more bullying
they set off on the five minute walk to the local greasy
spoon. As they pushed open the door steam from huge
boiling pans and non stop frying since 6am coated them in
an oily fug.

'I'm not that hungry to be honest, just wanted to get
away.'

'Well I am.' Ralf ordered lunch from the large over the
counter menu board while Mark sat hunched, nursing his
phone.

'Bought you a coffee, c'mon, you gotta lighten up.' Ralf
sank into the chair opposite to await his lunch, folding his
arms on the table and leaning in close. 'I guess you told him
then?'

'This has got to be it, he won't handle this, Thompson is
such a bastard, they can't stand each other,' he flipped his
phone over and over in his hand.

'No one will understand, you're getting paranoid, it'll get
lost amongst all the other stupid gags, I promise you.
Anyway I told Mike the script needs a rewrite, it's too
complicated. Besides the guy's far too smitten, I mean, way
outside my area of expertise of course, but if we stick to *stats*
you are probably in the top 10 to 20 percent of people
considered to be vaguely appealing. He ain't going to give

you up that easily, and he might be worried you'd spill the beans if he dumped you. He'll keep it going until the end of the year, then curtains. Sorry mate, I know it's not what you want to hear but it's kinda obvious. I mean the bloke's getting *married*. It's all going ahead, I know it is. Suzanne's sister, right, goes to school with this girl whose mother is making the bridesmaid's dresses.'

'What?'

'I'm trying to tell you that meanwhile, while you two are fucking each other senseless, or whatever you do, matters are proceeding. Little girls are having their little pink dresses made. And choosing bouquets and stuff to put on their heads. All that shit.'

'He never talks about it.'

'Well he wouldn't would he?'

A gust of icy air hit them as the door opened and a crowd of builders jostled noisily in and stood, heads tipped back, to quote the menu over their heads like a favourite poem, expressing camp derision at each others choices. Mark watched them intently over his coffee cup; a job on a building site may not suit, not if he couldn't even take the current wind up. Ralf, his back to the builders, continued to relate his latest attempt at finding somewhere quiet and dry to pursue his love life.

'Not still hanging round the country park are you?'

'He's started to come home with me a bit. Mum, well you know about mum.'

Ralf's image of Mark's mother was of someone issuing a list of instructions as she disappeared through the door. 'Fuckin' *bliss*, you have no idea. Mine never seems to go out.'

The phone rang which made them both jump. The call lasted a few seconds, 'I think I might have some lunch after all,' Mark said as he stuffed it back into his pocket with a grin.

'Well?'

'Sorted.'

'Far too smitten, didn't Uncle Ralfy tell you?'

Mark joined the short queue and out of the corner of his eye appraised one of the builders through the steamy mirrors covering the full length of one wall of the café. Quieter than the others he noted his large hands, small straight nose and sharp jaw line and watched as he pulled the Sun, rolled into a tight tube, out of his back jeans pocket and started to read. But what would we *talk* about though, he wondered?

'I just wanted to hit him, to punch his lights out. I said I understand there's some sort of running joke in the script about Mark and I and he said only an in joke, only a few of the sixth would have got it, don't loose your sense of humour over it. And I said then why put it in, *five* times? If they don't understand they'll ask and someone will tell them, school, staff, parents and he said he was going to take it out, the thing needed a re write and anyway tell them *what*? Shit, I fell right in it. He said I'm not accusing you of anything, what exactly are you saying I'm accusing you of?

'Shit.'

'He's being saying things, you know, like Mark's waiting for you by your car, or, are you waiting for Mark? Very casual but unnecessary and pointed, stuff like that. I told him, we walked your dog, that I liked dogs, that we had stuff in common, that sometimes blokes my age were a bit dull, him for example, no, I didn't say that. It was that bitch Julie Hope, she told him she thought she saw you kiss me in the park.' David had remembered the moment precisely; tucked behind a tree trunk Mark had held out one of the ear buds from his phone. 'What is it?' 'Try.' Mark had placed the bud in his ear, simultaneously kissing him hard. It was techno trance, pulsating and hypnotic, the sound filled his head and the kiss whipped it through his synapses. 'Nice?' he'd asked. Nice? Did bears? Now the bloody country park would be out of bounds.

'I'm sorry I but didn't know what to do, I should have said something, but he's staff Dave, d'you understand? What would you have done if I'd ended it?'

'Dug a hole, got in, and died,' he said, surprising himself how genuine it sounded.

'Don't be daft.' Mark compared Ralf's wedding information uncomprehendingly against this earnest commitment to their relationship.

'You don't know,' David said quietly, 'how I can go down, how I can sink.'

'It's hard for me too, you moron. I get it at school.'

'What, what d'you get?'

'That I like boys, nothing nasty, just teasing I suppose. That's why I've stopped using the networking sites, stuff gets on them. All I want is to tell them that I have a boyfriend, that it's you and that you fancy me, that you *want* me, like their stupid girlfriends want them. Only Ralph and Suzanne know and none of your friends know do they?'

'I can't possibly tell anyone.'

Mark watched David swallow hard and slid his hand between the car seat and the small of his back. This wedding, there was something dynastic about it; like two families protecting their wealth, had he misunderstood? He slipped his hand back into his lap, nothing was straight forward: whenever he called time on the relationship, however half heartedly, how quickly and reassuringly David gave in. There was always the hot builder to admire though; another café lunch tomorrow was a temptation and Chris, how easy that would be to retrieve. At the lights David felt for Mark's hand and replaced it in the small of his back.

David settled himself inconspicuously halfway down the hall amongst the lower school, deliberately keeping away from the sixth and any staff. He had considered staying away but Mark had insisted, 'just look cool.' The school Christmas play in which staff and pupil roles were reversed was now a fixed event and looked forward to by all but the most persecuted. Though not surprised he'd not been given a role this year considering who the playwright and director were, David was nevertheless a little disappointed. Last year he'd played the head boy, a keen scholar with a reputation for being very charming and diplomatic. The play had taken the school through a series of catastrophes which the head boy proves he cannot deal with, finally dissolving in a sobbing tantrum. It had been a triumph, he had managed to caricature him without humiliating him and the head had stamped his feet in delight at the end. Stretching out his legs and leaning back in the chair he considered his position, these events were integral to the functioning of the school, he must be seen to participate fully. The curtain rose to a hushed and expectant young audience, glancing at his watch he hoped Mark's backstage role would not keep him late.

He appeared in the second act and it took a few moments for David to recognise him. His locks, that had been curling very nicely round his ears, had gone, replaced by a severe short back and sides, he was wearing a grey suit and had a camera slung round his neck. He marched purposefully onto the stage and started to order around a group of cowering staff dressed in uniform, 'come on, move along, this isn't a *care* home, let's see a bit of action!' His movements were quick, even jerky and he raked his fingers through his hair almost shaking with impatience. Sarah, looking disconcertingly provocative in a short school uniform and the new English teacher hovered dreamily, gazing upward and twirling their hair. He swung an imaginary racquet energetically at imaginary balls, snapped away with his camera and David followed him, mesmerised, around the stage. Then someone who looked like the head of languages, sporting a long blonde wig, complained petulantly about the weather on a forthcoming fieldtrip and received a sharp lecture on dressing correctly. The penny dropped, he saw the eyes of every child around focused on him, watching intently for his reaction and, entirely from shock, his face remained impressively impassive. Quickly he forced the delighted smile he knew was now expected.

What on god's *earth* was he doing? He'd extricated them from one outing, was this some appalling joke to bring the whole thing to a very public end or just a massive attack of naivety? But the children were loving it, yes, sir was just like this, and here he was, sitting amongst them, looking satisfyingly stunned. The play continued relentlessly on, David maintaining a fixed expression of enjoyment throughout, but the end could not come soon enough, the fact that other staff were being heavily lampooned too hardly registering. When a chubby and feisty second year look alike bellowed the head's familiar assembly call to arms David was completely forgotten.

By the end his heart had given up pounding, it was just good casting, that's how everyone would see it, why should they see it any other way, that was the point of the school play, for one afternoon the staff had their comeuppance and as the curtain fell he stood up, grinning widely with relief, clapped enthusiastically and Mark, with a majestic sweep of the imaginary squash racquet, bowed deeply in his direction. Mark Derby was only enjoying for a brief moment on stage a little power over a member of staff with whom he played a bit of squash. The children crowded round.

'That was *wicked*, sir, he was well like you are.'

'Did you mind, did you mind?' someone begged hopefully, but the concern in Oliver's 'you won't be mad at him will you?' appeared quite genuine.

'I will issue him with a series of evening detentions, it was an *outrage*,' David replied pompously but they were already moving on to the refreshments. His phone buzzed, an anxious text but he let him sweat until he dropped into the passenger seat beside him ten minutes later.

'Don't mind?'

'Am I *really* that nerdy and needy?'

'Sort of.'

'So what's a cool dude like you doing with me then?'

'Your dorkyness accentuates my sophistication. Anyway it got them off the scent, I seriously took the piss out of you in rehearsals, double bluff eh?'

The haircut was a lasting reminder of the performance,

their association was now confirmed as comedic not romantic; '*so* good, I *had* to laugh, don't take it to heart Dave,' being ridiculed had never felt so good. The anxiety eased, he mentioned Mark's academic progress in the staffroom, he slept through the night. Far from driving wedges between them and making him question the effort these little crises were bringing them closer, each one further cementing the bond. He was so fucking happy, if only he could tell Clare how happy he was.

Booked during the confused days of early October David was blocking out the skiing holiday over Christmas with Clare's parents. As soon as he got back from the factory visit Jack had started to copy him into all his emails and he ignored them. It was when he saw that he was the only recipient that panic set in; what did he think? Jack asked, what was his advice?

'Looks interesting and I really don't know' only sufficed for a couple of replies so he became more inventive in his meaninglessness; 'I'd go as far as to say this appears to fit the bill; notwithstanding the previous reply I'd be interested to see how this one follows through', and; 'could definitely be taken further, or not; keep me posted how this pans out.' And Mark's contribution, 'let's touch base on it offline.' In fact quite a few of them were Mark's, he was amused by management speak and David wondered how many jokey drafts had been sent without his approval. If Jack was latching on to the joke he wasn't letting on and they kept coming until an invite to a meeting in Düsseldorf arrived and stupid replies didn't seem a good idea anymore and he made it clear it was completely out of the question, it was a school day.

It was the time alone with Jack on the holiday that he was really dreading, the early evening drink 'to let the girls get ready,' dated masculine bonding that he hated. Watching Jack grunt and gasp his way out of an armchair gave David hope that the bloke might have to stick to the lower runs or even the cross country track this time so no chance of getting stuck for hours with him in a high altitude bar. Now, barely a week away he put on some semblance of enthusiasm in front of Clare for this extravagant holiday. For Mark he painted a bleak picture; a long walk to the lifts from the poorly located hotel in painful ski boots, long, cold, boring queues for the uncomfortable pomas that he regularly fell off, crowded slopes with beginners using you as brakes. Mark was none the wiser, skiing was a mystery. He was working at the garden centre and there was no doubt from the little information he offered David that the celebrations in his house would be modest. His mother appeared to take full advantage of the unsociable shifts for extra money and David, so at home with guilt about Jack's largesse these days, let the festivities in the Derby's house sink to some Dickensian nightmare in his imagination. Left to his own devices the whole Christmas business would start and finish on the 25th, with an assault on the shops the Saturday before. This year however the shops and catalogues stuffed into the Sunday papers for men's clothes and gadgets captured his attention weeks beforehand, but it was all out of the question, the boy was becoming touchy about money. He'd agreed to the hotel though; beer, 50 channels, sex and wrestling, they left exhausted.

Mark saw him amongst the Christmas crowds after David had left for Switzerland and felt compelled to stop and watch him for a few moments and then allow him to approach. It had all begun with tiny gestures of interest and encouragement from him at the pool; a thumbs up acknowledging a good personal time, a towel tossed over casually at the end of a race, coming to sit next to him in the café afterwards. Eventually an invitation to check out some new video game and they fell on one another as the bedroom door closed, Jason astonished that he wasn't exactly the first. They were inseparable for six months.
After a few minutes of stilted conversation Jason suggested a

coffee bar.

'So, where d'you meet him then?'

Mark shifted uncomfortably, the tables were small; they were too close, too suddenly and he concentrated on the baristas working hard behind the bar. The settings for their entanglement had been exclusively the pool, which was legit and Jason's bedroom, which had not. Jason's stubbornness about keeping apart in public had even included separate buses.

'You know, the usual.'

'No?'

'School, I met him at school.'

'Not a fucking *teacher*? You're joking!'

Mark remained silent.

'Dirty bastard! He could get into serious trouble, my god look what fucking happened to *me*.'

Mark felt contempt and imagined David's infuriation at his admittance - it's private, why are you telling him? Being grown up and having coffee with your ex was a bad idea. He rallied, 'I'm eighteen now.' And he trotted out the explanation he himself had been offered; it wouldn't last long, he was off to uni anyway, Manchester was his first choice, he would never see him again. He could barely comprehend how it functioned himself, let alone explain it to Jason.

'This guy, if anyone gets wind of it he'll be sacked, his career will be finished.'

'I know. It's just a bit of fun, it won't last, like us.'

'It wasn't nice, didn't it affect you?' Jason caught his eyes and held them.

'It's all a bit blurred now, I was told it was wrong, so I felt guilty.'

It was the county championships and Jason had won the backstroke final. Mark had been desperately eager to get close to him, it was a personal best time for Jason and all he could do was wave frantically from his bench. Ten minutes later his team was second in the freestyle relay and as he rushed to join him he saw a little huddle around Jason including his mother and trainer and it had looked fraught and Mark guessed that it had something to do with him. She had guessed, Jason had said, she had been asking questions. Standing, scowling, a towel round his shoulders, his arms folded it had been the last time he'd seen him. The decision not to return to the pool was his own, it would have been very different if he had been one of the stars but he wasn't and he later leant that Jason too had pulled out of the team. Nobody said a word to him about it, it was as if it hadn't happened.

'Are you seeing anyone?'

'Not really, a few casual things.'

Jason moved the conversation into mutual friends and acquaintances and Mark relaxed back into the chair. Those curls, the pool chlorine had turned them almost white at the tips, now they were darker but still one of his best features. Their knees bumped as they slumped in their chairs and Mark straightened up, unable to mask a smile.

'Fancy a jar one evening, now you're legal,' Jason asked.

Within twenty-four hours of the encounter with Jason, Mark's confidence in his affair was plummeting and lying motionless on his bed in the dark he struggled to orientate himself in David's life. Clare, her glossy hair swinging like a curtain as she turned to call to David that afternoon after his car accident and the condescension in her expression. How *sweet* that one of his pupils had turned up, be *nice* to him, he's come all this way on his *bike*.

As the hours passed, lying motionless on his bed, only the awkward, difficult moments surfaced. The tender moments lost their tenderness and turned to taunts. How was he expected to behave, should he modify his chatter and act more mature? David's bleak details about his skiing holiday left Mark unconvinced and he had Googled the five star hotel and resort and regretted it. 'I'll phone you whenever I can get away,' David had said and his own pathetic rejoinder;

'Christmas, it's nothing, same old, same old.' Where was he now? In a queue for a poma lift? Whatever that was.

Sitting with Jason again a few nights later, someone he now recognised as not much older than himself and possibly even poorer, he saw the gap between them had virtually disappeared. There had once been talk of going to the USA together and Jason casually raised it again, confident having heard the end of Mark's affair drawn so clearly by the end of the school year. Mark had already sent in his application and they agreed to try for the same camp. At the end of the evening it was no surprise that Jason made it perfectly clear he wanted to sleep with him.

Leaving Clare to her lessons on the nursery slopes and Shirley and Jack to the cross country tracks David was relieved to find how much time he would be spending on his own. Wouldn't he be lonely Shirley wondered but there was no point feigning reluctance, Clare saw through it instantly. Every morning he clipped on his skis at the hotel door and skated down the gentle slope to the cable car station, exiting at the top and taking a chair lift the long last steep stretch to the start of the top runs. One morning he found himself sitting alone with another man, a Dutchman, Johann, who, like David, had left his family on the nursery slopes. Usually tightly packed on the seat besides chattering friends he appreciated sharing it with only one other, an opportunity to appreciate the gentle swing of the chair, the low hum of the power cables and the expectance of the run that the snowy swish of the skiers below brought. They soon fell into conversation and discussed the high temperatures that season, the effect of global warming on the ski industry and the rights and wrongs of snow cannons. They said goodbye as they launched themselves off the chair at the top and set off down the run, Johann in front, but David found himself keeping up and they reached the cable car station together. He readily agreed to joining him for a drink at the restaurant, it would delay the lunchtime rendezvous.

They sat in chairs on a deck overlooking the lower slopes and the sparkling mountain opposite; across the valley they could see the nursery slopes, the children's ski school and the lines of skiers weaving behind their instructors like baby ducks. David released the bindings on his ski boots with a sigh of relief and lay back, the view was simply glorious, a world away from the lower slopes, the icy cannoned snow, the crowds. He would bring Clare up here for lunch, he saw non skiers walking back down through the trees in the deep natural snow, she would like that. Into his second beer however his thoughts soon drifted to home, he turned to his new acquaintance, 'do you mind if I make a very quick mobile call' he said, 'I don't seem to be getting much of a chance,' he added lamely. The phone went straight onto answer phone as it had every time since he arrived, 'hi, missing you, leave it on this time tomorrow eh?' He searched for texts and finding none stared at the phone momentarily before putting it into his jacket. He turned to Johann, 'not answering,' he said with no attempt to hide his disappointment. Johann smiled and raised his eyebrows a little.

'Girlfriend?'

'Boyfriend.'

'Oh,' said Johann pleasantly. For a second David wondered whether to turn it into a joke but it felt too good, he loved saying it. If I *told* someone, he thought, if I put it into words, if I heard my own voice explaining it so someone else would understand maybe I could make some sense of it.

'He fell for me and I fell for him.'

'Attraction is a very strong afrodisiacum, is the word the same?'

'Yes, almost. I'm not sure who fell for whom first. I look back ad nauseam, trying to remember the first time I noticed him, you know. He lives with his younger sister and his mother who never seems to be around, always working, I think money's short, there seem to be few luxuries, no holidays anyway. I don't know what sort of a Christmas he's going to have, I know that he and his sister will be alone most of the time and he will be doing most of the cooking and looking after her and he'll be working in a garden centre. And I'm here and I thought I'd enjoy the break but to be honest, apart from sitting here with you, it's an increasing strain. I'm with my future in laws, it was their idea, I tolerate them for her sake. We're having five courses a night and he's, well, he's probably fine, its ridiculous to feel guilty, its obviously what he's used to but his bloody phone keeps going to answer phone. We agreed to speak, I don't understand.' He stared dully at the mountain range ahead; thank god he wouldn't be seeing the man again.

'He sounds like he's very important to you. You seem to care about him a lot.'

'Increasingly, I feel like I've abandoned him, like leaving a dog in kennels, it's absurd, that I've got myself into this situation, I'm normally so, well friends would say I'm not impulsive and they would think this totally out of character and I'm confused, you know, him being, him being a bloke. I don't know what's going to happen.'

'And how does he feel about you?'

'He's very keen, there's no doubt about that, I'm afraid that he's getting too involved though.'

'If you don't mind me saying this, maybe you are dependant on him too?'

Johann possibly hadn't translated dependent correctly from the Dutch David decided.

Half a dozen aircraft, each packed with impatient passengers, waited on the tarmac for a stand in the heavy post Christmas Heathrow air traffic. David was beside himself, yet again Jack had assumed he would appreciate his company for the two-hour flight. Barely bringing himself to acknowledge the crew's polite thank yous at the aircraft door he told Clare he needed the toilet and rushed down the corridor to the baggage hall. Choosing the last cubicle he pressed himself against the wall. Mark answered straight away, and David couldn't hide the pleading in his voice.

'Bin busy.'

'Too busy to *text* me? Listen, I can't talk here, I'll see you at six, usual place.'

'No.'

'What? What the hell's wrong?' he put down the toilet seat and sank onto it.

'I'm busy. I've got a date.'

'Come on! I don't believe you,' he scoffed, his stomach lurching violently.

'Sorry.'

'Meet me at six. *Please.*' The adjoining cubicle door crashed shut, 'Have to go, see you at six.' It took five minutes to compose himself before he emerged. 'Dodgy stomach,' he told them, in fact his whole central plumbing system had virtually dissolved with the fright.

The return journey home was interminable and finding an excuse to go out again rather than relax and watch TV with the others a serious test on his creativity. His car battery had been playing up and he wanted to give the car a run as it hadn't been used for over a week. Sitting in the pitch dark he reminded himself miserably; better to have found and lost than never to have loved before and prepared for the worst.

Mark turned up a fashionable and agonizing fifteen minutes late, slumped into the passenger seat, lifted the lever and jammed it hard back to its furthest position with a violent shove of his booted feet requiring David to twist back to look at him and deal with the way he was dressed without showing a flicker of surprise.

'I really missed you, I didn't call much because I couldn't get a decent reception,' he lied, 'why didn't you text me?'

'I've been working, and I've been with Jason.'

'Right.'

'He made me see reason.'

Five hours ago he'd had a final, early morning ski on the

nursery slopes around the hotel. With the prospect of seeing him that evening filling his thoughts he'd spent a pleasant hour teaching him how to snowplough, how to stay on a poma, how to stop; he couldn't wait to do it for real, maybe next year.

'I'm only a temporary plaything,' said the badly dressed teenager in his passenger seat.

'You didn't seem to mind my going, it didn't seem to bother you in the least.'

'What choice did I have? I can't afford to go *fucking* skiing, what's in all this for me? Waiting at home for you to get back after a fucking *luxury* skiing holiday with your girlfriend? I'm just getting the fucking leftovers!'

'Mark, I'm incredibly tired.'

'Tired? You've been on holiday!'

David took a deep intake of breath and shut his eyes. I'm *tired* of trying to make it work, he thought, and now some scraggy penniless university student comes sniffing around again and you haven't got the wit to see him off and hang on a week while I turn myself inside out to keep this whole ludicrous situation on the rails. It's as good an end as any though and you've been decent enough to virtually do the job for me; hair poking up in vile gelled chunks, stupid bleached tips, the crotch of your jeans pinning your thighs together like it makes you cool and that purple and sick coloured hoodie, it's the look I loathe, you couldn't have tried harder. And to cap it all when I get home, there they'll be and I'll have to act out some story about needing petrol and meeting up with one of the staff and then that appalling man will suggest a night cap – and he let his breath out in a long sigh. The sigh saturated the silence; they sat stubbornly waiting for instructions from each other.

It was only twenty four hours since David had been sitting with Jack in the hotel dining room and estimating his consumption at seven glasses of red, one more than the night before and watching as he heaved himself out of his chair and steadied himself momentarily on its back before making his way to the lounge. On proposing a night cap as if it was a novel idea and not the inevitable conclusion to every night that week, Shirley and Clare had disappeared like they'd been let out of school early. Last night's story had surfaced again, he was too drunk to even inquire if he was repeating himself, though he was clearly trying to be entertaining.

'You can't imagine today how glamorous it was to be able to buy a sponge cake filled with cream and jam packed in a box with a photograph on the front and present it for afternoon tea. Women were going out to work but they remembered their mothers baking and our cakes were a godsend, they could still have it all. Dad was very excited by automation, demand was high and labour was expensive. Today we've returned to hand decorating but then, to make and package a cake without the human hand thrilled my dad.'

For David, barely sober himself, Jack's stories which were quite interesting on their initial outing, were now tedious. He'd tried gallantly to imagine the thrill of the production line and asked questions about cakes per second and quantities of jam to keep to stats and away from family history. Last night Jack's story of filial duty and sacrifice (he'd have gone into the air force if things had been different) had struck miserably home, he was expected to produce the heir that would keep the business going so all Jack's sacrifice had not been in vain. David was also beginning to doubt Jack's sacrifice, he was beginning to see an unadventurous man, pleased to leave school at sixteen and join the family firm.

'Say something, *say something*,' Mark broke the silence.

'You aren't a plaything Marky, you're an insurance policy,'

'Whaddya mean?' He hoisted his jeans, zipped the hoodie up to his chin, threw the hood over his head and thrust his hands into its pockets, David watched, it was quite a useful garment really, in a plain colour he probably wouldn't have noticed and he was as hungry for the body inside it as ever.

'Against me forgetting what's possible in life.'

'I don't know what you mean, all I want to hear is that

you….'

He liked romance, give the guy some slack, give him some romance, it might not save it but it was a nice way to end. David closed his eyes and returned to the slopes.

'I hate the thought of never picking you up after another fall and dusting off the snow and retrieving your ski and clipping your boot back into the bindings while you hang onto my shoulder and pushing your skis parallel with my boot and setting you off down the slope again in front of me ready for the next tumble.' He started the car; Mark made no attempt to get out, he let out the clutch slowly, the boy didn't move.

They made it up in the only way that was available, no meals a deux, no public displays of affection, no cosy evenings in front of the telly with a take away, no supporting cast of mutual friends in crowded pubs to distract or fill dull moments of familiarity. Armed with Mrs Derby's shift schedule David spent a little more time in Mark's bedroom and finally he fucked him, an act that ended any remnants of denial he could claim about the nature of their relationship. Trained to teach the social responsibility and personal development course that all the school took from year one he was far more up to date on all matters of sexual health than most men of his age, and here he was confronted with the same tough issues he challenged his pupils with. 'No,' Mark replied grumpily, he had not slept with Jason over the break. It was early January, Jason would now be safely back at university, it must be his final year and he would, David fervently hoped, be a very busy young man.

Chapter Nine

On the first day of the spring term David set up his cafetiere at eight o' clock, sank with a contented sigh into his office chair and opened his paper to the weather forecast which, along with the strong black coffee signified the formal start to his day. He relished living on a small island in the path of four weather systems; their downright defiance of following a predictable pattern, their capricious refusal to allow anyone to plan ahead. It's made us adaptable and quick witted as a nation he claimed as yet another holiday cottage week was spent drying gear over inadequate heating appliances. But they also bestowed the surprise of a warm early November, a sparkly dry February, a ground quenching August downpour. There was now though a new edge to his interest in the forecast; he tailored Saturday's activities around the closeness of the isobars.

Before leaving for registration he drained his coffee cup and glanced at his watch noting that at that precise moment Mark would be sorting out his books in his locker ready for the morning's lessons and Clare would be turning on her computer, opening her emails and sipping a take away cappuccino from the coffee shop on the corner. Periodically mentally checking their whereabouts he moved through his day, holding them like eggs in spoons, checking each was securely in place, moving toward a finishing line that he could not bear to imagine. When his nerves failed him he called Clare with queries about bread and coffee purchases and the 'I'm about to go into a meeting,' replies brought his pulse back to normal immediately, she was safely a long way away. He kept his diary meticulously using a code based around fictitious extra curricular duties; detention supervision, pastoral matters, catch ups with individual students to timetable his time with Mark. Other parts of his life too were treated with similar attention to detail, if everyone got exactly what they wanted from him then there would be no chance for idle gossip he reasoned. James this Friday evening and every alternate Friday, Sarah; an afternoon tea break in her office Tuesday and Thursday, Mike's teaching timetable committed to memory for guaranteed absences, the crowd's weekly, monthly and yearly programme of get togethers, replying immediately to Jack's regular emails, the Sunday 6.30pm call to his parents and scheduled bank account, magazine subscription, utilities and car documentation checking. He explained his system to Mark, partly as a joke and partly to reassure the boy that he had everything under control. And regretted it.

'The – Mas - ter,' Mark had Darleked coolly.

The boy hadn't clue how complex and fragile the structure of his life had become, he was only eighteen, he lived one dozy minute in advance.

The hospital staff rota; pinned in the Derby's kitchen and in code in David's diary, set the evening routine, though David was still not entirely convinced about relying on it. Mark put on an excellent show of confidence portraying his mother as a whirlwind of work and social engagements and he also strived to give David the impression that she was entirely aware and supportive of his private life.

Life had not turned out for Angela Derby as she had hoped and planned but she did her best to hide the fact and to make it clear that the current situation was only temporary. Temporary is a flexible concept and as her salary failed to keep pace with the type of property she had once been accustomed to she remained, trapped between neighbours who thought her stuck-up and colleagues at work who all lived in the best parts of town and she felt unable to invite home. Her pride kept her off the benefits system but it also kept truths hidden and friends learnt to let the declarations that the estate was a *marvellous* place to live with space to play, generous room sizes and a large garden to go unchallenged.

She was aware of David, and her son's opinion of him even before David's own thoughts had been troubled by the boy. Even without the clues left around the house (two used coffee mugs, three dirty plates, The Guardian, an expensive ballpoint) it was obvious something was going on. Mark glowed, he smelt good, he was hovering somewhere just below the ceiling most of the time and nothing his mother said or did disturbed his protective shield of love. Abi was clearly harbouring a secret with such excessive precaution she was becoming a parody of herself, stopping significantly halfway through sentences with 'oh never minds' and 'it doesn't matters.' By the end of January Mrs Derby finally admitted to herself that her son and his teacher were having sex but outrage was only one option, there was great deal at stake. Mark had emerged from the end of the swimming pool liaison sour and resentful, spending most of his time in his room. She had encouraged him to mature quickly and to be happy with himself and had confidently believed that this approach would prevent the worst of teenage angst. However the humiliation at the pool had kicked started Mark's teenage revolt and she was unprepared. There was ample evidence as she drove through the estate at all hours of a generation that had fallen through a hole in the education system; she identified gangling versions of the young boys Mark had once played with drinking and bunking off. Although he was clearly trying to be careful she had picked up the intense smell of marijuana on his clothes in recent months but that had now been replaced by aftershave. Torn cigarettes had stopped appearing in the bin too, there was a strong possibility this man had something to do with it. Another confrontation could send Mark, well she wasn't entirely sure where; to drink, hard drugs and *London*. Only too aware that her neighbours would be clocking David's movements against her absences she kept them at bay by dropping the fact she had engaged a private tutor as they lingered to talk to her over the fence. This information spoke volumes about her opinion of their own offspring, unburdened by exam success, and sealed her fate. As she drove in and out of the estate she had grown to loathe, she determined that nothing would disturb her goal which was now in sight; a large semi near the hospital and her son with four As under his belt and on his way to university.

One Monday morning in early February year nine were starting weather and David gathered together some of his most dramatic photos to entertain them and spark discussion but weather lessons were always a challenge; one of his enthusiasms which sometimes failed to transfer well to his students. Weather symbols required a bit of effort and the kids were used to TV computer graphics and 'anyway sir, it's either *raining* or it *isn't*, yeah? Wassthepoint?' The course book did its best but he knew he could do better.

A look out of the classroom window that day was hardly inspiring; a soggy dampness that no painter had ever claimed as inspiration, the same as the past three days and probably the next three. It was snow that flipped their switches; the enticing possibility of early school closure, the thrill of skidding cars and abandoned buses, the snowballs stuffed down the backs of shirts and frankly, if they were honest, the sheer loveliness and silence as it fell, but no snow was forecast.

Accompanying his words with bold diagrams that made the pen squeak on the white board he reached one of his favourite weather phenomena.

'Thunderstorms occur when low pressure is enveloped by high pressure. There is a rapid upward movement of warm, moist air and as it cools it condenses and forms cumulonimbus clouds that can reach heights of 10 km.' A change to a different coloured pen and more squeaking. 'As the rising air reaches its dew point, water droplets and ice form and begin falling and colliding with other droplets and become larger. Sometimes the water falls as hail stones which can be as big as your hand. During a storm in the year 1360 they were so big they are reputed to have killed scores of men and horses in the English army.' He drew a quick army being felled by giant hailstones. 'What causes the thunder?' he asked, 'yes, lightning. Lightning is like a giant spark, it's so *hot* it causes the air to expand at an explosive rate which creates a shock wave that turns into the booming sound wave we know as thunder. Lightning is six times hotter than the surface of the sun.' He handed round photos of hailstones the size of grapefruit people had stored in their freezers and pockmarked cars beside shocked owners which they enjoyed. The usual eager diagram copiers copied, the rest stared, eyes checking the clock, another twenty minutes before break.

'However,' he turned conspiratorially to the class, 'there is an interesting *phenomena* associated with storms; the storm chaser, an individual so obsessed with their quest for the ultimate storm they will risk their lives and family relationships and squander all their money to follow them.' He held up some photos of said obsessives, wild eyed as they drove manically into the path of tornados. This raised a flicker of interest, did they ever die, and how? How much did they spend and what happens to them when they have no money left? Have you ever done it sir?'

'No, no, I'm far too chicken, I just watch their You Tube videos, you can storm chase in the UK too you know, it's just not nearly as exciting.'

Intense rain, advancing like a victorious army, firing into the soil and ricocheting high off pavements, David would shiver with anticipation even thinking about it. One day, aged seven or eight, they'd shot out into a rainstorm in their pants; like ice cream and hot chocolate sauce on their tongues they'd squealed and stamped with cold and excitement until they were hauled back inside. It was one of his last happy memories and he held onto it hard and it was here that it got complicated with the boy, where, having finally opened the box his expectations were getting out of proportion and mixed up.

He raised the matter with Mark with care explaining he wanted to see if he could take some decent photos of storms. Storm chasing UK style, with congested roads and no reliable storm season wasn't quite the Great Plains, Tornado Valley experience David explained but there was always a chance of something local, they had to keep their eye on the forecast. He broached the clothing issue with even more care, Mark had his kit off in a thrice in public changing rooms, no problem there but it was the cold and wet part that could cause problems; the boy even got him to drop him at the main school door if it was drizzling.

'And for a laugh we could whip our kit off to intensify the experience. Only a suggestion.'

Mark reacted like he'd missed a new trend, '*nude* storm chasing, is it like, a *gay* thing?'

'How the hell would I know? Anyway are you up for it? When one's on the way you can't dither, you have to drop everything and be ready to chase, the other bit's up to you.'

'Hey, it's so *random*; I could be struck by lightning or get hypothermia, or be *seen*. Is this nude stuff some sort of penance, you know, like a hair shirt, for being a naughty boy with me?'

'For*get it*. Fucking for*get it*.'

The long range weather forecast did not look promising for snow he advised a disgruntled year nine, in fact the weather was ridiculously mild for February, the grass on the pitches was starting to sprout he noticed, there was an emerald gloss that had not been there last term. Dire warnings that a sudden frost would kill off everything that had been confused into starting spring like behaviour accompanied pictures of daffodils in the paper. How often had he heard this old chestnut, nature always worked its way round the weather, that's what nature did, it was adaptable. So far, well at least during his lifetime there had been no mass extinctions because of an early spring. Be adaptable like nature, move round the constraints, work with them, a bit like he was getting good at doing he decided.

Despite the clement weather the dark evenings cut out cycle rides and they agreed the gym was the best place for their Saturday afternoons. Last year he had joined one of the private gyms in town but he was getting irritated by the emails and flyers pressing him to renew his lapsed membership. He imagined that they would be recognised as a couple very quickly there as the staff were trained to give personal service if only to build up loyalty in the client. The council run sports centre on the far side of town was now an obvious choice; cheap, with less likelihood of bumping into people they knew and despite the hordes of customers under four foot, the stink of chlorine and the lack of customer care from receptionists untroubled by targets or commission it was OK.

'I'm too thin, aren't I?' Mark had said anxiously at the first session in the weights room, the mirrors mercilessly throwing their reflections back at every turn. Compared to whom? David wondered with amusement, you're a bloke, I'm with a bloke, I'm hardly going to start comparing you with previous bedfellows now am I? He'd hovered his chin near Mark's shoulder, 'have I complained? Have I been inattentive?'

There was a full size 30 metre pool, a cold blue rectangle of water with numbers on the walls to say how deep it was and tall stools with people sitting, watching and waiting in case the water overcame the people who were fool enough to venture in. That's how David saw it but Mark was a swimmer and the pool was included in the entrance price. At first the workout and the sauna and steam room consumed all the time David had but the sparkling water and empty lanes were too tempting for Mark, finally after a few weeks he'd said 'swim?' coaxingly and let it hang for a few seconds. 'Dave, its OK, I just assumed you can swim.'

'I can.'

'You just don't want to.'

'Babe, it's not that simple.'

'Explain.'

'I will, I know you miss it, you go on, I'll go in the gallery.'

Watching over his paper he swam every stroke with him, and when Mark looked up from the water and waved, his return wave was that of a man drowning with anxiety. The smell, the echoy shouts, the splashing, he sat it determinedly out and watched the guards, were they really watching or were they day dreaming or recovering from hangovers? And when they were outside by the bike stands and unobserved he held him tightly, breathing in the chlorine from his damp hair, tasting it on his skin with his tongue even though he'd showered, almost weak with relief that it was all over.

The gym became their safe house, here they could be themselves but not in the isolation that was bothering Mark. They used a personal trainer sometimes, bouncing remarks off him and he would glance quickly between them, unsure whether to acknowledge the possibility of their togetherness. And the trainer himself, fit and tanned, was a source of amusement and competition between them, a test for the possibility of their roving eyes which, on David's part, did not exist.

The shock of Tony Peterson's appearance one Saturday afternoon made David judder the arm weights back onto their cradles. He feigned pleasure at seeing him and they talked private gyms and reassured each other that this was a sensible solution. Mark was a few machines away, far enough for an introduction not to be necessary but he stopped and came over to meet this rare being, one of David's friends.

'This is one of my year thirteen, I bumped into him in here.'

They continued to chat and Tony gave the silent Mark a longer and more interested look.

'Popular teacher is he?' he grinned.

'Not with everyone.'

David didn't like him overmuch, mainly because he suspected Tony didn't like *him* overmuch. At university he'd kept out of his way and they only met as part of a crowd these days so the matter was never put to the test and his reputation for being hugely hospitable prevented David from expressing his view that he thought he was also a bit arrogant. Tony did not seem to be in a rush to start his work out and Mark, transfixed with indecision about staying or moving back to his equipment listened with interest to the detailed knowledge this man had of David as they chatted about stag dos, rented cottages and mutual friends. Eventually Tony moved off to the running machines and David finally looked at Mark, 'sorry,' he mouthed; his carefully separated worlds had collided. As they left Tony called out, 'see you two chez moi this Saturday.'

James had felt a frisson of anticipation when it was decided Tony's new place for dinner next because Tony's neighbour had been added to James's extended list of possibilities. She probably wasn't interested, he knew she probably wasn't interested, but the point was she was on his list and the longer the list the better he felt. There were currently three; the girl who came into the sandwich shop, only seen twice, a Kiwi temp but that was fading fast and this one. It kept him entertained he joked, it also kept him depressed. Tony greeted David and Clare enthusiastically at the door wearing his striped butcher's apron and oven gloves slung over his shoulder. Clare kissed him and said how professional he looked and how nice it smelt and handed over the wine, Tony complemented her on her silky tunic top and asked if the boots were new and she said they were and said how long she'd spent choosing them while David moved into the lounge. The men knew the contents of Tony's flat pretty well; a few months ago they'd helped him move from his rented flat. Most of the furnishings were new, all they had to do was take off the wrapping and lounge in the matching sleekness of it all. After the move James had made a metal note to get rid of his cheap sofa, get some decent storage and start putting things in frames; the latter a right of passage from blue tack that he had not yet made. It was all very, well, *masculine*, this was not a flat a woman had had any influence over, a real bachelor pad and they were all impressed. David loved it, the squareness of it all, the lack of squidginess and space to move round; there was nothing unnecessary, if he had his way that's how he would live but it looked unlikely apart from a study, he would have his own way over his study. He quickly identified the square reddy brown leather chair that he had admired in the move that was positioned, he noticed, so no one would be sitting directly next to him. He sunk into it, they would be eating on their knees thank goodness, not stuck facing someone across a dining table all evening.

These evenings always started with a catch up as the girls called it but to David it had a feel of the inquisition about it and lately Clare had been answering for him which thankfully seemed to satisfy everyone. As an observer it was pretty clear everyone was only waiting for their turn for the floor and the girls poured their hearts out while the blokes, well apart from James and Naseem, didn't really give much away. This evening though he was not to be let off lightly.

'So, any juicy stories from the coal face of teaching?'

'We do our best to keep a lid on the anarchy.' There had been a certain novelty value in the early days of finding his friends entertained by the goings on at school but that had now entirely gone.

'Don't even try; you'd think he'd signed the official secrets act,' said Clare. 'I don't want to bring it home,' he'd said, 'you don't want to share it,' she'd said, 'I don't need to,' he'd said, 'like I do?' She'd said, 'yeah and I don't mind, honest I don't,' he'd said.

James pulled his chair closer to David, 'put on a nice spread, as per,' he murmured appreciatively. It was one venue they all looked forward to, it was in the details; the plates hot, the bread warm and the deserts home made. 'Do you think he takes notes so he improves each time? I can't begin to compete.'

This gradual raising of standards amongst the group was something David was dimly aware of. 'Don't worry about it, keep your standards nice and low, don't raise the bar for the rest of us.'

'He's very *interested* in that sort of thing isn't he?'

'What sort of thing?'

James leaned closer, 'there's never been a *girlfriend*, has there?'

It had occurred to David occasionally but good food, good location, decent furniture; not having a girlfriend didn't seem to be holding him back.

'D'you think, when we aren't here, that there's someone, you know, *here*?'

'If there is he clearly doesn't want us to know,' it wasn't something he wanted to pursue and noticing Alex helping himself to a drink from the table in the corner joined him.

'Are you going ahead with that off plan property you mentioned a couple of weeks ago?' Alex, on the property ladder for some time was, in David's opinion, a bit ahead of the game. He was not yet entirely convinced about this form of investment.

'Yup, just reserved another one for £500, a 10% deposit next month and they're sorting out the mortgage. With the property market the way it is by the time the thing's completed it will have gone up 25%. I'll sell immediately and reinvest.' He positioned his mouth closer to David's ear, 'everything I'm touching is turning to gold, you can't loose.'

Showing mild interest at the time David had flicked through the brochure; tower blocks in Leeds and

Manchester, great views and within walking distance of the city centres. With a complicit nod and a raise of his eyebrows David returned to his chair. It was amusing to be seen as a kindred spirit, but his true motivation would have seriously surprised the man.

Clare was sitting with her shoes off and her legs tucked comfortably under her talking about their wedding and David leaned forward to indicate some involvement.

'I just can't believe how long ahead we have had to book practically everything, I mean the venue was booked over a year ago, by the time we get married it will have been booked *two years*.'

Everyone listened patiently to the details of the organisational mountain being climbed, those that had already married, and there was only one couple, had done little more than pay for the license and whether this thrift was a triumph or a regret they were keeping it to themselves.

'I mean you start wanting something modest and it just gets out of hand, you go a bit over the top with one thing and then something else looks, well, *skimpy*.' She gave a few details in a throw away manner which dragged her into revealing costs, eliciting a few gasps. 'And anyway its ages away, Mike's next.' She untucked her legs sharply and David sensed her discomfort.

'It's *your* wedding; it should be what *you* want.' Everyone, except Lucy, got it that it *was* what she wanted and in the silence everyone hoped no one was drunk enough to say the unthinkable, that Lucy was jealous. Clare lifted her chin, 'I know it all sounds a bit stuffy and over the top but it was really difficult and somehow ungrateful to refuse my parents' generosity.' It was well said; David remained silent but smiled at her which was the most she expected from him.

Once all the mains plates were collected Tony emerged from the kitchen with first a large pie dish and then a tray of filled glass dishes, 'lemon upside down pudding and chocolate mousses with ginger snaps,' he announced and someone sighed 'serving us the usual old rubbish then?'

'Not too sweet? Lemoney enough? Would anyone prefer a teaspoon for the mousse?' David tuned into Tony's culinary concern and general attention to detail and for the first time, along with a few other recollections, he reconsidered James's remark. Had they been reading him wrong for all these years, would he have ever thought it if, if he was himself not now, *exploring* his sexuality. There was nothing inherently feminine about him, James for example had far more stereotypical feminine qualities, like the way he unburdened himself so easily, yet the idea of him with a woman seemed, for some inexplicable reason, unlikely. Anyway, gastronomically at least he was a hit with everyone. The desert plates collected Tony appeared with chocolates and leaned unexpectedly over the back of David's chair, proffering the box.

'You've got a young fan there then,' it was for David's ears only and he felt his breath on his neck.

'What?'

'The lad at the gym, nice looking boy, bet he turns heads.' David's heart somersaulted but he managed, to his surprise an equally quiet 'turned yours then?'

'Pardon?'

Barely audible but the tone made James glance sharply sideways to see Tony and his chocolates had moved swiftly away and David staring blankly at the floor.

'What?'

'Twat.'

Suddenly Tony's neighbour was leaning over James with a cup of coffee, smiling rather nicely, he thanked her but the chance for connection was lost in his confusion.

As they left the men remembered to make final arrangements for Mike's stag do in Brighton. Yours next they reminded David, nowhere too pricey mind, Brighton's bad enough. David assured them his would be in town and on him, no one protested, he was marrying a bit of cash and though he wasn't the sort of bloke to want strippers they'd make sure he didn't get away with it.

Meeting up once a month had begun in the union bar all

those years ago, except then it had been nearly every night. These days decent wine and three courses had replaced beer and a take away and an upmarket rented cottage in Cornwall the camping weekend in the Peaks. David joined the arrangements over the years largely out of laziness, dipping in an out according to his current partner's social commitments, a diary comfortably filled forever. But the equality forced on them by university life soon changed as they took up life at different speeds. Suddenly one of them had a mortgage, a half decent car, a full set of white goods, a cleaner; year on year they leapfrogged each other up the asset ladder. Occasionally David fretted to James of stagnation, a discontented niggle that left him unsure of why he wanted change and how to make it.

'This is the way it is from now on,' James would say, his voice thick with complacency, 'the best is behind us, it's a slog to retirement now, knuckle under mate, bow to the yoke and accept it.'

'*Jeese*, pass the fucking kitchen knife.'

'Seriously, what do you expect, just look around you, it's a well trodden path, no deviations allowed. You may not have noticed, *at the time,* but the best days are behind us.'

'Yeah but all I hear from you is *getting off the treadmill, jacking in your job, travelling, writing.*'

'Booze talk. I'm tied like a runner bean to a cane until I'm taken down in the autumn of my life by the great gardener in the sky. Apart from a lottery win that is, not *too* much so I'd lose me mates, just enough.'

He's only waiting for someone David would think, waiting for his Princess Charming to carry him off.

'Dave, it's just not possible to fit all the viewings in before one o' clock, it's going to take at least half an hour to get to the one in the village,' she was stacking the plates from the dishwasher more noisily than possibly necessary. He said nothing, waiting to see how far she'd take it, then, a sharpness to her voice that he rarely heard, 'can't you miss the gym just for once? You're always so knackered afterwards and there's no point in trying to fit in anything in the evening because you come home later than I do and I know its all extra curricula and department stuff but…' She tidied up briskly and left the kitchen and he heard her run ominously fast up the stairs and he called breezily, 'OK, let's book some viewings for the afternoon.'

Pouring over OS maps on Mark's bed the previous evening they had agreed to put the bikes on the car rack and drive to some forest tracks outside town. He stood motionless in the kitchen, it had to happen, it had all been going too smoothly, the key now was to pretend to *her* that Saturday afternoon was no big deal but to appear seriously upset for *him*. In the event Mark appeared unconcerned about the cancellation, it was someone's eighteenth so he would start the celebrations early.

Once they had set off he was glad he'd given in so quickly, it would get a significant number of viewings out of the way in one hit. To his annoyance she was still debating between town and country; he'd made his position quite clear here but decided on this occasion to be ambivalent to avoid conflict. As they drove from viewing to viewing he expected wedding plan talk but she seemed to have given up, his only role now it appeared, apart from turning up, was the band and the music.

It was Malcolm and Natalie's turn to host that evening. They ate the lasagne and garlic bread on their knees in the couple's compact central flat but squashed onto small saggy sofas and bean bags the slightly stodgy meal was making waistbands uncomfortably tight and a suggestion to go out for a drink was greeted with relief. They emerged from the flat into streets swaying with underdressed noisy youth and hurried into an upmarket bar where there were seats and cocktails and they could hear themselves speak. David spent the evening with a soft drink having offered, as usual these days, to be driver and they all set off back to the car park behind Malcolm's flat at eleven.

'Sir!' Suddenly they were surrounded by faces familiar only to David. The swaying boys waved bottles in the air and the underdressed girls clutched their handbags and each other as they staggered about on spiky heels, shrieking as their ankles gave way.

'Hello *sir*, 'avin a nice evening *sir*. We're *celebrating*, aren't we, it's Lee's eighteenth, is this your *girlfriend*, sir?'

Entirely sober he grinned sportingly, with a few drinks inside him he might have twirled round them a bit and shown he could still party, 'you're all a bloody disgrace,' he said good-naturedly.

And then he stepped into view, his arm round Suzanne's waist, so beautiful that David never to his dying day forgot that moment and the way his body had reacted. His slender legs, encased in sheer tights balanced on strappy heels disappearing into a short red clinging dress cut deep, exposing his neck and chest. They had swept his hair back into diamante clips with matching earrings and his face, no more made up than the girls, but enough, enough to emphasise features that none of the girls could match.

'Doesn't he look *gorgeous* sir?' they giggled,' doesn't he make a well buff girl?'

Their eyes met briefly and as David passed him he smelt perfume and Suzanne unhooked her arm and stepped aside, as if acknowledging some ownership, he's all yours it seemed to say.

'Come and have a drink with us sir!' the girls hooked their arms through his, 'it's only early! Come with us!'

The rest of the group had moved on and Clare was looking back, waiting for him and showing no interest in being introduced. He wished Lee happy birthday, regretted they had to get home, 'busy day tomorrow,' and waving cheerily expressed a hope that they would behave themselves for the rest of the night. He caught up with Clare, took her hand and walked as fast as seemed reasonable back to the car.

'My god, did you see how *drunk* those girls were?' She said scornfully and the stab of loyalty to the people he spent his days encouraging and nurturing made him drop her hand. Inside the car he made angry futile stabs at the ignition and finally locating it crunched the gears noisily into reverse and then sent Clare flying forward as he engaged the clutch too sharply. 'Sorry,' he just about managed. His two carefully separated worlds had collided yet again and the sight of him, so shockingly erotic and the girls adoring him and the boys? Where were they going? How would he get home? Did anyone else *want* him like he did? They hadn't agreed to meet the following day but he woke early, waiting impatiently for the boy to sleep off his hangover and picked him up. There was still mascara on his lashes, the perfume was still on his skin. 'I'm not coping,' he thought, holding him and kissing him with a new possessiveness.

Chapter Ten

'It's the overall *impression* that's important, it gives buyers confidence that there won't be any hidden horrors.'

'They're not going to notice the *hall* though, it's the kitchen that really matters,' Replacing the brown swirly patterned wallpaper with calico paint had made a huge difference, Clare had been right, but it clashed with the white skirting boards, or so she said. It was early February and he had arrived home edgy and exhausted, dumping his case on the dining room table and pulling out his marking. It looked like marking, painting, dinner or was it painting, dinner, marking? Even the effort of raising his voice to reach her in the kitchen was exhausting, he could happily crash onto the sofa and stay there till morning and probably would if he still lived there alone.

'I'll start on the skirting boards tonight.'

'Not *tonight*, I'm watching TV in there; I can't stand the smell, could you start sanding the hall doorways?'

'Alright, but it is odourless paint.'

'I'm sure I can still smell it.'

'OK, I'll start on the hall.'

'Lazy bastards, we should at least leave something for them to do,' he shut his eyes, almost too tired to walk to the kitchen. There had been a staff meeting over lunchtime about school discipline and he'd had to give a little pep talk to one of his form after school about bad behaviour, he didn't have any problems with the boy himself and he didn't care enough, not these days. Bottled up till he took him home at five he'd poured it out to Mark, standard for all his school frustrations now. All he wanted to do now was sit, motionless, to recover, he wasn't hungry but she would fuss and wonder if he was unwell so he would have to get a beer, it looked better than just sitting doing nothing. He wandered into the kitchen where she was pouring the sauce onto the spaghetti and took a beer from the fridge, squeezing her shoulder as he passed. He'd had spaghetti for lunch too and the packet sauce was cloying and tasteless and halfway through the meal he paused, wondering if he could leave the rest without offering an explanation. Clare was hungry, she only ever had a sandwich for lunch and he watched her sweep her hair expertly behind her ears a number of times as she leaned over the bowl to eat. He mused that sweeping Mark's shorter locks behind his ears was a pleasant distraction but he guessed if he should attempt the manoeuvre with Clare she would probably pull away quickly and say it needed colouring or cutting again as though his gesture had been a criticism, so he never had. The hair sweeping was extending to other things too; tie straightening, shirt tucking and sleeve rolling. Was it intimate or fatherly? He replayed a few pleasant shirt tucking moments and concluded it was a bit of both.

'Let's plan the rest of the work on the house in our diaries, then we know when we can get the agents in.'

'No,' he said sharply, he was not going to be distracted from the hospital shift schedule, 'I'll just fit it in, I've enough timetables without a DIY timetable.'

She stretched her hand over to his and held one of his fingers for a moment. 'When we move, no DIY OK, we'll buy something completely finished, someone else will have done all the hard work, everything will be so much better, we'll have more time to do all the stuff we don't have time for these days. I know it's hard but it'll all be worth it, this is just something we have to get through.'

There she went, hurrying to get today out the way and

forgotten with because tomorrow would be better, even though tomorrow would soon be today and to be got over with too. And there was he, living for today because he was starting to dread tomorrow. She opened her diary and started flipping through the weeks, stopping, as he knew she would, at the second week in September, their wedding day and on impulse he stood up and moved swiftly to the other side of the table and took her in his arms for a slow, clumsy waltz, all trodden toes and giggles until she pushed him away.

'You're seriously going to have to improve, or we'll have to do something that doesn't involve any touching.'

'What?'

'Our wedding dance, you have to start the dancing at your wedding.'

Her favourite hospital drama was on the box that evening, she patted the sofa and he slumped beside her. Anything but starting work on the hall.

'This is nice,' she tucked her legs up under her and leaned into his shoulder. 'I know I'm out a lot too but I do think that school takes advantage of your dedication, I mean at least I get paid overtime.'

'It's not just school, you know how it is, everyone suggests a quick drink afterwards.'

'You could be a bore and say no sometimes,' she said lightly but he felt her body tighten against his.

There was four or five interlaced story arcs, some new, some ongoing and David was soon baffled.

'How can they do such a high octane job with so much sexual tension, my god *they* are going to need the trauma department by the end of it.'

'Come on, it would be dreary without it, just like a regular night down the local casualty.'

'You'd come in, broken and covered in blood and be faced with half a dozen love affairs about to start or about to end. *Excuse me* nurse would you drag your heaving bosom and lustful glances over here before I leave this mortal coil.'

'It's not *that* bad, what's got into you?' she grimaced at him and poked him in the ribs. 'Dave?'

'Mmmm?'

She slipped her arm round his waist. 'Shall we stick it on the market at the end of the month, the agents keep asking when we do viewings.'

He snapped the ring pull on another can and it frothed and he had to hold it over the coffee table which meant she had to fully disengage from him which was exactly what he wanted because choosing a time when she knew he couldn't walk away or call 'let's talk about it next week' from the anonymity of another room was underhand.

'We *have* to sell it first,' the TV drama forgotten she shifted sideways on the sofa so she was looking at him, 'OK we'll have the money for our wedding present from my parents but we'll still need the money from this house, you know, to get what we want in town, because that's what you want, to live in town.'

'I know.'

'I know you love this house.'

'I don't feel *that* strongly but it's my home, I like it, I feel comfortable here. A bit of me can't see the point in moving.' It was step one, they knew it was step one, if he couldn't take step one how were they going to get to step two, like getting married? 'But I'm sure that once it's gone and we have somewhere else I'll be OK.'

'We can afford something wonderful, it will be yours, ours. It will make this place seem like a hovel.'

'Thanks.'

'Sorry, sorry, I just want you to be excited about it.'

'Ok, but lets just get a bit more of it finished first eh?'

There were a lot of boards up in the road but the market was buoyant and people felt about the road as he had, it was a decent place to live and it would sell easily. And the gift from her parents, over fifty percent of the purchase price, but a gift with strings, and those strings would be pulled hard that coming Sunday in Hampshire; he must finally put his cards on the table.

Although only ten miles from a commuter town once you left the main road, a visit to the Chandler's house became a challenge. The last two miles, along a winding lane, were so densely overhung with trees they were best negotiated on full beam at any time of day. David's first impression of the house, as his new Golf's exhaust shortened its life in the long potholed drive, was how huge and hideously outdated it was, rotting slowly into the English countryside.

David attempted to use the Chandler house to deflect James's view that he was marrying serious money. 'It starts,' he explained, 'with a pokey kitchen at one end and each room, bit like a child's attempt at architecture, has been added getting progressively larger as they get progressively less useful. Here's the kitchen and oh, here's the pantry, and we need a breakfast room, oh yes and we need a boot room and another room for the dogs and how about a morning room and a dining room and oh I forgot about the living room. It was designed for a small army to run and now they live in the tiny kitchen, the rest of the house is packed with hideous furniture and full of junk they've accumulated over the years and can't sling. I mean there's these ancient vacuum cleaners like weird dead bodies under the stairs and jars of ancient tooth brushes but the weirdest is a box of soap slithers in the bathroom, you know, to melt down to a new bar, you'd think they were destitute but there's a top of the range Range Rover and a huge, new, Jap four by four parked outside.'

James was rather looking forward to a visit, he thought it sounded very Country Life and he'd never been in a Country Life house.

'It's not *uncommon* for the rich to make trifling economies and act like they're broke; it makes them feel more comfortable with the hoi polloi. Maybe you should take some soap slithers instead of a bottle of wine, to help bond. Anyway, why does it bother you so much?'

'I haven't found out how to fit in, I refuse to pretend I'm poor, I don't feel comfortable being given money and I'm not entirely convinced that they *are* rich. Maybe the soap slithers are an unconscious cry for help and they're borrowed up to the hilt?'

'I think you should chill,' James said because he was looking forward to being best man at a very expensive wedding.

'Clare mentioned you were thinking of going back to college.' It was lunchtime and they were squeezed round the kitchen table, the labrador's head resting hopefully on David's knees.

'Yes, an MSc, it wouldn't necessarily mean a better teaching job, but that's not why I want to do it.'

'And what do you want to study?'

'I'd like to study the weather in more depth than I have, I'd like to learn more about geoengineering, that's weather modification in particular, it may become a serious option to reduce global temperatures if we fail to control emissions.'

'I don't hold with this carbon business,' broke in Jack, 'I mean the world's climate is changing all the time, even I can remember when a winter was a *winter*, when the drifts were over my head and we had to dig ourselves out of the house. A dusting of snow these days and the country grinds to a halt. And look at the middle ages, they grew vines in Yorkshire, every schoolboy knows that, the weather's always changing.'

'Well whether it's us or a natural phenomenon some countries will try desperate measures to increase rainfall if their crops keep failing. It's happening already, I'm interested in the technology and the implications for the world's weather patterns.'

'All sounds a bit barmy to me, I have to admit I'm a bit fatalistic, all this business about bees dying off and terrorism and nuclear proliferation or whatever they call it, at the end of the day, if it's going to happen, it's going to happen. But there's one certainty, we all have to eat, food is a recession proof business, it's a business I'm glad to be in.'

'In the future millions of people will start migrating to find food and water if we don't modify our behaviour.' Here we go again David thought but this afternoon they were both sober and when sober David got irritable quickly.

'That's all very well but as I said it's factories like mine that keep this country fed, nobody ever listens to me,' and here he gave the indulgent self-satisfied chuckle David had come to loathe,' I have vision, which is sadly missing today.'

David waited for the two women to say something, anything, but Clare had that fixed preoccupied look she adopted when she was with her parents and he decided petulantly to tackle her about it on the way home and Shirley was very busy at the sink. Jack continued with complaints about the accountant and marketing manager, they weren't listening to him; did he have to do everything himself?

'We're thinking of going into town for my birthday next week,' Shirley said brightly from the sink, 'maybe the cinema. I haven't been out anywhere for ages, the drive home at night along the lane puts us off these days especially after last month's scrape with the Range Rover, have you two seen anything good recently?'

'You should see Lord of the Rings if it's still showing,' said Clare, 'we're going, aren't we? We want to see it on the big screen.'

He had wanted to see it so much, had talked about it for so long and there was no way he would go with anyone else and his excitement had affected David and so they'd worked out detailed manoeuvres because they'd probably know half the audience. They'd arrived together, Mark slipping in first to find good seats and left separately, meeting up at the car parked in the far corner of the car park. And there, suddenly, there had been clinging and frustrated resentment; the film had left his emotions running sky high, so much valour and unconditional friendship, so many courageous deeds and self sacrifice, such stunning CGI in one evening, and then, time called on his personal allowance of David. He would be dropped for the hundredth time outside his house to watch David drive back into his real life. The memory made David's heart thump a little; he took a mouthful of tea and nodded in agreement to Clare behind the cup. That had been difficult, bringing it back from the edge once more, he'd promised another whole night together and they could see it again, *please*, he'd begged Mark, bear with me.

'How about this afternoon? We could go to an afternoon showing in Guilford and you two could drive straight back home from there,' David's face fell as Shirley's rose at the prospect.

'Mummy, David still has marking to do; we wouldn't get home till well past midnight. Go with Dad next week.'

Shirley turned her back and carried on washing up and Clare left the table and flopped into one of the saggy armchairs in the breakfast room next door, disappearing behind a Sunday paper. It was nearly two, they must be off by three at the latest, he would put his foot down a bit on the motorway, it should be a clear run home at that time. He would send Mark a text about seven, must try and remember Jack's best moments to amuse him tomorrow, let him practice a few three point turns and reverses on Monday night, he was still too anxious for anything else in case of an accident, Mrs Derby on nights, Clare at pilates, could stay till nineish, which will end up as tenish of course.

Taking the left over food on plates into the pantry he stood for a moment alone in the quiet cool, Mark would love this room; plenty of space for all his ingredients, not all squashed together in tiny cupboards like it was at home. Shirley appeared at the door. 'It's great that you still use it and haven't turned it into something else, it's a perfect temperature.'

'It's facing north and has that tiny window, we hardly need a fridge, yes I like it too.'

He listened patiently to the story he'd heard from Clare about how long the house had been in the family and how many people used to live in it and how many live in servants. A family home, with memories in every scuff and tear and crack but it means nothing to me, Shirley he thought; it's a big hole that you don't seem to be throwing enough cash into.

'I know it's in desperate need of a bit of updating, Clare thinks we should knock the kitchen through and turn a few bedrooms into bathrooms, is that the sort of thing you would do?'

I'd flatten the mouldering heap, he thought, 'it's a problem I'm unlikely to have, my parent's home is very modest.'

'There's too much furniture too, big heavy brown stuff Jack inherited and can't seem to let go of, I'd sling the lot apart from the kitchen chairs, the painted ones, I painted them myself when I first moved in and some of the head boards on the beds. I've seen painted chairs like that in trendy shops in London, a bit Bloomsbury isn't it?'

'I don't know much about that.'

'All *ménage a trios* and *homosexuality*,' she said raising her eyebrows conspiratorially and pulling a naughty face.

'Sounds fun,' he replied coolly, god, where's this going?

'I just did the chair painting part. I never got round to the sexual shenanigans, I don't think anything like that happens round here, or if it does I don't hear about it,' she laughed and David expelled air in what he hoped sounded like a laugh. 'All I've had is all the voluntary demands that living in a village involves, you have no idea what a village expects if you live in a big house; committees, fetes, shows, never ending, no Bloomsbury fun though!'

David moved quickly to closely examine the chairs, painted in pastel colours with flowers and leaves trailing across the backs and down the legs, not his taste but they were nicely done and he knew someone who would like them. 'I think they're nice, can I take a photo of them?'

'That sounds a bit final, you will be coming here again?' she teased.

'For a friend's sister, she's painted her bedroom chair a bit like yours, she's very proud of it. She's twelve,' he added.

They went out in to the garden after lunch, its size and complexity seemed to him like a penance, an unending chore he could see no point in. He had memories of his parents labouring over their modest patch, he had never been sure whether as a duty or pleasure and at home they had a mere twenty feet of lawn. Clare had added a few pots on the patio and there was a young wisteria struggling up the too orange stained wood panelled fence. Last summer had been so wet they had barely set foot in it and the BBQ, a gift from her parents, had produced one charred meal. Although it was his second visit he was shown yet again the copse, the orchard, the fruit garden, the vegetable plot, the hen coop with another story about a recent fox raid, the formal beds, the meadow, the pond, the mature trees and the new saplings ready to replace them one day. He saw only chores; mowing, pruning, thinning, digging, weeding, cleaning, trimming and wondered if gardening crept up on you slowly or if you woke up one morning and it all suddenly fell into place and seemed like a good idea.

The prospect of inheriting this time-wasting, inheritance-gobbling heap of sentiment, because that was what all this trudging about was in aid of, he presumed, made him resentful. What am I doing here Marky? It's everything I don't want, how did this happen? He accompanied him everywhere now, he wanted him to see, to experience the dilemma first hand, he wanted him to say 'I understand completely why you're doing what you're doing. Don't worry, don't fret, we'll be OK.' He wanted him to appreciate the compromises you made as you got older, how you fitted into an unsatisfactory world and made the best of it because the world didn't revolve around you. He's eighteen, he reminded himself, the world revolves around him and all you can do is protect him from it.

'Is you mother still teaching?' Shirley was asking, 'is that where you got your interest from?

It wasn't, he replied, she had played no part, expressed no opinion, offered no encouragement, and there had been no mentor, no special teacher.

'Would you recommend it, as a career, to someone younger?'

'I often mention it to the older boys and they laugh, but when they get to know the reality of a lot of jobs, it'll seem more varied and less stressful than many professions, hard work during term but long holidays to travel and do your own thing.'

'Oh,' she smiled at him,' the teachers I know all moan about the paperwork and the marking and the lesson preparation.'

'I don't,' he met her gaze and she gave a quick half smile and turned to talk to Clare. He was rattled, and rattled that he was rattled and crouched down to take some close up shots of the pond they were standing next to so it didn't show. The more people questioned his career choice the more he defended it to the point he didn't know what he was defending anymore except his pride. They returned to the house and David caught Clare's eye and pointed to his watch. She mouthed 'dinner,' and he held his hands one above the other to indicate a tall pile, 'marking' he mouthed back and pointing to the car held up three fingers. Shirley attached herself to him once more as they walked back to the house.

'I sense there's a bit of a rebel inside you,' she said, again with that conspiratorial face and David swallowed hard and looked, he hoped, slightly amused and bent down to stroke the labrador. It was almost three and he headed purposefully for the car and as there was no opposition from Jack he suspected Clare had been negotiating behind his back not to stay for dinner. Before getting in David leaned toward Shirley and their cheeks brushed in a very quick, almost combatative movement, the closest yet to a kiss.

'They like you a lot.' said Clare as they thumped down the drive.

'Your mother has just suggested I'm a rebel.'

'Oh, I just think she means you're not conventional.'

'I couldn't be more conventional.'

'OK, she means you have strong opinions then.'

In the lane David backed awkwardly into a shallow passing place to allow a car to squeeze past, scraping the paintwork against the hawthorn hedge. In other circumstances, in other times, being described as a rebel could have been flattering, now it only pressed his guilt buttons. He must learn to trust himself, he had given nothing away and she was only referring to his uncompromising attitude to teaching. She and Jack had no idea of the firewall he filtered everything he said to them through. He resolved that there would be no more trips to Hampshire, not for a long time and that cheered him up.

It wasn't often they travelled together in a car these days and neither made a move to switch the radio on; the engine hummed them into a thoughtful silence until, deep into his plans for the following week, Clare spoke.

'Dad left school at sixteen you know, there was never any question of his not going into the business and the pressure to keep it successful has been huge.' The confidence that usually filled her voice was missing and he wanted to say stop, I don't want to know, this isn't anything to do with me.

'Dad says he's worried about peoples' change in tastes and he keeps looking at new products and new machinery and thinks the company should keep moving to keep pace. He doesn't accept that the tried and tested staples like the fruit cake bases only need to be marketed better. It's a huge risk to move into completely new products with loads of competitors. And I think he's missing out on the muesli bars stuff, we already use loads of dried fruit and all this fancy German stuff, it will be hard to break into the market because they're bound to do it better. I've no idea about the company finances, he'd never tell me, it would seem almost *grubby* to ask and I can't bring myself to find out. Also I wish he'd really think about the future, he needs to start stepping down and let the people who will take over make these decisions.'

Tried and tested staples like the fruit bases? 'I hadn't realised you'd given it so much thought Clare,' he said, genuinely surprised. Weird how cars made you open up. Mark had opened up in the car; it's how it had begun.

'Mum and I talk, but he won't listen to me, he still sees me as if I was eight, that was when he was happiest, when he took me to ballet and riding lessons and we chatted about school and animals in the car. I want the best for him and the staff but when I got involved it gave him hope. I'm not *capable* of taking it on because I'm not interested and I want to stay in the career I've chosen, like you. You see, on the one hand I don't understand why you don't say you're not interested and in some ways I don't want you to because the pressure would fall back on me because he wants to know it's staying in the family and if he knew it wasn't going to happen he'd eventually lose heart and it would have to be sold and it would be the equivalent of selling family portraits and antiques. So I sit on the fence, like you, I act like it will all be OK, I prevaricate about me and about you just hoping that something will sort it all out and it won't be *my* fault.

Her words alarmed him, he didn't want to know how much her dilemma depended on him for deliverance and he felt his burdens double. The extreme vigilance that shaped his every move and word these days now rendered him silent, almost anything he said might raise hopes or worse, reveal more than he cared. It was one of those moments where a simple hug would show understanding and solidarity without giving anything away but they were in the car so he gave her knee a pat. He had to understand that she had lived with the company all her life; it was as she said like living in an ancestral home. Big albums at the house showed the Christmas parties and the May Day company picnic which had not taken place for a few years now. There was even a photo of her working on the lines in the holidays as a teenager and endless birthday photos, it was a company tradition, they celebrated everyone's birthday in style. They were going to be man and wife and that had been his choice and he must try to appreciate her situation; it wasn't going to go away and he was also accepting the family's increasing generosity, There was something slightly *weak* though about entering your wife's family business, he disliked the image intensely but at the same time it would solve *her* dilemma in one move.

'*Shit*, sorry, I've missed our turn off.' She hadn't noticed either.

Chapter Eleven

The Toll Gate was regularly brought back from being a pub closure statistic by a landlord willing to adapt and change to keep the doors open. Ten years ago you entered with a buzz of anticipation through the swing doors, instantly embraced by a hot fug of beery bonhomie, hugged by default as you squeezed between standing drinkers, noisy enough to make you sexily seek your companion's ear to ask what they wanted and on tip toe to see who else was there. In those days you'd arrived, now it was where you met and soon moved on. Attempts to attract new customers, women in particular, meant a coffee franchise, a calorie-lighter menu, sofas, newspapers and it hung, indecisive of its clientele, waiting for the next trend. This was where they came some early evenings, it was far from school, there was a corner they could sit close on the original leather banquettes made shiny and slippy from thousands of polishing coats. David chose it for his confession.

'Funny place,' said James when David returned from the bar with two pints. He picked up the coffee menu propped against a flower vase on the scruffy beer stained table. 'Lost its way a bit hasn't it? Anyway, how's life?'

'Y'know, manic.' It bought David enough time for a few long draughts of beer and for James to embark on his regular account of minor work disasters, always more entertainment than reality, and David sat back and enjoyed the tales of misinterpretation and misinformation. James treated his love life in a similar fashion, the recent list of three possibilities was now down to two but this evening David didn't go down the usual unhelpful road of reducing the matter to a maths problem; he needed the guy on his side. Another round and David launched into his regular set to put off the dreaded moment; DIY sagas, the marking, the field trip, a disciplinary issue, but there was clay in his mouth and the real story lay leaden in his stomach.

'How's the house sale going?'

'Losing interest to be honest.'

'Oh? And the old wedding plans?'

'Proceeding.'

'That much fun eh?' The evening was dying on its feet but James dug gamely on, 'anyway over six months away, um…time to sow some wild oats and all that bollocks. Not that you'd do anything like *that*, I mean why go out for hamburger when you can get….' his voice trailed.

'What?' Christ, he'd guessed.

'Well, she's got the lot, Clare, that's all I meant,' James said awkwardly.

They drained their glasses, David felt uncomfortable about smacking the man's blameless conversation entrées down; if he wasn't going to spit it out he might as well suggest an early night. He looked at the door, willing him to walk in so he could introduce him and say, simply, this is the person I can't stop thinking about.

'By the way I'm thinking of jacking in my job,' said James, it was tired but somehow a relief.

'C'mon, you say that all the time and anyway you know you can't afford to.'

'No, really, I've had enough this time,' and off they pottered into mortgages, interest rates, mortgage holidays, buy to let: the song of the noughties. They were such reliable topics David's responses came automatically and his mind wandered; yesterday, on this very banquette; sport, music, school, and just a tentative mention of the summer camp and travelling, Mark clearly testing David nervously about what life might be beyond the end of the school year.

Then, towards nineish, when the regular topics had been completely worked out, the alcohol flushed his secret out like a foreign object in his mouth but without the confidence and assurance he'd rehearsed. The barest detail, the only detail that was necessary. He was a pupil, at his school. James drained his fourth pint and placing it very carefully back on the table gave David a swift, awkward look.

'I'm being boring aren't I?'

'No. It's true.'

'It's OK to say it's because I'm being boring, I *am* being boring, I know I get boring after a few pints, that's why its time for me...'

'You're not, it's true.'

'You've done this before you know, to wind me up and it's OK, I can take it but things aren't so *great*, with me, to be frank. I exaggerate, you know, the sexual interest but to be honest there's nothing doing, absolutely *nothing*.'

'It's true,' softly, holding James's eyes, he'd never held James's eyes before.

And James said 'why?' which on the face of it was reasonable.

'I didn't expect it to... it was a complete surprise.' Please just believe me and we'll leave it there he begged inside.

James's glass was empty, not even a last mouthful to drain to distract him, he felt numb, how dare David wind him up with sexual intrigues when his own sex life was so non-existent, it hurt incredibly. He stared at the scratched and stained table, he must try to be amusing, he was after all, an amusing fellow.

'A *surprise* is a, a Christmas fucking hamper, a *surprise* is when my motor passes its MOT, if it's true, *this*, *this*, is *appalling*, are you having a *breakdown*? Is the comprehensive system cracking you up?'

'No.' David threw back the rest of his pint and bit his lower lip. He had been living with it a long time now and

133

had adjusted and conveniently shifted the parameters of normal. Now, to feel so strongly like he did was normal, sometimes an evening with Clare and the bathroom catalogues didn't seem normal. But what in god's name had he expected? The ready acceptance of the friendly Dutchman who had even offered practical advice.

'I had to tell you, you're the only person in the world who knows apart from some Dutch bloke I'll never see again, I needed to tell someone, sorry it had to be you.'

'I don't understand,' and there was anxiety in his voice and the space between them yawned like a ship leaving port.

'It just happened,'

'I've known you a very long time and well, to *date*, it's been er… *girls*. And, um, if it's just *experimentation*, and there's no harm in that, don't get me wrong, I'm as open minded as the next but why not someone, well, *not* in your school?'

'That's how you meet people isn't it, at work? That's how I met him, at work, I'd never have met him in any other way, it would never have happened, I wasn't experimenting, I wasn't *looking*. And if it was a girl, would it be different, would it be OK?'

'Dave, I'm a bit pissed and I can't quite get my head round it, I mean, *Clare*, you're asking too much of me, bloke or girl, you're due to get married this September and I'm you're best fucking man. It's just something I would never have expected of you. If this really is true, and I still don't believe it, you gotta sort this, I mean is it *legal*?'

Their pints drained David suggested soft drinks for the next round and as he began to sober up Mark disappeared from his side and he felt very alone. The details he had wanted to give, the reassurances about how he had it all under control and that they both knew what they were doing and how it was not going to change anything stuck in his throat. They managed to return the conversation to James's job, his next car and the potential relegation of the team he supported. But a cold dread had replaced the fleeting elation and relief of telling someone, as Mark had asked him to.

James was fully involved in their life; they had asked him to be, how naïve and foolish, he wanted to rewind the evening back into its spool.

The beer woke James in the early hours in the middle of a large shambolic event which it appeared he was supposed to be in control of. A bizarre version of David laughed loudly and made flippant, unhelpful remarks and the venue grew and shrank around them, eventually completely losing its roof. Stumbling to the loo he could not recall the boy being part of the tableau, he probably would be once he'd met him he thought dismally envisioning the dream being frequently repeated. It was Saturday, not a day he looked forward to much, the dream had made him nervous and he went out early to buy a newspaper which failed to distract him. He rang Tony, he couldn't tell him anything obviously but a little light conversation might be soothing. They chatted for a while, talked about arrangements for Martin's stag do in Brighton next month, yes he was travelling down with Dave, should be a good night, club had great reviews, hotel top notch, not that they'd get much sleep eh? Yeah, love life messy of course, what about the latest house price figures eh? If my equity keeps going up like this I'm taking out another further advance for that Beemer!

The call over, James flung himself violently back onto the sofa and slammed his feet down repeatedly on the armrest, 'meaningless shite and pointless bollocks!' he raged. Hot prickles of humiliation, a regular companion, hovered. The brief altercation between Tony and David last Saturday now took on a crushing significance, interesting and exciting lives were being actively and secretly led under his nose while his love interests were born and died without the intended even being aware. He lay immobile on the sofa, his resentment expanding into the emptiness of the afternoon; David, always sought after, taking a *boyfriend* to spice up the final months before a brilliant marriage. And Tony, his singleness always on display, almost flaunted, but secretly entertaining members of the same sex once he'd seen the hetros off the premises. He reworked the phone call to Tony; I don't want to go to Martin's tedious stag do, and if I *was* seeing anyone I'd certainly give these tedious Saturday get togethers a miss and if anyone mentions house prices once more I'll fucking *leave the country.*

James slept for a while and woke up feeling slightly better about life and read his paper which brought other equally unsatisfactory lives satisfyingly to his notice, but he sensed something had slipped very slightly away and he rang him. 'Just checking that last night was for real, I still can't believe it.'

They had just showered after the weights room and David walked out of the changing room and spoke in the corridor.

'It was, he's with me now.'

'Jeeze, I do not *believe* this,'

'Don't then, but I wanted to tell you.'

'I wish you hadn't.'

'Too late.'

'Then tell me, *tell me* how *I* deal with it.' He knew the answer; it was really none of his business, so joke about it, that was the way they'd always dealt with tricky things. 'What about my *speech*, a little jest about your latent homosexuality, or better still why don't you simply cut out the middle woman and marry *him*?'

'By June he will have left the school forever, he's going travelling and then he's going to university. By September he'll have completely forgotten me, it won't be necessary to change your speech, I'm going to let it rock on till it comes to a natural end for both of us.' It sounded very cool and plausible and David hoped his annoyance was muted, he hadn't wanted sympathy exactly, just an ear, someone to bounce his confusion and anxiety off, it was called a friend wasn't it? But having to coldly describing the end like that, out loud, was horrible.

'Just a final fling then?'

'If you like.'

'Don't forget the stag do in two weeks.'

'I honestly can't think of anything worse.'

He returned to the final fling who whispered on his mouth, 'the steam room's empty and there's no one around,' and slipped his hand under his towel. Oh my god, OMG.

James woke early on Sunday to rain and the recollection that he was now sole repository of a piece of gossip that the others would have handed their title deeds over for. He stood frozen with misery looking out onto the soaking lawn of the ground floor flat below. The pleasure of being Dave's best mate and best man shrivelled, the burden of *knowing* would now turn every social event into an agonising awkward ordeal, it hurt more than he could have imagined, it was almost physically painful.

He'd spent Saturday night on the internet, nothing had been arranged for the evening and anyway he'd decided he didn't want to see David for a while. A niggling voice told him it was time he made some sort of move on his wish list but there was always a crowd in the pub after work, there never seemed to be an opportunity to move in on the Kiwi. He would go to the sandwich shop at one o'clock on Monday and hang around outside for a bit. He nursed a second unwanted mug of coffee until it was lukewarm then forced himself to dress. A brisk walk down to the canal, along the towpath for a bit then back, then ring round to see if anyone, except David, fancied a pint and pulling on his jacket he set off feeling more positive. His thoughts turned to Clare, he liked her now, but it hadn't been easy. She was sometimes a little sharp for his liking, she was everything he couldn't possible want because he was everything she would never give a second glance. Her wish to confide in him as the best man, once flattering, now made him feel sick.

And then what was it like, with him? Was it really close and special because he was a bloke too? Apart from the obvious difference was it a bit like being really good mates like he and David once were when they were students. God knows how many hours they'd clocked up in the pub before the dinner party days. At closing time he'd say 'c'mon old man' and they'd step out into the night, shrugging up their jacket collars as the cold hit their necks, walking silently and companionably home. They'd stagger around the kitchen a bit and agree to put on a video and put the cans on the table ready for 'a session' and then 'shouldn't have had that last pint' and 'pr'aps I'll make an early night of it this time' then quietly head to their beds. Did hanging around together mean you were friends, were they friends now only from habit and a shared history? If he left town would they bother to keep in touch? Was there something missing from their friendship so that he'd taken up with this bloke? What in god's name did David have in common with Clare anyway; sometimes they barely spoke to each other, if you didn't know you'd think they hardly knew one another. If you were engaged you were supposed to be inseparable weren't you, otherwise what was the point?

Reaching the towpath he headed for the lock gate hoping a boat would be passing through. There was and he leaned on the lock gate arms, pleasantly warmed by the sun and watched the boat rising steadily and satisfyingly up inside. Reaching the water level of the canal the elderly owners accepted his help in opening the gate and as they chugged off with a wave he sat on the arm letting melancholic thoughts wade back in. I bet they're saying to each other 'he looks like a lonely fellow,' and I am *and* I hate my job *and* my car's a heap of crap. Everything he knew about relationships was second hand he decided, he'd never really had one, not really and it was the only thing he did want, very desperately, he was spending too much time thinking and worrying about other people's lives, it was time to make a move on every front and he'd start with Dave, he would pull out of his best man role. There was no reason to put himself through it, David could not expect him to now, he'd put him in an impossible position, in fact he would suggest Tony, Tony would be ideal to take over.

Chapter Twelve

David toyed with the idea of inviting Mark around to help with his weather station readings and he'd tried out in his head a casual 'here's the boy who came round after the accident, remember?' It could be the start of one of those *arrangements* he'd read about though maybe he was getting mixed up with the belle monde, and on good days with something upbeat playing in the car he was halfway to convincing himself that one was possible.

In the first weeks of April he was tired of the bland weather charts and dingy uninspiring dampness, it was time for some action in the skies he told Mark, or else he was upping sticks to Idaho. Doubts, however, about a joint storm pursuit were setting in on both sides.

'I hoped you'd forgotten about all that,' said Mark pulling a face. Spontaneity was critical to catching a storm and Mark wasn't playing; should they keep their shoes on? Should they take towels and a fresh set of clothes? Wouldn't it be too cold to stand for even a minute? David accepted that without the right attitude a man could lose his sense of humour in sheet rain and saw two bedraggled figures rushing back to the car, Mark shivering and grumpy as they drove home. It niggled more than expected and was a warning that you couldn't mould a bright eighteen year old no matter how keen he was on you.

Then in mid April the weather charts changed, the isobars were nice and close and yes, the short range forecast drawings had lots of black clouds with lightning symbols. A heavy rainstorm one morning on the way to work - wipers lashing, the low thunder on the roof, then emerging from it into bright sunshine - cheered him up. A few days later he checked again after the late news, thunderstorms in the afternoon, suddenly it became terribly important and waiting until Clare was in bed texted Mark, 'cd b storm tomorrow'.

The following day started with blue skies but by midmorning it had turned light grey and by mid afternoon a slightly darker grey. A tingle of anticipation made him lose concentration and David glanced anxiously out of the classroom window hoping the action wouldn't start until school had finished. At three thirty Mark was waiting at the car, his arms folded and a scowl, it wasn't looking promising.

'What are you expecting, some sort of religious conversion?'

'You don't have to join me; you can sit in the car with the heater on and listen to Radio 4. Granddad.'

It started to rain as they drove out of school and David drove faster than usual, heading towards the darkening sky over Radley Hill where, if you slipped off the footpath into the fields, the panoramic view might be a perfect backdrop for the advancing front. Nobody would be walking their dog in this; they'd have the place to themselves. Off the main roads he uncharacteristically whipped the car round the tight bends, Mark clutching his seat dramatically. 'Storm chasing UK style Marky; windy roads, hedges you can't fucking see over and bloody trees blocking the horizon, Nebraska it's not.'

Parking the car at the top of the hill they ran into the woods, taking the footpath for a short way then veering off it to emerge into the steep pasture that hung over the landscape below. They could hear faint thunder and lightning flashes were visible in the distance, if the lightning came any closer they'd agreed to leg it back to the car. Then, as they stood, unsure of the direction it was all moving, the sky blackened behind them and they saw a solid block of rain pounding towards them, a thousand celestial power showers.

'Here it *comes*!' David bellowed, and tore off his clothes as the first giant droplets hit them.

David adjusted the two big tweedy cushions he'd bought for Mark's room against the headboard and they lay down on the bed, towled dry and sleepy.

'You really are an uber nerd with extra nerdyness.'

'There's more.'

'Somewhere *hot* this time, somewhere I haven't been.'

'Haven't been? A medieval peasant was more travelled than you.'

'But not travelling is very s*ustainable.*'

'So you *were* awake in my sustainable tourism lesson.'

'Don't kid yourself travel's anything other than self indulgence,' Mark quoted.

David tucked his hands under Marks armpits and hauled him up so his mouth met the boy's ear. 'Let's go travelling. I'll take you where…. where we can walk barefoot on burnt ochre and russet rocks baking in a Mid West afternoon. I'll take you where we can run out into a warm Asian monsoon then watch our clothes steam as they dry. We'll lie in rooms with closed shutters and high ceiling fans stirring humid air waiting for the cool evening then we'll go out for drinks and dinner in tiny backstreet restaurants that only the locals know. I'll take you where we can ski in deep fresh snow then sit with hot chocolate in a high altitude bar with breathtaking views getting warm again. I'll chase you, naked of course, up and down steep Nubian sand dunes until we collapse exhausted from laughing and then we'll come back to Blighty and I'll hold you tightly on a cold windy Norfolk beach in winter and we'll stagger into a steamed up cafe for bacon sarnies and mugs of tea. How's that?'

'Sounds like a fucking geography field trip.'

'They're supposed to sound romantic and exotic you

philistine.'

'I want to travel, I want to go with you, you idiot, it's you that has other plans,' he pulled the duvet up over his shoulders and turned his back.

'Don't you *see* Marky, you can do anything you want, you can't imagine how different everything will be when you leave school. You're going to the Americas, you'll meet amazing people, then back to uni, get wasted every night, stay in bed all day, there'll be a queue of suitors outside your door.'

'I do that already, when I don't have to haul my arse out of bed to see you. Yeah and the queues won't be full of people like you.'

'That's nice of you to say so but a queue of people like me would be very dull, I mean exciting, sexy people with drive and ambition.'

'You're just so fucking jealous you make up all this crap, don't you?'

'True.'

It was the start of the spring term and this year's exams now had a personal edge for David. Mark was expected to do very well; while keeping his opinions to himself, David was overhearing from other staff that his concentration levels were high and that he was achieving excellent marks. If the boy did badly any blind eyes that may currently be being turned would focus on him. He needed, if necessary, to be able to walk away with a clear conscience at least about Mark's academic results. There was a suggestion during a meeting of sixth form tutors that Mark appeared more cheerful and that he was more confident with *whom he was*. Actually *who* he was was not specified although David listened, frozen with foreboding for any suggestion. They were either very circumspect or, like him before it had been made lavishly clear, they hadn't a clue. The whole year was on course for excellent results and the Head frequently expressed his satisfaction at the prospect of a good bump up the league tables.

The meticulous planning needed to keep everything on track continued to run satisfactorily. Mark required a delicate balance of support without being stuffy, and buckets of attention without it becoming too much of a distraction. Clare needed an ear as she unpicked her day, with suitably supportive words and evidence of DIY and thankfully not the sort of attention that Mark now demanded almost daily. Rigour and precision he mused was the key; contain everything in boxes, close one before opening another, predict and plan for every eventuality. Basic risk assessment in fact, if you can do it for constructing skyscrapers surely it could be applied to keeping two humans happy.

Walking the dog one early evening he gently tried to contain Mark's fervour.

'Isn't it time you ditched the Gollum answer phone voice and stop *texting*, for chrissakes.'

'Why?'

'I just have to keep deleting them, and you know *why*, just don't send so many.'

'How else do I contact you, *for chrissakes*? You won't let me phone and email, fucking *semaphore*? Write you a letter?'

'I shouldn't imagine anyone your age has ever written one.'

'That is like *so* patronising and *so* unnecessary.'

'I see you everyday except Sunday; you can text me on Sunday.'

'Everyone texts.' he moved closer and slipped his hand under David's jacket.

'Babe, it's the digital footprint, the curse of the 21st century affair, lets avoid that, look how long we've kept it secret.'

'They *know*,' Mark murmured,' don't kid yourself, they *know*.'

'How? *How*? All anyone sees is me giving you lifts home. Big deal.'

'You have no idea have you? They know what's going on;

they're like bloodhounds, hoovering up the trail of clues.'

'Bollocks, there's no *trail*.'

'But that's *it*, it's what you *don't* do they notice. I've been keeping this from you but some of them have given us nick names, Ralf told me. Alexander and Hepheasion for example and the two G's, Greek gods, on account of us being gorgeous like, but that's the girls. The Greeks, you know, they liked boys.'

'It's more complex than that.'

'The ped and his rent boy.'

'Who the fuck?'

'Longman, he's just an arsehole. You *do* pay for everything though.'

They walked in silence. David was shaken. 'I try to treat you the same, I try so incredibly hard not to let it show.'

'You try too hard sometimes.'

'This *paed*ophile isn't sleeping well and he can't keep up with his rent boy's demands. This *paed*ophile, hasn't seen his best mate in weeks because he was so damming and this *paed*ophile can't imagine the future without his rent boy.'

'The rent boy doesn't know what to say.'

'*Alexander and Hepheasion*, quite sweet.'

'D'you think they slept together on bearskins in a tent?'

'Not sure about bears, maybe goat skins. I think those campaign tents got pretty crowded.'

They kept pace with Fletcher trotting briskly ahead towards his treat in the car. Mark's thoughts drifted to a huge animal skin tent and placed half a dozen silent slaves inside holding wine and delicacies on large gold platters. On a vast bed with ornate canopies the open mouth of a bear welcomed them onto its furry body. No, maybe not the head. Would the slaves stay or leave, probably stay; they weren't considered human but then exhausted dusty messengers would probably keep turning up with bad news and there'd be generals waiting impatiently outside for instructions, and didn't they keep their favourite horses in the tents as well?

The image faded and the tent turned into something lightweight. He saw them travelling, carrying the very minimum so they could pack up quickly and set off early. They'd find campsites on coast paths and wake up to hear the sea crashing against the rocks below in the morning. After a fry up for breakfast, they'd throw crusts at bossy seagulls and stand on the cliff edge and squint out across the sea to the coastline in the distance and decide where they would be the following night. But the dream crashed quickly; he was leaving in July to work on a camp in America and now, barely two months away neither of them could bring themselves to even mention it.

Back at the house he settled himself comfortably on Mark's bed and stacked the year 10 workbooks neatly on his left and balanced each book on his drawn up knees. Corrosion, abrasion, attrition, hydraulic action, percolation, plunge pools, meanders, ox bow lakes; he ticked and commented alongside each painstakingly and not so painstakingly drawn diagram, the pile on the right quickly growing satisfyingly larger than the one on the left. He sat close enough to Mark working at his desk for his fingertips to reach out and touch him occasionally until the pile on the left had dwindled to just two and, to warn him, he gently tugged his shirt out of his trousers so he could place the tips of his fingers on his warm skin.

'Nearly done?'

His fingers drifted round to Mark's stomach and he let his middle finger dip into his belly button as the last oxbow lake received its tick and the exercise its mark. With a pull the boy's waiting body was next to him and in moments they were naked, their swift movements causing the books to slide, one by one onto the floor beside the bed. This was the very hardest part, harder than any of the deception and lies because that was all under control and faultlessly managed and this was not. His tired and in love body had now decided it belonged here, in this bed, for the night. To make love, fall asleep and wake in his arms the following day was obsessing him.

There was one part of the wedding celebration David was really looking forward to. He'd chosen The Forevers to play, a band that had been formed when two bands combined to give a huge range of sound and music that had impressed him at a 50th bash they'd been invited to last year. Whatever else he felt about the arrangements and size of the wedding at least he'd make sure there would be no complaints about the music, there must be something for everyone. His email to the band to book them resulted in complementary tickets to one of their gigs, he chose his two companions with intent.

There had been a short sharp discussion on the phone and James threw words like inappropriate and betrayal in for forms sake because really he was very intrigued. He and Mark were introduced, drinks bought and he stood on the other side of David as the ten man and woman band came on and launched into a medley of recognisable sounds.

'I've arranged to have a word with them about our do,' David announced at the break and disappeared backstage leaving Mark and James alone together. A bloke ten years his junior was possibly the least likely person James would want to talk to these days. Like the grads at work; take the piss a bit, offer a bit of friendly advice to feel generous and superior but basically leave them alone and he was good looking and taller, you didn't stand next to tall good looking men.

'Good choice isn't it?' Mark broke the silence and in the mill of people buying drinks they managed a reasonable conversation about the music they'd just heard, not *their* taste of course but absolutely spot on for a big wedding.

'They're going to play kids stuff at 3.30,' laughed Mark, 'you know, teddy bears' picnic and stuff like that.'

'At the wedding?'

'Yes.'

'Not bother you then?'

'It's OK. People come and people go, I know that.'

'How? You're only eighteen!' how dare he talk in such a worldly way, what were his comings and goings, he'd barely had any himself at thirty, was he just repeating what he'd been told.

'He wanted me to come this evening, he insisted I came, we listen to a lot of music.'

'It's a bit hard for me. You know.'

'Yeah.'

James bought him another drink and asked him the sorts of questions you ask a guy about to take his A levels and go to university and wondered as Mark described his plans whether David knew as much and when the man himself arrived back and placed his hand reassuringly and protectively on the small of Mark's back it didn't seem quite so inexcusable. By the end of the evening they were all dancing, it was difficult not to and in the mêlée David swung Mark around by the waist.

Only a nasty accident or something contagious would get him out of the stag do and neither seemed likely so David tagged along with James's arrangements. The real downer though was it meant a weekend without him and somewhere a countdown had started to a date he refused to calculate. He knew there would be strippers and foolishly he'd told Mark who had taken the opportunity to tease him and he'd got cross and they'd argued and David now despised the event even more. He travelled by train to Brighton on Saturday with James, wanting to have time to appreciate the sea air before being forced into the dark confines of the nightclub, the camaraderie of the gig had faded and they stuck their heads into their papers on the train. 'I don't want to get ratassed tonight, these days I feel so shite the next day,' he muttered.

After lunch in the town they wandered into a fashion chain and David bought a T shirt and shorts with a confidence James had not seen before.

'He's a smooth dresser, I have to keep up.'

'I thought Clare had taken on the role of dressing you.'

'I dress myself these days.'

'You're not looking forward to this do are you, too hetero for you?'

'That's nothing to do with it, they've never been my thing, you know that.'

'Plenty here,' James wasn't in the mood to let go and he waved his arm at the crowds, 'Londres Sur Mer, gay capital of the UK.'

'It's only him.'

'Sorted out your exit strategy yet?'

'I know what I'm doing.'

On the seafront the sun flashed and bounced off the sea, just like it should, they shaded their eyes and leaned contentedly on the warm metal railings, squinting into the far distance to watch the container ships in the Channel, the dingys and windsurfers in the bay and the buzz of activity on the beach in front of them. The beach and the town, bikinis and coats, lilos and shopping bags and despite the sun it wasn't hot but the faintest possibility of a tan encouraged some to expose pasty winter flesh. David watched the children on the beach in front of them, as content with the Brighton pebbles as if it were sand. He made a snapshot of this moment of contentment in his memory, in case of difficult times ahead, seasoned with a salty tang and a flash of sunshine, and then captured the scene on his mobile, I'll bring him here soon, he decided. He sent the photo, receiving one back a few minutes later of an open text book and showed it to James. 'Swotting while I play.'

Bright sunshine from un-curtained windows woke him the following morning and as he rolled away from the light his hands lept to his head to hold his rolling brain still. He stood, he staggered to the loo, he vomited, he felt a little better and James watched his return from the bathroom with a smile.

'How ya feeling?'

'Truly vile, did I enjoy myself?'

'No, not really. You'll be delighted to know that *I* feel *fine*.'

David lay very carefully back on the bed and felt a little uneasy, he remembered girls, very very close to him, and lots of laughter and shouting, his resolve not to drink had failed. He crawled up the bed and lay alongside James.

'I behaved myself, didn't I?'

James remained silent for a moment.' You rang him, right in the middle of it all.'

'Fuck. Did anyone notice?'

'Tony. Me.'

James rolled over and straddled him, caging him in with his knees. 'Probably because you were *trying* to keep out of their way, the girls were all over you and you didn't seem too pleased. In fact you pushed one away a bit *too* hard so I told them you were feeling sick and to leave you alone and then you grabbed me and said you wanted to talk to him and I said it was too late and not a very sensible time and you kept on at me so I found your phone and found his number and rang it for you.'

'That was decent of you old man, did he answer? I can't seem to remember.'

'Yes and you shouted that you were missing him and I took the phone away smartly and turned it off. D'you know something, I kinda envy you.'

'Not disgusted anymore?'

'It's insane but I can't deny I'm intrigued. I mean *logistically*, how do you manage? And what about that exit strategy?'

'Something'll turn up, fear not. He wants me, very, very much at the moment but he doesn't see the future like we do, he's too young, he doesn't see how it'll wear off, put a few hundred miles between us and expensive mobile calls and lots of cute guys around. One look at the sort of house were're going to buy and he'll see it's over. Everything's transitory for all of us at the moment, Clare lives for the future but when we move she'll settle down because it'll be her house and we can start to seriously enjoy being together.' He had it off by heart now.

'Honest, it's nothing to do with him being a bloke, I'm over that but you can't carry on like this right up to the very end, you need to exercise some self restraint *now*. You say he's going off travelling, to uni, like it'll end, just like that for him. But I've seen the guy, he's clearly besotted. He said to me 'people come and people go' like he was some old codger reminiscing, what experience has he had? What if he *really* thinks its just going to carry on and he can't handle it when it doesn't, what if he gets upset and *tells everyone*?'

'I want him to do brilliantly at A level, I've tutored him for hours in geography and maths. I try and make myself think of him as an amazing creature I've had the privilege of knowing for just a short wonderful time and accepting that one day it will be time for him to leave and explore the world. I've told him often enough what it will be like, how quickly he'll forget me and I believe that's what'll happen.'

'What *bollocks*, it's not what you said last night.'

'What did I say?'

'You said you couldn't keep your hands off his cock.'

Chapter Thirteen

'David, its Doug.'

'Doug?'

'Doug, from Chandlers, we met when you visited the factory, I thought it was time to catch up, we have a lot to talk about don't we? Jack's very excited about you joining the firm now you're going to be part of the family. Congratulations by the way, I'm looking forward to the big day, Clare, fantastic girl, you're a lucky man! Reason I've called, David, is about looking to the future with the company, Jack's been talking more about easing back recently, and there's been mention of you playing a part in this and I'd like to welcome you into the fold, if that's not too premature! And talk about how you see taking the company forward.'

'I think this *is* all a bit premature.'

'It's a first-rate company, outstanding potential and I'm fully committed to my role in taking it forward into the new century, breaking into new markets, brand leader role, supplying the big retail players etc. You see I see no harm in us putting our cards on the table, being prepared for future openings, how you see your role, how you see mine. There are big strategy challenges ahead and I personally see myself as a *shaper* in the company, the ideas person and you, with your background in teaching as a *team* player, someone who can pull everyone together and put those ideas into practice. We need to make sure Jack's retirement, and our relative positions at that point in time, are robust.'

'He's not mentioned retirement to me.'

'David, can I be frank? We may be in a buy out opportunity situation here. Jack is very committed to the firm staying in the family, when he lets go I feel confident that with you fully on board he will be more open to negotiations. There are currently a few *issues,* relative to the business; operational control matters, product base questions, payment stretching concerns and, we could have a falling market situation which will be beneficial to a purchasing opening.'

'I think your view of my having any influence is misguided.'

'Jack wants to keep the business in the family Dave, and I appreciate that but I think he's unsure of the *process* of managing *change.*'

'I'm a geography teacher at a secondary school, I don't know anything about the bakery business and Jack hasn't mentioned retirement to me.'

'Dave, of course I'm not party to your discussions with Jack but all companies need to review their position in a competitive market, what I'm saying is that there are opportunities for both of us but we must be equipped to take them forward.'

David leaned back into the cushions, even his voice sounded overweight; diabetes two, stroke, heart attack, you need to review your product quality control intake mate.

'How about if we touch base, one to one, I know a very nice hotel off the M4, excellent food, it would be halfway for both of us.'

'Fer fuck's sake,' he sighed when the call ended, dropping the phone onto Mark's bed.

Mark turned from his books, 'who was that?'

'I think I've been sounded out for buying out the bakery business with the lardy marketing manager. Did I sound disinterested enough?'

'You sounded like you didn't know what he was talking

about.'

'I didn't. I'm going to keep my head right, right down.'

The head in the sand approach didn't work with Doug, the man's determination to draw him in should have been warning enough. But making something polite out of the word no defeated David and he found himself on the M4 heading towards Doug's equidistant hotel the following Saturday. David dressed seriously down; his old Saturday afternoon attire from the time when looking good didn't matter.

Doug struggled to launch himself out of the sagging depths of a chintzy chair to shake David's hand and fell back as if given a hard shove while David perched on the one opposite to indicate he wasn't staying long. They ordered tea which arrived with a few cakes which prompted Doug to make a fuss about diets and temptations yet he still tucked in. His health problems poured out; the high cholesterol, the dire warnings that he wouldn't last much beyond fifty, his breathlessness and difficulty sleeping. He repeated his phone conversation almost verbatim and David listened silently then sat back with his tea and told a few school anecdotes just to remind Doug that he did in fact have a career. Doug listened and then sighed and explained finally in plain English that the fruit slabs weren't selling well, there was too much in storage and Jack's desperation, couched as vision, to start more continental lines was flawed. 'People want tasty moist individual cakes they can eat at their desks or with a quick coffee that don't squidge cream everywhere yet we have this brand new depositor for the éclairs and cream cake selections, and that hasn't even been switched on yet because a part's missing.'

Doug described some ideas he had; mini celebration cakes for two, boxed cakes ready cut and individually decorated for office birthdays and bolder, more modern cake decorations for adults, the staff were highly skilled; give them tougher challenges on the decorating lines. It all made perfect sense,

David thought of Mark's little coffee shop treat when they escaped at lunchtime; a chocolate muffin, what had he said? This is the sort of thing those buggers should be making. Doug showed David what the multiples were actually stocking and the new websites springing up with small firms making bespoke cakes. Face to face the planned responses David had been rehearsing all down the motorway didn't fit so he expressed his appreciation that Doug was sharing his concerns and ideas but made it clear his complete inexperience in the business world let alone the bakery business. Doug complimented David on his ability to see the challenges and opportunities ahead and said he thought there was definitely scope for a profitable working relationship. David spoke of his interest in writing and the possibility of a PhD. Doug said he would send him more details of production costs and profit margins for the celebration cakes and invite him to the next trade fair. David said how lucky Chandlers was to have someone like Doug who could make changes that fitted with the company ethos, kept staff employed and didn't require huge capital investment. On their respective drives home neither were quite sure what, if anything, had been agreed but were confident they had made a good impression and had got their respective messages across.

Inevitably David's point blank refusal to make another trip to Hampshire meant Jack and Shirley would soon turn up and in the last weekend in April they arrived at midday on Sunday, their four by four filling the narrow driveway. David and Clare stood at the door as they unloaded bag after bag and carried them into the kitchen. There was the usual frozen fruit and vegetables from their garden which always welcome, but this time a puzzling amount of dated kitchen equipment, ornaments and containers.

'If you don't want it just throw it away,' Shirley said breezily, Jack hates throwing anything away that might have a use. I'm trying to de clutter, you're starting off in life and there may be something that might come in useful.' He watched her as she bustled about, she had had her hair cut he noticed, a bit severe at the back but quite stylish. He considered mentioning it, but the moment passed.

'You won't have anything left,' he said instead, attempting to sound amused but felt nothing but annoyance as it piled onto the kitchen table. Once you're out the door the whole lot's off to the charity shop he thought and looking at Clare pulled a face which she ignored.

'The girls came round the other night to try on the bridesmaid's dresses, they looked amazing,' Clare enthused.

'How exciting, can I see them? Are they in the spare room?' Shirley asked eagerly.

'No, she took them back to alter them a bit.'

'Did *you* like them Dave?'

'Yes, the girls looked lovely; they didn't want to take them off.' She knows damn well the dresses aren't here, he thought, recalling a protracted conversation during the week about the alterations between the two women.

'I'm pleased you liked them,' said Shirley with the faintest query in her voice which made no sense to him, they were little girl's dresses for god's sake, he wasn't that Grayson Perry bloke. All he wanted to do was get on with his marking or rather hide behind his laptop and pretend he was doing his marking. He was still traumatised about finding the Lonely Planet Guide on Mark's bed the previous day flagged up with post its, discovering a lover's note would not have hurt less. He'd picked it up reluctantly; even the weight had been disturbing, a big book for a huge continent where anything could happen to him; abduction, accidents, completely forgetting about him because he was having such a good time. In the few moments he'd had before Mark returned he'd turned to the post its, they were all blank, merely page markers apart from one, marking Sao Paulo, it was covered in phone numbers and web addresses and parts of the text were underlined. The city was nowhere they had ever talked about visiting and it was hardly a tourist destination. He guiltily memorised a few of the sites and replaced the book as he heard him coming up the stairs. Mark's silences about his plans for the summer were equal to David's about the wedding but he finally asked, as casually as he could muster; the date and number of his flight, the address of the camp and phone number, the final day of camp. He wrote it all down in his diary in a business like fashion and then, speechless with misery had held him, burying his face into his shoulder. Mark was leaving in the last week of July, marked only with a large dot in his diary; they were now both incapable of talking about what happened next.

Clare and Shirley disappeared into the living room leaving him in the kitchen with Jack and he started stuffing the fruit and vegetables into the freezer.

'Your *car* David, I noticed it in the road, none of my business of course but I thought, after the accident, you'd buy, well something more substantial. I'm sure we can come to some arrangement if finance is the issue.'

'That's really not necessary, but thanks. I'm not using it much at the moment; I'm using my bike a lot.'

'It's a decent enough car; you won't have any trouble selling it.'

'I'm not selling it.'

'Well the offer stands, and once, well once a family's on the way well, you'll be needing one of those people carrier things or something like mine. Only have to ask and I'll see what I can do.'

The freezer was filling up and he hauled out one of the shelves and started to repack it on the table.

'Anyway, what d'you think of the German offer eh? Marvellous website isn't it, wonderful photos; I don't think it would take much to get us tooled up ready for production. I know you're very busy, James has said so and Clare, well she says you're working very hard, on the house. Had you thought of getting a Pole in? They're tremendously skilled so

I've heard.'

'Yes I'm incredibly busy. On the subject of money, about the TV licence and the water rates and the house insurance, I mean there's no *need*, we aren't poor.'

'That was *supposed* to be just between us and Clare, just a small gift to help you starting out in life, everything's so expensive now isn't it?'

'It's just that I've budgeted for these bills and suddenly they've all been paid. Clare doesn't say anything because you don't want her to but… its, its confusing.'

'Can't we just be practical about it?' Clare had said as he expressed his frustration, 'spend the money on something else, save it. Dad thinks we should start saving for school fees.'

He'd been aghast, *school fees*? 'When did we ever discuss private schools? I'm not working at a *state* school and sending my kids to *private* school.'

At the end of the month there was now a substantial amount of money left in his account, a new experience and at first it sat ignored but now it meant that he in turn could be generous.

The suspicion that some sort of stage management was at play and that the visit had more significance than their regular Sunday visits continued over lunch. Jack and Shirley appeared unusually co-operative with one another, she would say something and he would agree and then he would say something and she would agree, he hadn't witnessed this before, in fact it was so odd it made him question his opinion that they led separate lives.

'Must get on,' he ventured as Shirley piled up the plates,' I have a bit of marking to do.'

'There's just something we need to go over, all together.'

'Won't take long.'

'Your opinion is so important.' All three were looking directly at him, there appeared to be a bit of teamwork going on. Clare produced a list he hadn't seen before and proceeded to go through the wedding from the arrival times of guests in their respective hotels to the final invoicing arrangements and he was left in little doubt that this was entirely for his benefit and it was a revelation.

'When did we decide to have it videoed?'

'Ages ago, you'll regret it if you don't.'

'I didn't know you, we, were having a page boy, who is he?'

'My cousin's son.'

'I'd no idea so many children were coming.'

'That's why we've hired an entertainer.'

'An entertainer? I thought children were supposed to join in, dance on adults' feet, fall over their dresses and be sick on cake and the dregs of champagne.'

'In *comedies* maybe but I think we can do better than that.'

'David,' said Shirley,' is there anything you particularly want to go through?' Three pairs of eyes held him and he blinked nervously.

'Only Mum and Dad, they aren't great joiners in as I've explained, but James and I have been over this, he will be checking on them constantly.'

'He's been wonderful, you know we have given some thought to a gift, cash, we know he'd like a new car.'

'Well that's up to you but he really won't consider it necessary, I hope to do the same for him one day, if he gets his act together.'

It was customary to take a walk after lunch and David had prepared for the event by piling workbooks conspicuously in the lounge and leaving his laptop open displaying a dull looking table. If any of them noticed the hint wasn't taken so he made it clear that he could only spend a short time out and they'd have to take two cars hoping this would do the trick. Again there appeared to be teamwork at play, they were quite definitely ignoring him and outside, to his surprise, Shirley got in beside him leaving Clare and her father in the other car.

'As you know there's quite a bit left to do isn't there?'

'Clare seems to be in control of everything, I trust her completely.'

'She's asked me to help out a bit.'

'That's decent of you.'

'How d'you feel about that? It's interfering and I know enough about you to know how much you dislike that.'

'Then don't.' *Too brusque*, but he didn't retrieve it.

'Don't think for one minute that it's been an easy ride for Jack and I. It's all involved a huge amount of work, and I've certainly worked hard, over the years and things, they aren't necessarily how they look from the outside you know.' She spoke quickly as if knowing she only had ten minutes before they reached the river.

'Oh?'

'All I want is her happiness, I know we give her a lot of material things but it's her *happiness* that's critical to me.'

'She is, isn't she?'

'Yes, yes of course but I know how hard it can be, you know, the final run up, the pressure and the expectations of the day, things will be very different when it's all over, you'll be able to laugh at the difficulties.'

'What difficulties?' His foot drifted off the accelerator, oh god, has she guessed something, was she firing soggy warning shots over his soiled bow.

'I, we both just want you *both* to be happy. Clare is *nervous* of course, she's trying to keep that from you but you've probably noticed and I've said that you'll be more relaxed when it's all over and you can just be together. Nothing ever stays the same, I mean I was a completely different person when I married Jack, we haven't necessarily kept pace with one another but Clare knows you, she knows that you are an individualist, you don't follow the herd and she understands that.'

Herd? A lone wildebeest about to be picked off by a crocodile or a successful entrepreneur? Neither, they weren't happy with him and they had clearly been discussing him, at length.

'James has been marvellous of course.'

'Mmm... you said.'

'Some of the arrangements, as you know, have been very complex and he's taken a bit of the burden, off *you*, with all your pressures at school.'

Say what you bloody mean, come on *say* it! I'm not pulling my weight, I'm disappointing you all and he exaggerated his mirror checking at a junction to appear busy and unconcerned. 'The whole thing has become bigger than I envisaged, I hadn't anticipated it being so unwieldy.' He managed to say it like he was disappointed in *them* which was staggeringly underhand and worked like a treat.

'All I'm saying is that it'll all be worth it in the end,' she flustered, 'and we think that you have a great future together, you're very suited and all the, all the *bumps* you're having now will fade into nothing when you get settled in the new house. Those pupils of yours, they don't know how lucky they are to have someone like you putting so much energy into their futures.'

'I really appreciate your support and thoughtful observations Shirley,' he said as if he'd come across a year ten miscreant who'd accidentally done something he could be praised for for once and he swept into the car park, scattering gravel.

Catching up with Clare he slipped his arm through hers, a show of togetherness was essential and she hugged his arm back and comfortingly linked they strolled along the river bank. He let go of her to lean over the bridge and Shirley came up beside him and they discussed how sluggish the water was and how you could see how high the river had reached in the April flood by the flotsam still hanging halfway up the willows. He looked round for Clare but she had walked ahead with her father and overcome with a muddle of guilt-induced gratitude he found himself wanting to say, 'you've all been, all three of you, incredibly good to me,' but didn't.

Chapter Fourteen

The key scraping around the door to find the lock woke him instantly, then the front door slamming open against the hall wall then closing, comically quietly. A bit of stumbling then a handbag tumbling to the floor and the slow ascent of the stairs, probably on hands and knees, a pause between each tread, accompanied by laboured breathing. God she must be seriously drunk, drunker than he'd ever known her to be, he should really get up and help her but instead he sat up and waited wide awake with a sickening foreboding for her to appear at the bedroom door. Finally there she was, a white face staring in his direction, searching for his face in the darkness. They looked at one another for a minute as she hung onto the doorframe for support.

'Do you still want to marry me?' It was no surprise.

'Yes.'

She took a step toward the bed with her arms stretched out and finding the edge felt her way slowly with her hands along the bottom edge to her side where she kicked off her shoes and groped up her back with her right hand, searching for the zip tag. Her question and his answer paralyzed him; he made no move to help. Finally she fought her way out of the dress and sat heavily onto the bed in her underclothes and he caught her shoulders before she collapsed forward onto the floor. He rolled her onto her side, moved her limbs into the recovery position, pulled the duvet out from underneath her and carefully covered her. He listened as her breath slowed and soon she was asleep.

Rigid with shock he remained sitting up, staring into the darkness and churning through the previous day for clues to where it had come from. It had been an ordinary day; he hadn't even been home late. In fact everything had been going so well generally; no disagreements and not another word about how he spent Saturday afternoons. He trawled back through the weeks to recall how every late homecoming, every bike ride, every quick nip down to the shops had been received. In fact she'd been out a lot herself what with beginners Spanish and pilates and endless birthday and leaving dos. She was always so open when people asked personal questions, he knew she'd reply 'no, he's not particularly involved in the wedding arrangements,' or 'he's always busy the whole of Saturday,' but Lucy would have jumped on these revelations, happy to stuff uneasiness into any tiny gaps in her confidence.

What about aftershave and hairs, always the giveaway in TV dramas. No, the house still stank of paint and glue and white spirit and Mark's hair was too like his own. His diary? No, even Bletchley Park would have difficulty there. His phone? Possibly when he was asleep but he was religious about deleting.

At this point he was forced to confront himself with last Saturday; he'd left the house at six for 'an early morning cycle ride before the traffic built up.' Mrs Derby not back from nights, the key under the mat, waiting for him, hot and sleepy. But was Clare noticing, if not the lack of sex, they were both falling exhausted into bed, but his emotional absence? It was said that people having affairs became more attentive, that was the giveaway, could the hours he spent sanding doors to a porcelain finish be considered attentive?

Initially he felt defensive; another Saturday afternoon in should do the trick and certainly no more early mornings, that really was going too far. But as the night wore on this belligerence faded. She had never questioned him or challenged him; she had always trusted his actions and judgements and never shown the slightest jealousy. Challenging him under the cover of drunkenness and avoiding the row she dreaded, she was giving him a second chance. But everything he did and said from now on, every late homecoming, every evening out, every night away, every nip down to the shops, she would be watching him and how he justified it, his manner, his tone, his guilt. Everything would have to be scaled down; home earlier, more time on the sofa with her, more wedding talk. He rolled towards her, now snoring slightly and stretched out his hand, laying it gently on her arm.

'James?'
'Dave, hi.'
'I've done it.'
'Done what?'
'I've ended it.'
'With *her*?'
'With *him*.'
'Blimey, how did he take it?'
'He was really pissed off; he kicked the dashboard and broke the catch on the glove compartment.'
'Oh. So that's it then?'
'Yup.'
'Thank goodness. It's a vulnerable age of course and isn't he taking his exams pretty soon?'
'He'll be fine.'
'Not concerned he might, you know, spill the beans?'
'His word against mine.'

He had parked right outside his house for the first time ever so he had only a few steps to go, so he could at least see him go into the house where there would be Abi and the dog. He had had the early hours to rehearse what he was going to say, watching over Clare to make sure she wasn't sick.

He wanted him to understand that by simply asking him to confirm his commitment she had avoided a scene and given their relationship a second chance. He wanted him to know that despite confirming his commitment to her the trust that had given him the freedom to spend so much time with him had gone forever, from now on he must devote all his time to her and there must be no more secrets. He explained that financially and socially his life was already irrevocably tied with her's; marriage would make very little difference now. They had had some great times together, he would never forget them and he hoped he wouldn't either but they were at totally different stages of their lives, there would inevitably come a point, when the differences between them would be insurmountable and when the novelty and insecurity that fuelled their desire would die. He was getting married in four weeks time, it was going to be huge, the entire factory had been invited and the staff had been looking forward to it for a year, it had effectively become their annual party. It was costing a fortune and he was contributing almost nothing, her parent's generosity was overwhelming. They were about to sell his house and they would be buying one of the big Georgian properties in town; it was what she wanted and as her parents were paying for a substantial part of it he was in no position to disagree. He said he had thought about it very very long and hard but to continue to have even a friendship with him would be painful for both of them and to continue their relationship would destroy his marriage. He told him that visiting him would not give them time to get over each other because in time they would. They really would.

And he gave the when you go to university speech again, the exhilarating freedom, finding friends for life just like he had, the chance to find himself, to make mistakes, to experiment and the more he said the more sense it made and he imagined his measured words, painful though they were, were beginning to make sense to the boy too. Then, assuming the silence as slow acceptance of the situation the timbre of his voice again took on that of the schoolmaster that he stopped using with the boy when they were alone. He continued that of course he was still available to help with revision, just come along anytime but he had no doubt he would easily achieve the grades Manchester wanted and in time, because time was a great healer, maybe they could take Fletch for a walk when he came home for the holidays, he would miss those walks and it would be nice too to keep in touch with Abi but then his mouth had suddenly seized, frozen in revolt at the odious cant.

Starting as gulps Mark began to sob and lifting both feet brought them down violently onto the dashboard in front of him over and over until the car shook and the glove compartment flew open, the CDs they had bought together over the year flying out onto the floor. He'd try to slam it shut viciously with his foot a few times but the catch had broken and it hung open and the boy had paused; the damage had shocked him, the year rolled back, he'd damaged a teacher's car. But it was his car, though he didn't know it, the handover now cancelled forever. As he fumbled for the familiar door handle and felt for his rucksack on the floor he turned.

'You *fucking, lying, cheating, closeted, ponce*, just a bit of *twink* before you settle down eh?' because he knew it really was the end.

David had accelerated away fast, smashing his exhaust on every single speed bump, wanting to shed the estate and all it had represented like a dead skin but reaching the main road he'd jammed on his brakes, shuddering with dry sobs of shock. He had made the banal a joy, the simple a feast, he had become his all, he had given him, for nearly a year, the teenage years he had lost, the sex he had always dreamed about and allowed him to give the love he had always wanted to give.

In the first few days, like an injured animal, adrenalin pumped through him getting him out of immediate danger until he found somewhere to quietly recover. The natural boost was heady stuff at first, his heart sped, he half ran everywhere, all his classes went smoothly, nobody messed around, he was in control again, reprieved, the decision finally made he could really breathe. He joked with Mike, flirted lightly with Miss Kenyon, tidied his desk, suggested the cinema to Clare, he worked on the last hard to reach bits of unpainted skirting board, cleaned the brushes properly right down to the hilts and went for a morning run. He rang round the lads to fix up a night out, took the car in for a service, joked with the mechanics and phoned his parents.

James was impressed, 'well well well, I thought I'd have to pick up a few pieces, how's he taking it?'

'Dunno, he'll be OK, he's got plenty of mates, he'll soon get over his decrepit old teacher. Anyway he's taking his exams in three weeks that should keep him pretty busy. I've got so much catching up to do, *god* it was time consuming.'

'*It?*'

'Fancy a pint after work tomorrow?'

'I've been holding back a bit on this one but we have some things to sort out about the wedding.'

But on the fourth day he woke at four am and lay, bereaved and empty, his tide had gone out. He hadn't seen him at school for days and in deciding to keep out of his way was not aware that he had not in fact come in at all. A geography revision class was scheduled, his legs shook and the seat the boy normally took throbbed with his absence, a black hole in the middle of the room and he could not deal with it. He sensed censure from the class, no greetings, no smiles; it was after all just about their final revision session and it should have bubbled with their anxiety and high spirits. His leaden arm drew shaky diagrams on the board; his hopeless jokes were met with silence and his questions with cold disinterested responses. He struggled through, offering final tips and advice and his availability throughout the coming weeks of exams and revision leave, he would be in every day, he was always available and hoped, expected, to see them in school during that time for support and help; he was begging them to love him again. But Mark was not there and therefore there was nothing and nothingness and by the end he felt as though he'd run a marathon and watched in disbelief as they filed out in silence. As Ralf left he sought his eyes and the boy remained reluctantly in the room after the others had gone. Quite unable to control the tremble in his voice he asked where he was and was given a vague reply that he had decided not to come in.

Each day piled on the punishment. The rest of year thirteen appeared regularly around the school, using the library, the gym and canteen; they had a comfortable common room with excellent study facilities and a kitchen and were to be found in the pub at the end of the road in the early evening. But he was never among them and obsessed David began to make a daily detour to drive past the house at dog walking time. He saw Abi frequently but after a week still no sign of Mark and he parked near the house, watching in his rear view mirror for a sight of him. Returning home each evening after these fruitless vigils he indulged in the mindless distraction of painting the thirty two newly installed banister spindles; an undercoat, two top coats with a sanding in between each, unable to look at Clare in case the despair showed in his eyes. He had made a terrible mistake, he was no more able to walk away from it than anything you love to distraction and that was what he did, he loved him to distraction.

Anxiety and misery set in like an ice age, he dragged himself through the remainder of the school year; set written revision tasks in class because anything more than a flat monotone required a super human effort and he began to wonder how he had ever enjoyed the job. Who knew? Mike showed no sign but they were barely on speaking terms anyway. He listened in the staff room to find if any other staff were concerned about Mark's absence, his name was mentioned occasionally but without concern, he imagined they were all looking at him, accusing him of dishonouring the profession to further his own perverted pleasure and ruining a young life. He trembled with terror at the prospect of him flunking his exams and the unspeakable guilt that would follow. James advised him to speak to Ralf and after another tortured week he sought him out in the library and asked to speak to him in the corridor.

'He's working, he's OK,' Ralf said coldly, he phoned him every day, he was at his books but he would offer nothing else, probably as instructed. David was barely able to stop himself from clutching Ralf in desperation but he betrayed nothing of his inner turmoil yet felt a faint relief.

It was Sarah, yet again who noticed the change; she was busy with displaying final pieces and sketch books for the external examiner and peered in at him sitting in her room at lunchtimes, clutching his mug, hiding behind a paper that didn't seem to get read. This time, under great pressure herself, she presumed he was anxious about results, he was just more conscientious that most of the others. And she informed Gail Kenyon, who had told her in the ladies what she'd just heard about David Ashbourne and Mark Derby, that it was only pathetic gossip and that he was just the sort of teacher to make friends with the sixth. He was attractive and sporty, a good role model, it was only the unpopular old frumps that couldn't see that these days there was no need to act like you were a different species.

Never before obsessed by his mobile, David glanced at it constantly and slipped it under his pillow at night, his texts, once a minor irritation, were now ached for. It was about midnight, two weeks after he'd ended it and when they'd been asleep an hour, when it rang. He threw himself out of bed and took the call on the landing, it was the police, his number was an emergency contact in the diary of a boy they had in custody for being drunk and disorderly and could he come in? He hauled on his clothes with deep relief. He would see him, he would take him home, he would talk to him and confirm that he was confident and capable of taking his exams. It was an opportunity to break the appalling deadlock, they would re establish contact maybe, who knows. He told Clare James had had a car accident, very minor; he was just a bit shaken up and need a lift home, she sat up and began to ask questions anxiously but he threw himself down the stairs and into the car. Yet another favour to ask the man, god he deserved a medal, he would have to ring him early, before Clare got up, she was sure to want to find out how he was, they'd got so chummy over the wedding arrangements.

It was drizzling steadily; on-coming headlights bounced unpleasantly off the wet shiny road and after a few yawns he turned up the radio and drummed the palms of his hands hard on the steering wheel to wake himself up. Binge drinking scenes from the TV news filled his head, he imagined him stumbling and weaving, knocking into innocent passers by, he saw the police grappling with him, his abusive response and, having no alternative, frogmarching him struggling and kicking to a police van. So, he'd been on a bender had he, got wasted, rat arsed and what was that quaint term he used? Over refreshed. So, without his guiding influence Mark was no different to anyone else, just a stupid drunken yob and where in gods name was Ralf this evening? Sensible to the core, had he given up with him? He slammed his way up through the gears on the by pass and jammed his brakes on dramatically at the speed cameras. What would they think when he turned up, should he be his dad, his uncle or his brother? He would act furious, actually he *was* furious, being called in the middle of the night, a bit of humiliation would put a stop to it ever happening again and if he threw up in his car, god help him.

In the town he anticipated weaving through drunks prostrating themselves in front of his car, but the streets were almost empty, clearly, along with Mark they been swept into another part of town or into the police station. As he parked some possible repercussions struck him, would he get cautioned? Fingerprinted? His DNA taken? A record? The implications of his arrest grew, he must have a story to tell, a plausible story; there were family problems, divorce, debt and a home about to be repossessed, it was hardly surprising he'd finally hit the bottle, how could anyone that age take such pressures? It wouldn't happen again, as a close family friend, and school teacher, he'd make sure it didn't, he wanted Mark to be able to walk away from this, so he could too. At the desk his teeth were almost chattering with nerves, it was no longer a case of just taking him home, he had an act to put on.

The duty officer seemed relaxed, 'we found him lying on the pavement, he's been drinking very heavily, and he seemed to be alone. The officer who found him was concerned about his safety and welfare, he's been very sick, is he eighteen yet?'

'Yes, he's eighteen, the officer said drunk and disorderly on the phone.'

'No, just dead drunk, it's unusual for a young lad like this to be alone. Do you know him well? You must if you're his emergency number.'

'Yes, I know the family well.'

'I think you should tell his parents that there may be some underlying problems, he's told us nothing. He's free to go, there's no official caution except to caution him about the health risks of drinking to excess and wasting police time, I'll go and get him.'

He appeared a few minutes later, his eyes firmly fixed on the floor, his favourite jacket shiny with vomit and stopped as far away as he could from David.

'I didn't give them your number,' he said sullenly.

'I know, I know, it's OK, come on I'm taking you home, you're free to go.' He walked up to him and slipping his arm supportively around his shoulders held him close for an awkward moment and noticed the desk sergeant watching them curiously, trying to establish a relationship, he assumed. Outside Mark allowed himself to be lowered gently into the passenger seat of the car.

'Why were you on your own, for chrissakes? Why in god's name did you get into this state?'

'Just did.' He turned and dropped his head on David's shoulder as David fastened his seat belt.

'Mark, one day very soon I'll just be an embarrassing memory, please don't do this again and please stick with Ralf and the others when you go out.'

He drove as if the car was full of eggs, expecting him to throw up, thrilled to have him beside him once again. Helping him out he walked with him to the front door. 'I can't possibly go in; I'm going to have to leave you here.' He took his key and opened the door for him and found Abi, holding Fletcher, standing in the dark hallway in her pyjamas, she helped Mark in and closed the door firmly in David's face.

It was the worst, the very lowest moment, nothing compared, he loathed himself.

Chapter Fifteen

After that Mark barely left his thoughts, he now took complete responsibility, how much was the drinking incident to do with him? Binge drinking was a national sport, a product of not much else to do and alcohol cheaper than bottled water. He was morbidly terrified that he might do something; he imagined a bottle of weed killer, a non stop train at the station, a bottle of spirits and a handful of the assorted drugs he seemed to acquire. Images of Mark swinging, falling, throwing himself, or lying comatose on his bed lay in wait for him at unguarded moments and eventually he could only sleep at night if he confirmed he was alive that day. He resumed his daily trawls along his road but never saw him, the temptation to call at the house intolerable but he never gave in. Seeing Abi ambling along with the dog at the usual time, chatting on her phone, was his only reassurance that matters were as usual in the house. He wanted to believe she would ring if anything happened, so every phone call now sent his heart racing. He'd rescued a dog, loved it and then left it out on the street because it had become troublesome and interfered with his lifestyle.

In the days leading up to the start of exams David threw himself into work, making himself as available as possible, his door wide open to any one who sought him out, and he finally managed to be more tolerant of Mike if he was around. As he coached, encouraged and supported everyone who came through his door he desperately hoped that the months of individual tuition that he had given Mark would pay off. They had battled over it, he had put aside part of every week for him alone even though it was rejected frequently as taking up their precious time for sex. His arms wrapped around his shoulders he had half joked that his tutoring was his lovemaking too.

The night before Mark's first exam he did the usual trawl, tucking himself between two cars in a road that ran at right angles to Abi's dog walking route. She was late and when she finally appeared the craving to speak to her was overwhelming but he squashed it and drove home to a lousy night's sleep arriving exhausted at school at 8.00 the next day. Fretful and unable to settle in his office he paced between the exam hall and the main school entrance, it was still too early for anyone to have arrived and the hall door was still locked so eventually he positioned himself next to a wall so he could see the bus stop without being seen and smoked as an excuse for his lingering outside. By 9.00, on his second cigarette he heard his name and turned to find the Head standing behind him.

'Go and collect him please. He hasn't left home, go and get him, just get him here.'

It must have been his mother, she must have rung the Head, he must be refusing to come in, the Head would have just found out, maybe his mother had just found out too, he would deny everything, nothing had gone on, nothing at all, he had ended a flirtation weeks ago which had got out of hand, these things happen, he had decided not to inform the Head as he felt able to contain and deal with it. Yes, contain was a good word, nothing remotely sexual about it.

The front door was wide open when he drew up and Abi was standing stony faced in the hall. 'Make him a sandwich and a drink,' he said and sprinted up the familiar staircase to his bedroom. The room was dark, the curtains closed but he could see he was still in bed, his head turned away from him.

'Get the fuck up!' he hissed, swept the duvet off him, took

his arms and hauled him to his feet. Mark fell against him, hot from his bed, his hair standing up in dirty clumps, his sleepy eyes downcast.

'*Please*, get your clothes on, I'm taking you in.' Completely familiar with the room he pulled a shirt out of the wardrobe, pants and socks from the drawer, found his grey suit trousers on the floor and the shoes he wore for school under the bed. David tugged and pulled the clothes over the impassive body; the hard flat chest, the wide bony shoulders, the height, the form and the flesh that he wanted.

'Lets go,' he whispered and taking his hand they clattered down the stairs past Abi in the hall hanging onto Fletcher barking hysterically, uncomprehending at the tension in the house. There was no sign of his mother of course, probably keeping out of the way in the kitchen. Abi handed Mark a sandwich and a bottle of drink and met David's eyes briefly. He drove almost light headed back to school, his precious passenger, a delicate repository of knowledge and opinions ready to pour onto an exam paper, was sunk into the seat. David said nothing; nothing must disturb this fragile state of affairs.

'Fuck, my tie!' he yelped suddenly as they reached the school entrance and David tugged his off and handed it over.

'I'll be in the car park afterwards.' Between classes he managed to peer through the windows into the assembly hall once, Mark was still there, head down. He waited in his car for the exam to end and Mark appeared immediately he noted with intense pleasure, he clearly hadn't stopped to discuss the paper with the others.

'How d'it go?'

'Fine, quite well, nothing unexpected.'

'Be OK tomorrow?'

'Yeah,' he paused, 'come home with me.'

David's stomach lurched, the directness was erotic and he was desperate to obey. He turned his head so Mark couldn't see the battle with his conscious play out across his face, to see his mouth fall open slightly, to hear his breath shorten with excitement. I want him, life's for living now and he's magic.

'It's impossible, you know why…'

The car door slammed.

It wouldn't happen again, he knew, Mark's risky and desperate last attempt at getting him back had failed. He turned up on time for the rest of his exams and David did his utmost to keep completely out of his way, reluctantly avoiding the end of exam party and drinking sessions. Suzanne, probably the only one with enough social skills and maturity to express her disquiet with his absences appeared at his office door one evening as he was preparing to leave; he stumbled through stupid excuses about paper work to complete.

'Thanks for being such fun,' she said, 'thanks for helping us so much, for always having time for us.'

'Thanks, I really appreciate that. I know you'll all do very well and have fantastic futures ahead of you.' He waited for the big smile as she left for her fantastic future but she stared at him.

'He worshipped you, he lived for you. Lucky you.'

Lucky? The Head wanted to see him.

The Head claimed, frequently, to have his finger on the pulse of his school, his daily rambles and unannounced visits to classes were unnerving for some and reassuring for others. However from the moment David finally acknowledged his feelings for the boy the man made him shake and every jaunty greeting he threw at David on his perambulations round the school gave him a sick jolt in his stomach. But he had got away with it; it was extraordinary that so many had at least some suspicions yet the Head, along with his pulse, had remained in the dark.

At 9.15 the following day he set off for the Head's office, his resignation letter in an envelope in his hand. He had of course given a term's notice but would assume that the Head would want him off the premises as soon as possible so he would offer to cover until a suitable replacement had been found. Before the Head had the chance he would a, acknowledge that he had let the profession down, b, jeopardised a student's career and c, caused the Head unnecessary distress. He would explain his intentions to do a post graduate course but hoped that the Head could see how committed he was to teaching and give him a good reference so he could continue teaching when his studies were completed though, of course, in the further education sector. His hands jammed between his knees it tumbled out and he only managed to meet the man's eyes at the end, losing eye contact in the ensuing silence.

The chair squeaked as its tubby occupant leaned back, pressing his fingertips together in an arch, the floor was now his; he'd had to wait for it.

'I have known the Derbys for a long time, I remember Mark, a scrawny little thing on his first day with us, the pride of his junior school, we were very pleased to have him. I can remember Mark himself, sitting in that seat, telling me, after much persuasion that he was being regularly bullied on his journey to and from school and I can also remember Mrs Derby, a year later, again sitting where you are sitting now, upset over some incident with an older boy. His father walked out on them, as of course you know, left her with heavy debts but instead of retreating to the benefit system she threw herself into her career and is now, I understand, in a position to buy a house close to her daughter's school. I saw, from very early on, that he was enthralled with you. In fact as hard as you tried to cover it up, he let it be known, constantly. Nothing direct, he was keeping a secret too, but what you underestimated was how proud he was of you and how much he actually *wanted* us to know that you were in some way together. Your name and your opinion dropped into every conversation and as Mrs Derby told me, the day you appeared on the scene their lives were transformed. Mark changed from D grades to As, bursting with confidence is the way staff described him, his mother said she was able to completely stop worrying about him. He blossomed from someone sometimes not entirely happy with his sexuality into one of our brightest and one of our best. And he was eighteen, a man, it was consensual, he also made it clear to me in his own way that he had initiated it and as I said we are talking about a relatively sexually mature individual here, I made the decision therefore that I would not treat it as a breach of trust.

No David, there's no need for resignations although if that's what you want then I accept. No, what I do want to say is how *blundering*, how crass, how selfish your decision was to end a relationship you had allowed him to become so dependent on, weeks before his final exams. He barely left his room and he barely spoke, his mother was distraught. I visited him a few times, I was satisfied that he was ready to take the exams and that he had been working. I mentioned you briefly; just enough to reassure him that I would expect you back next year, for his sake you understand, not yours. His mother and I were prepared for some incident like the morning of the first exam, he had threatened, it was no coincidence that I was waiting for you. He'll do well in his exams, you and the other staff prepared him well, summer camp will do him good, and he'll forget you, very quickly. As for your position here, I'll leave that up to you but a term's notice will not be required and the further education sector may be a better choice. And I understand you're getting married in two months time? Congratulations!'

'I'm going to supply teach and see if I can get on a post graduate course, the same money will come in, I still want to work in a school close to the centre, nothing much will change. I'll talk to your dad, you know, about the opportunities, I just needed a change, you can't imagine how stressful it is working in a school like that.'

'It's not that I don't understand, about the school and the pressures it's that we haven't talked about it, when you don't talk about things how do I know when things aren't OK?'

David wrapped his arms round her rigid body and hugged her and rocked her until she relaxed against him but this wasn't the person he had become accustomed to confiding in. Mark had quickly become the repository for every gripe, they piled up during the day and spilled out the moment they were alone. He'd apologise for offloading, convincing himself he was preserving his best side for Clare, it hadn't struck him at the time how every confidence had glued them more tightly together.

The solution to relationship crises in these cash rich times was a weekend away and he managed to fuss over the hotel and departure times to convey his commitment to the event. Leaving town, albeit only to Salcombe on the coast, still signified to David his continuing severance from Mark. The weather was reasonable, grey but not actually raining and although the appearance of the sun occasionally might have lifted his spirits more he put in the most tremendous effort, holding himself under surveillance for good behaviour. Nothing was too much trouble, he agreed to everything; the afternoon teas he couldn't stand; the gift shops and galleries where he managed a few purchases himself but she was making an effort too; agreeing to ten mile walks when he knew she'd had enough after three miles. They debated the species of seabirds squabbling over their sandwiches, read the guidebook out loud to each other and for once she made the effort to map read with him instead of waiting for instructions. They resumed their sex life and he ensured a frequent and regular pattern was maintained so there could be absolutely no possibility of any doubt or uncertainty on that score entering into any future girl talks.

There was a thank you from the Head in assembly, a card and gift, a goodbye on the school website with photos from the school plays and the expectation of a leaving do at the local which he did not fulfil. The Head's all seeing all knowing smugness that he'd known about them all along and chosen to let it run its course was shocking and humiliating, however the bugger had got one thing very wrong, Mark's father was actually dead, why had Angela Derby told him that nonsense, for sympathy? He composed an email to Sarah, rewrote it and rewrote it as it swung from an apology to a cheery goodbye to an invitation for a drink. He imagined her bewilderment and annoyance; why didn't you tell me she would ask, why didn't you stop me asking divvy questions about your inner peace when all this turmoil was going on? I'm not just a tea making machine, you'd have found me sympathetic and helpful.

The long summer holidays, seen by some as the whole reason d'etre to be a teacher stretched ahead like a prison sentence, in fact a stretch in the nick he decided might even be a diversion. Anything would be better than this, which was buckets of nothing, even hearing something second or third hand would ease the misery. He and Mark had isolated themselves so much there was really only Suzanne and he couldn't bring himself to get in touch. The only link now was Abi and after the sullen looks on the exam day he'd have happily kept out of her way too but if there was one thing he did have experience of it was sullen teenagers. He'd contemplated crawling after her in the car as she walked Fletcher and drawing up alongside her but he didn't like the image. Now the only living creature who might still like him enough to help was the dog, he would have to use Fletcher as bait, it was sneaky but he could see no alternative. It was a week before Mark's flight to the USA, a cheerful goodbye, a handshake and a promise to meet up when he returned would be mature.

He positioned himself on the regular dog walking route at the side of the pitches behind the Derby's house and saw Fletcher running ahead of Abi off the lead and one call had him bounding enthusiastically towards him. He grasped him, ruffled his thick coat and buried his face in his neck whispering his name over and over and kissing his floppy ears. After a few minutes he looked up and saw Abi had stopped, she called Fletcher back and the dog ran in her direction then shot back to David, now *two* playmates he seemed to say, David walked towards her hesitantly.

'Abi! hi! , how's things?' He hadn't really seen her close up for a few months, the little stick he had met a year ago appeared to have filled out and her hair, usually scraped into a tight pony tail was loose around her shoulders and was there a touch of eye make up he wondered as he got closer. 'Fletcher's looking well.' David crouched down to stroke Fletcher and even this felt creepy, please god no one was watching. 'How are you both?' he stood and began to walk, knowing Fletch would follow and Abi trailed behind.

'Talk to me, you always talked to me.'

He pieced together a story which was as bad as he hadn't wanted to imagine. No speaking, not coming out of his room, dope. Worse was the back story that he'd never been told. Crying in his room after school because they were horrible to him on the bus, walking the long way from the bus stop, taking his books and his lunch. How his appearance had made everything better.

'He stopped talking to *me* and since you left everything's been horrid and shitty.'

'I was very stupid, I thought things could carry on, that's what people do sometimes when they get into a mess, they pretend it's not happening and that's what I did Abi, I pretended it was all going to work out right in the end. 'I just want to know how he is, that's all.' What did she mean, since you left? He hadn't lived there, she watched TV and played on her computer, he barely saw her. She was holding the clip on the lead, ready to attach it back to the dog's collar but he hung onto Fletcher, 'please Abi, is he still at home with you?'

She fiddled with the lead; looping and unlooping it round and round her wrist.

'He's gone to live with Jason, they're going to America next week, *together*. He will be *really* mad if he finds out you're trying to speak to me.' He detected a note of triumph, that he'd specifically sought *her* out; he would make the most of it.

'Abi,' he said and now held her gaze,' I've made a lot of mistakes but everything comes to an end eventually and Mark's probably forgotten about me already. I'd like to make contact with him though, as an old friend and I can only do it through you.'

'Do you still love him then?' Love, was she discovering it? Just to walk the dog she'd changed out of her school uniform and was wearing tight jeans and flat white pumps. It brought it home to him that she knew pretty much everything and now he had all the information he needed it was time to put it all on the footing he wanted it to be on from now on. Standing up he folded his arms to create a less friendly look for the benefit of anyone watching. 'Abi, we were great mates, we enjoyed each others company, we liked doing things together and he was great fun. That's all.'

'But, I thought,' her voice quavered uncertainly, 'he loved you, he told me he did, he told me before, before you started coming round.'

'Yes, OK, but things are *different* now and as you said he's back with Jason and that's great and what happened in the past is well, in the past, and it's just between *us*, isn't it? But that doesn't mean I don't still like him and want to keep in touch.' He took a piece of paper out of his jacket pocket 'Here's my email address and my mobile number. Don't hide it from your mum, tell her I just want you to let me know how he's getting on occasionally. And can I have your mobile number, you know, for the maths help, if you still want some that is.'

She took his proffered diary and wrote her number in it and then took his paper, put it in her coat pocket and clipped Fletcher back onto his lead. 'He said he's going to email us regularly so I'll let you know.'

He strode back to the car, it had gone well and he now had the information he wanted. And yeah, it was love of sorts but Mark was a vulnerable and demanding youth, what could he, in such an exposed and professional position have done and yes, there was fondness but it only worked as a short, secret fling, giving up a normal life was out of the question. This rational held the shock at bay long enough to get across the car park where dogs and bikes and children were spilling out of hatchbacks, long enough to get to the privacy of his car where it felled him; insane, pounding jealousy, exploding in his chest, firing up the blood vessels in his face and taking his legs from under him. *Waiting*, like a fucking *snake* under the floorboards to slither out when the going was clear, touching him and kissing him and everything else. *Shite. Shite. Shite.* He sank into the car and forced himself to breath deeply, the memory of the classroom panic attack, how totally debilitated he had been, how he thought he was going to die, it must not happen while he was driving. He needed to calm down before he set off, any upset, and god there were plenty of them these days and memories of the accident returned and made him nervous at junctions and lights.

He begged himself to be bigger than this, to be generous for once, Jason clearly cared about him, there was no need to worry anymore, he would look after him, he'd waited long enough. Give thanks that they were both moving on, be relieved that things were now working out for both of them. These noble sentiments calmed him and he sat watching the children pedal off down the paths and the dogs scoot, noses to the ground, into the undergrowth and his heart beat gradually slowed. This must be the last emotional rollercoaster; it couldn't be good for him. Now all it needed for that fabled closure was for him to send a cheery email via Abi and when Mark returned from his travels they'd go for a drink and he'd suggest he meet Jason. Taking out his diary he flicked through the weeks, Mark was due back in late September and would be moving straight to Manchester to start his first year. He'd be back for the Christmas break and they'd be settling into their new house and he could maybe suggest a bike ride and show him round the house.

Throughout the early weeks of the summer break David settled into a pattern; rising late, doing simple household tasks and waiting for her to return home, so he could open the wine. He became easily tired and took frequent double intakes of air because his breathing was too shallow and he stumbled over nothing and found himself staring vacantly into space. Sometimes he managed to pull himself together enough to have the evening meal ready for her. She was surprised at his bolognaise.

'It's yummy! What's in it?"

'A teaspoon of sugar and a bit of chorizo sausage.'

'Who gave you that idea, an old girlfriend?'

'A bloke actually.'

'Bet it was Tony.'

'Yeah.' No, it wasn't Tony, actually.

Although he just about managed to fill the weekdays it was Saturday afternoons during that summer that hung bleakly in wait all week for him. To keep up the pretence for Clare's benefit he carried on doing the things alone that they'd done together; cycling on the ring road cycle path, the weights, the running machines and hating every minute of it. A few people asked after Mark, 'haven't seen your mate for a while.' Mate was reassuring. 'Travelling,' he'd say indifferently, 'alright for some.'

Apart from James he was morbidly convinced at least one of the crowd knew or had suspicions about him so staying at home until the big day was the safest strategy, no drunken questions to field and it looked committed and domesticated. There had been no mention of the stag do, even Clare, her hen party two weeks away in a London hotel, had kept oddly quiet about it, it looked as though he had got away with it. Now diaries no longer had to be cross checked because he wasn't doing anything or going anywhere but Clare struggled, both pleased and anxious with this new man. Alone at home David held endless imaginary conversations, practicing repositioning the affair in his future. Would the Head break his promise of silence? Would Abi's loyalty hold? Would Tony finally come out and drag him along too, and which one of Clare's friends had twigged? If he was going to take on responsibilities like a Headship or a role in the local community the moment of madness scenario was out of the question, it was now a comedy classic.

The midnight confrontation was never mentioned, but the care with which they now treated each other demonstrated the watershed it had been. To fill the time and stop his thoughts wandering David decided to go into town and buy something weighty and distracting from the bookshop. He hadn't been since the last foray into the uncharted territory of his sexuality; this time he decided to investigate the Second World War section; it would give him something to talk to his father about who read nothing else. Yet again once he was safely inside he snuck downstairs to just run his eye over the self help psychology section. He knew what he didn't want, there would be plenty of the loving and accepting who you are guff, even Sarah had tired of that. No he needed a boot camp book, he needed to be terrorised into behaving himself. He wanted someone to rage at him and say that he'd been a fool and that the consequences next time would be very different, he had got away with murder.

The basement was empty and quiet and he was drawn to the familiarity of the geography section and settled into something new on cities and as he debated whether or not to buy it the rather nice assistant he'd noticed on his previous visit appeared with a customer and David watched him discretely from behind the book. There was an earnestness that was attractive and he liked the careful way he handled each book he pulled out and the way his T shirt didn't quite meet his trousers, exposing a narrow and enticing band of creamy skin but most of all he liked his face; he was pretty. Except he was a bloke, maybe that was it, he liked pretty; pretty dogs, pretty girls and pretty boys.

He wandered over to psychology where he picked out a popular lightweight study on gender differences, and flicked through. The spatial awareness differences, the hunter gatherer debate and that old staple, reversing.

'What d'you do when I'm not here?' he'd say to her when they changed seats at a tight parking space.

'Find a bigger one.'

Mark wasn't too brilliant at reversing himself but then he was a learner. He, on the other hand, could back into a tight space in two sweeps of the steering wheel, so that was OK then, his brain was wired up nice and straight, or more realistically, he'd practiced more. He snapped the book shut and took out the cities book again, barely able to look at the assistant as he paid for it but unwilling to leave he mooched around the three for two stacks near the door where, to match his repetitive thoughts, he picked them up, turned them over and put them back. Their relationship had never got off the starting blocks, it had never been tested, how long would it have taken to reach the practical compromises he made with Clare? He and Clare had already made all the day to day adjustments of living together, they had established an optimum contact time that suited them both and ironed out the irritations of allocating domestic chores, that was why they were so confident that marriage was the obvious next step. He lifted a book to read the blurb and replaced it suddenly as one of his uncontrolled memories swung in like a demolition ball and socked him with the backswing; a memory of being *taken* by him, of entirely letting go, physically, sexually, emotionally, of being wholly in the now with him. And that couldn't last of course and he strode briskly out of the shop.

'Hello sir.'

'Oh, hello Michelle, hello Chloe.'

'It's a pity you aren't coming back sir.'

'Well that's kind of you.'

'Are you going to another school?'

'No, I'm doing some more studying.'

This puzzled them and he explained and wished them a nice summer and as he walked away he could no longer imagine ever teaching again. There was a weakness, the boy had seen it and mined it and at all costs it couldn't happen again.

After the bookshop he went into the outdoor shop in town they liked to visit and where they'd fingered the fine merino base garments, admired the thick socks softly padded at toe and heel to avoid pressure on long walks, checked out the lightweight camping gear, been impressed with the solar powered equipment. Unspoken but somehow implicit in these visits had been that they would one day be needing all this gear for their travels together. He bought a South America guide, maybe he could trace his travels from the emails Abi said she would forward.

A good offer was made within days of the house going on the market so the half hearted house hunting took on a new urgency yet she was still vacillating about the location. In his misery his world had narrowed, the clamp round his heart kept him pinned to the security of the town and familiarity, 'I don't want to be stuck out in the middle of bloody nowhere!' he exploded one evening from a deep dread at the prospect and for the first time he saw a wariness of him in her expression.

It's said you make the decision in the first five minutes of the viewing but she had made up her mind when she opened the agent's brochure. To his immense relief it was in town and they arranged to see it the following morning.

The door opened to reveal three children. 'We're going to show you round,' they announced,' Mum's tidying up upstairs especially for you.'

'Sorry, you're one of the first,' muttered the agent,' the novelty will wear off.'

They followed the children down into the semi basement, a vast kitchen with enough work surfaces to accommodate a dozen cooks.

'We spend all our time in here especially in the winter because the rest of the house is *freezing*.'

Clare was ecstatic, 'I really want a big kitchen, and what fantastic big patio doors, onto the garden.' The children obligingly flung them open and she stepped outside.

'We get foxes, they come in and eat the cat's food and one of them has mange.'

On one side of the kitchen was a huge pine table covered in a recently abandoned craft activity and paintings and collages decorated every surface.

'Do you three come with the contents?' David asked chummily and they looked at him blankly. As everyone trailed out of the kitchen David lingered and looked back into the sunny room and the elder boy remained beside him. 'This room was probably originally four separate rooms, you can just see the ghost of parts of the walls on the ceiling. It would have been much darker in here, full of cooking smells and the only window would have been high up on the back wall and there, in that corner, would have been the scullery. A poor maid, not much older than you would have been scrubbing pots in there all day in soda, her hands and arms red raw. You probably wouldn't have been allowed down here you know, it was just for the servants, your mum and dad would have stayed upstairs. I wonder what they would have thought of how we all live in the kitchen now eh?'

'Are you a school teacher?'

'That obvious? Come on.'

'It's a lot of stairs, its *all* stairs, mum wants somewhere with less stairs, stairs keep you fit, I fell down the stairs when I was little, *twice*.' The agent, her lips pursed, closed the living room door sharply leaving them behind in the hall. David was conscious of her glancing at him as Clare continued to make very positive noises.

'The Aga in the kitchen is on all day and the heat rises up the staircase making it a very warm house, and there's also a new condensing boiler.' She glanced at David, expecting approval but he was staring out of the front window, it looked like rain and he wanted to go for a long cycle ride.

On the second floor David walked into an en suite

bathroom and pulled up the window blind to look at the view. The window faced east and he stood quietly looking out across the roofs in the direction of Radley Hill and then looked at his watch, it would be 8.30 at the camp he calculated, he would be having breakfast with the children, would he be wearing those long plaid shorts he'd bought him that he liked so much or a camp uniform? What would their first activity be? What was the food like?

'That's the window the burglar got in.' said a voice behind him, 'he climbed onto the conservatory using a ladder that we'd left out and climbed through this window which someone had left open. These houses have lots of ledges and drainpipes and are very easy to climb up.'

'Really? What did he take?'

'A laptop, a camera, money, you know, easy to carry things. Mum reckons he'll come again because he knows how to get in now.'

'You know I don't think that's the sort of thing you should be telling me. Why are you leaving by the way?' Might as well make use of his loose tongue.

'I've been told to tell you it's because of Dad's new job.'

'And what's the *real* reason?' it was just too tempting.

'It's because of Dad's new job. Why are you standing in here?

'I'm thinking about someone.'

'A celebrity?'

'No.'

'Are they on TV?'

'No, it's nobody well known.'

'Then why are you thinking about them, then?'

'Come on, let's find the others.'

The boy didn't move, 'are you going to buy it then?'

David folded his arms, 'we'll have to weigh the investment potential of the property against alternative investment opportunities for our capital, take into consideration the maintenance implications of such an old house like the condition of the wiring and plumbing, the state of the roof and if there's any damp. We'll have to consider the utility bills, factor in parking permits. Is the roof insulated? Are the windows double glazed? What is the energy rating? Are you on a water meter? Do the drains get blocked? What council tax band are you in? It's divided into four flats next door; do they party into the night? You don't enter into a capital commitment of this size without *considerable* research, *do you?*'

'Oh,' he said.

Back home Clare immediately laid all the details out on the kitchen table and sat quietly as he fiddled around making tea and emptying the dishwasher.

'It'll go very quickly, 'she said eventually.

'No rush.'

'It's everything we want.'

'Five floors, seven bedrooms, one point two million. I need to think about one point two million.'

She was sitting perfectly still, staring fixedly ahead, her fingers tightly laced on her lap, white at the knuckles, red at the tips. He waited for the bright smile, the bounce with which she always greeted his negativity.

'*Drag you*, that's all I seem to have done over the past months, *drag you, drag you!*'

The word did not immediately make sense,' what d'you mean, *drag me?*'

'*Every, single, fucking decision* has been *mine;* it's been like hauling a block of *concrete* behind me, every *inch* of the way!'

They sat in shocked silence, he couldn't look at her directly so he gazed at the dark roots of her hair; he supposed she would have it done just before the wedding. It wouldn't bother him if she didn't have it done, he couldn't care what colour her hair was, in fact he couldn't care less about the wedding or the house or his job or anything much any more. And *concrete*, there was something very dead about concrete.

'OK, put in an offer,' he said coolly.

As David was gazing out of the house towards Radley Hill, Mark was doubled up on the floor of the cabin he was sharing with two other councillors and ten boys. It had been a disruptive night, some of them had refused to settle down, excited by the start of the camp and were now testing their boundaries with the staff. One boy in particular, fighting tiredness, refused to get up, then to get dressed, hurling shoes at Mark who was the youngest of the three men. At first Mark tried to treat it as a joke not fully understanding the boy's real aggression and he dodged or caught the missiles. 'Come on, get dressed,' he approached the boy with his T-shirt and attempted to pull it over his head but the boy thrashed his arms wildly and swung punches which Mark ducked.

'Hey Mark, leave him,' one of the other councillors moved towards them in the cramped room, 'leave him, he can stay.'

It was too late and the kick in the groin floored him, quickly the other two men pulled the boy away. '*Fag*,' the boy sneered.

Getting slowly to his feet his instinct was to get out of the cabin as fast as possible, the boys were all staring at him, startled by the attack and the word reverberated around the room. How was he acting, how was he behaving that had made this boy say that? He felt a friendly arm around his shoulders, his main concern was they'd think he couldn't cope but the other two men had taken control and the boys filed out obediently and set off for the dining hall. He followed and suddenly Jason was at his side.

The boy was taken out of his cabin but it made little difference, the homesickness he was keeping at bay overwhelmed him and he was ashamed of it. That afternoon, during the few hours they had off Jason took him away from the camp in one of the pickups.

'I've made a mistake.'

'It's a one off, the boy's got problems and the camp knows that.'

'He called me a faggot where did that come from? He's

hardly had anything to do with me.'

'Probably because you were trying to be kind, it's a pretty common term of abuse, don't take it literally.'

'I've made a mistake, I can't cope.'

'Course you can, I'll spend every moment I can with you. It's not so long and then we can be together for two months. If you go now I'll go with you but we'll have to pay the air fares back.'

It was Jason's second summer camp in the States and he had chosen carefully to make sure the problems he'd encountered at the first were not repeated. He wanted good facilities, better pay, not too isolated and his swimming and sailing instructor certificates had got him a specialist post which meant he didn't have to sleep in the cabins with the children. It was a responsibility taking Mark, it wasn't the easiest way for them to start again but it meant they could travel round America together afterwards. After a couple a days of acclimatisation for the staff the children had arrived and a tight daily schedule and the high level of responsibility in a camp obsessed with safety was leaving them little time together. Jason had access to the camp vehicles and the day after the incident they drove to town to pick up supplies. They took the long way back, Jason finding deep ruts to make the elderly vehicle bounce them high on the wide front seat, forcing laughter out of Mark.

'Right!' Mark yelped as Jason instinctively took the left carriageway on an empty road.

'It's like when I drove off the Eurotunnel into France, no problem in traffic but when the road was empty my brain slipped into UK rules.'

'I'll be your US brain.'

'Cute councillor in cabin 4.'

'Not bad.'

'Play your cards right…' he danced the steering wheel making the truck lurch.

The battered pickup, a pencil straight treeless road stretching ahead, heat shimmering on the horizon. If Dave could see him now, part of an American cliché, or rather Mark's American cliché. What was the homesickness all about when he'd fantasised about this for so long and the final weeks at home had been a lousy confusing mess? It was only the familiar he was missing and that was difficult to grasp. School, the gym, the pub, his bedroom, they were blurred black and white images, fading fast. But David remained vivid. Jason had told him what to say to wreck his career and when he refused; 'you're letting his party carry on,' he'd said. And so, in his imagination, a party, a sophisticated, urbane dinner party with beautiful people sitting around a long kitchen table drinking wine and eating interesting food, carried on in a loop. And when he placed himself in the image they looked up and stop talking and stared. He slammed his fist into the worn leather.

'Fancy a burger? The sign's a fucking disgrace but I've heard they're good.'

Jason parked as far away from other vehicles as he could and slid across the seat to kiss Mark lengthily. Mark relaxed into his broad hold, there was no denying he was a very sexy man and he pulled him so he lay on top of him along the seat.

'Not too much stubble?'

'No, I like it.'

'Going to be difficult, to be on our own.'

'We'll find a way.'

As they walked across the car park Mark snapped the ridiculous billboard on his phone.

There was only one place he wanted to be now, quite desperately. He called through the door into the kitchen that he was off for a spin and would be back in time for their meal out that evening but there was no reply, he supposed she was on the phone to the estate agent, making an offer. Without the usual brake adjustments and touch of oil he lifted his bike over all the junk in the garage and set off as if late for a vital meeting. The derailleurs changed like silk, he got his head down and pushed himself reaching that man and bike union that was the closest he got to spiritual and he arrived at the start of the footpath sweating and shaky after the final pull up the hill. Leaving the footpath in the usual place he lifted his bike onto his shoulder as he negotiated the undergrowth and headed through the trees to the field and the familiar spot behind the hedge where he lay his bike down and sat on the grass. He could see nothing moving apart from an occasional tiny coloured dot of a car, the flicking of Friesians' tails in the shady corner of the field below him and, if he held his head very still, insects, faster than cheetahs, catapulting past. The packet of cigarettes he took out of his jeans pocket was the same packet from their first time and the same packet from the exam morning, there were two left. He'd claimed he'd taken it off Mark to stop him smoking but soon it became impossible to throw it away and like his brother's penknife and favourite Hornsby train engine he'd secretly hidden it.

He smoked them both as slowly as he could, taking long pulls and staring out intently across the county laid out before him, reading it like a 1:25000 map. They had cycled through all the villages he could see from this vantage point on their Saturday afternoon excursions, stopping for pints and peeping into the churches if they were open. Their spires still gave each village the sharp definition they had for centuries, still dominating the settlements clustered tightly around them, the separation between villages rigorously maintained by planning law since 1947, islands in a grassy English sea. Today the sky was cloudless, there had been weeks of dry weather and the charts were dull, he'd started turning his attention to the rest of the world for a bit of weather action.

He took off his T shirt and lay on his stomach, the rays, directly overhead, immediately got to work on his white flesh and he anticipated a touch of sunburn, of wincing as he leaned back in a chair tomorrow, the pain would be faintly comforting he decided. He dozed on, unwilling to return home, if that's what it still was. The purchasers, living in rented accommodation and eager to move in had come round the day before to measure up, which would have been fair enough but he heard 'far too much cream' and 'could do with brightening up' and he'd disappeared into the garage to stop his depression finding its voice as rudeness.

An ant, laboriously negotiating the cracks in the bone dry soil, began to hold his attention, his breathing slowed, he tuned into the heavy insect hum, picking out individual whirrs and drones and slowly tuned out of the now and into that afternoon four months ago.

Braced against the wind they'd seen the villages to the west still lit by celestial searchlights but to the east the sky was charcoal black, the tempest pounding towards them like an army of storm troopers and they'd watched fascinated as acre after acre below them succumbed. Within a minute it was on them, 'this is freaking *crazeee*!' Mark had howled then pulled off his clothes too as the deluge hit, blinding them, leaving them gasping for air, filling their mouths as they tipped back their heads and sending hundreds of messages of icy delight onto their skin. As the storm moved on they laughed at each others dripping, muddy nakedness.

'Next time, somewhere hot?' he'd pleaded.

They had had nothing in common really, apart from school and maybe music. He'd taken up David's political position and shown an interest in his hobbies to keep him and because he was young but all that would have changed with time. His interest in clothes though was one area he was his own man. There was freedom to accessorise beyond the regulation dark suits for the sixth and Mark had taken full advantage. A very thin tie, a new belt, narrow shoes and one morning a tight pink V necked jumper with teal trim under his jacket. 'You *smooooth dandy*,' he'd whispered in his ear as he passed, the words demonstrating he knew the details were for his eyes and approval alone.

Then there was that faux dependence that he loved and that confused him. 'I can't open this jar,' Mark would say like a bloody girl and hand it yet the same big hands could replace his bike chain with a flick or swing his bike effortlessly, one handed, over a gate. David felt himself jolt involuntarily as he remembered struggling one minute to pin the boy's arms over his head, the next having a docile rag doll in his arms, sweetness and brawn switching on and off, it enslaved him and his eyes sprang open with the memory. How would Mark be when he was older, would he continue to have the confidence to play or would convention and the unkindness of partners pin him to behaviour that conformed to an expected role? He would never know.

Rolling onto his back he took the envelope out of his pocket, he had kept it at school until the end of term and then in his bike maintenance box, the sheet, so crisp and thick it leapt out like a spring. He knew it by heart, a little crushed in the middle where he had pressed it against his eyes in distress, a letter, a real fucking letter, written in real smudgeable ink, the envelope and the paper even matched.

'I know I'm just a twink, I know that I don't have anything much and that I'm just going to be a bloody poor student soon but is there any chance that we can still be together because you are the world to me. Everything that was ordinary you made the best and I'm sorry that I seemed so ungrateful, I didn't mean it, it was just that I had nothing much to offer back. I can deal with it, whatever you can deal with I can too. I wanted to tell you something important and now this has happened, I can't go through with it without you. I want to get back with you.' He laid the letter beside him letting the sun, now low in the sky, fall on his face, how we Brits crave the sun, right to its dying embers, he mused.

And then his shadow falls over David's face and David looks up at him and smiles in welcome. Slowly he lies down on top of David, his bones and his muscles settling gently down into David's contours as he lets his arms release his full weight. David can feel his heart beating, his breath fills his mouth, he smells his shaving cream, his weight makes breathing difficult. He gives one of his slow grins and David lets his legs slip between his and smoothes his hair behind his ears just as he likes it and then wrapping his arms round him he rolls him over onto his back and smiles at him because it is all over and his mind is now made up. 'C'mon,' he whispers, 'lets get going before it gets dark.'

Chapter Sixteen

His life would change absolutely, James would be the only one to understand; all the others would be uncomprehending. She would take all their friends with her, his personal life would die, instantly, and he would lose everyone. He would have to start again and he was prepared for that. They might assume some sort of breakdown and this would be tolerable, it would give him space and time and no one would ask for explanations. He would be letting a great many people down, they would consider his actions completely reprehensible and for a short time it might be so indescribably dreadful, so atrocious that he wondered if he shouldn't disappear himself, maybe spend a few months out of the country, to give time for people to forget and for her to get over it.

He had absolutely no intention of revealing to anyone and Clare in particular a year of deceit, despair and happiness of an intensity he could never have imagined, the wound he was inflicting on her would be terrible enough. The truth came from somewhere she could not have dreamt of because it would have made no sense based on the man she thought she knew and its unimaginability had allowed it to flourish under her nose and for it to still have unlived life in it. He would offer no explanations and take whatever was thrown at him because there was no one to blame, it had all been self inflicted. He would take full responsibility for his inability to resolve their incompatibilities, he would not blame her in any way and he must sound confident to show how sensible and right it was, how it was the only way forward. He was in fact doing her a favour.

In order to be best prepared he carefully predicted what to expect; sobbing, rage, possibly she'd try to hit him and he would let her. He assumed, from what he'd read, that after the initial shock she would become abusive, possibly hideously abusive but as she never had behaved remotely like that it was difficult to imagine. He would let it all happen, try and maintain his dignity, not argue, hear her out and wait until he felt he could say his little piece, his explanation that would make it clear that it was for the best for her as well as him, better now than later when they were inextricably linked.

It was nothing like that, when was anything? Wanting the end of their relationship to emerge as a natural and obvious conclusion to a controlled discussion he rehearsed the issues; not agreeing over the size of house and its location, incompatibility over lifestyle choices such as his wish to take time out to do further study and travel, that he was not ready for children, that their interests were completely different and neither was prepared to compromise, all proving that to continue would only bring unhappiness and that he should release her so she had the opportunity to find the right person.

He chose his parents and their self imposed detachment from the wedding celebrations as the starting point in order to gently introduce the matter of all not being well. She acted surprised and argued that James had ensured they would be centre stage the whole time, he said her family and the factory employees would dominate, but he had agreed all this she said, the business was part of the family and some had known her all her life, they were friends, family almost. It's all for Jack, it's what Jack wants he began to wine desperately but she was right, he had accepted all of it. The adrenalin surge that had carried him this far had not properly factored in her negotiating skills. He could feel himself sliding down an oily slope of reasonableness and compromise. There simply wasn't time, not with only a month to go, the longer they dragged it out the more ghastly it would be, every day, every minute mattered.

'I'm sorry, I don't want to get married anymore.'

His voice did not let him down; there wasn't the slightest tremor of doubt and this time she remained silent. No sobbing or throwing or hitting; shock and disbelief rendered her quiet for a long time, her mouth fell open and she appeared to sag as if what kept her upright had been removed. They were standing in the kitchen and holding onto the table, she sank onto one of the two hard kitchen chairs in slow motion as if onto feather cushions. He remained standing throughout the ordeal, rigid, not even allowing himself the kitchen surface to lean on, taking it standing up, like a man.

After a while a little saliva dribbled from her open mouth and she took short jerky breaths. She said why and why and why sometimes a squeak, sometimes a growl, it was such a shock that she could only understand it in the context of the argument they had just had as if it was only based on the frustration with that single issue, as if he had made a sudden spur of the moment decision. Then, regaining her composure, she started to babble saying she completely understood his concerns, she would speak to her parents, they would change the speeches, keep the business guests in the background, the whole organisation had bored him hadn't it? It had gone on for too long; maybe they should have just had something more intimate sooner because that was the way he was, wasn't it; men weren't interested in that sort of thing were they? He was that sort of man and that's the way she liked him. All he had to do was turn up and then they would be alone and starting their life together, it was only a day, it would soon be over.

She had still not understood, she had rationalised it to something as trifling and easy to resolve as the colour of the table flowers. Whatever explanation he offered would be dealt with in the same way, only by opening the very core of his being would she understand and he was not prepared to do that. So he repeated, over and over, that he no longer wanted to get married, that he wanted to end the relationship, that it was for the best for her as well as him until she started to scream and rage and sob, hurling whatever came to hand; a cup, smashing against the wall and spattering dregs of black coffee all across his new cream paintwork, a cookery book which caught his shoulder and cut his ear but the table kept them apart and he made no move, remaining stricken behind it, beached in his kitchen, speechless, watching the death throws of his relationship until, weak with screaming and shock, she dragged herself into the living room and broke the news to her parents.

She packed and went to her parents that evening and the quietness of the house soothed him into persuading himself it wasn't going to be anything like as bad as he'd imagined and that his agony about the impact was possibly unfounded. He wiped the coffee off the wall in case the purchasers came round again and rang the agents. They didn't happen to have a terrace, no chain, near the station and requiring no renovation work, not even a lick of paint, did they? They did.

'Why aren't you answering your fucking phone, what the *fuck*?'

Angry over a poor team performance or a crappy manager and James's face would be animated with outrage but the face at David's door was pale and immobile. He stepped inside but remained at the door.

'Why didn't you tell me? Why didn't you say? They're blaming *me*, you know, because they think I should have known you were going to pull out. They're ringing me, night and day because they can't get hold of you, they won't believe I didn't know.' He eased his rucksack off his shoulders onto the floor. 'Do you have any *idea* what has to be cancelled? Did you know that two of the guests have already arrived from Australia, admittedly on an extended holiday but based around your wedding. They've couriered me the paperwork, it's like stopping a fucking *container* ship. I keep telling them, I *didn't know*. But it's not true, is it? I know why, I *do* fucking know *why*.' He opened his rucksack and pulled out handfuls of loose sheets, their very looseness adding to the drama.

'I'm incredibly sorry, it didn't occur to me they'd…you know, and it really isn't any of your…responsibility. I'll turn my phone back on.'

James leaned against the wall. 'This isn't, isn't a, you know, a traditional last minute bout of cold feet, is it? You know, all I need you to say is that you've had last minute nerves. I can do everything, I can hold your hand for the next four weeks.'

'It's not.'

James remained leaning against the wall. He was one of life's scapegoats, a sponge to fill with someone else's guilt. He shut his eyes. 'Why am I acting surprised eh? I *know* why, I'm as guilty as fuck.'

'Tea? I can do tea.'

The details of James's last two days made David cringe. Before he'd set off for work and in his lunch hour and as he ate his dinner he'd taken the full brunt of her grief. She wanted an explanation and as she hadn't had anything that made any sense from David she wanted it from him because he was his best friend and he was their best man and he must have known something was wrong; she refused to believe that he didn't. And she wanted him to agree, she begged him to agree, that they were made for each other.

'So I've had to agree with her. I've had to agree with every piece of twosomeness she dredges up, you know, about your compatibility, the way you finished each other's sentences….'

'We didn't finish each other's sentences.'

'Fuck, I couldn't tell her *that*, if I display a microbe of doubt she'll be onto me that *I - know - why*. Was there something she'd missed? Was there something I saw that she hadn't? It was my job as best man to counsel you through the pre-wedding nerves. She wants me to tell you that she knows it's got too big and that you can have a small wedding. She'd planned for rain Dave, not a catastrophe.'

'I thought they would handle it better, I was hardly a good catch.'

'You were marrying *her*, not *them*.'

'By the end I'd lumped them all together, I stopped differentiating.' With only a few days distance the last year struck him as madness, why had he battled on?

'You know, I thought it was going to be *fun*, being best man, I saw myself as the man of the day, mien host, all faultless organisation, lots of happy faces.' He paused and screwed up his face. 'It was kinda an important day for me too.'

'So sorry I spoiled your day.'

'Fuck. Off.' How could he explain that when accountability was sought he threw himself on the pyre?

They wandered into the kitchen and sank onto the chairs and the balloon of self righteousness James had arrived with gradually deflated. Clare's absence from the house and possible permanent absence was remarkably pleasant. He noticed a large brown stain across one wall and didn't want to ask. Surely there was no chance of him taking up with the boy again, so hopefully there would be a period of bachelordom with boozy nights in front of the telly. David enjoyed quietly drinking his tea with James, could he ask him to walk away from the mess, as a final best man duty? And the brown stain needed painting over he decided, before anyone noticed.

Despite the responsibility word hanging threateningly, James thought one last best man duty was necessary, for forms sake. 'Listen. OK, you'd only just split up with him, you were bound not to be feeling, well, *weddingy*. Phone her, tone the do right down, go away on holiday and when you come back you'll move into a new house and it will be all different and you'll have forgotten about him. A year from now you'll laugh if I mention him, honest, you'll be *embarrassed*. There's time to retrieve it,' he paused long enough to give away his true feelings, 'that's if you want to.'

'I tried incredibly hard, I really did but it was impossible, it would have been wrong to go ahead; it would have been cruel to her. I'm really sorry, I just hadn't realised that you'd get so dragged in, I didn't expect it, I'm prepared to admit that was naïve.'

The following evening they spread the paperwork across the table and the impact of his decision was made agonisingly clear. It was more complex, involved more people and, looking shakily at the figures, more money that he had assumed. There was a copy of every email between Clare and the companies that were providing goods and services, even the one liners. Was that Jack's secretary? Following orders with possibly some satisfaction, only the invoices would have been necessary. He started to read some of them but stopped because the commitment to their day and the preparations that were already in hand made his hands sweat. The complexity of the discussions between Clare and the florist passed belief. The matrix of colour themes, flower varieties, sizes and numbers for bouquets, buttons, bridesmaids' headdresses, table flowers, marquee flowers, church flowers and flowers for the inside of the wedding vehicles. Barely a day seemed to have passed when they hadn't been in contact; they appeared to have become best friends.

They sorted amongst the papers for the cancellation terms and conditions, what deposits would have to be forfeited and what invoices would have to be paid in full. The Chandlers, via James, expected him to cover all these costs and, having had no emotional involvement with any of them he did not feel obliged to take into account wasted time; business was business. The venue was easy, it was just a building but the catering was different, he was putting a small army out of work and then he got to The Forevers, and it became personal. The Forevers; Beatles, big band, chart, they'd rattled off their repertoire with drum rolls, challenging David to find something they couldn't play. It was a great break for them, a great chance to showcase they could send sleepy children off to bed and keep the party animals going all night. Everyone would have remembered the great band long after they'd forgotten everything else.

'I'm finding this bit hard. Do it for me.'

'Just tell them, they're big boys, they have the deposit, give them more if you feel guilty'

'I was looking forward to them playing, they were going to play my all time top ten,' David wined and finally they managed to smile.

'More like *his* top ten as I recall.'

'I could go through with it if you drugged me, just for the party.'

'Too late, venue's cancelled and have you any *idea*, how *many...* '

'Shut. It.'

And the bridesmaids; two pink dervishes twirling ecstatically around the living room and endless discussions about whether they should have their hair up or loose, curled or straight, it must have been difficult to explain and he mused on how Clare might have done it; 'sometimes in the grown up world things don't always work out like you want them to and you have to not let it upset you and think about other nice things,' He was curious too about how the Chandler's had told the guests.

'They're telling everyone it was down to some two bit schoolboy from a council estate with a *very* nice arse.'

It made him laugh and that felt incredibly good, 'seriously, you twat,'

'They're saying it was *unforeseen circumstances*. This is middle England mate, nobody is asking *directly* for details and the paps haven't contacted me; it's worth being a total fucking nobody sometimes.'

His phone now back on she rang that evening and he said nothing but sorry, and again sorry and sorry. What a handy word it was, it even sounded sorrier without the very and the extremely; sorry I spilt the milk, sorry I ruined your life. He said it like it was a bolted door but ignoring his tone she spoke of regret and loss with puzzlement in her voice and no hint of anger. Recalling her own advice to others he supposed people were persuading her he'd change his mind and not to burn her bridges.

Hi David, got an email from Mark and he is having a fantastic time but says he's very busy and sent me these 3 photos. Fletcher is sitting on my bed and sends his love.
love
Abi.

Hi Abi,
Lovely to hear from you, let me know if you want some maths help. btw just to let you know I'm not getting married anymore.
Best,
Dave.

Taking a deep breath he opened Mark's photos expecting to see Jason in at least one of them. No people at all, the tatty interior of an old pick up truck, a polystyrene cup in the gutter with a long view of an empty road stretching into the distance behind it and a hideous peeling bill board with a hamburger dressed as a cowboy. Very Eggleston he thought, photographing nothing much and making it interesting, the boy had taken on one of his enthusiasms then.

Hi Abi,
Here's a few photos to send back, he knows the place.
Best,
Dave

The boy had been made to apologise, Mark's cabin team mates were dealing with the late to bedders, he'd tried ice hockey and baseball and the weather was improving but his malaise had set in hard and the thought of another six weeks was crippling, he wanted to go home and the humiliation was intense. He had no complaints about the food but the clamour in the dining hall and his low spirits killed his appetite. At lunchtime on the third day after the incident he sought Jason out and they escaped to the seclusion of the dense woods around the camp. He could not go on, he said, every day was now a fight, the job required endless enthusiasm and he had none, everyone was noticing. Jason, his dream in tatters, fought to hold back his disappointment but he was as smitten with him as he ever had been and found it impossible to show any anger. He blamed himself he said, it had all been his idea and it was only an air fare and they would find work as soon as they got back and maybe go travelling in Europe. They walked back in silence and Jason resigned himself to leaving, letting the camp down and forfeiting a good position. The predatory schoolteacher had ruined his summer too.

After a miserable evening meal, watching food he would normally have enjoyed eaten enthusiastically and noisily by his charges, Mark left for the computer room to get a few moments of time before the hoard rushed in. He wanted to warn his mother of his imminent arrival but within minutes he was sprinting back to Jason still in the dining hall, 'I'm staying,' he said breathlessly, 'I've changed my mind, sorry to be a pain.'

A few hours later David received an email direct to him, not copied in. Photos of plates of food, grinning kids, it didn't make much sense except he was happy. And he knew. David sent some pictures of the dog down the road with a stupid grin and the inside of his fridge which was mainly full of beer. Take it easy he thought, like dealing with a skittish colt, not that he'd dealt with one, don't frighten him off.

They exchanged emails for a week until one said simply that he and Jason had decided not to travel on together and David asked, as casually as he could, 'can I fill the void?'

Chapter Seventeen

Sao Paulo was the rendezvous city Mark had chosen with the explanation that he had got a cheap connecting flight. David wasn't convinced. Why were there so many post it notes flagging the Sao Paulo section of Mark's Lonely Planet Guide? It would have been simple to ask but every mention of the future had become increasingly fraught. And Mark's emails, though now frequent, could have been written to his mother. David supposed Jason or the kids were shoulder surfing so he kept his emails bland too.

It was huge leap of faith or rather it wasn't entirely rational to expect someone barely out of their teens and surviving out of a rucksack to be reassuring about reigniting their relationship on another continent. The familiar organised structure of their lives was over. They had lived their lives over the past year on the same stage with the same players. At the time it had seemed impossible, now it seemed a breeze. To lessen his anxiety about the reunion and its location he decided to take a holiday in Belize, a real holiday with reps and excursions and sports. It would deflect questions like why are you going on holiday to Sao Paulo? But as he was rapidly finding out there wasn't anyone now to much care whether he took a break in Mogadishu or Siberia. The Saturday crowd hadn't met for weeks so James informed him, the Dave/Clare break up had been a bit of a watershed for all of them, each with their own opinion on why it had happened and comparing it nervously against their own unsteady outlooks.

David's expectations of armchair travelling with Mark as he made his way south to their rendezvous were proving disappointing; it was all grumbles about how long he had to wait for the bus, being hassled by hawkers and things in his bed. He usually forgot to say where he was, who he was with or where he was heading for, was this some sort of geography defiance or was one dusty town, grotty bus station and uncomfortable bed with small unwelcome bed companions merging with another?

The Sunday 6.30 pm phone call to his parents was a model of reassurance. They had taken the breakup news with almost speechless incomprehension and then his father had asked quietly why had he left it so late? David burnt with shame.

'Yes Mum, everything's *fine*. The house I'm buying is really snug and I'm taking a bit of a break so I can concentrate on writing and studying and I'll be supply teaching. Yes she's fine, she's got loads of friends and has accepted that it was the right thing to do and James has been fantastic of course. I'm having a holiday in Belize and then I'm catching up with an old friend in Sao Paulo and we're going to go on and do some travelling in South America. Yes, it was the right thing to do, I've absolutely no regrets, bit like closing down a factory but we're there now.'

The outdoor shop was almost empty and an assistant smiled in recognition as he came in.

'Finally,' he grinned, 'it's the big trip. I need quite a bit of kit and I wouldn't mind some advice. The guy I used to come in with, he's in America now and I'm meeting him in Brazil, he'll only have summer gear, we need some warm stuff for the mountains so I'll be buying two of some things.'

'Well you're about the same size so that should be easy, let's start with the base layers.'

'He's a bit of a wimp when to comes to cold and rain so I want to kit him out so he doesn't complain too much. He'll make a fuss about how much it all cost but I'm sure he won't have much more than T shirts and shorts in his pack.' She was smiling so encouragingly words tumbled out. 'When we used to go cycling he'd turn up in a hoodie and no gloves then it'd start raining so I always set out with extra gear to lend him and he'd say he didn't need it and then he'd start shivering and end up wearing all of it. He never seemed to learn and I suppose he did it on purpose to be honest. He likes clothes though, fashion clothes, he's always buying something new but nothing practical though, in fact it's hard to imagine him slumming but he's been living out of a rucksack for months.' Stupid, stupid, it made him sound like a child.

'All this gear is designed to dry off quickly, there's no longer any need to be cold and miserable.'

'I'm sure he'll have changed.'

'When did you last see him?'

'Ages, four months, I'm really looking forward to the trip; we've sort of been planning it for, well as long as I've known him. And I need something warm and lightweight to wear on top, he will probably too, something we could wear, you know, in town as well.'

She walked over to a stand and held up a jacket, 'these are just in, they're breathable, warm, compressible, forward set shoulder seams for when you're wearing a pack, yes they're expensive but it's all you'll need. They come in dark grey, taupe and navy, which colour d'you think your boyfriend would like?'

Boyfriend? He managed an impassive expression, she was taking a risk, he was only buying clothes for a travel companion, maybe he was fussing too much but the recognition was faintly thrilling. He tried a jacket on, had he ever bought clothes for Clare? Nope, he wouldn't have dared. The jacket wasn't bulky, a little bit fitted, Mark would like it, the dark grey one for him and he would take the navy, he'd have to lie a bit how much they cost, he could pretend they were in the sale. Then two long sleeved merino base layers and two pairs of walking socks and clever things for covering necks against sunburn that converted into hats or face masks against wind and blowing sand, sunglasses with retainer straps, a solar charger, tablets for purifying water, powerful sunscreen, lip balm, insect repellent and a first aid kit. 'Call in when you get back,' she said, 'tell me how you found the gear.'

'And you?' He asked, 'planning any travel?'

'Well, you know us Aussies, long haul gypsies. I'm off home for Christmas but I'll be back, one day I'll make up my mind, where I want to be, meanwhile I just kit out lucky guys like you.'

The move into a chain free terrace behind the station went without a hitch and he left without unpacking a teaspoon. Belize did its best to distract him but the timing was all wrong. He threw himself unenthusiastically into the excursions and diving and sat in a cocktail stupor all evening. His anxiety about the next month increased to paranoia as the emails from Mark failed to appear. With still no message from Mark, Belize City to Sao Paulo with a change at Dulles was an expensive and lengthy trial. In his anxiety his self image collapsed, the single, free spirited, rucksack bearing young man that left Heathrow arrived in Sao Paulo with the spring erased from his step. That evening, holed up in his hotel he finally received an email from Mark with the address of a downtown youth hostel.

Sao Paulo, eighteen million people in the metropolitan area, the second largest metropolis in the world, eight million cars, a humid sub tropical climate. At home he could put his hand on the stats straight away; birth rate, infant mortality, GNP, migration into the city, literacy levels, life expectancy and knock up a decent essay on the city's role as financial powerhouse of South America with plenty of global comparisons and contrasts. More fun stats were that the weather could be quite poor, it had the highest helicopter use in world to avoid kidnappings, appalling traffic and the largest Japanese's population outside Japan. But they spoke a language he couldn't even say yes or no in and nervous of the city's reputation he felt intimidated

The following morning he arrived at the hostel to discover Mark had already stayed two nights but had checked out the previous day. David anxiously checked his email on the terminal in the hostel reception and returned to the reception desk, 'there's no message from him, it must have been a last minute decision, he would definitely have left a message for me.' The receptionist who had checked Mark out appeared and confirmed he'd wanted a private room but they were all full and he hadn't left a message.

Of course they wanted a room to themselves but where was the message to say where he had gone? David persisted, could she remember a note, had she possibly forgotten? No, there was no note, he'd paid and left, there was no mention of anyone meeting him, but she remembered he had said he was unwell. She had given him a map of local hotels she said and handed David a copy. A crowd of backpackers trooped in and he automatically searched for his face among them. Something had gone wrong, he checked his mobile and email again then asked for a taxi with an English speaking driver. Even this was fraught, so few spoke English it took half an hour before one pulled up outside, driven by a man with an expression suggesting he wasn't in the mood for anything complicated. His face remained blank as David tried to explain he wanted to check every hotel within a couple of kilometres but he was unwilling to be separated from his vehicle to get some translation help from reception. Confidence drained, the traffic roared, the language intimidated, the city frightened him but as he stepped back from the taxi to let him drive away the driver leaned over and opened the passenger door. 'I take you.'

Holding up the map he attempted to give directions but with a few swift lurches they were outside a small hotel. Inside the receptionist shook her head at the photo on

David's mobile and this continued for the next half hour, crawling through the city's permanent rush hour, it would have been quicker to walk but to his shame he didn't dare. Eventually they drew up. 'This man very poor?'

'Well yes, he's a student.'

He let a dramatic minute pass, as though drawing upon a deep well of local knowledge and setting off with another lurch they shot back past the hostel and round the corner. 'Very cheap,' he waved his hand at a brightly painted building with a sprinkling of plastic chairs outside occupied by customers who were definitely not tourists. It was some sort of B and B or guest house but there were no signs in English and it wasn't on the map from the hostel. As David sat uncertainly in the taxi the driver came to life, leaving his precious car he greeted the assembled with hearty handshakes and guffaws of laughter. After a few minutes of jollity that left David frantic with frustration he returned, 'this man, he here, very sick.'

David and the driver followed the owner through the door into a dingy room full of empty, tightly packed tables and chairs. They weaved their way through to the back of the building and up a flight of narrow stairs to a dark landing of closed doors. Without knocking he opened one and indicated for David to go in.

His eyes slowly focused in the gloom; there was a bed against the far wall and a wardrobe in the corner and on the bed was a body. In two strides he was beside him, leaning over his face, yet not his face. A tan was to be expected but he was grey under week old stubble and his eyes looked like they'd aged twenty years.

'Hey!' He took his shoulders, expecting his eyes to fly open and his mouth to break into that grin that he wanted back in his life. 'Mark,' he shook him gently, then roughly, *'Mark!'* and turned in panicky disbelief to the driver, 'I think he's unconscious.'

An uncoordinated scramble between the three men took place. David attempted to scoop Mark up by looping his limp arms over his shoulders, pulling him into a sitting position and wrapping his arms around his waist while the other two went for his legs so he hung suspended between the three of them, going nowhere.

'*I'll* carry him.' He'd thrown him over his shoulder in play but he'd been cooperative then and balanced his weight correctly, now taking all his weight in a fireman's lift David wobbled and held the door frame to balance himself before taking the narrow stairs one at a time, his knees trembling with the weight and with fright at what he had discovered. The bitter smell of stale sweat and urine told some sort of story about the last few days.

'Hospital, *hospital*,' he barked as they emerged outside into the sun. They laid him on the back seat and even in the confusion David remembered that people needed paying. He handed the driver his wallet, indicating the hovering guest house owner who handed him a bottle of water through the window. In the car he held him upright, trying to pour water down his throat and succeeding mainly in drenching them both.

Standing on the other side of the blue plastic curtain that had been shot smartly round he felt queasy from the drive in which the driver had given his best demonstration of off road rally driving with a heavy reliance on the horn. He couldn't complain, they were at a state of the art hospital (one of eighteen in the city he recalled from his guidebook) in less than five minutes. The driver was still beside him, again David remembered payment and fumbling in his jacket for his wallet realised the driver still had it. He handed it back, 'my name is Juan,' he said, 'I stay.'

David sank into a nearby chair and watched the movement and listened to the talk behind the curtained bed. As the minutes passed his head cleared and a detached coolness replaced the panic. This was his punishment, to be there at his end and to wonder for the rest of his life; what if he had arrived sooner, what if they had never arranged to meet, what if Mark had stayed with Jason who would have looked after him and got him medical attention sooner.

During the taxi ride he had bargained frantically, now, as the minutes ticked by he closed his eyes and surrendered. *OK, have him. Go on, take him why don't you? Don't leave me with anything, it's only what I deserve and at least I'm here; at least I can say he wasn't alone.* He imagined the activity behind the curtain would suddenly stop and someone would emerge with the news, in Portuguese of course, but regret would sound the same in any language. The repatriation of the body would be his responsibility; he would do whatever was necessary including travelling home with it, the British Embassy would tell him what to do. He would finally come face to face with Mrs Derby.

The curtain swished aside, to reveal a young woman in a white coat. 'He's very dehydrated, his blood pressure is very low, we are giving him liquids and antibiotics, he'll be OK,' she said with an American accent. 'How has he got into this situation?' David lept to his feet, oh god she thinks it's my fault; she thinks I didn't notice he was ill or I didn't care.

'I've only just found him, I had no idea,' he flustered.

Shaking with relief he made arrangements for Mark to have a private room and sat with him until he was asked to leave for the night, watching his chest rise and fall with every breath. His hair was so different, long and curling round his neck, David leaned over and moved a stray strand off his face. He noticed a necklace of small seeds they had taken off him on the bedside table and then the thin white tan line it had left on his neck. He felt sickenly happy and relieved, finally here they were together again but with an unexpected respite before the explanations and pleas for forgiveness and grovelling that he had spent the past month rehearsing. Here in this quiet room they would have time to get used to each other again before they set off. Sitting with his forearms on the bed as Mark slept on, David considered how to portray the preceding nightmarish months; Mark would definitely want to know what had happened. The truth was out of the question, as it always had been. Protecting him, as he saw it, from the reality of a man preparing to marry in a very expensive and public manner had become second nature over the past year and now it had all turned very nasty the same applied. Everything must be perfect, they must start afresh and there was certainly no need to tell it all. Of course, he would say Clare had been terribly upset but she was relieved that the tensions between them were now all over and she could move on. Mark stirred a little but remained sedated and David took his limp hand. 'Hey,' he said softly, 'everything's going to be OK.' He'd read how patients were talked out of vegetative states with stories from their past, or was that one of Clare's TV hospital dramas?

'Remember when we cycled over to Lower Gidding that really hot day and that barking couple in the pub. We thought they lay in wait to trap innocent travellers so they could entice them back to see their vintage sweet wrappers collection and you made up some mad excuse about having to get home to bottle feed the kittens and they were full of sympathy and we cycled home like loonies, giggling. And we Googled them and discovered they were bloody famous and people travelled far and wide to see their collection.' A ridiculous and happy day. He looked at the shape his body made under the sheet, the bumps of his knees and feet yet the sight of him so close had no erotic effect, it made him feel decent and then it turned to anxiety that his feelings had changed.

The next morning, delivered by the same driver because at least the man knew which of the eighteen hospitals Mark was in, he peeped in through the corridor window, he was awake. With a deep breath he went in and sank quickly and nervously into the chair beside the bed, resting his arms on the sheet.

'Hi.'
'Hi.'
'How you feeling?'
'OK.'

'How long have you been ill?'

'Weeks,' he stared ahead. 'I don't know if it was food poisoning or a virus, I was sick, I had diarrhoea, I was constantly tired and feverish. I'd start to feel OK and then feel crap again. I wasn't drinking enough the doctor said; my kidneys could have packed up. Sorry about the hostel, I couldn't stand it, seven others in the dorm, I just needed to be quiet and sleep.'

'If you'd stayed there you would have got medical help sooner, why on earth didn't you tell them where you were going, so I could have found you?'

'Someone in the hostel overheard I wanted a private room, they said there was a cheap place round the corner, I could hardly walk and anyway I almost forgot you were coming I felt so ill.'

'It's so wonderful to see you, so bloody wonderful,' he couldn't stop smiling.

'Yeah.'

'And your results, they were fantastic, god I was so happy, so fucking happy. I knew totally that you could do it. How did you hear, did you phone school?'

'I rang Ralph.'

David stretched out his fingers to touch his hand but stopped and curled them back into his palm. He had to explain, Mark deserved an explanation, he needed to see that now was different, he'd got rid of every obstacle.

'Your letter, I almost wore it. I've got it here, in my pocket, it's kept me going, it's got a bit grubby, you'll have to write another it's getting so worn out. I remember teasing you about writing letters, yeah I know, I didn't reply but I wanted to wait until I had got everything *clear* in my head, I didn't want there to be any more misunderstandings, I wanted to be completely *free*.' There was no reaction. 'It must all seem such a long time ago now,' he added lamely, 'all the things you've done, and people you've met. Abi has been great, a bit *off* to start with, but I charmed her, well you know about my charm don't you? Anyway with or without her

217

we'd have got here one way or another eh?'

'I dunno.'

'James has been a brick. I thought at first I'd pissed him off so much he'd keep out of my way but he came round in the end, he's acted the voice of sanity in the storm, or rather hurricane. You can't imagine how shite it's been, don't want to tell you too much but I don't recommend it, not with four weeks to go.'

'Your choice.'

'I didn't *choose*, it was always you, I just didn't *manage* it all very well.' He finally took his hand and laced their fingers but Mark's hand didn't co-operate and he let it go and laid his hand alongside his instead.

'I'll look for a decent hotel tomorrow, out of the city, somewhere you can recover properly, somewhere with a pool.'

'That's not necessary, I think you're being a bit heavy, I'm not ill, I just needed re hydrating, that's all. There are people coming in here with serious gunshot wounds all the time, I saw a sheet pulled over someone's face, I feel a fraud.'

'Mark, you were in a very bad way when we found you, I don't want to upset you or anything but you could easily have....'

'I wasn't fucking dying! It was a stomach bug that's all, all the tourists get it, you get it and you get over it.'

'Mark? His mouth was dry with the shock and he reached for the water glass. 'Mark. I've resigned from my teaching post at school, I'm single, we can travel together, like we planned until you start at Manchester, wherever you want to go.'

He stood up and tentatively leaned towards him. It had been four months; of course it would take time to adjust to being together again, and it had been him after all that had dealt the final blow. But it wasn't a good look, hovering uncertainly over him with nurses around, and he sank back into the chair. Who was he now in this boy's eyes anyway?

'You've come to take photos for your text book.'

'That's not *why* I've come, I've come to be with *you*, I've thought of nothing else, *nothing*, since we ended.'

'Did she find out, did she dump you?'

'No, I ended it, I couldn't carry on, all I ever needed was some time.'

Mark turned his head to face the opposite wall, 'things have changed for me, things haven't worked out like I hoped.'

'What things?' He knew; but tell me he begged silently, tell me all the same, you'd tell me all your marks, even the poor ones and when you cried when you twisted your ankle and about the guy in the coffee shop who winked at you. Why did you keep something so important a secret?

'Private stuff.'

'Mark, now we can be together properly and do all the things we used to talk about. I know you must feel lousy now but you'll feel differently in a few days time when you're better and while you're recovering we can plan where we want to go, I've brought a few guide books, there are some places I really want to see but it's up to you, we can go wherever you want.'

'I didn't *want* you to give it all up for me, it was your decision. I know this isn't what you expected but as I said, I wasn't really sure but over the last week things have really changed, I want to be on my own and do things my own way.'

The strap slowly constricting his breathing tightened another notch. 'You shouldn't *be* on your own in this state, you *need* me, when you get out of this place you'll feel different.' Oh god I'm begging, like he begged me. Let him have his moment of triumph, give him a few days, he'll come round.

'I'm not the Mark from school anymore. I'm meeting some friends from the camp next week and travelling on with them.'

'But we arranged to travel together, the two of us.'

'Sorry, I've kinda changed my mind, stuff happens.

Anyway it was you that always said I'd feel differently once I'd left school, that's what you told me at the beginning and that's what you told me when you dumped me and that's exactly what's happened.'

David pushed his chair back sharply and stood up, shoving his hands into his jeans pockets. 'You're ill, you *need* me.'

'I don't *need* you.'

All the times he'd clung to him, his mouth open and teeth gently gnawing his shoulder, letting himself be gently rocked, how he loved to be held and comforted, any excuse; a cold, a hangover, a late bus, a crappy day, unselfconscious and greedy for every morsel that David allowed him. Seconds passed, David fixed his eyes on the floor, let him kick at the traces a bit, there was no rush.

'I'm tired.'

'I'll come back later.'

'No need, I'm on the mend.'

He slipped his hand into his pocket and felt the car key, he'd put it on a neck strap so he could loop it round the boy's neck and the prospect of his delighted smile had helped him bear the long tedious flights. The car, he had intended to say, it's waiting for you, taxed and insured and serviced and the glove compartment catch has been mended. Grasping the key he pleaded with himself not to attempt some pitiful presentation. Get out, get out.

'I'll sort out the bill.'

'Don't, I have insurance.'

'They'll want it up front, claim when you get back, I'll keep the receipts for you. Here's some cash, pay me back if you want but I don't want you to.'

'I don't want it. I don't want your money.'

It represented a fraction of what he had already spent on flights but he felt no temptation to take it back. He stuffed the notes into the pockets of the jacket he had bought him and lay it alongside him. There was no response, Mark's eyes were latched onto something on the far wall.

Returning to the hotel he lay motionless for hours in the curtained gloom of his room waiting to time his call to James's morning alarm.

'He doesn't want to know,' and all the assumptions about the trip that poured out made him sound deluded and inexperienced, like the end of a two week holiday romance.

'He's only done *exactly* what you told him he'd do.'

'I didn't *mean* it, I didn't bloody *mean* it! I said it so it wouldn't happen, that's what you do isn't it, say it so it doesn't fucking happen!'

'Come home you daft bastard, no point in prolonging the agony.'

As David re positioned his head around the bed the next morning trying to find a place that slowed the throbbing he found his letter lying where the letter's recipient should have been and held it until he could focus.

'Why don't we just try it for a week, let's meet up with your friends, if they don't mind, it will ease us back into being together. Where had you planned to go? I thought we could go to the Iguazu Falls and then head to Buenos Aries, then over to Mendoza, Salar de Vyuni and on to La Paz and Lake Titicaca. If we head for Banos, we can see Volcan Tungurahua which is still active after the 1999 eruption and still spewing out gas and steam, there could be another eruption any time, it would be fantastic to see an active volcano. I've bought everything we might need for trekking in the Andes, I know how you like to be warm and dry, those clothes I left on your bed are the ones we were looking at in town.' Further down there were a few unintelligible words and a scrawled signature.

Two wine bottles, one empty and one almost empty stood in a dried puddle of wine on the bedside table. He lay staring at the light fitting in the ceiling, there hadn't been the slightest sign of uncertainly or hesitation, the bloke had barely been able to bring himself to look at him, or disguise his irritation. He honestly hadn't expected passion, not after all this time and a dose of the local lurgi on top but there had been undisguised distaste. David's stomach curled with embarrassment, his hangover drained him of every optimistic thought. He was a naïve schoolteacher who'd not had the maturity to deal with a confident schoolboy and had thrown away his future because he couldn't resist a bit of flattery. He threw himself out of bed and shredded the letter furiously into the bin, flakes of paper missed and floated across the room.

The hangover pinned him to his bed. He lay facing his denial that he was hanging around waiting for a change of mind or the stomach cramping ignominy of trailing him down to Rio, waiting for him to fall out with his friends. Corny, humiliating and desperate, it pretty much summed up the past year.

The hotel had a roof terrace and eventually he took the lift up to find a breeze. Looking out over the city he calculated how soon he could be back in his little house sitting amongst the packing cases. A waiter lingered to practice his English and the effort to smile and be friendly broke the deadlock. He was in Brazil and he'd never been to the country or even the continent before, how he would despise himself later for flying in, holing up nervously in an international hotel chain and flying out. He phoned the airline and booked a flight which gave him four more days in the city.

So, things hadn't worked out like Mark had hoped. The web addresses on the post its in the Lonely Planet guide and the Head's complacent revelations had made everything clear weeks ago. It hurt that Mark had kept it a secret from him but now it was all over and England and his previous life seemed less real than this vast city. A touch of belligerence drove David's next decision.

It was a matter of pride that no local transport systems had ever got the better of him but today's challenge would be quite enough. He called Juan to pick him up, the guy seemed decent enough, if grouchy and his English was sufficient for basic directions. After the drama of the previous day David sensed a little bonding between them as they crawled through the traffic the following morning. His English had improved quite remarkably overnight, 'many peoples travelling four hours a day to working,' he told him, shaking his head, 'very bad air,' and he gave a rasping cough to demonstrate which sounded completely fake. Sitting comfortably in his air conditioned taxi David wondered at the state Mark must have been in travelling to the same destination on public transport he assumed, unwell and undoubtedly deeply anxious. Not prying was something he took pride in yet here he was intruding on an intensely private matter that was now even less his business than it had been the day before. A glass or two of beer might make it seem like a good idea. After an hour Juan announced they were close and leaving Juan to his paper and probably a sleep David got out of the car and set off on foot and following the hotel receptionist's instructions found the café in an adjoining street and settled himself with a drink. Positioned facing the door he read the day old English newspaper he had bought, holding it low so he could easily see everyone as they came in.

There was no mistaking him, an Anglo Saxon amongst the Latins, the familiar narrow face and eyes were instantly recognisable. He watched him make straight for a table in the corner, probably the one he took every day and examined with interest his lean frame, slight stoop and heavily lined face. He waited until the man had ordered his meal and to his relief saw that he clearly intended to lunch alone, with a local newspaper. His mouth went dry, it was now or never and folding his paper he took a deep breath, pushed back his chair and tried to make his walk look confident. It was important that his nerves didn't show and his prepared story was partly true, it could even be entirely true. Excusing his intrusion he introduced himself as a schoolteacher from the UK taking a rather belated gap year. He had seen the school website, wondered if there were any vacancies and had taken the liberty of asking the receptionist if he might have a word with him over lunch as he was only in the city for another day and understood that he was busy all day. The man reacted with a smile, holding out his hand.

'Of course, yes it's a busy day but I take a Latin lunch and my receptionist knows I'm always on the lookout for native speakers,' and David's anxiety swung from fearing rejection to the prospect of being interviewed for a teaching post he definitely did not want.

He ordered the same meal the man was having; steak, rice, beans and salad, more than he wanted but it looked sociable to order the same he decided. As he ate he listened attentively to the man's advice about working in the city, opportunities for English language teaching, how much he might earn. With interest he watched his mouth move, his hand gestures, how far his hair had receded and the unevenness of his lower teeth. Is this the sort of detail Mark would have picked up? Possibly too unwell to take in much detail, the sort of detail that Abi might want though. The man was clearly more than happy to talk so David gently probed under the guise of someone looking for a new start in life and soon the mystery of Martin Derby was revealed by the man himself.

After leaving the UK twelve years ago he said he lived in Spain for a short while and then met a Brazilian who said his country might suit him, he hadn't formed any ties in Spain so he went. The first few years had been very difficult, not speaking the language, living hand to mouth; he seemed quite prepared to admit the hardships.

'I never intended to stay, I kidded myself I could go home anytime I liked, every year I talked about when I was going back but year after year I never did. At first I never managed to save the air fare then the UK got more distant, more expensive, I think I dreaded it, let's say I wasn't expecting a warm welcome. And once I spoke Portuguese pretty fluently and settled down with a woman and her children, well, it just got more distant. If you want to escape, to get away from something, it's a great place. No, I didn't rob a bank, something far more mundane.'

'Failed to file your tax return?' He said lightly.

'Bankruptcy, marriage failure. There's counselling and advice these days to help you, well there was then too I suppose but I… well I ran. I left a heap of problems behind. At first it was heady and liberating, then I sank back into the depressive state I'd come from but as time passed I became my old self.' He paused, 'I don't want to intrude, but as we're on the subject, are you leaving something behind yourself?'

'*No*, nothing like that!' Yet what was the harm in telling him, everything, he'd never see him again, and if he didn't like what he heard, Juan was only round the corner ready to whisk him away. He concentrated on the steak, cutting it into smaller pieces because it was becoming difficult to swallow, did guilt narrow your throat? Martin continued, keen to show that the streets had contained a little gold. As he became more competent with the language, he explained, he'd moved into IT, then management consultancy and training and more recently had added language teaching. He was setting up franchises and shortly moving to larger offices. He was always on the look out for people he felt he could work with, assuring David he could get someone like him up to speed in the language pretty quickly. He was a persuasive talker and as the third glass of lunchtime beer was working its tricks it was surprisingly tempting, there was simply no reason to return now, not a single reason. But the bakery fiasco loomed suddenly, just *tell* him, Mark had said of Jack, just *tell* him you aren't bloody interested. David politely conveyed his undecidedness about his future to Martin but still kept the door a little open to be agreeable. Tucking Martin's company brochure into his jacket he moved the conversation to his own plan that had taken shape as his plane had swept over the city to land. He wanted to visit a favela the following day and asked Martin's opinion; could someone like himself just walk around? They continued their lunch amicably, then, breaking into David's observations on overstretched sewage systems Martin said 'I had another unexpected English visitor a few days ago.'

David gave a politely curious, 'mmmm?'

'Yes, it was a bit of a shock, but not totally unexpected. Anyway it put a few ghosts to rest for both of us. My life is here now, with my family, I have no reason to return to the UK except for a visit and I've lost a lot of contacts. It's a bit late now but deep down I feel very guilty, not that I told him, no, I was possibly a bit offhand but what can you say, after so long? I have to admit though, I've hardly stopped thinking about it since, it's shaken me.'

'Sounds like a difficult situation, did you agree to keep in contact with this person?'

'We exchanged email addresses, it was all very awkward but maybe it's for the best for him, he can move on now, as they say these days.'

'Well, have mine too,' David wrote his email address on a post it note from his diary, he could hardly claim to be job hunting without leaving it. Attentive to the advice about life and travelling in Brazil he continued to watch him curiously, the way he took his lower lip as he thought, was he looking for similarities that weren't there? A few photos would be best, he would show them to Abi when she was old enough to know the truth. The deed was easily done, Martin none the wiser as the waiter lined the two of them up, 'I'm a keen photographer; I like to keep a record of everyone I meet,' said David.

When Martin announced that even the Latin lunch was over the warmth of his handshake left David in a guilty hole. Juan was where he had left him, asleep with his newspaper over his face and after a shot of coffee to get him fully awake for the rigours of the traffic they set off back to the hotel.

'D'you know anyone who lives in a favela? D'you know anyone who can show me round a favela tomorrow?'

In a few days he would have left this city with only the depressing memory of it being the place Mark outgrew him, only something extreme could blot that out and a Brazilian shanty town might do the trick but he needed a guide.

'No! It very dangerous! It not for tourists! It for very poor people!' Juan hit the brake emphatically, pitching David forward.

'Juan,' he said, not expecting him to understand any of what he way saying but wanting to talk, 'I live in a nice city where I can drive with the windows down and I can stop at red lights with the doors unlocked and I can walk around alone at night and nobody bothers me for money but d'you know, I was too frightened to go out when I left. I was frightened in case I met his friends or her friends, or the woman who made the dresses or one of the staff from school. All those people who once liked me, would they cut me and leave me out of all their parties and holidays because they couldn't think what to say. In lessons at school I tell the kids about shanty towns but I've never been inside one and I'm ready for a few uncomfortable situations, so take me to a favela, guaranteed no one will know me and that's my idea of heaven at the moment. And I'll pay you double.'

'You speaking too fast!' Juan drove on for a while, concentrating hard on the road, both hands uncharacteristically on the wheel and David let himself appear distracted by the view from his window. Finally, '*very* bad this, very bad, very dangerous. You say pay double? OK, I know very poor woman, she living in the favela.'

Martin's reaction to his interest in the city's favelas had been polite but dismissive. He said his housekeeper and cook lived in the nearby favela and had stories of the gangs and police raids and fears for their children's future. He heard gunshots regularly and one of his gardeners had been injured during a shooting, he himself wouldn't dream of going into one but he had heard of people being shown round favelas in Rio, it was known as slum tourism wasn't it? Maybe some were safer than others. He jokingly likened it to visiting a run down council estate in the UK, you wouldn't would you? Not unless you were some opposition politician looking for a photo opportunity. OK the sewage system might work but he'd read there were gangs and anti social behaviour and it wasn't safe at night, weren't they in fact just British slums? There was a touch of defensiveness in his voice, David had said nothing, he must have appeared naïve to Martin, like he thought it was a theme park. At the time, wanting to move away from the subject he'd missed the comparison but now it hit home; didn't he know *anything* about them? Hey, your two kids live on a crappy council estate, they've lived there ever since you buggered off, I've seen the photos of the nice house you used to live in and Mark in his toy car in the front drive.

He ran through everything he had seen and heard that afternoon with Mark's eyes. Surely Martin would have played down his success but Mark would have seen the reception with the staff photos on the wall and brochures and fresh flowers and comfy chairs to wait in and he must have mentioned his new family, even the website would have given plenty of clues. But if it was delight and remorse Mark had come all that way for, it looked like he might have been disappointed. And then a nasty little stab of possibility; was *he* the intended go between? Is that what Mark had meant in his letter; facilitating the reunion and bringing his Dad back home? Now Mark was living with a wrecked dream and instead of an adventurous father leaving to seek his fortune he'd found a settled businessman more interested in his plans for expanding his business than his son. He thumped himself back into the seat making Juan glance sideways in surprise. As for tomorrow, gunshots, dealers, stench, poverty, bring it on, the retelling would certainly add some colour to his geography lessons. At the hotel, heart thumping, he asked if there were any calls; nothing. He killed the evening in the bar hiding behind his day old newspaper.

Warned that it would take an hour to get to the favela David decided to pass it by telling Juan his story, mainly to get the volume of the radio turned down and to stave off the misery that was coming in increasingly painful waves. He took it slowly and with disbelieving shakes of the head Juan enquired at every point the exact worth of the deal he had walked out on. The girlfriend; 'blonde hair, from a bottle,' the Hampshire house; 'about three million US dollars, it needs a new roof,' the family business; 'not a successful business,' his job; 'about fifty thousand US a year, enough to live on,' the wedding; 'about seventy thousand US,' the wedding gift; 'a couple of million US.' All given up for that *very thin boy* as Juan described him with some relish.

'He no like you now! I no understand, it mad, for that boy! I show you some very, *very* nice boys.'

Since there was very little point in trying to make him understand, a man with three children, holding down two jobs, living in no more than a tower block shanty town himself, David accepted his incredulity. Talking about it made him feel better, even positive and for a fleeting moment he imagined cancelling his flight, renting out his house, exploring the country, writing articles for the Sundays and academic journals. Juan's earlier dourness towards his puzzling fare had disappeared; he laughed and smacked his palm on the steering wheel, repeating almost gleefully the sums of money that David had willingly given up. This strange man who gave him a good tip every day and sat beside him as they drove was intriguing him.

Juan's poor woman, he guessed a second cousin, placed the DVD player he'd bought her on the pink plastic table next to the bed in her single room dwelling which barely had space for the three of them to stand. As she and Juan talked David examined the room, she was clearly someone with a sense of fashion and close inspection of her walls revealed collages of clothes and accessories, painstakingly cut out from magazines and glued into collections by colour and mood. It reminded him instantly of Sarah's office walls covered in pictures and objects she found inspiring from every conceivable source. She showed him her scrapbooks and drawings and Juan said 'she want being fashion lady,' and David said 'yes, fashion designer.' Two lean feline rat catchers slept on a narrow ladder at the end of the bed leading, he could just see, to a low ceiling mezzanine for the children's beds and starting with them he took some photos as they blinked sleepily. He expressed interest in her montages and asked to photograph them, subtly taking in the plastic and china statues of the Virgin Mary tucked into corners, cheap jewellery hanging on hooks, family photos and neat piles of magazines. Finally, after much giggling and with some persuasion from Juan she piled her hair up, found her fluffy mule slippers, applied some eye makeup, hooked some big loopy earrings through her ears and posed in a plastic chair in the doorway. Juan said something to make her laugh, the sun caught her earrings and the interior of her shack behind her looked cool and homely.

It took a lot of persuading by Juan that school children in the UK really did have to know about how shanty towns worked for her to agree to him photographing the cheap plastic hose with a shower head over a bucket, the two cooking rings connected to a gas bottle on a rickety table, and the plastic toilet, sitting in the corner, unconnected to any sewage system. It was always the ablutions that fascinated children, or anyone really, the communal toilets in medieval monasteries, the terrifying drops from cantilevered holes to the moat from Welsh castles, luxury portaloos hired for outdoor events. He heard himself explaining to a class that she simply emptied the plastic toilet into the open sewer, yes, just like in medieval times, yes, it stank and hearing their howls of disgust. When it rained, she said, they put basins under the drips and the narrow street outside turned into a filthy river. But she had a TV connected to one of the two sockets dangling from the ceiling, the other fitted with a bare light bulb and the cuts in the 'borrowed' electricity supply didn't happen *every* day. She was proud of the one inside tap but when that didn't work they used the standpipe in the street and when that didn't work either they carried water bought from the tanker parked in the nearest road up the steep rutted streets. She worked as a cleaner in a block of flats close to the favela during the day and in the tiny café opposite in the evening.

Even in the marking pile Mark's urban metropolis assignment last summer had stood out, nice cover and thicker than the rest and he could see it was a tour de force. Extensively researched and full of photos he'd learnt a lot himself, if only that it couldn't possibly have been a joke, this was surely some sort of courtship. But, as he sat, a cold coke by his side, looking out into the filthy, dusty street he saw what Mark had missed out and what he missed out in his teaching. Inside the tiny shambolic plastic, cardboard, corrugated iron and rough brickwork construction, aside from the fact they had no title deeds or any ownership rights, it was a real home to six people; cooking, sleeping, chatting, watching TV and keeping pets like anyone else.

Neighbours approached to be introduced, shaking his hand vigorously and practicing their few words of English. He learnt that the authorities were gradually concreting over open sewers and connections to the electricity and water supply were slowly happening, evidence that favelas were having to be accepted as mainstream housing for working people and here to stay. He had read about the gangs and factions and drug dealers and police raids but that wasn't what his visit was about and it seemed inappropriate to bring it up amongst all this friendliness and hospitality. He played the geeky urban geographer, on all fours to view the sluggish sewage channels and marvelled at the range of building material. 'I want to see how the favela has grown,' he told Juan, 'I want to see how it's changing, I want to see how people adapt to living in a way we would think impossible.' He had his smallest camera with him and took discreet shots, switching to video as often as he could. The little party wandered around the narrow dusty streets, up and down tight curving staircases and squeezed between buildings, stopping to shake hands with friends and acquaintances. Juan's cousin appeared to know everyone, this small section of the vast favela was her village. Aside from brightly coloured shorts, t shirts, flip flops and baking heat he tried to imagine he was in a real medieval city, not the sterilized modern version. The street used for waste disposal where semi feral cats and dogs rummaged for a meal and slept in corners, the pungent air and tiny shops set up inside doorways. Juan tapped David's arm and silently pointed out a pockmarked breezeblock wall used for target practice and he noticed alongside it a brave attempt at a garden in pots in a doorway. Further on he saw three small faces peering wide eyed though barred windows, tiny children locked in for the day while their mothers were at work, probably looking after other people's children.

Superficially everything looked fairly solid but walking further up the hill away from the more established lower sections they showed him a small localised landslide. Known as a slump, he could just see the scarp or cut at the top where the ground had broken away caused by heavy rain lubricating the ground and taking everything with it. Someone was retrieving wood and breeze blocks from the mud and debris, desperate or optimistic enough to have another go at claiming, what appeared to have been a rubbish dump, as real estate. Proximity to this localised catastrophe made him feel queasy, the ground giving way suddenly and running down the hillside like oil, out of control with you and your family and possessions inside, he hoped they'd got out in time. Maybe they'd been attempting to add another storey to the house. He scribbled a few notes, 'the ground sighed with relief as it gave up the Herculean task of holding up yet another hundred breeze blocks on flimsy stilts,' not his usual style but it matched his mood.

Apart from the chance to mention the English football league no one had taken much notice of him. A cool breeze blew, what would it be like as darkness closed in, he glanced at Juan who, despite the double time, was looking like it was time to leave.

The day had surprised him, moved him, life appeared

more positive. He remembered Juan's opinion of Mark, '*Very thin*!' he mimicked and threw back his head and laughed.

'Yes?'

'That boy. And broke, spent all his garden centre wages on clothes. And demanding. Endless bloody texts and would I stay a bit longer and could I come a bit earlier, I never had a moment to myself. And time wasting on a continental scale. I've come all this way and I'm supposed to understand, you know, not in a phone call before I buy my ticket, no, I've come five thousand fucking miles and he tells me what he could have told me a few months ago. Hey, he's grown up, and surprise surprise his old schoolteacher is a bit, well *embarrassing* now, I mean following him all the way to South America. Cree-pee.'

Juan, understanding little except the scorn in David's voice got the idea and warmed to the theme. His passenger, a day in the favela and he'd come to his senses, 'and no big house and no money, this is *very* bad mistake, I think you go back to this woman. Take present; say you are very very sad. Is she good cooking? My wife is very good cooking,' and he patted the stomach straining the buttons on his shirt.

'Not particularly.' Unless pasta with ready made sauces and bought quiches and broccoli and, well, bought most things and broccoli was good cooking, not that he ever complained, he couldn't do any better. 'Now the *very thin boy*,' he grinned at Juan, 'now *he* can cook.' Mrs Derby was clearly a stranger to the ready meals aisles, Mark only ever had raw ingredients to work with. David smiled to himself at Juan's continuing disbelief at such a terrible decision.

David wound the window down and let the early evening air battle with the air con. He began to enjoy the drive back to his hotel, the traffic had sped up a bit, he could have been in any world city, it was clean and the Paulinistas were hurrying home from work looking well dressed and prosperous. He attempted in simple English to explain how the favela and the modern city co-existed, needing one another to survive and then Juan tempered it with his personal viewpoint of living at such close quarters to the drug dealers and guns and how he told his children how lucky they were to live where they did and not in the favela.

He had three more days in the city and he poured over a map with Juan before he left him at his hotel. That evening he forced himself out into the evening crowd to eat in a busy restaurant where the people watching was too good to waste by hiding behind his paper. His fellow diners would be surprised to know where he had spent his day. Would Juan's cousin's cousin be cooking a meal beside the makeshift shower for her family before she settled down with her two cats to watch a pirate DVD on her new player he wondered? No, she had probably already sold it, or the electricity had gone off.

'Cool jacket.'

'Someone's cast off.'

'So what did you do in Sao Paulo then, just meet up with this guy who lives there?'

'Yeah, more or less.'

'I thought you had something special to do there, man?'

'Just meeting this guy.'

Would you mind waiting in the corridor, call me when you arrive and I'll come out, he'd said on the phone. Peering into the smart reception, shaking with nerves, so bloody tired, the slow creeping dread that this man, his Dad, was only being polite and wanted him kept out of way of his staff. Mark had worked his way through the whole range of emotional reactions he might expect from the man from rage to abject apology yet the reality had been a bland mix of politeness and formality as if he was being interviewed for a job he wasn't going to get. Returning from the reunion the stress and dehydration had brought on a vicious headache and he had become disorientated on the subway, taking the wrong line. Eventually finding his way back to the hostel he vomited and lying on his narrow bunk trying to ignore six noisy room mates an irrational and raging loathing of David grew by the minute.

'This guy, from school, was he like, keen on you?'

'Yeah, but I'm not interested, he can go hang.' He threw back the rest of his large glass of blood red wine which was mixing entertainingly with the meds they'd given him when he left the hospital and refilled all three. One of the boys raised his full glass, 'to Bolivia!'

'And Chile!' said the other.

'Wherever the fuck they are!' Mark laughed and laughed and thought himself remarkably witty.

It was eleven, the party city was only just waking up and they were hungry and drunk. The steaks arrived, hanging over the edges of the plates, food he could barely have looked at a few weeks ago he now attacked eagerly. All three were silent for a while as they ate, watching the steady stream of people strolling past their table. God he felt better, his view of South America was changing minute by minute, it was now exciting and fun with endless possibilities. He grinned at his two cute Canadian companions, getting cuter with each glass, thankfully they had decided to stay longer in the city or he would have been stuck. And thank god for the cash, his fingers involuntarily sought his money pouch hanging round his neck and he squeezed the thick wad. Without it he couldn't have gone much further, certainly not to Bolivia with these two guys, he hadn't factored in the Sao Paulo diversion generously enough. He'd pay it back one day of course, in fact as soon as he returned, write him a thank you note, or something.

Chapter Eighteen

For his whole life to date the month of September signalled a start; school, university and then school again and always fully into the swing of it by October. But here he was in October, 8.00 in the morning, jet lag an excuse he couldn't hang onto any longer and a completely empty day ahead and he set off on a brisk bike ride to block out the rising panic. As he pumped the pedals he talked himself in and out of a new teaching job; he could manage without the money for a while and hadn't he promised himself a sabbatical for years? Now was his chance to get to grips with drafting the text book that had been put on hold during the past year, to prepare himself for the MSc and even start considering a PhD. The future was exciting, finally he was completely free, this could be the break he was really looking for, didn't everything have purpose? Didn't everything turn out so for a reason? And now there was absolutely no one to make any demands on his time.

As he pushed his bike through the front door on his return a short elderly man greeted him cheerily from next door. He welcomed him to the street and told him about the previous owners of his house and how sad he was they'd left. David listened politely, it was at these moments Clare was at her best, she'd have said all the things the fellow wanted to hear and made him feel better about a new neighbour while he would have busied himself bringing in the shopping and locking up the car. He listened to complaints about noise after closing time, loud music from open windows at number 14 in the summer and dog mess. He inched his bike slowly through the door as the man continued to talk, the house might as well have been in the middle of a field for all he cared about neighbours.

He was missing washing up sponges, energy efficient light bulbs and the external hard drive to finally back up all his photos and work but he was reluctant to disturb the neatly taped packing boxes. They could stay as they were for a while, he'd try living in a more modest way, surely you didn't need much more than a pan and a knife and a plate. In the fraught final hours of their life together, speaking with icy civility they had divided the contents of the house and she had carefully listed the contents of his boxes down the sides as if she bloody cared about whether he had a garlic press or a juicer. She didn't need any of it, her own flat was equipped for a TV chef, and why on earth had they bought all this stuff with their endless pasta dinners? The boxes contained a previous life; he imagined peeling back the tape and the air from their last miserable hours being released into the house. Making a half hearted start on the boxes he found one of her embroidered cushions that he had disliked so much and wondered whether there were any of her clothes and shoes nestled amongst his and what he would do with them.

They'd had a complex recycling arrangement with four different coloured bins which he appeared to have inherited, he assumed, deliberately. He heard her call; 'You've put the plastic fruit container in the *tins* bin,' and his retort, 'why bother to recycle if you only get 23 miles per gallon out of your car?' 'It's not the *same*,' she'd call back and they'd bicker amicably on. In a couple of moves the four coloured bins were tied up inside bin liners and in the street. Climate change, who cared, he'd just cost the planet nearly 2000 tonnes of CO_2 in his transatlantic flights. In tender moments, curled up on Mark's bed, they'd planned their fantasy world tour, carefully off-setting the environmental costs with tree planting but now saving the planet seemed utterly pointless; the human race could hurry up and bloody die out.

At a pinch he could probably get the basics he needed in the corner shop but the town was close enough to walk, one of the reasons he'd chosen it. Between ten and twelve would be the best time he reckoned, everyone would be safely tucked behind their desks, the chance of bumping into kids and staff and parents and friends would be minimal. He set off with a notebook intending to sit in a café and sketch out a few ideas for his text book, something he'd never settled down to do in his cramped school office, burdened with paperwork. He felt cheerful; the South America fiasco had achieved a brutal but final rupture with the past and was going to kick start him into a new and productive future. The pleasant walk into town through the park and back streets once again confirmed he'd made the right choice of location.

Getting most of what he needed from a couple of shops he headed along the high street and stopped automatically at the outdoor shop, they'd never passed without calling in. She'd probability be there and recognise him and want to know all about their trip and if they'd liked the gear except he'd told her they wouldn't be back until January and she might remember and ask why he was home early. He hesitated at the door and a surprisingly sharp chest pain made him turn away and want to get home desperately quickly, the café lunch and writing moment forgotten. Of course, it was going to take time, you didn't get over the sort of upheavals he'd been through in a few days, he'd have to take it more slowly, pace himself; the local shop had everything he needed in the short term and he'd be off travelling again soon anyway.

Yet by three the following day a nervous tension drove him out and he emerged from the corner shop into a gaggle of school children. Year nine he reckoned with a smattering of ten, not his school, his ex school rather, but same familiar white shirts and dark skirts and trousers. To his surprise he felt compelled to exchange a few words with them, casual stuff about their school and staff he might know but he wondered if they would think him weird and notice if he was around the following day and then that would be another part of the day he'd have to avoid going out. It was only how anyone would feel after leaving a job; missing the familiar, everyone would have some twinges of regret, it was only natural.

Nasty hot stabs of memory, temporarily blotted out by exhausting cycle rides, unleashed themselves as he lay in bed waiting for sleep or sat in his chair. He'd wiped out the future he had wanted and a future he could have adapted to with time, how in gods name had it happened? Five in the afternoon was the worst, it arrived like a nail whacked in his heart, no waiting boy with a CD ready to shove into his car's player and stupid jokes, endless questions, cheek and drivel and would he do this and could they do that. In fact nothing really, terrible nothing.

James prepared himself to be upbeat on his first visit to David's terrace. Everyone he knew was upsizing, not downsizing and he guessed David would see through words like 'compact' and 'cosy' and 'perfect for one.' So for once he said nothing and rationalised it must be the ten packing boxes stacked in the living room that made it look so small and politely pushed some to the side so he could get a better look.

'To be honest I thought you might pull out of the sale.'

'It all happened in a rush before I went to Belize and buying this place released nearly £100 thou which lets me pay off a few debts from the cancellation and to study next year, so I decided to go ahead, I didn't want to stay anyway.'

James followed David into the kitchen and looked round with relief, 'very smart, now I see why you bought it, unpack and it'll be great.'

'Of course, after what happened, over there, means I've had to rethink my plans.'

'It was for the best, really, for both of you. Sorry, I know that's not what you want to hear, it must still feel raw.'

'Yeah, a ridiculous waste of time, and money, Belize was great though, really great.'

'Crap about his Dad not being interested.'

'Well he gave me a good kicking to make himself feel better. Anyway, I'm glad that little episode's over.'

'No contact then?'

'Nah. His loss, the little idiot. An interesting entanglement and one I won't be repeating. So much for wanting me to travel the world with him. A hundred places to see before you start going to the shops in your slippers did not include the ward of a Sao Paulo hospital as far as I was concerned. Or even Sao Paulo.'

'Getting over it then?' The man hug he had considered giving if David got shaky was shelved and James felt oddly let down; personally he hadn't moved on from that desperate long distance phone call at 7am nearly two weeks ago. He'd got his bed settee ready and filled the fridge with six packs but the man hadn't appeared back in the UK for a another week and then moved straight in to his new house. Over the years he'd built a small reputation for mopping up misery but in this case it didn't appear to be required and they were straight back to light badinage.

'Yeah, I had an interesting week in Sao Paulo, excellent compensation for being dumped by the twat.'

'I've been dumped too you know, I'm a dumped best man.' He raised an imaginary champagne glass, 'I'd like to say what a wonderful girl you *didn't* marry and how happy I know you will both be *without* each other.'

'Very funny.'

They wandered back into the living room, David slumped into the only empty chair and James put the books filling the other onto the floor. They pulled the tabs on their cans, two packing cases lay between them, one labelled books and the other miscellaneous, James considered offering to unpack at least one, maybe not the books because there weren't any shelves but miscellaneous might be a diversion because he was irritated by David's flippancy and irritated because he was irritated. He gave one of the boxes a hard shove sideways so at least he could see the man. He was sensing revisionism creeping in, 'remember,' he said stubbornly, 'when you said that you had just borrowed him for a while…'

'C'mon, I was *drunk*.'

'That that was all someone ordinary, like you, could expect,' James carried on defiantly, 'and you weren't drunk, actually.' He'd be claiming he'd been drunk for the entire year in a minute. He leaned forward, resting his arms on his knees and stared at the floor, how did you become so wanted by someone or for that matter what was it like to want someone so much, even the suffering involved was *something*. He would not let David dismiss the last year so casually, it belittled him and the burden he'd had to carry with the wedding arrangements and now, as go between. The light was fading, the boxes were casting deep gloomy shadows, it was the sort of moment when you stood up and said it was time to go, but he wasn't ready to go, he could run the affair into the ground too.

'Of course, I realised it was only a *short* term thing, you said yourself often enough that it didn't have a shelf life beyond the end of term…'

'OK, at the time, at the *time*, things were different, I was confused, I was blind to the consequences, I was struggling. I mean he *threw* himself at me, literally, I was stupidly flattered, they say attraction attracts, it's an aphrodisiac, a drug.'

Almost a minute passed, James stared coldly back at David through the gloom.

'They were determined to get something out of me you know, endless glasses of wine and meals I could barely eat, it was a Home Counties Guantanamo Bay, it was like being tortured with frightful decency. Superficially they treated me like a member of the family while steadily humiliating me.

And for what,' and his voice rose to an unfamiliar pitch, 'a bit of *confusion and flattery*?'

'James, I had no idea,' David shot forward in his chair; James without the jokes and the self deprecating manner he was so familiar with unnerved him. 'I'm incredibly sorry you had to put up with that. I shirked my responsibilities; there's been no shortage of shame and guilt I assure you, d'you want to hear it? Would that make you fell better about it?'

'No, I only want to hear it was *worth* my keeping my mouth shut.'

'It was, it was. Sorry, running it down makes it easier to deal with. Once it had begun, and I'm confused about how it began, but from the second it begun, I had no intention of it ever ending, ever. I had every minute of the rest of my life planned with him.'

It was enough, it was all James wanted to hear, if it hadn't been real, of everyone, he would have been the biggest fool. 'You see you're very good at something, I'm not exactly sure what it is or even if it's very useful, I'm certainly no good at whatever it is, I mean look at me, no one's ever sobbed over me.'

'Don't try so hard.'

'That's it, is it?'

'I dunno, I dunno.'

They drank on in silence, they could barely see each other now and James's thoughts drifted to his list, now back to two with another vague possibility which could bring it up to a reassuring three. Was being in love and being loved back a sort of skill and could you learn it or were you born with it? Not trying was the hardest advice to take, he longed for directions and rules. Or to have someone *throw* themselves at him.

'Anyway, he might come round, when he's back in Blighty and he's happy he's inflicted enough punishment on you and he's come to terms with his disappointment.' That's what I'm good at he thought, putting a positive spin on *other* people's lives.

'And the shit's run out of money. You should have seen me in the hospital, I was like David fucking Attenborough creeping towards the gorillas, all whispering and proffered hands and extreme caution; will he, won't he, tear my head off.'

'Hey, imagine if you'd started out and then had this massive row on some deserted crumbling inch wide Inca trail and you'd both tumbled into the impenetrable steaming jungle below. Never to be found.' It kind of summed up his view of the whole South American continent, in fact anywhere outside Europe and he waited for an enthusiastic defence of the place but the beer and darkness had brought David right down.

'I didn't expect it to happen, the whole thing took me completely by surprise, it was a wobble, give me break, everyone has wobbles.'

'You've got to stop hawking that surprised business around; it doesn't wash anymore, well not with me anyway. And people are forgetting, life goes on, crises come, crises go, it's your *next* move people will be watching.'

'People will have to wait a loooong time.'

It was what James wanted to hear, it made his own situation more bearable and now he was ready to go because another can and he'd have to leave his car and call a taxi but there was one small matter though, he couldn't leave without touching on it, his last best man task. How long ago was it that they'd shared a house? Seven years? It had taken James, struggling with his own insecurities a long time to realise one day that David was in trouble and no one was bold enough to suggest turning down invites to the pub and spending long hours in his room was anything other than studious behaviour because he had a reputation for being brusque. It was an episode James had almost forgotten about, and how it had ended. There were times since then too when he seemed to disappear but not so obviously because they weren't living in the same house. A small predisposition to depression someone had once suggested, he'd no more suggest it to David than accuse him of being an alcoholic but some of the signs weren't good.

'Keep busy eh? Unpack, it'll make you feel more at home, two break ups and a house move, can't get much higher up the human stress scale. Don't *sink*.'

'I'll be OK, I just need some time, I've got a few plans, you know, moving on and all that shit. I'm starting at the garden centre tomorrow, only temporary, to help Alistair out.'

James absently counted the empties piled up around David's chair, chucking them in the bin for him was possibly too interfering. 'How about some light? Which box are the lamps in?'

It was during Easter when Mark had put a week in at the garden centre that David had got to know Alistair. Although a man generally considered to be socially challenged David presumed even he had guessed about his relationship with Mark. Not many blokes turned up at the end of every working day to help a friend in the last hour to shift bags of pea shingle off a lorry and then take them home. He had offered David work immediately and on his first day David volunteered to restack the back yard to make space for the Christmas stock. Turning down the offer of the fork lift he swung and released 25 kg bags until something told him that if he carried on he wouldn't be able to get out of bed the following day. It was practically self flagellation except he was getting paid and he wasn't getting a shortcut to heaven. The break from his repetitive thoughts however, didn't happen and each day he corkscrewed further down. It was a quiet time of the year, there were only four of them and they gathered in Alistair's warm shed for breaks but even that was too much company and when he didn't appear one morning Alistair brought his tea out to the yard. He didn't try to encourage David back to the warmth of the shed and company but sat quietly with him drinking his tea. Alistair, the funny bloke who answered simple gardening questions with complicated answers with lots of Latin, Alistair in his dark green overalls, straggling hair he didn't wash quite often enough and filthy nails, in fact he and David were beginning to look rather alike. They sat on compost bags, tucked into the corner of the yard; the tall stacks like a sepulchre in the quiet dimness of a church. A confession duly tumbled out.

'You see, I don't like myself much at the moment. I'm ashamed of myself and it's getting increasingly harder and I don't know when it's going to stop. I have repetitive thoughts and they paralyse me, small things frighten me.'

He looked at Alistair clutching his mug in both hands and the man's eyes dropped immediately to gaze silently into the liquid as if searching for a response which David was happy not to get, saying it out loud was a relief in itself.

'You may find,' there was an agonised pause as he struggled with the personal, 'that it will get better with time.'

'Yes, I know it will, well I think I do but meanwhile I think I should disappear, not too far, somewhere in Europe and teach English and polish up my French and German, I could easily rent the house out, I've enough money to keep me going for a while, and when I come back, well, people lose interest don't they?'

'That might not help,' Alistair said uncertainly, for whom a trip into town was, if not an ordeal, an event. 'What are you disappearing *from* Dave?'

There was the boiling shame of course which he felt in waves but there was, he was ashamed to recognize also loss of face and status. Once in the Georgian town house (perfect for entertaining) he would have become a member of the local history society, chair of the resident's association, member of a political party, a councillor, a committee chair, invitations to everything, a bespoke family Christmas card with their photo on the front and a round robin letter inside to keep everyone abreast of their relentless social ascent. He smiled; at least it made him smile.

'Nothing specific, maybe it's the notoriety, I'm a private person and you're right, time will cure everything.'

The next day he worked through without a break and Alistair persuaded him to leave early and he cycled to his old spot in the country park and sat by the river in the weak evening sunshine to return a missed called from James.

'Bit of a shock coming old man but I think you should know, they've gone into *receivership*, I couldn't believe it, I mean there was a new van outside the house last time I was there with fancy new logos and him bellyaching on about his German partnership.'

David sank back onto the grass, 'I'm surprised it's staggered on this long to be honest.'

'You're kidding me?'

'I'll email you.' It had gone down faster than he'd ever imagined, it was more rotten than he'd dared to think. He had no reason to feel in any way responsible but all the same he did and stretched out his arm and felt for the crepe wrapped handlebar of his bike lying beside him and held it for comfort, going over and over all his misgivings about the whole set up until the light disappeared and he started to shiver. On the ride back he looked forward to the opportunity to explain to James in an email his predicament over the past year.

'When I got back from that visit to the factory,' he wrote that night, 'I couldn't let it go, nothing made sense, no intelligent person could have sat through that meeting and not thought something was seriously wrong. You know me, I like the facts, I like to get to the bottom of things don't I? So I did a search at Companies House and sent for the company files. Then I worked out the profit margin, 10% is a good level but Chandlers hadn't made any profit for the past three years. Then Mark and I went and did a bit of on the ground research. We went to the really big supermarkets, all the places Jack had told me they supplied and I didn't recognise anything I'd seen on the lines or in the catalogue. So we did a bit of ringing round. I pretended to be a start up bakery, all enthusiastic and entrpreurial and asked questions about suppliers and the sort of products they were wanting and then mentioned Chandlers saying I'd done some training there and Marks and Waitrose and Tescos, well at least over the phone, said Chandlers wasn't a supplier. That might have been a standard response but we did everything to find out where the bloody stuff was being sold. So we decided it was very small scale just local shops or it was being stored, they weren't actually selling it. And then, when we were visiting the Manor House, that time you came with us to go over menus, one of the waitresses recognised me from that visit. And I asked her if she'd left and I got all this 'I shouldn't really say' stuff but she told me they were cutting down the lines and reducing hours and that was why she left. All that idle machinery really was idle, not being serviced like he said. That ridiculous meeting with the marketing manager in that stuffy hotel pretty much confirmed I never wanted anything to do with it and then the bloody account manager rang me, just before I set off for Belize. A whole different character, he said he'd wanted to confide in me for ages but wasn't sure if he could trust me but now I wasn't marrying her anymore it was different. He told me the bank was threatening to call in the loans which were huge and he didn't know if next month's wage bill could be met, including his. Jack wouldn't listen and wanted to sign a contract with the German firm because he thought they'd save the company and he'd been asked to paint a rosy picture and fudge the figures. The German company did their research, just like I did and pulled out. He wanted to know if that was why *I'd* jumped ship! What could I say? If that's what he wants to think, he can.'

As he had typed it had sounded casual but on reading it back to himself it had a defensive tone, wariness had set in with James, the balance of their friendship had shifted very slightly. There was no way any blame could come his way of course, the Visigoths were well on the way to the business by the time he had turned up and he had only done what anyone would do if they were being pressed into making a life changing decision, it was everyone else who'd shown an astonishing eagerness to spill the beans.

James rang immediately, 'you could have told me some of this before.'

'It's only recently become necessary.'

The short silence was like the cold downbeat of a wing, James had the same tour as David and he'd seen and heard the same story from Jack except he'd believed every word of it but he said, 'if you'd told me all this I'd have understood your decision to end it better.'

'It had nothing to do with it, *nothing*. As I said I never did anything more than look politely interested. All I did was check on the facts; I had a right to check on the facts didn't I?'

'It was another reason to get out, a reason I didn't know about.'

'James, it *wasn't*, if anyone knows it wasn't it's you, you know *why* I got out.'

Of course James knew, but at first he'd been flattered and impressed by the Chandlers, David had never been flattered, never impressed.

The back yard was now cleared ready for the Christmas trees but instead of joining the other staff as they unpacked the Christmas stock and prepared the Christmas section, Alistair gave him a greenhouse to sweep and pots to scrub, away from the yuletide conviviality. Here, alone under the sun warmed glass he tried to distance himself from Chandler's financial problems and failed. Family firms were closing all the time, maybe the bank could find a buyer and anyway the factory site, close to the town centre, would be worth a packet. 'We all told you what you wanted to hear you stupid fool,' he said out loud to the empty green house, confirming both its emptiness and wanting to hear the reassurance in his voice. It hadn't been in anyone's interest to tell the truth, maybe it was the way all businesses collapsed, who was he to know.

He got everything looking very organised and tidy in the greenhouses ready for seed propagation and hoped Alistair would keep him on; he liked the idea of watching for the first shoots and potting the seedlings on when they were bursting out of their nursery accommodation. And Mark would be back soon of course, not guaranteed he'd want to work alongside him but he was prepared to make it work and together they could help Alistair effect a few changes to encourage customers to spend more. Once all the Christmas stuff was taken down a big garden bird feeding display should go in the same place he decided, so it was the first thing people saw when they came in. All the bird feeders should be hung filled so people knew what seeds to buy for which feeder and all the manufacturers display material used so they could see what birds they would attract and the bulky seed sacks should be piled away to the side so customers could get close to the products and there should be plenty of special offers. But there was no sign of him.

Christmas was dealt with in a few lies,' I'm spending Christmas with James,' he wrote to his parents and 'I'm spending Christmas with my parents,' he emailed to James. The handful of cards went straight in the bin and apart from a few obligatory seasonal exchanges on his way to the corner shop on Christmas Eve it passed unnoticed.

The temperature dropped suddenly but he still kept the heating off and felt quietly triumphant to be in control of the temperature in his home once more even if he was wearing all his base layers, snow boots and jacket in the house. But in mid January it turned really bitter, and it was a relief to go to work where a ancient smelly paraffin heater kept his greenhouse cosy. On his days off he paced the streets at regular intervals, too wary of patches of black ice to use his bike. As usual, checking his weather station and plotting the figures was a pleasant distraction and the fact that the temperature inside and outside barely differed was perversely consoling but eventually no matter how many layers he wore it became intolerable and the pain in his feet no longer made him feel any better about himself. Reluctantly he put the heating on, low, pressing himself with relief against the radiators as they spluttered and glugged into life. To keep the thermostat down he moved the chair to face the radiator so he could press the soles of his feet and hands flat against it like a gecko on a wall. He balanced his laptop on top of a box in front of his chair and got down to the backlog of filing and backing up his work as a priority, when that was finished he could finally get on with the text book.

The TV aerial and radio were missing, presumed in the boxes but the tape sealing the lids had a permanence he was now unable to disturb. He stopped buying a paper, apart from natural disasters nothing much caught his interest and when it did his concentration failed him after a few paragraphs. He knew it was Tuesday because of the racket the bin men made at 7.30 in the morning and Sunday because of the church bells; in between he lost track. Used to an edited but action packed school week, the Sunday call to his parents, none the wiser about his resignation, was proving difficult. He invented a forthcoming trip to India where mobile reception would be bad he assured them so he'd keep in contact with them through James as they weren't on the internet. Not that he'd heard from James, admittedly the charger for his mobile had disappeared and there was no time to open his emails.

The front garden was only six feet in depth and he felt too exposed to the street, noticing with annoyance how his neighbour would automatically peer in as he passed, sometimes three or four times a day. He tried repositioning the boxes so they broke up a direct view through the window but allowed a couple of narrow gaps shaped like arrow slits in castle walls so that he could see out, but not be seen.

Returning late from the garden centre one evening, (Alistair had agreed to longer opening hours finally), he turned on the hall light and a handwritten envelope stood out from the pile of colourful junk mail and typed addresses on the floor. Instantly he recognised Sarah's bold handwriting from her school reports and notes she left and he tore it open as he stood in the hall, instinctively knowing its contents.

She wished him well, said it was a pity there hadn't been a chance to say goodbye, would miss him and their tea breaks together, thanked him for all his help with the photo competitions, hoped he'd enjoy his further studies. It ended, 'I told people, over and over right to the end it wasn't true, that if anyone would know it would be me. Why didn't you tell me? Is it because you guessed I cared about you? I wish you'd said something, it could have made it better for both of us.'

He held it so it didn't fall but barely enough to feel it. His face burnt, cared? They'd stuck exclusively to art and the weather and staff gossip, but the recollection of Mark's words, delivered with such reluctance and received by him with huge irritation made his breath short. Some of the school thought she fancied him Mark had said. Oh god, surely he'd treated her like a mate, retreating to her office because she was so, well, neutral. How the hell was he expected to guess if she never said anything? He screwed the letter up tightly and threw it into the bin but fretfully, for the rest of the evening, recalled the tea breaks and lunchtime chats, his body language, the way she had looked at him.

After that he let the pile build up under the letterbox for a few days but another envelope with a handwritten address was sitting on the pile as he let himself in one evening. He watched it disappear under more mail for a few days then one evening lost his footing on the slippery stack as he tried to hurdle it and it lay exposed once more. Finally, on hands and knees, without disturbing the pile, he read the postmark.

It was six pages, typed with one finger; he'd seen him in action. Beginning in a formal and almost dignified manner it expressed their shock and distress at his decision. 'It was beyond our comprehension, there had been no pressure, the marriage had been entirely his decision, they had merely offered the love and support they considered appropriate in welcoming him into their family.' An inventory followed of the generations of local families that had worked for the company, the awards and customer plaudits, the breakthrough into biscuits in '56, the new ovens in '84, the M and S order in '91 and the new decals on the delivery vans last month. Then good wishes for the future, so laboured and proper they bordered sarcasm but David guessed some old fashioned decency had been mined.

A confused and repetitive journey followed, of poor and untrustworthy management, of high interest rates, escalating overheads and changing consumer tastes which were familiar from Jack's dinner table ramblings. But now there was a new focus for his blame. 'You admired our company photos,' it continued querulously, 'you saw the factory at work, I opened every door to your scrutiny, I hid nothing. Did you resent us? Did you compare us with your own modest background?'

By this point he could just about cope, it was only to be expected from someone shattered by financial failure, maybe he wasn't the only one to get a letter like this he thought desperately. As he read on though it became harder to distance himself; it was personal; he had snooped into company records, retailers had been contacted and were consequently unwilling to make orders, he had spread rumours about the company's finances and influenced the bank's decision to foreclose on the loan. He was accused of speaking to staff and rocking their confidence in the company despite their longstanding loyalty and they had consequently left, highly skilled staff that could not easily be replaced. And the German company had found out, he spoke German didn't he? And now they'd pulled out of a partnership ending a long year of delicate negotiations. And Doug, Doug who had sung his praises, Doug with a wife and two children had lost his job and was looking worried and ill.

Rooted to the floor David lifted his eyes from the sheets for a moment and dug deep into his memory, they'd all fallen over themselves to confide in him and he'd thought nothing of it. How remarkably easy it was for them to twist his common or garden decency and good manners into scheming sabotage as the bad news reached them.

The email to James flashed before him and a hot flush washed over him. He ran through it in his head, its contents would have let James completely off the hook for having known all along about the boy. He saw James perched on a chair in the huge lounge they rarely used, in front of the best china, with this new evidence that would finally prove he had known nothing and offer him the guilt free exit he so desperately wanted.

The letter raged on, he skip read to the last paragraph where it ended with a list of his 'qualities'; manipulative, scheming, deceitful and clever. 'You took us in, you gave no indication that anything was amiss. Had you planned it, from the start?' And finally, the advice of a solicitor was being sought, for slander.

Shaking, he went to shred it, but instead found himself folding it carefully back into the envelope as though Jack was watching and remained motionless and disconnected in the dark kitchen for along time, fighting for his self-belief and in doing so his thoughts turned to Clare in mounting bitterness. You drew me in, you positioned me to take the blame when you knew it was all collapsing. A powerful urge to confront her boiled up, to both rage at her and to seek reassurance that her father had lost his hold on reality but snatching up his phone from the work surface he remembered it wasn't charged. Instead he stumbled to the living room to collapse into his chair, drawing up his knees to his chin. 'Basterd, basterd, basterd' he whispered, and cried.

The letter terrified him, for hours the accusations pinned him to his chair like knives. How easy it had been to say he'd fallen out of love, who could argue with that, where did it say, anywhere, 'thou shalt stay in love.' From that point he was untouchable but the internet searches, the supermarket hunts, the debates with Mark were all true. He'd treated it like a research project; using as many primary sources as possible to find out if the company was financially viable and had a future and if not, why not. It had been fun, yet he had dug himself two holes to fall into. By confiding in him he had built up Mark's confidence that their relationship was more significant than his relationship with Clare and he had given Jack his scapegoat for the final collapse.

Later, as the beer and the quiet undisturbed solitude of his little house calmed him he recognised that there was one thing missing from the tirade, something he genuinely wasn't proud of and that he couldn't deny. From pots of paint, glue, packets of sandpaper and drill bits to a new wood floor, tanks of petrol, the TV licence, car insurance and the skiing holiday he had, with various degrees of protest, accepted it all, yet Jack hadn't mentioned it. It was such an obvious target and he sensed a row and that his endless protestations had left Clare, even in her grief and fury not able to blame him for the onslaught of their generosity. He started writing a list of items paid for by Jack that he could repay but most had been enjoyed by both of them, he had even given Clare a share of the equity in the house. He made tea and held the cup in both hands, spreading his fingers, trying, as usual these days to extract the maximum benefit from the heat. He knew that if he could control his impulses the best thing to do would be nothing, from nothing comes nothing sprang to mind, which was hardly a dynamic to live by but had its uses. Sipping the tea he let a memory work its way through to the surface. He'd waited in the car for him, more nervous than Mark had been about his driving test and he'd watched the boy's face intently in the driver's mirror for a clue as he walked back from the test car. 'Move over,' Mark had said casually at the driver's door, breaking into a huge grin as he dropped into the driver's seat David had vacated. That's where some of it went Jack, driving lessons, in fact it's probably being spent this very minute on rounds of Bolivian beer.

The small pleasures he was managing to conjure up during the day from the uncomplicated job, no demanding lover and no DIY were deserting him in the early hours. A deep foreboding now woke him at four am every day and he struggled in a dark place for what was only minutes but seemed hours. At that hour, notorious for bleak thoughts, he was unemployed, unemployable and sexually isolated; he was living in the world of the damned. He would try and get up but end up sitting on the edge of his bed, rocking slightly until the waves of panic subsided. He'd been there before of course, it wasn't unfamiliar territory but now the support structure was missing; no dog pressed lovingly to his teenage feet, no fun university flatmates to hang silently round, no Clare planning their weekends and their life. Yep, he was on his own with this one.

He struggled on at the garden centre, Alistair leaving him alone to take the whole day to do things that should have been achieved in a few hours and he tried to convince himself the steep dip in his energy levels was down to the manual labour which he wasn't used to. He refused his pay packet from Alistair one Friday and they stood mute and embarrassed, two troubled men defeated by language. He filled each day with work, beer and sleep, narrowing the opportunities for thinking, then one morning depression pinned him to the bed, he didn't want the day and the day didn't want him. Alistair rang about ten and in a stilted exchange he said he'd strained his back and would let him know when he was better. From then on, released from every obligation, he let the days and nights gradually merge. Clothes became confusing; when to change out of pyjamas and when to change back until a mix of the two saw him through the day and night. Drunk for at least part of the day the stairs would soar dizzyingly above his head when he was tired so he took them on his hands and knees until he abandoned his bedroom altogether and by abandoning upstairs he also abandoned the basics of hygiene and did little more than wash his face in the kitchen sink.

Now he was finally fully in control of his time. He had time to do things properly, to make coffee as it should be;

the right amount of grounds, the right amount of water and the correct length of steeping time. Time to keep the kitchen clean with everything in its place, the washing up sponge alongside, but not touching the soap and the tea towel folded into four, the corners satisfyingly adjusted for symmetry as he hung it on the rail. Now breakfast could be enjoyed, not shovelled down as he rushed out of the door; there was time to mix his cereals correctly and butter the toast properly into the corners. Taking things carefully, not missing out on any details the flurries of panic began to subside. This was all he needed, a bit of time to himself to adjust to his new circumstances and get everything under control once more. Moving systematically through his chores with no chance whatever of anyone being let down, expectations being raised or anything unexpected happening he drifted into a dozy calm. No timetables, no targets to meet and assessments to write, no one to keep happy, no guilty secret to gnaw away at him his life slowed to a bearable crawl. He craved this state so much, put such score on its returning him to normality that the slightest deviance or intrusion in his ordered day brought back the panic, instantly.

Without Clare's four bin recycling system every wrapping and container left him frozen with indecision. Now he accepted it might have made sense but he'd got rid of the bins and the discipline of setting it up again defeated and annoyed him. Shoving everything into a bin liner would have been the solution but now he hovered indecisively over each piece of packaging, the decision getting harder every day. Finally, as the pile toppled onto the floor he flattened the boxes and plastic containers neatly and they lay in segregated piles on the kitchen surface which soon took up too much space and he bound them up tightly in carrier bags transferring them and the cans and bottles temporarily to the living room, pending a trip to the recycling centre.

It was around the end of January he started to hear cautious knocks and the letterbox snap and one day, peeping through the gap in the packing boxes saw Abi standing on the pavement, shading her eyes and looking intently through the window then wander off. She was probably after some maths help, well he didn't have time. The soft polite knocks became louder and on a few occasions his name was called through the letter box. Someone even stood in the front garden and cupped their hands against the window in an attempt to see into the dark room, it was unbelievable how determined people were to interfere. His neighbour was a particular problem; surely he'd been cool enough when he first moved in to show he liked to be left alone but the bloody man stood outside for a few minutes nearly every day, whistling loudly and tunelessly like a bait to entice him out. Sometimes, later in the evening the noise from next door increased, as if volumes had been cranked up, did the bloke's hearing deteriorate as the day wore on? The post and junk mail piled up, he ignored it all, everything was on direct debit. It was also useful as evidence that he'd gone away, you could see it if you peered through the letterbox, in fact it was all very satisfactory, a disruptive and expensive move abroad hadn't been necessary.

One early evening in February, after half a dozen sharp knocks he heard the squeak of the letterbox being pushed open and a firm voice filled the house, bouncing off the bare floorboards.

'Dave, its Tony and Liz. Listen, none of us have heard from you and we wondered if you'd like to come out to the pub tomorrow night, a quiet drink, just a few of us.'

He held his breath, Tony would have been able to see the large pile of post on the floor but there had been no uncertainty in the tone of his voice, they would be at the front window any second. Sinking onto the floor he crouched behind a box.

'Dave, your neighbour said you haven't gone away, he saw you yesterday. It's all history now mate, everybody's asking after you, they want to know if you're OK.'

There was an edge to his voice, a 'we're not going until we see you or we're taking further action' sort of edge and

David stood up like a guilty schoolboy. As he took a tentative step towards the door he was suddenly conscious of what he was wearing and pulled off his scarf and ski jacket then attempted a brisk walk as though they'd caught him in the middle of doing something.

'Hi.'

'Hey, good to see you, how are you?' Tony rubbed his hands together as if he'd popped round for a cup of tea on a freezing day.

'I'm fine!, I'm just really busy, I'm doing a bit of writing and I've an editor's deadline coming up.' They smiled with their mouths, their eyes flicking from his head to his feet and then into the house behind him. A few more pleasantries tumbled out about the location of his new house and the weather, their forced and breezy tone comical and shocking.

'You know,' said Liz earnestly, turning to look fixedly at Tony, 'it's all water under the bridge now isn't it Tony and we wondered if you'd…'

'I really appreciate your coming but as you can see everything's fine. I'm going abroad for a while but I'll be back in circulation as soon as I get back but thanks for calling round.'

Its very reasonableness left the two visitors wordless. Liz rubbed her hands together briskly, 'gosh it's freezing isn't it? Well, nice to see you, we'll be off then, everyone sends their best wishes.' She caught his eye, their visit had not been undertaken lightly, some had not been supportive. 'We haven't seen her for a while you know, it'd just be us,' she blinked anxiously at him.

'Oh, by the way,' Tony pulled an envelope out of his jacket, 'let me know if you're interested.' With quick smiles they hesitated a further few moments then said goodbye. He closed the door and ran his hand self consciously through his hair, he'd run out of shampoo and washing up liquid was OK but made his hair, now down to his shoulders, a bit dry and stiff. He glanced down at his pyjama jacket, maybe he should have kept his ski jacket on but it was plain, it looked like a shirt. Back in his chair he fingered the envelope anxiously; if it expected a reply not opening it might bring the bloke round again. It was an invitation to a club night, a gay club night, with a scribbled note about meeting up beforehand for a drink. Tony knew and he was bringing him into the fold. Incensed he burnt it to ash in the sink.

By the end of February he was living entirely and contentedly downstairs, laying three chair cushions on the floor in a row when he wanted to sleep. This required him to keep very still; even with a sheet tucked round them to bind them together they shifted and separated requiring adjustment throughout the night. A breakthrough came by exchanging the duvet for a sleeping bag and by clenching his stomach muscles and drawing up his knees he could soon turn over with minimum cushion disruption. Trussed up in his bag and severely limited in his movements he continued the pleasures of self denial into the night.

The visit, and the possibility of another, made him anxious about his appearance. His previous bathroom had a large mirror over the sink and an illuminated magnifying mirror which he used for shaving, cleaning his teeth, combing his hair and generally checking he was a good looking guy. There were no mirrors downstairs in this house and he was using one of Clare's handbag mirrors he'd found with the kitchen equipment to shave. He quite liked his hair longer and in combination with the stubble he was looking less recognisably himself. The slight softness his face had been developing had gone, the shadow was back under his cheekbones but he looked away, even the tiny reflection was too much.

The post continued to pile up, he ignored it all and he positioned a packing box a few feet from the door to add support to the case that he was not in residence. The front door was now difficult to open so he abandoned it for the back door, walking down the path through the overgrown back garden to the gate in the rear fence. This opened onto the narrow alleyway behind the terrace and he slipped out during the early evening when he assumed everyone would be eating and watching soaps. Sometimes, temporarily free from alcohol and its after effects he ached for company and lingered in the local shop. They clearly liked him, he spent all his money there after all and they smiled at him very hard but didn't say much and his attempts at conversation, mainly the weather, never progressed far. I'm a schoolteacher, he said one day, would the children like any help with their maths, he didn't want paying. They smiled even harder but said no thanks. Occasionally he searched unsuccessfully for the phone charger, picking over the contents at the top of the two boxes that he had opened and pulling open the empty kitchen drawers. He thought about another trip to town for a charger and books, something new on climate change, maybe the latest political diary so he was up to speed when he moved back into the social milieu. Not the old one of course, that was dead and gone, the new one and fuelled with self confidence from the first cans of the day he saw his text book as recommended reading in the Times Educational and a new crowd occupying his contemporary sofas in his open plan flat and inviting him over to sit on theirs. It was, however, a journey too far and he remained in the security of the fortified living room.

A stretch of an arm and he had his laptop, his weather records, his beer packs and his wine. It took two minutes to convert his chair to a bed and a quick dash down the corridor and there was his blue plastic bowl in the sink and the pink plastic showerhead which was attached to the tap. He turned the tap on twice a day, to fill the kettle to shave and for his coffee in the morning and for a cup of tea later on in the day. Every couple of days he filled the bowl for a stand up wash. His day was punctuated by a small travel alarm clock which sent him scuttling to take his weather readings.

Beer was becoming a problem though, he was running out every couple of days and the twenty minute walk to the off license opened up the prospect of meeting people he didn't want to meet, in particular his neighbour who seemed to spend his entire day patrolling the surrounding streets. Never a big beer drinker the quantity required to get him to where he wanted to be was making him bloated and nauseous so he started on 14.5% Shiraz which did the job. Tins soon replaced his pasta and sauce staple, no prep; his unsteadiness made it difficult to stand for long and once he'd smashed a hole big enough to extricate the contents he could manage three minutes standing next to the microwave. The variety was surprising; ratatouille, curry, soup, beef stew, treacle pudding, he was back at his chair with a steaming bowl and spoon in minutes and no bloody debate with Clare about calories, nutritional content, food miles and whether it was fucking organic or free trade. He didn't give a shit.

Chapter Nineteen

His neighbour was now resting dramatically on his zimmer frame on the pavement outside David's window two or three times a day, painstakingly adjusting his shopping bag hanging from the frame then quickly squinting through the window. The man was a bore and a pest, David had to crouch low as he moved backwards and forwards between the two rooms in case he saw him. He could tell the bloke he was going away but even that engagement was too fraught; he would ask where he was going and how long for and did he want him to come in turn lights off and on and close curtains? If the old codger thought he was away then inquiring visitors would be put off. This meant keeping the lights off but in the dark he was banging his head and his knees against the furniture and boxes so he moved them to create a corridor and started filling the gaps between them so even the most determined wouldn't see any movement through the window.

His laptop, balanced on the box in front of him soon became no more than a light source, in fact his only light source in the living room. Burdened with viruses it had been slowing down for a while but it hardly mattered, topping himself up with Shiraz and beer throughout the day, he could barely gather his thoughts together long enough to write a sentence. One evening he consumed the beans and sausages cold and straight from the tin, too drunk and absent to transfer them to a bowl to microwave them and collapsed into his chair to come round hours later to relative sobriety and a crushing depression. Wretchedness ate any vestige of energy, his breathing was shallow, his chest hurt and reaching for his weather notes he struggled to raise his left arm from his side. It was pitch dark outside and he heard a few chirrups heralding the start of the dawn chorus; he supposed it was about three.

How they would have smirked over their beers with Tony and Liz's information about unwashed hair and still in his pyjamas in the afternoon. He would be the hot, the only topic. How his detractors would enjoy presenting their case; his aloofness and slight superiority. Supporters might fall into two camps; those who automatically took the other side, whatever it was, and those who saw the best in everyone. He inserted himself miserably into their midst and tried to make his case but self deprecation is only funny when things are going well and he removed himself quickly.

Lying in his makeshift bed, wide awake at 4 am he summoned them; friends, colleagues, the in laws and the business associates that never were, in an orgy of loathing. Dredging up every slight and magnifying the trivial he dammed them for their meaningless displays of friendship that hid their miserable ulterior motives. He picked them off, one by one.

Did daddy's girl know about the letter? She would certainly know how it would terrify him, she knew he shrank from confrontation of any sort and that defamation and slander, in fact anything legalistic was totally foreign territory to him. She was spoilt, money cushioned falls, there would probably be a Caribbean holiday to forget and recuperate.

James, always eager to please. They'd have picked him up from the station in the Range Rover so he wouldn't have his car and couldn't make an escape. Had the offer of a new car as a thank you been quietly dropped? As for their friendship, it had had its day, it was of a time and place that had long gone, the man would have to live with his big blabbing mouth.

And Mark, the catastrophe of their affair grew by the day but the details were becoming hazy. He was loosing track of the sequence of events; who had said what to who and who knew what and when. In the first sentimental flushes of drunkenness he fantasised passionate doorstep reconciliations; carrying him to bed, tearing off his clothes, which were counterbalanced later once he'd sobered up by images of unpleasant little exchanges in the street. But the truth was he'd heard nothing and a cheque for the hospital expenses had arrived without even a note. One evening, a bottle of Shiraz fully in occupation in his system he began to shout, the sound seemed to die in his mouth so he shouted louder until his throat hurt, so he knew he was shouting. 'Fuck you! Fuck you!' over and over and the voices and laugher from next door stopped abruptly but returned after a few minutes, slightly muted.

'Everything alright, Dave?' His neighbour asked a few days later in the street, his aluminium zimmer frame flashing as he hurried to catch up with David who was setting off briskly for supplies, 'I heard a bit of shouting, my telly's not too loud is it? And don't mind the cat, he gets everywhere.'

The explosions of hate became tempered with fear that soon they would start turning up. The street lights threw shadows of people walking along the pavement in front of the house across the curtainless room. He watched for recognisable shapes; Jack, bulky, arriving by taxi, hand delivering paperwork with those accusations of slander and defamation and god knows what else business people did that would destroy his confidence and his future and empty his bank account. A solicitor would be pleased to cook up something for money, however hollow. In preparation he attempted to make notes but again could not recall who had said exactly what. Doug had probably taped their meeting and given the transcript to Jack and a crack team of solicitors had forensically dissected it.

Tony was any trim male figure that passed, he would

definitely come again. James, from whom a confession could be extracted merely by the pressure of an afternoon tea, would have told Tony the truth about his gym buddy. There would be more invitations; Gay Pride next week? A threesome? Or a gossipy chat about how had it started, was he the first and how long had he known he was gay? Tony would have to kick the door down before he let him in and if you want the truth matey; no he wasn't the first, whatever the *first* means; the first touch, the first kiss, the first fuck?

Sarah would be easy to spot, not a keen walker she'd drive and find a meter. He sank behind the box as any larger female figure passed and waited, it would be five seconds before the door knocker rattled. He had a story ready about what you don't know you can't worry about and how it wasn't the sort of thing she'd have wanted to know anyway and she would look mortified and ask why. And what if she confessed, about how she felt about him, the possibility of such an exchange made him flush hot and he rehearsed feeble replies that only dragged him deeper into the hole he'd dug for himself.

Shirley would come because he interested her. He welcomed her visit, he wanted to shock her, she was asking to be shocked and he wanted to tell her, in explicit physical detail about his love affair. A real homosexual love affair right on her doorstep, not something nicely over and done with in the 1930's, all daring and bohemian and safely between the covers of some respectable biography. But what if all she'd wanted to do was to confide in him, the failing company, her failing marriage? And all he'd done was let her down like a selfish oaf.

He found it difficult to imagine his parents' elderly dark blue estate arriving and there was a very big bit of him that wanted it to happen and for them to quietly pack him in the back with the Jack Russell and take him home for a while. They would draw up and then pull away as confusion reigned inside over the parking restrictions listed on the pole outside his house. Unaware of visitor's parking vouchers they would trawl around to find a meter and finally return on foot to his door. To have got this far would have followed days of protracted debate after weeks of fruitless calls and there was probably a letter from them in the pile in the hall. All three of them had let each other down, united only by the unspoken agony they had shared in silence for so long after the accident. It wouldn't be long though before he'd be ready to drive up to see them, only a few more days and he'd feel himself again.

During March one low pressure over the country was quickly replaced by another and it rained relentlessly. Next door's blocked gutters were overflowing and the damp patch, covered by a quick coat of paint for the house sale was now revealing itself on the party wall. During the day David took readings from his gauges which showed rainfall to be well above average for the month. Asleep, the information he was collecting soared out of control and extreme weather conditions filled his dreams; saturated plaster, floating furniture, sodden photos, ruined laminate floors. A full bladder always woke him sharply in the early hours right in the middle of each disaster to find himself trapped and panicky inside his sleeping bag. Awake he checked with his hands for water penetration; his sleeping bag, the carpet, the boxes. Worst of all though, catching up on lost sleep in the afternoons, struggling like an ant stuck in resin to wake, his house slid, creaking and snapping down a mountainside.

Tinned food, once so convenient and surprisingly tasty no longer tempted him and the few remaining tins were mainly syrup sponge which made him nauseous. It was the last week of March, he had not ventured out for a week, he was rationing himself and was hungry, terribly hungry, returning again and again along the corridor to check the remaining tins and to search cupboards and open the fridge to find beer and only beer. His empty stomach teased his brain with phantom home cooked dinners, the smell of real food, the feel of it in his mouth; creamy, crunchy and crispy. If he had the ingredients he could give it a go, he could cook something, he'd peeled and stirred and drained as directed, surely he could put the whole thing together on his own by now? He stood motionless for hours at the back door staring through the glass panel into the dripping overgrown mess of the back garden, the concrete path barely visible between the lush weeds filling the joints in the slabs. The journey to the shop had to be made and he ran through it over and over in his mind. The sharp ping as the shop door opened; who would be on the till? The clever daughter, barely raising her eyes from her school books beside her, her mother with welcoming words but her eyes shifting suspiciously; she knew, oh she knew what he was living on, the watchful father and brother and his every move captured on the CCTV cameras. Back outside huddles of schoolchildren would stare, they would know by now who he was or who he *used* to be; a teacher! Oh my god! He's like a *tramp!*

It wouldn't take long, he could be back in less than fifteen minutes but could he leave the house for that long? The scuffles, bangs and creaks were almost continuous; he was struggling to put a rational explanation to any of them anymore. A new damp patch had appeared in the kitchen, it was getting bigger every day, how long before it joined up with the one in the front room. And of course once they knew he was out, oh yes, they'd come. Maybe they'd joined forces, told one another that he hadn't gone away, yes he was in there, hiding but it was quite easy to get in, all you had to do was break the glass panel in the front door to get to the Yale lock. He must get a mortise lock fitted on the front door.

By the last day in March David's life had ground almost to a standstill apart from the imperative of taking the weather records. It must have been over twenty four hours since he had last eaten and before that only sporadically, even the thought of the syrup sponge made him sweat with disgust. Waiting until it was completely dark before making foray to the shop he forced himself violently to his feet and fainted headlong into the boxes.

After a few dazed minutes on the floor he recovers and the shock of the fall brings some clarity. Pulling his wallet out of the back pocket of his jeans he finds a few coins and his debit card. He remembers he needs a number to use the card but then it's all too much, he's suddenly incredibly tired and falls back into his chair where he sits for a long while, dozing, trying to remember the number. It may be in his diary, in a code but he can't see properly in the gloom and flicks through the last pages holding it against the dull light from the laptop. Eventually he thinks he can remember the first two numbers, he must get cash, then he will be spared the embarrassment if the number doesn't work in the shop. There is a cash machine at the local petrol station, he hasn't driven for a long time, he can't remember how long but his car will get him to the petrol station. Too unsteady to stand he stays on his hands and knees as he heads for the back door and as he opens it a black cat bolts out into the darkness.

The car is parked close by, and he sinks with relief into the driver's seat. The soft clunk of the door sounds safe and familiar, everything will be OK, he will drive to the petrol station and get some money and buy some food. He starts the car and moves off, his body, though weak has not forgotten how to drive and the foreboding that has been hanging over him lifts. At the petrol station he is successful on the third attempt at the cash machine. In the shop the food confuses him, there are no fresh vegetables for his home cooked meal so he buys beer and a pasty and returns to the car. He dreads returning to the house. The passageway between the boxes has been closing in on him for days, it's getting harder and harder to move through it, the roof is gradually getting lower, the bending is restricting his breathing and he is afraid there will come a point he won't be able to get to the kitchen or once there, return to his chair. It has become a dank horror that is oozing water and the intruders who are scratching and burrowing will soon break through and get in. Leaving the petrol station he can't focus properly and stalls twice as his foot misses the clutch, he pulls into the kerb exhausted and drinks a can of beer. Then another. The seats are so soft, they tip back like a bed and the heater has warmed him up quickly, even his feet are finally warm. He can live in the car! The pasty is very, very nice, he can eat pasties. If he takes a long sleep in the deliciously warm car he will wake feeling better and then he can return to the house. A long sleep without any interruptions is all he needs. But now he can't sleep, he can't sleep.

There it is, waiting in the glove compartment. 'See,' Mark had said, 'you've only seen bloody photos, here's the *real* thing, Class A, Class B, I've been collecting them, I pick them up here and there, I get out and about more than you do. Keep yer hair on! I never touch 'em, I've been saving them, to show you.' David opens the small mint tin, tips the contents into his mouth and washes them all down with the last can of beer.

The light stung his eyes and he tried to turn his head away from it but it obstinately followed his feeble movements. He heard a voice, sharp and urgent but ignored it and then shaking, shaking, he lifted his hands to push whatever it was away, he was sleeping wasn't he? All he ever wanted was some sleep, who the fuck was this disturbing him? 'Fuck off,' he said but didn't hear it and tried again louder. Then hands, taking handfuls of his jacket and lifting and pulling and he reached out to grasp something to stop it happening, the steering wheel then the door but nothing was working properly. He struggled on as he was half carried, half lifted, then a face, close to his, 'what did you take?'

White, he was covered in a white blanket and the walls were white, everything white like a hospital. It *was* a hospital.

Was it the same one as Mark was in? That would be nice, was he in the same room? He turned his head to find him and felt very sick then was sick into a small papier maché bowl close to his face. In front of him people in white were bustling about and he started to ask about Mark but his throat hurt, then someone came close, speaking carefully and slowly. 'We have rung your emergency contact number in your diary.' He didn't have an emergency number, Mark had an emergency number, *he* was his emergency number. Mark was here wasn't he? 'Tell Mark I'm here,' he said firmly, and returned to sleep.

The next time he opened his eyes onto the bustle of the ward his mind felt much clearer and there was no denying that something fairly unpleasant had happened.

Someone took his pulse and adjusted something beside him. He looked at his hand and followed the tube up to a drip; he was attached to a *drip*. The house! It was empty, it was essential that he got back to the house as soon as possible. He must remove the drip from his arm and maybe when everyone was busy with another patient, quietly leave.

'Can you tell us what you took?'

'No, sorry, sorry.'

'We rang the contact from your diary; do you live on your own? There needs to be someone at home when you leave.'

'Who?' he asked but someone else was causing a disturbance in the corner, and the nurse left his side to help manoeuvre a drunk with a bloody gash on his head onto a bed. The sight made David shrink even further into his embarrassment.

And suddenly there she was, wearing the belted trench coat with the collar turned up that he used to call her spy look, her Mata Hari coat, which he told her made her look sexy. He shut his eyes in disbelief for two long seconds, she'd be gone when he opened them, she'd see the mistake. His eyes flew open as he heard the rustle of her coat against the bedclothes as she leaned over him, blocking out the harsh hospital lighting.

'Not expecting me? You should have updated your diary, it was difficult to explain to a busy nurse over the phone so I decided to come.' She paused and their eyes snapped on one another and her face remained expressionless.

'The nurse kindly introduced me to your first emergency contact, a little girl. Her number was in the front of your diary but they need someone who can take you home. This little girl told me she is your *ex boyfriend's sister*. I did suggest she had the wrong person but no, she seems to know you quite well and supplied me with lots of interesting details. Do I believe them?'

'If you want,' her coolness was admirable, it matched the coat.

She moved back, '*so*, so now I know, it's nice to know, isn't it? I think I have a right to know don't you?'

'If you like.'

'And what's all this in aid of?' She took one hand out of her pocket and flipped it dramatically in his direction. 'No, don't tell me, I really don't care any more. I'm over it, *well* over it, I've better things to do these days and I don't want to be here if the *boyfriends* start turning up now do I?'

He turned his head away and caught the eye of a nurse, watching them and then looked at the drunk being mopped up opposite and heard the jingle of car keys swinging defiantly from her fingers and turned his head to watch as she walked out, her heels cracking smartly on the shiny floor. No scene, thank god, she had the sense to see it wasn't the place for a scene, that they would throw her out. He guessed she would manage to get to the car and then collapse and sit sobbing till she could hardly see.

'Have a sleep, I'll leave it up to you to call the person you want to come and see you and take you home,' said the nurse.

He woke in a ward with the desire to flee quite gone. Even the encounter with Clare seemed remote and he watched serenely as the staff moved briskly around.

It was breakfast time and the tea and toast and jam he was

offered were like nectar to his starved taste buds. He felt the crisp, clean sheets and an image of nights spent struggling in a dirty sleeping bag made his heart skip a beat. A doctor younger than him sat on the edge of his bed and explained how dangerous it was mixing a bunch of unknown pills with alcohol and he was in bad shape physically, had he been eating properly? Any longer and he might have got alcohol poisoning or a chest infection or jaundice and if you carried on drinking like that sclerosis of the liver and they'd organise some counselling and some anti depressants would help. Sorry was all he could think of to say and he said it repeatedly to everyone that took his pulse and blood pressure and temperature and changed his drip and brought his meal and cups of tea. While he was sitting in the chair beside his bed waiting to be discharged a nurse in theatre uniform appeared and perched on the end of his bed. She asked how he was very kindly and before he knew it he was stumbling out some story about the car breaking down and falling asleep and getting found by the police and she checked his drug chart and told him to take the pills and when she'd gone he guessed. It was the way she looked at him, as if she knew him very well indeed.

James took David's key and met resistance as he opened the front door, shoving it hard a few times first into the mound of post and then the packing box.

'What the fuck?' He pushed it all aside to let David in. 'I'll make some tea,' he said heading for the kitchen but stopped in astonishment at the living room doorway. The bloke had let his living room to a fucking tramp.

'Dave,' he said cautiously, 'Dave, when did you last go into your lodger's room? He's built some sort of *barricade* around his chair with beer cans and,' he moved further in, 'used your flattened *packing* cases attached with *duct tape*, round the other? And he's built some sort of corridor out of bundles of what looks like plastic packaging. It looks like an encampment that tramps build under flyovers.' He stopped to look back but David remained in the hall. 'I don't want to upset you mate but he's laid fucking *newspaper* on the floor! And there's this sticky yucky mess next to the chair where the dirty bugger has spilled his beer and food.' He stepped back into the hall, 'Dave, who the fuck are you renting this room to?...' but stopped, to watch his friend working his way up the stairs on his hands and knees with the effort required for a vertical rock face.

Abandoned now for over two months, David crawled into his bed with intense relief. James followed him upstairs and watched him as he lay, barely able to keep his eyes open. Didn't they sometimes find people, decomposing, weeks after they had died and wonder at the neglect of their friends? He guiltily pulled the chair in the room to the bedside and sat on its edge, leaning forward, elbows on knees, hands clasped as David dozed.

'Um, I think you might have had a sort of, well,' he dropped his head and said 'breakdown,' and examined the floorboards in detail as he waited nervously for an answer.

'I've been drinking too much, that's all, I've been on a bender.'

'The living room?' There was no lodger.

'Wh'bout the living room?'

'I'll give it a tidy up.'

'Leave it.'

The situation was seismically different to a shoulder to cry on and the bed settee for the night, what he had found frightened him. He wanted everything to be back like it used to be when he was the bloke's friend and a bit pleased with himself about it. He'd been keeping clear of the crowd and sulking at David's lack of communication after all he'd done for him. It had stopped him doing anything like forcing an entrance and had made the decision about Reading easier. He went to the shop and bought bin liners and filled them, furiously, with the detritus from the living room He repositioned the TV in front of the chair and turned it on to check it was working and found the aerial curled neatly in sellotape behind the screen. He fitted it, pushed the boxes into corners and hung the curtains from the box labelled 'curtains'. He woke him with a cup of tea.

'How you doing?'

'The cops or medics or whoever wrenched my arm as they were dragging me out of the car, it's really starting to hurt now the painkillers or whatever was in the drip are wearing off.'

There was no way to break the news gently, 'I don't want to make things any worse but that's the least of your problems, they're going to prosecute; you were drunk, your keys were in the ignition, it's not going to be nice, you're going to need a good solicitor and go down the total mental breakdown route. I promise, this time I'll be there, if you want me. It was a bit more than beer though wasn't it?'

David rolled onto his back and stared at the ceiling. What was left to hide? Tell him. 'It was what Mark called his box of delights. He put all the uppers and downers and ecstasy and whatever crap he got given or bought in this tin and he'd taunt me that I only knew what they were from pictures in booklets for schoolchildren and he was educating me, showing me actual real drugs. He left them in the car; I just threw the lot back.'

'It could have been worse, maybe some of them were only sugar, you know, he'd bought duds?'

'I think I threw them up before they did much damage to be honest.'

'Just as well your stomach's smarter than your brain. You weren't, you know….'

'Dunno, dunno what I was doing, seemed like a good idea at the time.'

'I think you may have got some things out of perspective…'

'I've had a letter, from Jack.'

'He copied me in for some reason.'

'He's threatening to sue me.'

'Bollocks, a desperate man looking for a scapegoat and

274

consumed with his own guilt and failure, lashing out at you was so easy. You opened my eyes to the problems; I did a bit of digging myself of course. We get letters sometimes like that at work from residents challenged in the art of reason, astonishing works of literature some of them, gives us a laugh anyway. Didn't take it to heart did you?'

'I'm being sued for slander. I had sex with a pupil. I've lost all my confidence in being a teacher. I let loads of people down. I lied and was deceitful to Clare and have ruined her life. I look at men. I can't leave the fucking house.'

'OK, it's not good, at the *moment*, but…'

'He trusted me, no, it was more than that, it was absolute conviction I would make it all right in the end. You see that's one of the privileges of being a teacher isn't it? The students trust you. Teachers don't stop in the middle of lessons and say 'I don't understand what I'm doing, I don't know what comes next, I don't know why I'm here.'

'Don't beat yourself up, the bloke's having a great time at uni. Like I said before, life goes on, you're old news. You will take the pills the hospital gave you won't you? No booze eh? You see I'd come over more often, now I know, but I've a bit of news. I've got another job, in Reading, in fact I'm moving next week into a rented flat, if you don't answer your phone and email what d'you expect people to do? I came round once but you were out. Anyway, let's go for a curry tonight.'

'I can't go out, not for long,' and he drifted off to sleep again.

Later that evening, with James's encouragement David made his way slowly down the stairs and the sight of the tidy up left him speechless at the living room doorway but the way it had been and it's purpose now completely escaped him.

'I found the landline stuck in a packing box, still connected.'

'It was ringing.'

'Well that's what they're supposed to do.'

'It was him, Jack, ringing and ringing but it's been quiet for a while.'

'Well it would be, listen, I guessed you didn't know, he had a massive heart attack at the end of February, his second it appears. Arteries like blocked drains from years of stress and cream cakes, I shouldn't think he'll be doing much suing, or much of anything for a while.' He ordered an Indian take away and watched David devour it with astonishing greed.

By early May he was back at the garden centre almost full time, but the medication slowed him down, he couldn't lift the 25 kg bags or shift the standard trees as easily as he had before so he agreed to take the till for half the day. There was the occasional parent who recognised him and a couple of members of staff he'd never known well who complemented him on his healthy lifestyle and sense in getting out of teaching etc. The days drifted pleasantly by and in the evening if there was anyone trying to get in he didn't hear them because the TV drowned them out and the medication ironed out every anxiety in its infancy. He began to buy a paper again, the political crises filling the pages six months ago had long burnt out and been replaced with new political crises, the bodies of the disappeared had finally been found and one natural disaster replaced by another.

Now he was back on line Abi had emailed to resume the maths help, encouraged it appeared by her mother, and it was turning into a trial. 'I don't want to talk about him,' he explained calmly from the start but she looked like him, she even sounded a bit like him and she'd witnessed the whole disaster. This was nothing though compared to the memory of the man with the pool boy, the gardener and Christ knows who else he employed for a pittance from the favelas; her very much alive father. The knowledge drilled holes in him, Mark clearly still hadn't told her he'd met him. Fortunately she seemed to have grown out of her fantasy future and was living entirely in the real world of Facebook. Letting Abi in one afternoon he watched her mother drive off, 'Mum got a new motor Abi?'

The answer didn't quite sink in to start with; it took a day, if not to cobble the truth together, certainly to admit to it to himself. No, it wasn't a new car, she'd had it for ages and yes she'd had it when he was paying his almost daily visits to the house and yes she'd known about him, possibly from the very start. It wasn't fair to dig it out of Abi but he did all the same and she finally admitted that her mother had turned herself as much inside out to keep out of his way as he had to keep out of hers. Not told him about the car change, not told him when she was in the house, all the ridiculous subterfuge when all along it was *him* Mark was hiding the truth from. What happened when he arrived? Did someone call 'he's here,' and were certain rooms vacated and doors closed quietly and did Angela Derby tiptoe around downstairs or drive off in the car parked outside that he had no idea was hers. It was a fast and furious rip tide of rage that crept up on him unexpectedly throughout that day. A fucking babysitter, that's all he'd been.

Totting up the amount of money he'd spent on Mark on the edge of his newspaper tweaked a nerve but the medication's mellowing effect allowed the truth to have a say. How many times had he said, 'what's mine's yours,' to stop Mark's money anxiety and he'd meant it because money was meaningless when you loved someone so much. As for the loss of Clare he genuinely struggled to place her now, a figure in the kitchen, a shape in the bed, his abiding memory was of her moving, her hair swinging as she busied herself toward her goal.

Now he was answering the door again but only if he could make out who it was through the frosted glass door panel. After a knock one Saturday afternoon he judged from the height it was his neighbour and opened the door with a smile ready.

'Just wanted a quiet word with you,' she said, with icy reasonableness, 'best if I come in.'

Without thinking he stepped outside holding the door almost closed behind him, he did not want Clare to see how he lived.

'Not going to invite me in?'

'There's nothing to say,' that would be enough; she was too polite to challenge his refusal.

'*Basterd! You basterd!*'

He let her in immediately, slamming the door behind her and once inside the shrieking stopped and now on his territory she seemed at a loss, as if a rehearsed explosion had failed to detonate. The decent thing would have been to take her into the kitchen but he stood his ground, not wanting her to see the unpacked boxes. However the hallways of late nineteenth century workers' cottages weren't designed for receptions and they were forced into an uncomfortable proximity. Just jeans and a jacket this time he noted but unable to meet her gaze he focused on her handbag, her birthday before last present from him.

'I want to talk to you. I want to tell you something, I want to tell you that I feel dirty, you've made me *dirty*.' He pulled an uncomprehending face and she proceeded, with almost medical accuracy, to list the sexual heath risks he had potentially inflicted on her and the consequences to her life and fertility. She had numbers and percentages to heart; level of risk, numbers affected, the side effects of cures, life expectancy. Did he know how many opportunities for the transfer of bodily fluids there were, quite apart from the obvious, such as cuts from vigorous tooth cleaning and tortilla chips? He was astonished, she's really read up on this he thought, really put some effort into it, she must have got it off the internet, this sort of thing, it wasn't anything they'd ever touched on, it was to do with other people, not people like them, like her. You gave something for Comic Relief and read articles in the Sunday magazines but it didn't apply to *them*.

Listening to her reduce his love affair to the passing of diseases, which he had apparently passed on to her upset him, unexpectedly so. Good memories resurfaced to counteract the onslaught. Clare's grubby interpretation of the happiest days of his life sickened him. She must be got rid of but her knuckles were white where she was clutching the strap of her bag and her feet were set slightly apart as if braced against an instinct to flee. The best thing to do would be to say nothing until she'd run herself dry he decided, try not to react, look vague, she must guess he was taking anti depressants.

She ground to a halt finally. Her voice, dramatically cold and steely while explaining the medical facts now suddenly spiralled into a miserable whine, 'you have no idea how terrible it's been!' Releasing leaden lumps of information between shuddering gulps she painted a picture of her daily mortification since August as people either avoided her or attempted clichéd words of comfort. There were short notes, phone calls, invites for coffee, but she had been too miserable to respond and it was only smugness and insincerity, wasn't it? And, despite the universal reassurances that it had been nothing to do with her, at first, she had taken full responsibility, blaming herself on a minute by minute basis for not understanding that the wedding and the money and the gifts had not been what he wanted, that he really wanted something simple, just the two of them. She described in wretched detail the incomprehension of the two bridesmaids; 'their little faces, frozen with misery and their struggles not to cry,' and the embarrassment of the dressmaker, left with her dress and the children's dresses that although fully paid for she had to take back because Clare could not bear to see them again, 'all the hours and hours of fittings and debates over the exact numbers of *bees* and *flowers* to be embroidered on the train. We sent back the presents that had already arrived and we had a little party for the employees so they could still wear the outfits they had bought especially which was excruciating and I've been for a drink with Naseem and Natalie and Sophie, who said they wanted to keep in contact with me but they said they hadn't seen you. Mum and Dad, they didn't understand, they couldn't believe it. Nobody could but they had to ring them all, three hundred guests, and every time we had to try to offer some plausible explanation - yes its all terribly shocking, yes out of the blue, no we don't know exactly why but respect their *privacy* about the reasons - when there was none,' and she lifted her head and spat, '*not then.*'

He braced himself. 'Dad,' she gulped and he forced a sympathetic expression but it took her a while to compose herself. 'Dad, why did you let that get so out of hand?'

This was too much, he held her eyes, 'you actively *encouraged* it!'

'I was only doing what I thought was for the best,' she whined. She wasn't blaming him for the heart attack she said, he was already on the transplant list but had wanted it kept quiet but the silent factory, the receivers wandering around, the sense of failure, it couldn't have helped. 'Dad asked over and over; "was joining the business the reason? He never said, he need only have said, I would have understood." But no, all along, *all along* you had been deceiving me, with a *boy*!'

'I'm sorry.'

'Oh my god, *oh my god!*' She stared, '*sorry?*'

The anti depressant cosh was dulling the impact, or was it all too long ago, Mark's rejection the only rejection he cared about or remembered any more. Should he tell her about the slow disengagement that he had been barely aware of, neither of their faults, hadn't she felt the same if she was truthful? It was called drifting apart and yes, they'd been a good team but that was teamwork, not love. We lived in the same house, slept in the same bed and dreamed on different continents.

'You simply don't *care*, do you? You just want me to go away.' She had moved slightly closer and he felt the 'care' on his face and moved back a step and the wheel of his bike, propped up against the wall, touched his leg. His bike, for a year the get away vehicle and a cover for his deceit, propped up in the hallway, awaiting instructions. He'd been about to adjust the brake cable, give the tyres a pump and a touch of oil to the chain, have a test run round the park ready for the ride to work the following day.

'I was about to go out for a bike ride.'

Expecting the indulgent smile of yesteryear her furious sneer finally made him concentrate on the matter in hand. She was going to hit him, across the face, but that would be OK, he could take it and it would mean throwing her out would be easier. Where have you gone, he thought, the person who made me think once upon a time, I can live with you, you understand me, you're secure enough to give me the space I need, yes, I can live with you. Everything has unhinged you, you're listening to people you wouldn't have given the time of day to before; it's taken away all the bits I liked so much about you. And then she put her hand in her pocket, and his teeth gave an involuntary clatter, she had a knife, in her pocket; she had come to kill him and the doziness of the pills was wiped out with a stab of fear. She was unhinged with grief and anger, she wanted revenge; there was no point in fighting back and risking a fatal cut, he would say whatever was necessary to get her out of the house, he would tell her exactly what she wanted to hear. Yes, yes, it had been a moment of insanity that he had regretted ever since, he had got caught up in it, could not see a way out, it was a mid life crisis brought on by stress and overwork at a difficult school and his selfishness over the wedding which had got too big and was not about him anymore. He would blame the boy; he had made emotional demands, threatened to do himself harm if they did not continue their affair, threatened to expose him as a predator, threatened his career. He took a deep breath, 'We just played a bit of squash, it took me completely by surprise...'

'Oh *shut up*.' Her voice sliced the air, there was a hint of satisfaction, she was getting through. 'Teaching, what *opportunities*, bet you even chose a mixed school as a cover, homing in on someone vulnerable, I hear he lives on the Hastings Estate, probably in awe of you. Like running off with your secretary or the nanny, they always say, men don't look far.'

Temporarily deserted by the medications the fear was causing his breathing to shallow, he stifled a deep breath; she would interpret it as a bored sigh. Surely he could easily overpower her but a quick exit by her hand would bring an end to the crippling guilt. She probably knew she would be convicted of manslaughter with extenuating circumstances and spend a few years in a nice open prison with friendly guards and educational opportunities. She could get that law degree she'd prattle on about after a few glasses of wine. At his funeral everything would be forgiven, everybody would remember what a decent guy he'd been, what an inspirational teacher, just one little off piste moment, it could happen to anyone.

And then she stopped and leaned back heavily against the wall and he saw how tired she looked. Faint purple stains under her eyes, her eyelids slightly heavy and he knew her well enough to see nights disturbed with weeping. Was she on some medication too he wondered and then thought not, it would have dulled her rage, now he was in a position to know. Her arms now hung by her sides, there was no knife of course, only her tongue. Abi's revelation had hit her very hard, she would have thought of nothing else. A boy. She would not have understood a boy. She could not live without confronting him about a boy. Another woman would have been just a good excuse to get out of the relationship; she must now see that a boy was completely different; a boy must have been love. Tell her, tell her the truth and she would go.

'D'you know, I could have almost accepted one of the girls, pathetic but obvious, a weak man easily tempted. But one of the *boys*, the *boys!* It was only sex of course, I mean what in gods name did you have to *talk* about with a *schoolboy* but as I said, it was convenient, you didn't have to look too far for it. Now I realise I was too stupid, too naïve, to realise you were *gay*, all along. I didn't notice any of the signs most women would have picked up on quickly, so I'm told, too inexperienced to have seen that I was just a smokescreen. You put on a good show for a queer, for a long time had *me* fooled.'

Queer? Nobody used that word and he'd never heard her use it, it was a word from the days when it was a crime, how extraordinary, a crime.

The time had come to say something; he was beginning to understand how often his staying silent had caused confusion and upset and to think of it as mature and controlled was cowardly. Look at her, the effort it must have taken to come to the house, it was brave and whatever he said must give them both a way out so they could part with a modicum of dignity, for once he must drop his own stubbornness and admit his mistakes.

'I haven't given you any sexually transmitted diseases Clare, you know I haven't, if you really don't believe me get yourself tested and see. I fell in love with someone else and if it makes you feel any better it's all over now anyway, he dumped me. Now please go, this is awful, for both of us.'

She stared blankly ahead, exhausted, and it brought back that terrible evening when she had faded with shock in front of his eyes. His calm words were working, she'd be gone in a few minutes, just let her gather herself together. But she put her handbag gently on the floor and his heart sank, there was more.

Softly, 'but what do you *really* want out of life. Look what we had, what have you got now? It's over with him, there's no one else is there? Can't you remember the good times we had, look how we worked on the house together, look how people wanted to *be* with us, look at the friends we had, look how we liked to spend evenings in together, just us. Why did you do this? For what end? And where are you now? This *tiny little* house, you're *unemployed*, no one sees you any more, your friends, *our* friends.'

He was recovering from a breakdown, she must see he'd lost weight, James said he looked haggard. She was bullying him, if she hit him he couldn't fight her off, his arms felt leaden as the adrenalin flooded away and the medication began to take hold again. Don't argue, let the decision to leave be hers, then she'd never bother him again.

'What do you *really* want?' she said again, imploringly, almost sweetly, as if the past five ranting minutes had not occurred. 'We've been through so much over the past months, neither of us is happy.'

Surely she's not, he thought, then again why not? Neither of them had anyone else, she was opening a door and all he had to do was walk through, it would be so easy. She would probably let him have his way about the house and taking a year off for his MSc in another city and delay having children and they could marry somewhere remote, James would still have his day, albeit a much smaller one. A great deal of humble pie would have to be eaten, a great deal of grovelling would have to be done and it would be pretty excruciating but they would get there. He wouldn't have to say too much, just look guarded and even broken as though he had been through a hellish personal journey to be finally ready for commitment. People would be very careful with him, for her sake, they'd let him quietly settle back into the fold. In years to come they would probably have a laugh about it, his blip, his one terrible lapse of judgement, but it had to happen, didn't it, to get that wayward streak out of the way, something he should have done as a teenager and now they were better and more secure for it. Or maybe it would just be dragged out in times of stress and used to bring him to order, to show him what he could have forgone and the life he nearly missed out on. Or it would hang over them, like a dead body for the rest of their life together, Clare watching for any more pretty boys lurking round her man, keeping him controlled and confined.

'I want my boyfriend back, that's what I really want,' he said quietly and she opened the door and was gone.

Chapter Twenty

Hi Dave, Jason comes back on 23, prefer not to stay with his parents can u put him up for a few days?
Cheers
Mark

It was a few days old, both outrageous and dull. But he stopped breathing as he read it, and reread it. Was it a truce, a wind up, a reconciliation or a bloke asking another bloke if his mate could kip on his sofa for a few days because he was short of cash? The enormity of how to reply, or indeed whether to reply, hung heavy and he sat almost incapacitated by the weight of this decision and by the infuriatingly unspeakable thrill of his email. The morning drifted by in a mixture of the luxurious daze of the renewed contact, spoiled by a needling voice. You arsehole, leave me alone, I'm beginning to get back to something like my old self, starting to manage just fine. He imagined him in a cheap internet café, surfing shorts, t- shirt, tanned, it would be hot and the fans would be stirring thick air and there would be a cold beer at his elbow. He saw him turn and break into one of those dizzying smiles. *'Plonker,'* he would say, 'can't we still be mates?'

Deal with it, whatever the reason he was at least thinking about him in some capacity. 'Start opening doors,' the NHS councillor had said, 'let the world back in, say yes to things.' Although she'd been careful about the specifics of his breakdown, these days psychological problems were prime time telly, soap story arcs and Sunday supplement staples and he knew what had happened to him. Now he watched and monitored himself for that behaviour he had lost control of though of course the medication had stopped it in its tracks. This time he followed his email send rules; he was sober, he'd given it plenty of thought, it was OK if the entire world read it. 'Sure' he typed, matching Mark's casualness and brevity, possibly leaving him, too, a little curious. I might of course be driven out of insane jealousy to murder him, he mused, but it will be a crime of passion, engineered entirely by you and I will do my PhD in a nice open prison.

It was September again and again there were no new starts. He had, following various advice, postponed his start at Manchester, he knew in his heart anyway that he wasn't ready, the low dose anti depressants were making him lazy and although he was only back part time at the garden centre in between his concentration was poor. He was managing to get the behaviour in control, he took a cleaner who stopped any hoarding in its tracks and he spent as much time as he could out of the house on his bike.

Jason was exhausted, he had barely slept on the flight back and his rucksack, full of souvenirs, had never been heavier. He was relieved to be returning to the UK, travelling had become increasingly hard work with his recurring bouts of illness and he longed for the same bed for a few nights in a row. It had been a great summer, he'd dealt with the split philosophically and soon found replacement travelling companions but now he was focused on getting his foot on the career ladder. He could have slept on his parents' sofa but his father would plague him with questions about starting work and the predatory schoolteacher was more likely to leave him alone to sleep off the jet lag for a few days. In fact he imagined himself spending most of the four days he was staying asleep, the bloke would be at work, they would probably hardly see one another. He would be cordial though, the guy was putting him up after all which was remarkably decent of him in the circumstances but those circumstances had completely changed for both of them. He vowed yet again to keep Mark off limits as a topic of conversation. As he walked from the station down the street of small terraced cottages he saw that his resolve to be distant might be difficult living at such close quarters and at the door his nerves seriously kicked in and he regretted his decision, it just wasn't a good idea any more. He knocked, ready with an excuse about a friend putting him up instead to be faced with a man who looked like he too had regretted his decision.

David had arranged with Alistair to work full time over the four days, an easy excuse to keep out of his way and Jason probably had friends in town, they'd barely see each other. He'd show him where everything was and let him get on with it. The churning jealousy that had overwhelmed him like a madness a year ago was difficult to recall precisely, he marvelled now at his being capable of such extreme emotion. Was the guy a sort of peace offering? Wouldn't that be so characteristic of Mark and so typical of him to think the worst? He'd said yes and he would stick to his decision, his councillor had been supportive. He spent the morning moving things around with the intention of achieving a homely feel but with half the boxes still unpacked it still looked liked he'd only just moved in.

The London train Jason was catching got into the station at one thirty, by one fifteen David was ready to leave the key under the mat with a note on the door and flee through the back gate to the camp bed in Alistair's shed for the duration. Did opening doors actually include letting thine old love rival doss for a few days in the spare room? It could put a lid on that whole episode though, a couple of beers and they would be laughing about it all. He opened the door to the knock damning his enduring pessimism. A towering rucksack, a tanned face surrounded by greasy dishevelled curls, the bloke looking as if he had made a terrible mistake.

David spent the day at work wondering if he would still be there when he got home. Had he been hospitable enough? Had he given him the impression he was genuinely welcome? Did he think he was merely curious about him and once satisfied would want him to disappear? By the time he got to his front door he was convinced that that there would be a polite note on the kitchen table. The rucksack was missing, he wasn't in the sitting room and he ran up to the spare room two at a time. The door was wide open, he was lying, his arms flung wide apart, abandoned to jet lag, partly covered by the duvet. David stood at the door, relieved, watching him for a while, his rival, his nemesis was just a tired bloke for whom things hadn't turned out as he'd hoped either, who had maybe wanted to assuage his curiosity about David himself. He watched him for a few minutes, how miserable the bloke had made him but now he felt nothing, possibly curiosity but even that was slight. He decided to wake him up so he would sleep that night and get back into the right sleep pattern; he said his name and touched his arm.

That evening David went through the cooker dials, thermostats, door locks and how Jason should help himself to the contents of the fridge and what time David left and got home. Jason was still emotionally in South America, he remarked how quiet the street was and how empty everywhere was in the evening. He told him a few stories that only emphasised what David had missed by not travelling with Mark.

'In Chile this guy showed us around his village and how they were using the wool to make hats and gloves and how the whole village was involved, he didn't want to show us the poverty but we could see it. That was kinda moving. I wish I'd taken more photos, you know sort of arty photos where nobody's looking at the camera, like professionals do. You're a photographer aren't you? You'd know how to do that.'

There had been difficult times though, he admitted to being pick pocketed and the anxious days spent getting money transferred and a night spent trying to sleep rough and being frightened by a bunch of drunks and sleeping all that day in the safety of a busy park hoping the police wouldn't move them on. David told some of his India stories like the Indian guide's anxiety over his prospective son-in-law wanting a scooter and a TV as part of his daughter's dowry and how worried the man was and how real it made the dowry system, like reading in a book didn't. And the man who designed wooden printing blocks with meticulous accuracy, someone had remarked that in another world he could have been a computer programmer. And Juan's cousin of course, her aspirations in the world of fashion.

David was trying to keep off the drink but Jason was filling the fridge with beer which was difficult to refuse and he worried his tongue would be loosened because he didn't want anything getting back to Mark. He didn't want it to look like he'd been fishing for information, like he cared for information. It only took two cans these days and he ended up telling Jason about the bedside rejection scene which he significantly abridged and managed to make amusing and even offhand. He wanted to hear the closing lines from Jason and Mark's relationship but there was no revelation, a couple of cans did nothing to Jason, he had to wait till after midnight for his inhibitions to fade even a little.

'Why haven't you unpacked?'

'No point, nothing I want.'

'So wassin the boxes?'

'Stuff I don't need, crap from the past.'

'Your neighbour...'

'Nosy fucker.'

'Said you'd been ill.'

'Can't remember much. I stayed in, drank too much, no harm in staying in is there and then I went to get some food and was having a kip in the car and the next thing I'm in hospital.'

'Why?'

'Police found me; drunk with the keys in the ignition.'

'Because of *him*?'

'Nothing to do with *him*.'

'You know, I thought you were like some fucking *paedo*, with a paunch and bad teeth and one of those kit bags full of home made porno videos.'

'And Mark would go for that type?'

'OK, it made me feel better.'

'Listen it was a one off, thassall, I thought why not? You'll never *know* otherwise.'

'Didn't it kinda fuck everything up? Didn't she have a bit of cash behind her?'

'They *thought* they did. No interest to me.'

'The girls hit on him you know, he kept it *very* quiet.'

'Spoilt it for you then?'

'For both of us. He was a *twat*, you didn't really know him.'

'I *knew* him sunshine, I *knew* him. Did he ever mention me?'

'Coupla times.'

'What d'he say then?'

'That you couldn't *Leave. Him. Alone.*'

'Other way round I'm afraid. Beggin' for it, *gaggin'* for it, never got a moment's fucking peace.'

'*Weren't* you the lucky one?'

'Then he wrapped you in a nice email and posted you through my door.'

'I'm not a fucking present.'

The next morning he dangled the car keys over Jason's slumbering form and said he was too hung over to drive and didn't fancy the cycle because it was pissing down and could he drive him to work but there wasn't much point in keeping that rubbish going, so he told him. A year, very lucky not to have got two the police told him as he emerged from the court room.

'You see,' he perched on the corner of Jason's bed, 'I'm a schoolteacher; faintly heroic, they hear stories and imagine it's like trench warfare in the classroom of the twenty first century. We're too precious, they want to keep us in battle theatre, no excuses like can't get there on the bus.'

Alistair dropped him home that evening and Jason was out, at his parent's he presumed. He stuck his gear in the washing machine, hung it up to dry, made enough dinner for two just in case, waited for him to come in, left the door on the latch and went to bed annoyed with himself and fell asleep waiting for the sound of the front door. But Jason was in the kitchen early the next morning still struggling with jet lag and as they cleared away dishes he bumped his forehead very briefly on David's shoulder as an expression of his fatigue. Neither mentioned drink that evening, they watched TV and then Jason suggested showing him some of his photos on the computer; the camp, the kids, fellow staff and a few of Mark.

The next evening he came home to find him asleep on the sofa which had been buried under books since he'd moved in. The flattened boxes were stacked in a corner, his bookcase assembled and filled and the kitchen cupboards and drawers full of cutlery and kitchen utensils. Even with James starting the process he still hadn't been able to complete the task and gratitude mixed with irritation at the interference. He sat in his chair quietly watching him for a long time then woke him again, not just to balance his sleep pattern this time.

On the morning of the fourth day, the day he was due to leave for London, David lay in bed listening to him packing his rucksack and, getting up, peered into the spare room, 'keep the fleece and the socks.' he said. They ate toast and drank coffee standing up in the kitchen and David ran up the stairs twice to check he hadn't left anything behind.

'You've been great, thanks a million, thanks for the clothes.'

'No trouble, thanks for unpacking the boxes, come again, you know where I am. Hope you get some work soon.'

At the door he lifted his rucksack taking its weight while

Jason balanced it on his shoulders, but the person who'd come through the door wasn't the person who was leaving and he laid his hand on a padded shoulder strap keeping it there, a goodbye and a question. Jason stopped. They stood for a heartbeat, then the plastic clack of buckles being undone and the rucksack slid down his back to the floor. Cupping his hand round his neck David drew him towards him and stumbling over the rucksack they sank against the wall together.

'Stay?'

Jason kissed him, 'what took you so long?' he murmured.

'Had to make sure.'

'I'll miss my train.'

'Just another day? I can take the day off. I want you to so much.'

He bent his knees and gently lifted him for a moment, grinning at him with surprise and pleasure then lacing his fingers into his he led him upstairs to his room.

'This is possibly a very bad idea,' Jason said, with no conviction a lot later, as they dozed in a jumble of naked limbs.

'You've found the right man there; I'm a bit of an expert on the bad idea. Let's see, bothering to try to convince people who sit in offices all day that bored fourteen year olds are worth all the effort, or topping up someone's cracked self belief in their falling business so they could throw it all back in my face when it didn't work out or hiding away from everybody when nobody was in fact looking for me. You, on the other hand, are a good idea.' He must tell him, and the sooner the better (because he had taken his last one two days ago, he promised himself) about how the pills lopped the top and the bottom off his emotions leaving a vanilla middle which was carrying him very serenely through the days and didn't do much for his erection.

'I've been on medication.'

'I guessed.'

'Apart from the obvious disadvantage it does make me

more, well, amenable.'

'No denying the irony of all this though.'

'Scratch a foe and find a lover; Dorothy Parker.'

'Isn't it the other way round?'

'Yeah but it doesn't fit that way.'

'We can't live on irony but I'd like to give it a go, I'd like to see you again, is that too heavy?'

'Jason, I've had delusions, I turned this house into my prison, I'm virtually unemployed and sexually, I'm right on that fence.'

'Is it over? That's all that matters to me.'

'It's as over as the Roman Empire, all that's left is the attractive ruins - me.'

He came up again the following Friday and wanted to spend most, but not the entire weekend, in bed so David was forced out, literally, into the world again. There was no need to be secretive, suffer hot attacks of guilt, to make elaborate plans to meet, to tremble with anticipation or to suffer the sweet angst of enforced separation. They were single men and nobody, frankly, gave a damn. It was going to be very, very hard.

Early morning lane swimmers ploughed up and down the main pool, he had the toddler pool to himself for half an hour and there was no one to see his deep reluctance. Inching his way down the steps he lay in the shallow water and supporting himself on his hands let the bath-warm water sway him around. He lowered his face so the water covered his mouth, it was OK, he could feel the bottom and see the side and with the instructor beside him he walked across the pool on his hands, his body floating. Now he was in it was fine, the hardest part had been emerging from the changing room, the - please shower before you enter the pool - the final gate, the luke warm soak ending any thoughts of legging it back in. Hanging onto floats he was soon kicking his way across the width of the pool beside the instructor and finally, taking a deep breath, immersed his head completely. He could not wait to tell Jason whose casual suggestion for a swim one morning had resulted in him booking the private lesson. The instructor, having anticipated hours of coaxing was delighted and obligingly David allowed him the achievement. The low dose medication probably deserved the honour most, along with a year of trauma that put a few things in perspective.

It had been remarkably easy to tell Jason. 'My elder brother drowned in a swimming accident. It was a really hot day and I was going to go with him but I decided not to in the end because I wanted to stay in the cool and not get on a bus. They think he slipped as he dived in backwards, his favourite trick, and banged his head and by the time they'd got him out it was too late and if I had been there, it wouldn't have happened because my simply being there would have inevitably changed the course of events. I could never swim again, for my parents, it was inconceivable to do that to them.'

His parents pulled down the shutters and closed shop. There was no cry for help, no outward sign of distress, it would have been unthinkable, simply offensive to suggest to such a strong family who demonstrated the ultimate in moving on that they might need help. Aren't they coping well, look how they support each other, how determined to keep things normal for David, even bought him a dog. Getting on with life, what an example to all of us when we moan at minor problems   And now, nearly twenty years later, none of them were any the wiser about how each other had coped through those dark lost years. The impact on all three of them was, of course, devastating. They each quietly died with him, alone, unable to share grief they could barely see in each other. He had carried on, he had the dog, he passed his exams, he wasn't picked up by the police drunk in gutters, no unusual behaviour suggesting drug use and he appeared to have dealt with it remarkably well. As the years passed any memory of how he had been before was lost, he had no idea if the way he was now, was him or him as shaped by what had happened.

'It never leaves me, I check everything I do against it, it has become the base I touch. Sometimes it's a torment because I can never let go because to do so would be disloyal to his memory of which I now consider myself sole custodian.'

Chapter Twenty One

'I can't spare you much time,' he warned Jason and proceeded to spend every weekend in the smoke with him, a world city on his doorstep he hardly knew. He was now completely off the anti depressants and trying to moderate his alcohol intake too but the recovery to the man he was before wasn't happening as fast as he hoped. The medications had put paid to the anxieties and repetitive thoughts but it was difficult to keep them at bay when he was alone in the evenings. He went to London because his prediction that she'd take all his friends with her - how meaningless at the time when he had his future mapped out with Mark - had come to pass. He was now David no mates and he was on the train every Friday night throughout autumn because a girlfriend was unimaginable, a teaching post filled him with dread and he took the post with him because he couldn't bring himself to open it without Jason at his side. The uni crowd had been shed; there were no stale friendships staggering blindly on, his little 'breakdown' kept them all away. If he'd had a car accident they'd have organised shopping and cooking rotas but no one liked a breakdown so there were no rotas. All there was now was Jason and the perverseness of it made him more committed.

One evening in October after a day of exhibitions and coffees and walks along the Thames they ended up in a club. The new crowd, David discovered was surprisingly the same as the old crowd; they cursed their line managers, calculated mortgage payments and checked airfares same as the old crowd but there was less football talk which was a bonus, but whatever he was looking for, he hadn't found it. He smiled, shook hands and swayed obligingly to the pounding beat for a while before pinning himself to a wall with a drink and a frown as he waited to be retrieved by the sociable Jason. They were silent in the taxi home and in bed that night David showed how much he liked Jason's body and how right it was for him. It was outside the bedroom he was struggling.

'My friends don't believe it's like this,' Jason said.

'D'you care?'

'No and yes.'

'I'm not going to put myself about to prove I'm the real thing either.'

'D'you still, you know, like girls?'

Girls, their complete absence from his current life if not exactly making his heart grow fonder was certainly stimulating his curiosity and he watched and listened to them at every opportunity. The way they laughed at themselves so easily, the way other things clearly mattered as much or more than their jobs, the way they supported and comforted each other, the way they held half a dozen subjects in play at once, the way you didn't feel you were competing with them, they were just too different.

One afternoon, dozing over beers outside a pub in that special enjoyment of late autumn sunshine David crooked his arm affectionately around Jason's neck deciding he wanted to say they were 'together'. He noticed that an interestingly side effect of this public show of affection was he instantly felt more confident looking at women and he let his eyes linger longer than he ever had. A pretty girl with tumbling shiny hair walked past and when she glanced his way he turned and pressed his mouth against Jason's curls like a child caught with his hand in the sweet tin. Women, had he really lived with one? Yet they were everywhere and he gawped openly with this new authorization. He was also waiting for a sign, a stirring of interest where interest was supposed to stir but nothing happened, it was both comforting and worrying.

'D'you look at women ever?' he murmured in Jason's ear.

'Only if they get in the way of the men. Why, are you looking at them?'

'It's like I've never really *looked* at them, so many varieties.'

'Like tomatoes?'

'Of course, exactly like fucking tomatoes. I mean now I've kinda got permission to look.'

'Only academic?'

'Course, don't fret. As a straight man there's protocols, unless you're very pissed. Now I feel I've got the freedom to check them out, in detail: what if she lost some weight? Or what about more subtle highlights? Is she hot or is it only the heels? I've never dared look like that before; I'm far too politically correct.'

'Girls always want my opinion; I say what they want to hear, what do I care?'

'Now it's like I'm watching videos of them. Close but not too close.'

'And you lived with one.'

And slept in the same bed with her every night and put the tampons neatly back in the box when they all spilt out onto the floor and debated when required how blonde she should go and suggested maybe *too* much cleavage for work and hung her underwear on the drying rack and tied her hair back with a band for her that time she was vomiting.

'I've never you seen you check out the guys. I like that and I don't.'

To order a nice looking lad came into view with a beanie hat which accentuated his jaw and a black puffa vest and unhooking his arm and his togetherness from Jason to reach for his drink David ran his eyes up and down him as he passed.

Bahrain had been mentioned at Jason's interview, they never doubted that a single man would be happy for a short stint and he'd agreed in order to get the job. Now a date had been set, only for three months but he was acting like they were sending him to the Gulag. David was getting uneasy, not about Jason himself, more that he was getting increasingly sucked into London life and the expectation that he'd move there to teach or do his MSc at a London university. Bahrain seemed like the natural break and he tried hard to get that balance between packing him off with relief and planning a holiday together in Dubai. In the end a long session with his laptop confirmed he was back in working order again. He was experimenting with a more challenging journalistic edginess and emailed the result to Jason who was enthusiastic.

During that last evening with Jason before he flew out tension was high, David had no idea what to do, it was impossible to explain how much he dreaded him going and how much he wanted a civilised end. He couldn't begin to shape a sentence that conveyed all the subtleties of his confusion about his sexual identity, how he didn't feel loyalties either way or that he really didn't care, it wasn't a priority and this all translated as silence. Without Jason to phone and email and fill his weekends he would start drinking again because he would be stinking lonely and that couldn't be admitted either, because it implied that he'd used him. They watched a TV comedy that didn't make them laugh and when Jason switched it off and they were sitting in a terrifying silence before going to bed Jason said quietly,

'I wasn't a present, actually I was a messenger.'

'What?'

'Yeah, I was supposed to give you a message, from him, it was *yes* to getting back together.'

'That's a shock Jase, yeah that's a shock, and when was it supposed to be delivered?'

'Pretty much straight away, you know kill the messenger? Well this was supposed to be; be nice to the messenger because he's telling you what you want to hear.'

'Must have been a *very* quick decision not to deliver it.'

'Instant.'

'That's nice. D'you think it would have made any difference to us, if you had delivered it?'

'Would it?'

'I dunno, isn't that what makes life so extraordinary?'

It was a generous thing to finally admit in the circumstances and it let David off the hook in once sense but on the other made it harder.

By the end of the year David had taken over all the day-to-day bookkeeping, invoicing, ordering and the payroll at the garden centre and had become that very rare item in the workplace, indispensable, and was very nervous about it. Since he had full access to the books, he could also see that the business was struggling, there were plenty of people coming through the doors but, like he and Clare used to, they were treating it like a day out, they weren't spending enough. His suggestion to put an, albeit horticultural themed, rack of greetings cards near the till threw Alistair into confusion and to disappear into a far off greenhouse for a few hours. David did the maths and placed the evidence in front of Alistair, the mark up was outrageous and they didn't need watering. However the warning bells had sounded, he was getting too involved.

No one worked particularly hard; they followed Alistair's measured pace and took frequent tea breaks especially during the week when there were no customers for hours. By February he was finding the paperwork repetitive and Alistair's glacial decision-making increasingly irritating. One rainy afternoon he stuck a deckchair in one of the farthest greenhouses, and sat at eye level with the pots and their youthful contents which stretched in neat rows to the end of the house.

He wanted to hear his voice, was it still steady and confident and did he still have that touch of humour? 'Well,' he said softly and then more firmly to be heard above the rain splattering on the glass, 'and how are we all today?' He waited to check if he was completely alone, no one appeared. There was no response from the five hundred plastic pots either but they weren't fidgeting so he carried on. 'Today let's look at the phenomenal growth of cities in Africa, Asia and South America, how are they coping with the influx of migrants from rural areas? How and why are people prepared to tolerate terrible living conditions and without them would the city be able to function? Do they need the city or does the city need them?' Eventually, the lack of feedback silenced him. He knew the topic well but now he would have his own experience and photos to liven his lessons up, he could do it, once he was in there, in front of them.

One afternoon as he was moving the bedding plants into a display at the door, Ralf appeared and put on a reasonable act of being surprised at seeing him. Was he on recognisance? Here was the man who had briefly had him at his mercy. David inquired if he was enjoying university.

'We've got some great bands playing this term and I'm in this crazy house share and we have these like *amazing* parties that start on Friday and just keep going and loads of people have been slung off my course,' David examined the slightly grubby, tousled look; so, he'd hauled his sad arse out of bed at midday and got his shit together enough to check out his teacher who'd like, resigned before being pushed. He was very different from the quite particular sixth former he remembered, or wanted to appear to be. This is what it would be like if Mark turned up he thought, exactly like this, it would be horrendous, appalling.

'Any career plans?'

Ralf mentioned the graduate milk round and possibly out of kindness, teaching. However the crisis at the end of the school year that had briefly brought them together was all David could think about, long forgotten by Ralph he guessed in the riot of university life.

'How's Mark doing?' It had to be asked for form's sake, he couldn't be sure the meeting would be relayed back but not to ask was suspicious. He braced himself, he didn't want to know anything, he really didn't.

'He's got in with a big crowd, really enjoying it. Have you, given up teaching?'

'I'm taking a break.'

They looked at each other and the gap between the teacher and his former pupil narrowed with a snap, it wouldn't be long before he and this confident youth would competing together in the job market. As soon as Ralf had left he rang Manchester and confirmed he would be taking up the place in the coming September.

Manchester suited perfectly. It was time he went north and it put distance from London and Jason when he returned from Bahrain and the course was the best fit. They were bound to bump into each other at some point but they were in different departments and so what, they had both moved on, in David's case to the ex who was also on the way to being *his* ex. What he wanted now more than anything was to tuck himself in the corner of a quiet library and monkishly engross himself in his work. If he got the reputation for being an old bore, bring it on, this time round he'd be a stranger to the union bar. However he had taken a step much further than make an application to Manchester, he'd invested in the place, he'd followed Alex down the path of buy to let and bought a flat in the city.

He did not renew the tenancy and moved straight in himself at the start of term. Enough time had passed for the reveal scene he'd planned for Mark to have faded, even so he ran up the stairs and jammed the key into the lock as unceremoniously as possible. There was still a reveal though, it was the first time he'd set eyes on it himself. Although prepared for the estate agent's tricks with a wide angle lens it was smaller than he hoped but light flooded in from the balcony windows and he went straight to open the doors to see the view that had sold the flat to him. It was OK, hardly Florence and the seven hills but different enough to the Victorian frontages at home to be exciting. Turning back into the room he admired the chairs, identical to Tony's and the kitchen, as specified, not too stainless steel, there was warmth in the painted wooded cabinet doors.

Dear David,
You may remember me; we met in a café in Sao Paulo nearly a year ago. I looked at your home phone number and by an amazing coincidence you live in my home town! Without going into details an incident last year has finally persuaded me to pay a visit to the old country, there are a few things I need to do and I feel confident about leaving my team to run the business. Maybe you're still in Brazil but if you have returned home, I wonder if you could recommend somewhere   reasonable to stay, not too far from the station. Maybe we could meet up for a pint, I don't know anyone in the UK anymore and I enjoyed your company. I'll give you a ring when I arrive.

Regards,
Martin Derby

David groaned and slumped back into his chair, his little con had gone so well he'd practically forgotten about it but like the scissors left inside after the successful operation it had now inched its way to the surface. He couldn't ignore it; the man had his phone number and email address and he had probably come across as a sociable and likeable fellow. David rehearsed his confession.

Listen, I've got to tell you something, meeting you in Sao Paulo wasn't what it seemed, it was a lie, I wasn't looking for a job, it was you I was looking for. Mark and I, we were lovers, but not anymore. So, you're welcome to stay but I perfectly understand if you don't want to.

This generosity of spirit lasted until the light faded and he stood on the balcony looking for signs of life in the surrounding flats. No beautiful people having a beautiful time, they had been bussed in for the photo shoot for the property catalogue. Alone, before the first glass of wine, his charitable offer died.

Listen, it's too late, they've managed beautifully without you, what are you expecting? To be greeted like a returning hero? All they ever needed was a bit of financial support and you never gave them a penny. No, they didn't tell me, they didn't have to, it was fucking obvious. Anyway it's all over for me; find your own hotel, you won't find anything cheap round the station, spend a bit of that cash you've saved over the years on child support.

Two weeks into term and he had established his special space in the library, in one of the far corners where he could still see who was coming in and out but the bustle around the main desk was far enough away. One morning he settled himself in early to complete an essay, it would have been as easy to do it at home but the silence of the flat was bringing him down.

There she was, not too close and not too far away so it was difficult to tell how deliberate her positioning was. Emma somebody or other, in the final year of the undergrad course, he saw her constantly round the department, they'd exchanged a few words at a seminar and he noticed she'd started to join his year at coffee breaks. Acknowledging her smile with a nod he turned back to his screen. It was difficult to tell but he thought she was quite petite under all the coloured layers, it was a world away from the bland corporate look Clare and his female colleagues sported and he wondered if he should abandon his suit this year for some distressed jeans and a sloganed t shirt. He carried on reading but remembering her easy laugh glanced at her again, he was, he admitted, quite interested.

She was also, as he expected, in the pub that Friday. He sat next to her and as they chatted drifted back to the night he first met Clare and how it had progressed. He leaned back and listened to her chatting to someone else, she could be his way back into the mainstream, he would take it very, very slowly, every decision would be hers. She moved away after a while though to talk to another man and the fact he didn't like it made him seek her out again and he got himself invited to a party that Saturday.

The chemical bitterness of the air freshener in the badly lit lobby made him hold his breath as he walked through to the lift. And why was the lift so pokey, and did anyone live behind the other three identical doors on his landing? Once inside the flat only worked with the curtains open and the lights twinkling on the canal below. Mark would have gone along with the place for a while possibly but he wouldn't have liked what it represented, the accumulation of wealth through buy to let, property ownership was a subject they avoided. As for flipping, the path Alex had encouraged him to follow, this was as far as it was going. It would be nice to be able to tell Mark that the past couple of years had put things more into perspective and he had a better idea of what mattered now and it wasn't the acquisition of property.

One evening, the lights off, he sat staring out across the water through his big glass windows, watching the bouncing lights. He'd run out of alcohol and the trip to the off licence along an empty road to an isolated shop at a cracking walk to demonstrate he wasn't an easy target at that time of night was tedious and worrying.

In a lecture one afternoon, the central heating too high and a subject matter that didn't engage him delivered in a quiet monotone, the reality of his current situation eased its way in. Sticking with his choice of Manchester, now that its original rationale had entirely gone, was plain stupid. The relief from his demons that he'd expected from applying himself single-mindedly to study was not materialising. Sex was troubling him, he was a freak, a body tourist, where was it all going? He would go and see a local GP for a low dose of what he'd had before, to see him through to the end of the course. No one would notice, he'd been declining a range of recreational drugs since he'd arrived, he would just be another dozy expression amongst a few other dozy expressions. Interestingly Emma had appeared quite keen for the joint being passed round when they first met though she too now declined, in line with him he supposed. They were settling into curry on the Friday night with the department crowd, the cinema on Saturday then back to the flat. One evening, sitting together on the settee he took Emma's arm for a moment and gave a few distracted and experimental squeezes.

'Hey! What are you looking for?' she laughed.

'Nothing. Your arms are so, little.'

'I don't go to the gym; did your last girlfriend go to the gym?'

'She did pilates.'

'How did it end, you and her?' It was the first time she had asked but it was so quick he knew it had been waiting.

'She died from Pilates-induced exhaustion; it's a pretty extreme sport you know.'

'Very funny, OK I won't ask anymore.'

It was all happening so quickly and David accepted he couldn't put it all down to her. By not telling her much she was filling the gaps with her own desires and hopes and these days, as he had a slightly better grasp of his own needs, he wondered was he doing the same. Dispensing with a couple of years you weren't proud of couldn't be dissimilar if you'd spent some time at her majesty's pleasure.

They appeared to be playing the same game; information was seized if it fitted or forgotten if it wasn't. They were sleeping together, it seemed rude not to, nevertheless brakes need to be applied.

'I can be a bit of a shit.'

'No you can't! Who said that?'

'It's been said that I'm selfish and avoid responsibility.'

'Well they don't know you.'

'And that I can't commit.' He told her about the cancellation of the wedding with all the drama of a cancelled hair appointment. She waited in vain for more to emerge; it was like he'd appeared out of the mist with a carrier bag. She Googled and found the school website, the journalism and the photos but no personal detail. Armed with this information, Emma delved.

'How long did you live in the favela?'

'A few weeks.'

'And you wanted to really experience living in a shanty town?'

'Yeah, so I could talk from experience for once.'

'So when you got back you decided to take a break from teaching to experiment with a more sustainable way of living?'

'Sort of.'

'That is so impressive, my friends and I are all talk, we recycle and ride bikes and turn the lights off but its pretty feeble, I mean you did the real thing!' Did you keep a diary; I mean you could write a book! So it was the favela that inspired you?'

'It wasn't easy.'

'Of course it wasn't, how long did you stick it out?'

'Oh about, about two years.' He downed another glass of Sauvignon quickly, the fabrication was getting easier as he worked his was through the bottle and it wasn't a *million* miles from the truth, was it?

'I'm so impressed! So many people talk about living like that but actually doing it? It must have been so hard, doing it all on your own and not being tempted to jump in the car or turn the heating up or buy a ready meal. You must have tremendous self control. And what about cleaning products and shampoo and razors, did you grow a beard?'

'Kind of.'

Only little lies but once he started they took a life of their own and it was what she wanted to hear. David's modesty was so enchanting Emma considered it her duty to release small pieces of information if only to demonstrate her special place in his life. A fable built up around him in the department, not only was he a published journalist and accomplished photographer but he put his money where his mouth was and had lived an alternative lifestyle, not with a camera crew in tow or in a protest camp but quietly, in an English terraced house.

Chapter Twenty Two

December 4th still brought him up short; its significance at the time had permanently burnt itself on his brain. How absurd it appeared now yet it had more of an impact than his own birthday. On the pretext of sending a birthday card he got Mark's address out of Abi then realised she'd tell him and he'd have to send one. He chose his favourite photo from Belize, a huge colourful parrot, sent it a day late and stuck his new address label next to 'all the best, Dave.' The effort to appear casual wound him up and caused lengthy self examination of his motives, OK, he was still holding a candle, albeit a guttering one but if Ralph's grungy appearance at the garden centre was anything to go by it would be out in seconds.

'I've got an old friend in Manchester; I haven't caught up with him yet,' he told Emma.

'Why not? Invite him over, I can cook for us while you chat over old times.'

'I was thinking of calling on him first, maybe this Saturday.'

'So why don't you?'

'OK I will.'

'Don't forget to show him your article, he'll be impressed.'

'Yeah, he'll be dead impressed.' It was highly unlikely he'd seen it, broke students didn't buy the Sundays, plus they were too busy sleeping off Saturday night.

The morning would be best, at eleven o' clock, they would

be up, just about, possibly getting dressed, ready to go out and having breakfast. By mid afternoon they'd be shopping, five would find them back talking about what to do that evening, he wanted to avoid an invitation to the pub, a refusal might sound superior and no invitation; disappointing. He would probably be invited to stop for a cup of coffee, which he'd accept saying he could only spare half an hour. He decided to go by bus so no chance of offering him a lift anywhere, that would be going too far. He really must get rid of the car, it wasn't sentiment that made him keep it though the car keys always reminded him of that appalling bedside scene but it was a good runner, why give that reassurance to a stranger for a couple of grand? He set off at precisely ten past ten; walk into town ten minutes, maximum wait for bus five minutes, journey time twenty five minutes with a five minute walk and five minutes for error. Please let it be chaotic with people asleep on the floor, let him talk like Ralf of uncompleted assignments and getting his shit together, let there be someone cute with his arm draped round his neck. On the bus he called Emma and arranged an early film, dinner and meeting up with his year in the pub.

The door was opened by a flustered girl with bare feet clutching at an untied dressing gown, 'they've all gone to work, d'you want me to tell him you called?'

Work? It hadn't crossed his mind, he'd always had a job so why not now. He stood his ground, 'could I leave a note?' She hesitated; he sensed she might refuse to let him in feeling vulnerable, half dressed. 'I'm a student here too,' he dug out his union card and swipe card. 'I'm a friend from home, David Ashbourne, he may have mentioned me.'

'Yeah, I mean no he hasn't but come in, his room's the one on the right at the top of the stairs, I've got to take a shower and I'm due at the restaurant at twelve, leave the note in his room.'

His bedroom door was slightly ajar and he hesitated before pushing it lightly open with his fingertips, not quite believing Mark wasn't inside. It was his bed that drew his eyes, a small double, he stared mesmerised. Why kid himself he thought, he just wanted to know how many people had got out of it that morning. The duvet was in a mound in the middle, there were two pillows, their positions not giving any particular indication whether they had been used by one or two heads. The bed had two side tables; one held the familiar clock/radio and a jumble of books, tissues and cups, the other, more books, again no indication of a regular sleeping companion. He instantly recognised the jacket hanging on the chair and other familiar items from his bedroom at home caught his breath. Moving further in he looked around and noticed a pin board on the wall next to the door. The parrot stood out from everything else on the board and it lifted his heart. That's enough, he thought, but it was impossible not to be curious and he stepped closer. Amongst timetables and notes there was a photo of Abi, Mrs Derby and Fletcher, photos of people he didn't recognise and the swimming photo, now he knew exactly which of the grinning boys was Jason. He smiled ruefully, Jason, familiar, charming, probably still in love with him, how stupidly nervous and jealous that photo used to make him. With an absurd touch of disappointment he could not see a photo of himself but there, together under one pin, printed on cheap photocopy paper were some of the photos he'd emailed him in America. They were a bit curly at the edges and he lifted them one by one, uncomfortable in remembering the part they'd played in rekindling their affair. The wardrobe door was open, he pushed the hangers along and found many familiar clothes and taking them out held them up like little ghosts. He could hear the shower still running and stood a while longer until the urge to lie on the bed and simply wait for him to return was so powerful he left the room quickly. He hadn't prepared himself to write a note and could think of nothing that in any way expressed how he felt. 'Thanks, I'll see myself out,' he called at the bathroom door; she may or may not remember to tell Mark he had called. If he still didn't know he was in the city he may not even recognise her description with an unfamiliar coat and hair that now covered his collar.

'A bloke came round looking for you this morning.'
'What sort of bloke?'
'About your height, dark hair, not bad, said he's a mature student. I was literally about to get in the shower when he arrived otherwise I'd have taken him into the kitchen, anyway he said he'd leave a note in your room.'

Mark launched himself up the stairs and at the door saw the room through David's eyes. Christ. It was bad. The gall of the bloke, the sickening gall to walk into his room when he was out. If he'd known he could have at least taken the pants off the floor and the dirty plates and the empty cans. His eyes swept the room, no note balanced on the detritus. He sank onto the bed, pulling one of the pillows under his head. Shaky with tiredness he closed his eyes; the restaurant had been full of children changing their minds, dropping cutlery, running around and disappointed parents wanting it to be a nice Saturday treat.

What if he'd been in? 'So,' he'd have asked, 'how's uni? Live up to my expectations?' It was tempting to say no and tempting to say yes, whichever way would be the most irritating. Truth was it was 50/50. The city itself had been engaging for the first two years, his first introduction to gritty Victorian architecture. And he himself had been a novelty; his faint West Country burr, the council estate, gay. But inside the student world his views were mild, other people's gap years more valuable, his final year at school something to be kept quiet about. Hall had been fun but this place was a dump; the petty disagreements over partners and guests overstaying and hot water usage and the last dregs of milk and whose turn it was to put out the bottles and clean out the fridge. All accompanied by the bluff bravado of the culpable; 'listen bro' and 'give us a break mate.' He got into arguments and harboured resentments then ended up doing it himself to keep the peace and because he couldn't stand the mess.

He wanted a car, a trip to Berlin, less housemates, money for rail fares, decent clothes. Worst of all he still had no idea what to do with his degree, something with people? Social work, housing, something vocational at post grad, he was waiting for it all to fall into place, he wanted to be one of those people who carried around their smug certainty about their future like they'd been let into a secret Ponzi scheme.

A photo on Jason's networking site rendered him silent for days. He had spotted David twice around the university, the second time with a small dark haired girl, not touching but talking intently. To have gone ahead and still chosen Manchester was, he decided, a sign of interest or spite.

'It's got nothing to do with you,' said a drunken confidant, 'he's got his own agenda and you're not on it anymore.'

He sat on the bed and picked up Bear who was tucked against the headboard. David had found the elderly beast stuffed in a box and insisted it had a place on the bed, sometimes interfering in their lovemaking, 'he gives great head when you aren't here,' always led to a pleasing tussle. He drifted back to the days they had spent methodically working their way through his childhood memorabilia, taking each item and assessing its nostalgic worth, placing it in piles for the charity shop, the bin, for storing or for continuing display. Amazing how much time he had devoted to the clearout, asking questions about each item, wanting to know its origin and how much he'd played with it, not pushing him to bin it, almost treating each piece and therefore his past, with reverence. He hadn't understood then that he was giving him his most precious commodity; time, that time equalled love. Here time was a loose concept, everyone claimed not to have any but had buckets and who needed punctuality these days when you could cancel with a text.

His phone rang, the guy he'd exchanged numbers with the previous night, did he want to meet up this evening? His on off boyfriend Tom would not be pleased; there would be another protracted discussion. He could easily blow all today's earnings this evening, just as he had done the previous Saturday and most Saturdays and then spend Sunday recovering. Two assignments lay unfinished on his desk. And where was the note? Anyway if he had left a note it would probably have suggested a drink or maybe dinner as well which would have meant a pep talk about keeping up with his work and a reminder about the good working practices he'd instilled in him and all that shit like he was still at school. It was so sneaky, spying on him, checking out his house and his room, the creep, the lousy fucking creep.

'Who was he?' Jackie asked later as he slumped in front of the TV, still not sure where his hard earned cash was gong to end up that evening.

'Oh just one of my ex teachers fer chrissakes, dunno why he turned up. If he appears again don't let him in, I'll tell the others.'

The monthly lunchtime talks were cosy affairs with an emphasis as much on the sandwich fillings as the academic rigour. Somebody from the previous session would be volunteered to organise the next which would be cobbled together at the last minute from a current, preferably controversial, news item. Occasionally someone interesting might be in town and be persuaded to give a couple of hours. Gordon, the departmental head, was on the verge of quietly abandoning them.

Most people in the department had read David's article, it had been referred to on the department website and a copy pinned to a board and it was no surprise Gordon asked him to do the December lecture. It wasn't often that the academics managed a crossover with populist journalism and made it to the Sunday supplements; there were jokes about geography as the new rock and roll or was that cooking or history or physics? His photos would certainly entertain but Gordon wanted to get a first-rate discussion going for once.

'If Gordon wants dry data I'm not the man,' he said to Emma, warming to a new popularist persona.

'Focus it round what we need and what we can do without in a resource-limited future.' She almost bounced off her chair. 'You can turn the shanty town round, are *they* showing us a sustainable way forward. And you can talk about how you tried to manage with minimum power and resources, for two years, I mean how many well off people have actually tried that. As the population explodes and most people live in urban areas will we be returning to a more simple way of life but still, as you said, be able to maintain all the positives of city life?'

He was bemused at the reinvention of his breakdown, but it didn't matter, by the time he'd shown the slides the usual suspects would have got into their stride and have taken the discussion over and his bunch of lies would be lost in the great future of the urban metropolis debate. He may even get some ideas for his next article.

A modest A4 poster on the department's notice board was all the publicity the lunchtime sessions usually got but Emma said why restrict it, hadn't the newspaper seen its universal appeal. It would be interesting to see how the discussion ranged if other disciplines were invited and he thought she was actually right and gave in quickly and the notice went on every student union board.

By ten am on the day, Emma, in charge of the catering, realised it was going to be wholly inadequate but more worryingly so was the usual room. David was sceptical about her figures but it was a filthy day and he'd been surprised at the number of 'see you at lunchtimes,' thrown his way that morning and as the minutes ticked to 12.30 Emma shot off for more supplies and Gordon stuck the poster on the larger lecture room next door.

'You know the stats, I knew the stats, it was pretty much all I knew and I wanted to see those stats at the micro level, the personal so here's Camilla.' And there she was, a big confident smile for the photographer, her guest from England, it was a brilliant opener to her immaculate and tiny home. 'First of all I thought, nice photos to liven up my lessons, the kids always liked my slides, they loved anything personal, but, well it was more than that and you don't take photos in the favelas, not if you want to leave without a few extra holes in you but I'm a photographer, and photographers take photos.' He showed them how he hung his smallest camera under his shirt and poked the lens between his shirt buttons and despite the very high failure rate the shots that came out painted a portrait of living with ingenuity and pride in one of the newer, more dangerous and less colourful favelas of Brazil.

Each slide of the interior of Camilla's house was partnered with a challenging analogy; the plastic washing up bowl: part of a simple camping holiday? The carefully placed ornaments; a proud display in a working class Victorian parlour? The fashion drawings glued on the cardboard walls; a St Martin's student? The uneven recycled wood shelves; today's ultra cool loft kitchen blending eco with the luxury of a bespoke fitting? And everything positioned and stored in the cramped space with the precision of a submarine. He took them on his walkabout, they saw the impermanence of the structures in initial land grabs being transformed to breeze blocks and brick houses, the original plastic sheeting and board mortared in but still peeping through like sandwich fillings to show their humble origins. He showed the astonishing spaghetti of cabling for borrowing electricity, the sickening reality of open sewers and the value of fresh water in the faces of those laboriously collecting it. He brought the misery and danger of the landslides close; photos of wooden supports poking out of the debris like broken limbs and close ups of soaking, irreclaimable clothes and toys stuck in the sticky mud. Here he spoke casually of his own attempts at minimalist living following the visit, seriously reducing his power and water consumption, no computer or car, simple food, making do. As he spoke to the attentive audience, the morsel of truth it contained and the reality of his mental breakdown behind it made his voice shake momentarily but he held it together surprising himself how such an appalling episode in his life could eventually be turned round. Then to end he flicked back and forth between the colourful three storey houses of the older Rio favelas that were beginning to attract tourists and the pastel frontages of Poundbury until it was difficult to tell the difference and they laughed. Why, at his best, he had kept the full attention of thirty fourteen year olds at the local comprehensive, he had this lot in his hand.

He turned to the group, numbering an unprecedented sixty and threw the discussion open, could they live like this, was it more sustainable than the way they lived, in the future would we all have to pare our lives down to such low levels of consumption or would the inhabitants of the favelas one day be the consumers that the middle class suburbs were today? Cities were bursting, the rural poor were continuing to flood in, how would they cope, how did people live at such close quarters, were the factions in the favelas a necessary evil? He sat back, it had gone well, the effort he'd put into making the photo sequence flow had been worth it, he let his eyes wander around the room, interested to see who had come along.

He was in the back row of chairs near the door, he saw him for a second before he shifted slightly behind the person in front. He saw him because he'd been looking for him, wanting him and dreading him turning up. David's eyes whipped away instantly back to his notes, he took a deep breath and tried to concentrate on the current speaker, focusing hard on her to minimise his peripheral vision. He'd heard his talk, he was listening to the discussion, everything he'd said, every throwaway line, every slight embellishment, every boast, knowing that it was all built on the outcome their failed love affair.

The lunchtime talks were usually quickly opened up into discussions, the original speaker, having presented them with something to chew over would sit back and let them chew. Today however they were interested in him and him alone, arms shot up, he tried to throw the discussion out but it was him they were fascinated in.

'Where was he going next? What was he currently working on? How did he see these metropolises in a hundred years? Had human habitation reached its zenith? Had we come full circle and would we return to hunter gathering, or live in nature reserves tended by robots more intelligent than us? Was he going back to teach in schools?

Then from the back, 'aren't you glamorising it? Comforting stodge for the Sunday morning colour supplement reading middle classes but it's a shitty, miserable way to live and they'd jump at the chance of something better, isn't it nicer to be a British organically reared cow?' There were a few sniggers.

'Interesting comparison from the back, I've seen some organically reared cows up to their hocks in shit but I'd like to think I was recording what I saw for those who haven't experienced a shanty town and that I was showing the ability of humans to be infinitely adaptable. The trend in the western world to single households can seem a lousy way to live if you've lived all your life six to a room. Humans are hard wired to live in villages, how many people do we really know? Real friends, not social networking friends, I think the figure is about one hundred and seventy. That's how cities work, thousands of villages.'

'You mentioned you'd tried to live more basically yourself, was this as a result of your trip? Is this something you've been considering for a while? Is it something you are continuing to do?' The same voice, not his but from his direction and David forced himself to look, it was the fellow sitting next to him. Had Mark put him up to it? David answered yes to everything; he gave the same answer and same story as he had to Emma who was sitting directly in front of him.

'I believe you own one of those new luxury flats at Salford

Quays? How does that square?' No sniggers now and people shifted in their chairs and someone growled, 'leave it *out!*'

'That's OK, I'm glad you mentioned that, yeah I do, a rash purchase I made a long time ago. Changing the way you feel about things can take time, you have to make a mistakes along the way, I've made mistakes along my way and I'm sure I've plenty more to make. If you want the truth I don't much like living there and won't be staying.' Mark remained hidden and his mouthpiece looked away.

After the longest lunchtime lecture to date, Gordon called time leaving disappointed hands still waving to ask questions and he thanked David who received enthusiastic applause. A little group formed immediately around David and Emma, with a disgruntled expression, sought out Gordon.

'What a spoilsport, I mean why turn up if that's your attitude!'

'Not at all, it livened it up, in fact it's the liveliest session we've ever had by far and that's exactly how I want it to be from now on. Over *sixty* people instead of the twenty usual faces, it's been far too complacent and inbred, it's time we got a bit of attention.'

Emma, confused, starts tidying up the paper plates and the group around David quizzes him about his plans for the future. He gives vague replies, his mind and thoughts are elsewhere, in fact they are somewhere behind him. The challenging remarks are clearly his friend's, he is too sensitive, there is no way he will disappear after those exchanges, he will have left his seat at the back and be standing quietly behind him, waiting to speak to him. David takes a deep breath to savour the moment, everything has its reason and it has worked out well. Gordon says he has to dash and David slips one hand into his trouser pocket and perches on a desk corner as he talks to demonstrate to him, waiting behind him, how relaxed and in control of the situation he is. He can handle challenging remarks, he's a published journo. When he turns round he will find him smiling hesitantly, unsure about the approach but his eyes will have that steady depth that made him so sure, all that time ago and he will shake his hand firmly, holding it a fraction longer than necessary. He takes another deep breath and swings round; finally they have both come to their senses.

He is not there.

Chapter Twenty Three

The women's clothing section of a large store might be an inspired film location to hold a lover's row between two men but the middle of a ploughed field would have been David's preference. He frequently used the store as a cut through as did a lot of other people and a few days after the lecture, on the way to a café lunch with Emma she paused to look at a new display. David waited, slightly impatiently in the busy passageway between the food and clothes.

His hands in the pockets of his flapping coat, *the* coat, he was coming the other way talking animatedly to a man alongside. By the time he saw him it was too late and too obvious to dive further into the women's clothes and to turn his back was hideous. David made sure he was the first to acknowledge.

'Hello Mark.'

'Alright?'

'Not bad, and you?'

'Not bad. Er.. this is Tom.'

'Hi Tom.' The mouthpiece.

'Hi,' Tom stared.

Emma had her back to them, holding a top up against herself, peering down at it, checking its length. The two men were clearly on their way somewhere, nice to see you and see you around was all that was necessary David decided.

'I hear you called in on me. Why didn't you leave a note?'

There he was, barely three incredible feet away. David saw

he'd been right comparing his appearance to Ralph's.

'I didn't know what to say,' he said in a tone that denied the tortured debate he'd had with himself as he stood in the room.

'You went in my room.'

'Yeah, very briefly but, well I decided to phone next time, or text.'

'I went to your lecture, pretty good, worth the trip to Sao Paul then?'

'Yes, it turned out useful in the end.'

'Crap for me, I think you know why.'

'Yeah.' He glanced across at Emma, hoping she'd move further away but she looked up and came over immediately and he introduced her. They all stared at one another, they were blocking the thoroughfare and David took a step closer towards the rails of clothes to get out of the way. Agree to arrange a drink by text, he thought, say goodbye and go.

'Enjoying uni?'

'Yeah, it's totally brilliant, just like you said it'd be.'

'That's good then.'

'Seen Jase recently?'

'I don't think this is the place… '

'Didn't take you long to get stuck in there.'

'Things happen. Listen I really don't….'

There was no corner to slide into, to say his piece in private, of all the fucking places to finally meet him, with Tom in tow and some woman.

'I changed my mind, Jase was supposed to tell you.'

'I don't know about that…' A woman flicking her way through the hangers on a rail beside them moved between them. 'I really don't think this is the place Mark….'

'That was the sickest thing, bet you had a laugh when you heard that.'

'Yeah, it's all been one long laugh.' David raised his eyebrows and drew his head back in mock distain, then leaned forward with his back to Tom, 'Didn't you hear the gossip from home? How shall I sum up the horror? I had a breakdown and haven't taught in a school for two years and probably never will again. Right, it was really nice to meet you again but I think we should all move on now.'

'Hey,' Emma pulled his sleeve, her head twisted awkwardly away from the scene.

They were beginning to become a small spectacle, people staring as they manoeuvred round them, the woman stuck between them sharply pulled a top off the rail and bustled away to the changing room, but paused before she got there to look back. With a few deft swings round the islands of railed garments, David was out of the shop with Emma trailing behind him. At the swing doors they struggled to get past workers on route for their lunchtime wrap and ready meal for dinner and found a quiet space to stand. David stood with his hands in his pockets, staring into the traffic.

'What was that all about?' she said, her voice wavering.

Who ever it was up there that was pulling his strings had really done a very comprehensive job this time, maybe the string puller was tired of leaving 'openings' because that was quite definitely *it* and as his heart rate slowed, a faint sense of relief waded in. He recalled a US general's dry opinion on moving into Afghanistan.

'That was the rubble of my broken heart being smashed into even smaller bits of rubble in full public view,' he paraphrased, impressed he could even make a joke of it, sort of. Not the closure he had hoped for though, the quiet transformation to the wholesome friendship it should always have stayed. All he ever wanted was a quiet life.

'Who was *he*?'

Have the decency to let her lose interest in you, very fast he ordered.

'I've been telling you what you wanted to hear, no, no that's *shite*. I've been *lying* to you. He's my ex.'

'Ex what?'

He told her enough to make her bite her bottom lip so it disappeared, for two hard creases he hadn't seen before to appear between her eyebrows and for her eyes to lose all their sparkle; yet again he'd killed the sparkle in someone's eyes. He didn't apologise or dip his head or make any gesture that conveyed any regret or guilt, she could make her own mind up about him and convey it to anyone she pleased. Finish your dissertation then get the hell out he ordered himself.

Chapter Twenty Four

It was through one of the district engineers in Deli that he met the Singhs and their lively younger daughter was happy to have her day documented for one of David's profiles. They offered their couch and their older son Ravinder was eager to interrogate his guest.

'It was a man wasn't it?' Ravinder asked cautiously as they settled into an evening beer a week into his stay, 'it was a man you left your fiancée for.'

'Yeah, it was, sorry; I wasn't sure how to play it, with your Mum there.'

'She would have smiled and been very polite and talked of nothing else once we'd left.'

'What gave it away?

'Um…tall, skinny, huge grin, liked arguing, it's not how we describe girls we like. And you didn't look very comfortable telling us. Tell me about your life in the UK, I really want to go there.'

'You could say I ran away from it.'

'But you're going back?'

'I have to; the money's running out, back to the classroom for me.'

Which was what anyone would expect him to say but did the classroom want *him*? How far had the gossip got? Would the Head's promise of a good reference hold? Frankly the prospect made his stomach churn. And the textbook was shaky. And he feared his favela article had been a one off, written when he was high on shock and could write pictures. The blog was doing well though.

'What are you going to write about tomorrow?' Asked Ravinder, 'I'm really enjoying it, my photo last week has developed a fan club.'

'Your lift attendant, the older one, he intrigues me, how he nurses that creaking old contraption up and down all day with such job satisfaction. And the little repair workshops in the market we went to yesterday. Everything in India is repaired; battered cases, jewellery, plastic shoes, cooking equipment all ingeniously given a second or third life.'

'What's the big deal about mending stuff? Don't you mend things in the UK?'

India. No matter another continent and the distraction of blistering heat, unspeakable toilets and constantly saying no to unwanted goods and services. No matter that from the moment he woke the sounds, sight, smells and especially the tastes of Asia occupied all his senses. In between the distractions David was disappointed to find he was still carrying around the same old guilty, confused and unhappy head. At the end of his day, after he had closed his laptop and before he sought some company for dinner from the guest house or the hostel, everyone from back home jostled in, most of them living lives at least three years out of date. His self imposed news starvation from home was keeping everything on the pause button and he was carrying old news round like a shell on his back. Did he want to know if Clare had a new boyfriend? That Alistair had followed his advice and found someone to manage the business properly and if Shirley had bought a flat in Antibes? He didn't.

Two more beers were ordered. 'Do you have a big family?' David grasped the glass and threw it back. The explanation about Jeff came out remarkably easily, Ravinder was sympathetic; they too had lost a sister. A quiet calmness descended, maybe India was working.

The bar door swung open, the two men turned in idle

curiosity as three Westerners came in and sat nearby. They were speaking English and David tuned into their conversation, trying to pick out their nationalities. One, David picked up a Dutch accent, looked up and caught David's eye. The following evening David separated the Dutchman willingly from his companions, took him to a back street restaurant and made love to him in a high-ceilinged room under a sluggish fan just like he'd once imagined whilst lying on a bed in a council house in England. There he discovered his companion's body was so perfect he could barely close his eyes at night and every ounce of denial about men he was hanging onto died as he held him in his arms. He kept him for as long as he could but the lad moved on, as backpackers are wont to do and it was a shock. The respite this incredible continent had given came to a sudden end. Where was he? What was he doing?

Mark slumped heavily onto a bench in Crewe station and tucking his rucksack between his knees prepared for the ten minute wait for his connecting train. It was not to be, the tannoy gave any credulous passengers one minute before announcing a half hour delay and he was experienced enough to know this was bound to be optimistic. The Victorian arches stretching the length of the station asked to be counted, that took about a minute, he felt for his paperback but he'd lost both his place and his interest and his phone wasn't delivering much joy these days either. The winding down of the house share was generating a lot of texts with complex figure work as they argued over remaining bills and the agreeably complicated love triangle he was mixed up in was now going nowhere as two of them drifted back home. Effectively Manchester was over, their lease had ended and no one he cared about was hanging around; rent free parental homes were calling them back like economic sirens. It wasn't how he'd imagined it. David's friends for life scenario looked as realistic as a certain long-running American comedy.

327

Alistair had rung, probably prompted by his mother. 'Did you have a good time? He'd asked as if Mark had been away for the weekend which was about as much as the man could bear to imagine himself or anyone else going away for. 'Can you start work on Monday?' It wasn't so much that he hadn't had a good time, it was more that he hadn't planned for it ending, endings were hard work. A lot of the three years were now very hazy, but it was over and the whole point of it all, to start on the career ladder, didn't seem to be happening. He should be investigating graduate training schemes and filling in applications forms but instead they were squabbling over the house deposit. The garden centre was his schoolboy past; he could not drift back as if the past three years had never happened.

The station was now quiet, passengers from his train had slunk to the bar to wait or were on their phones, he counted the arches again and with no other distractions sank into the disaster that awaited at home. Last year his father had made contact.

'All I did was email him back, you'd think I'd invited Hitler home, it was a bloodbath,' he'd said to his friends to try to turn something that had gone spectacularly wrong into something amusing. His mother's reaction had left him reeling.

'He's not coming anywhere near *this house*,' she'd hissed and money, a subject they'd rarely touched, broke its banks and the relentless penny pinching truth of the previous years poured out. Here Mark got confused, did she want Martin to see how she'd successfully worked her way out of the mess he'd left her in or did she want him to see she was still struggling, with a view to asking for a financial settlement? Mark knew that she knew Martin wasn't dead because the Christmas card from her sister in law sent without fail for eleven years said nothing in particular but was confirmation he was still alive, she would have said if he wasn't. She would hand it to Mark in silence every year, their secret from Abi. Abi had reacted to the news that her father was in fact very much alive and doing very nicely on the other side of the world like any good teenage girl; she had thrown herself into her room and sulked.

'If your dad had been around that lechy schoolteacher'd never have got a look in, easy pickings,' said Tom.

Mark had met his father in a pub as his mother wouldn't even have him walk up the front path and it was here Martin dropped the bombshell, 'I've made an arrangement to stay with a teacher I met not long after you visited me, by coincidence he happens to live in town.' Instantly Mark made the connection and as he struggled to take the information in, a cheque was proffered which was substantial enough to set him up in a rented flat for a year. Miserably he'd stumbled over it; it was as hard to accept as to refuse and asked for time to think. He wanted it very badly but it was the ultimate disloyalty to his mother, a great wodge of cash that reeked of guilt and was too late anyway, all the scrimping had been done. If he had found Martin a failure would that have been better? He imagined such a figure returning to the UK and touching him and his mother for money, why couldn't he be proud of the way his dad had turned things round? The temptation of the cheque, the hideous scene in the shop with David and his imminent return home were all undoing any satisfaction he might feel for his 2.1. He wanted to pay David back, not just the hospital bedside loan but the gifts and the meals and drinks because it would represent a final severance from the liaison which he could not place where he wanted it placed; in the past with his GCSEs and school tie and school memories. Handing over the exact amount, no more and no less, would buy himself back he decided. Tomorrow his resolve would be severely tested, Martin had returned for a second business trip. They were meeting up again where the cheque would probably be pressed again but he knew he would refuse it, politely.

Angela Derby had let Mark know David had had a

breakdown when he returned home after his second year. He didn't want to ask how she knew or what it meant exactly or how to express the correct amount of concern and indifference for her consumption. Not exactly understanding the condition the word breakdown became literal in Mark's mind; David's bones snapped, he fell to the ground, he broke. Whatever it was though Mark decided it had nothing to do with him but it made him wonder at his mother's complicit acceptance over the year. She had admired the makeover, heard the laughter from the bedroom, seen his grades soar and watched Abi's maths improve. During his final year, the urge for news agitated him, he googled David, then started regularly checking into his life. He cropped up in forums, he discovered an anonymous blog that seemed to fit him and then there was the academic paper. Mark saved them and hid them, like pornography, in an anonymous file.

The wooden platform bench was getting uncomfortable, he wished he'd set off a lot earlier in the day, he didn't have a key and his mother would have gone to bed early ready for an early shift. Home was now an unfamiliar room; his stuff in boxes.

Someone sank onto the far end of the bench he was sitting on. 'Any idea what's caused the delay?'

He'd noticed him get on the train and passed him on the way to the buffet, his head resting on his neatly rolled up coat like the man was used to making himself comfortable in uncomfortable places and a shape that suggested he didn't spend his days at a computer. There was a faded blue mark on his arm peeping out from his t shirt sleeve which suggested the services or ex services maybe. He's picking me up, thought Mark.

'Well it can't be snow or leaves on the line as it's June so umm... rails buckling in the searing heat? No, not that either, 'Mark smiled at him; a little teasing would test his interest.

'It'll be the light drizzle then,' a nice set of teeth grinned back.

The bloke would offer a cigarette and they'd wonder if you could smoke on the platforms and then he'd say how about a quick half and he'd find out where Mark was heading and he'd wonder if he might miss his next connection and whether it might not be better to give up and take a hotel, together, to save money of course. The tannoy announced a further twenty minute wait. Mark glanced at his watch and calculated how long and how much it would cost to get to his bed, factoring in the inevitable taxi the other end.

'Cigarette? Dunno if you can smoke on the platforms mind. D'you fancy a swift half?

By early June David had made his way down to Kerala where he wanted to experience an important event before flying home. He hoped that the silence of his kitchen table in the UK might stimulate something more creative than his laptop had been producing recently, the dream of earning a living through travel writing was fading fast. The teenage profiles for the textbook were being well received thank goodness.

He chose a decent guest house for his final week, the area was cheaper than Mumbai and he sometimes recalled how he might have traveled with Clare and the money they would have spent. In the garden, under the shade of a tree he forced himself to consider his return; with who and how he would renew contacts. A couple were standing on the hotel steps, British; he'd seen them the previous morning at breakfast. He smiled and indicated the darkening sky.

'When d'you think it'll start?' they asked.

'Within the hour, those dark clouds in the distance are boiling with energy, they can't get here fast enough, they are so *waterlogged* they can barely hold it in. I'm going to get a bicycle rickshaw into town, I want to see the drama. Do you want to come or will I be a gooseberry with the honeymooners?'

'We haven't got the plague, we'd love to come with you!'

He wanted relief from the oppressive heat and the smell

as much as any of the local people he'd met. He wanted to experience for himself, the transformation of the streets, people's reaction, the relief and joy that the waiting was over and the concern about flooding.

'We're not sure about how it works.'

'High pressure moves into areas of low pressure and here, in India, because the land is so baking hot the air pressure is very low so the high pressure over the sea rushes in picking up moisture from the sea on the way,' he explained as they bumped along. 'Don't expect light drizzle.'

'Are you going to stand in it, we want to stand in it and have our photos taken.'

'Then I'm your man. I have been known to whip my kit off in my enthusiasm but I think I may end up in the local nick if I do it here.'

'How long have you been in India, you don't seem like a backpacker, are you working here?'

'I'm helping update a series of geography textbooks for ten to fourteens, I'm doing research for a PhD and trying to get some academic articles published. And I've been keeping out of the UK.'

'Why, have you done something terrible?'

'Not unless making an art form of pissing people off is something terrible.'

'You seem too nice!'

'Precisely, it gets them every time. Sorry, I'm being rude. It got to the point where I felt it was better if I put a few continents between me and the UK.'

'So you're staying permanently?'

'No, I'm going back next week, I've got to have drafts ready in a fortnight so I'm hunkering down at home to finish them off.'

'And have you always done this sort of work?'

'No I used to be a school teacher, in a mixed comprehensive.'

'Bet the girls liked you!'

'Laura!'

'He knows what I mean, don't you?'

'It's OK, no the girls thought I was geeky, very uncool. Being a geek has its advantages, you could let a geek loose in a harem and they'd all be crowding round with their crashed laptops and he'd be going 'go to control panel, go to programs.'

'I bet there were some secret crushes.'

'You learn to deal with them quickly,' he leaned quickly out of the cab, 'how about we get out around here, it's going to start any minute.'

They stood in the street and watched the black rolling sky while around them people were dragging possessions undercover and to higher ground, the performance was about to begin. A few elephantine drops bounced off their heads and noses, they braced themselves and gasped as it arrived, so heavy it didn't seem real, as if some over enthusiastic film technician had set the rain machine on max. David felt for his camera, he could barely see, already they were paddling, he watched the drains fill up and little waves washed against their ankles as the scooters and rickshaw bikes struggled past. He took the couple's camera and snapped them laughing and motioned with his hands to draw them together for a drenched kiss. Braced against the onslaught he walked on and found a glistening cow, her long lashes blinking the rain indifferently out of her eyes, women lifted their saris a modest inch or two as they scurried along under makeshift head covers and people crouched under the awnings of their shops, anxiously watching the water rise towards their stock. The monsoon had finally come, he'd been waiting for it, it was time to go home.

Instead of a dash for the last train after his delayed touchdown at Heathrow David remembered Jason's exhaustion and took a hotel for the night in London and a late afternoon train home. There was no need to rush; he hadn't primed anyone of his arrival though he intended to renew a few contacts eventually. Finally he had achieved a genuine distance from the mess up, the dread of anyone showing any pity had gone. He had successfully reinvented himself and looked forward to presenting a fresh him.

Apart from a few tractors towing giant round hay bales on trailers the countryside struck him as virtually abandoned compared to India as it flashed past the train window. He had been away nearly six months; it was going to take a good few days to adapt to not being constantly part of a crowd and to being on his own at home. Martin Derby had returned to the UK and David's house for a second visit last month. After the first email Martin had duly rung to suggest a pint after he'd arrived in town. The pint turned into four and like some idiot David had vaguely suggested that Martin could stay in his spare room. Martin explained his real reason for returning; to re-establish contact with his children and David had revealed nothing, he was pretty sure. Martin's generous rent and company hadn't been so bad over the week he stayed and David felt confident to leave the man in his house when he set off. It was just after he'd arrived in India that he knew the game was up, in a short email Martin told David his daughter was coming round. There had been nothing else for a week then one line, 'I've knocked your back garden into shape, hope you don't mind.'

As he neared the house in the early evening he wasn't surprised to see the hall light on, Martin said he was going to leave a few lights on for security when he left. In some ways it might have been nice to overlap, the bloke wasn't a bad cook; he had a kind way of making too much as if it was a mistake. Opening the front door he stopped, the sound of chopping, sharp and rhythmic, was coming from the kitchen, oh well, the guy was still here, that would be OK, there would be dinner, he wouldn't have to have a take away.

'Hi,' he looked into the kitchen.

'Hi,' he says and puts down the knife. There's a pile of chopped onions on the board and chicken pieces and tomatoes and potatoes, some sort of chicken casserole is being made. The scene is so domestic, what limited kitchen equipment there is, he's using it. David's heart starts to pound, is some appalling joke being played, has he misread Martin, is the man finally getting his own back for being hood winked? Is Martin suddenly going to appear?

'Why are you here?' David says coldly, 'what are you doing in my kitchen?'

Mark puts down the knife and turns to look at him. David's forgotten that he's taller and there is no doubt that in the three years since he has been able to look at him closely he has changed. His face is squarer and there is a lot more facial hair to shave, the boyishness is going. This has got to be something to do with Martin, how else could he have got into the house?

'Well?' he meets his eyes, 'what are you doing here?'

'Dad said you get maudlin after three pints.'

'Always have done.'

'About me.'

'I've never mentioned your name to him.'

'He thinks you're waiting to get on with life, it's like you need rescuing, from yourself,' and he stretches out his arm and touches David's hand.

David swallows, he moves sideways so the hand falls away. There may not have been boundaries once but there are now, he'll be polite but Martin's interference after everything he's done for him is seriously out of order.

'Load of new agey mumbo jumbo, I don't need fucking *rescuing* from anybody, I'm tired of being made a fool of. Listen, it's been a long time, I'm not the person you once knew, I've had some very difficult times, I've been around a lot of blocks. Anyway you can't just pick up where you left off if that's your intention, *you* told me that a few years ago you may recall.'

'You're not brilliant at seeing the obvious.'

'Clearly not, what is it?'

His voice falters, 'you think you're the only person that has difficult times, you don't see that everyone makes the best of what they have. It's a struggle for everyone…'

'In other words I'm self indulgent, I wallow, thanks, but it has been said before.'

'I'll go.'

There he goes, David thinks, they could be back in his bedroom on that first visit, testing each other out, advancing and retreating. And yes, he admits he makes it hard work, for everyone including himself. But every nerve is screaming to give in, to pull him into his arms and hold him, but he can't, pain has become his companion. 'I'm back to sort out some business with my publisher then I'm going to Cambodia and Vietnam in four weeks. I'm sure you have a busy schedule ahead of you. I'm not quite sure what you're doing here.'

'I know you're going away again, I'm coming with you,' the hand is replaced on his.

This is quite unbelievable, why does he think that a few second hand sentimental drunken confessions mean anything? He doesn't deny he said things to Martin, the bloke encouraged him to drink more than he had intended but Mark should know by now that alcohol loosened stuff that should stay in deep filing. If he's suggesting that asking Martin to stay at his place was a way of renewing contact he only did it out of a sense of decency. His head drops, of all the reconciliations he has played with in his imagination this is not one of them. He can see a pile of chopped vegetables and wonders what he will do with them when Mark goes, he's still not good at cooking vegetables. Is there no end to this, at what point do they move on and what is keeping the thread alive? Any rekindled feeling would quickly wither in the harsh light of the ordinary lives they now lead, can't they just accept that what they had had worked because it was so exceptional, so *inappropriate*?

Mark lets go of his hand and places it on David's waist, it's a bold move but his hand is steady. When was the last time they touched, the day of the exam? How terrified he had been that Mark would refuse to go in, everyone ready to pounce on him and destroy him. He is still the same terrified person, he can think of nothing to do about it because he doesn't know what the right thing to do is anymore; he needs rescuing.

'You'll have to lend me some money, for the fare.'

'*What* a surprise.'

'I'll pay you back, promise, I'll get some work when we get back.'

David shuts his eyes and takes his hands out of his pocket and they stand quietly for a minute. He leans forward; a faint smell of onions, something soapy, a light touch of stubble on his cheek. Slowly his hand slips onto Mark's waist and he lets his fingers press hard enough to feel the heat of his body. His other hand does the same and he sighs as the body sinks against his. It is beyond wonderful.

'It won't last,' he murmurs into his hair, smiling and smiling.

Dear Reader,

Thank you for reading my book, I would be delighted if you reviewed it on Amazon or Goodreads.com.

If you would like an advanced reader copy of my next novel please send me your email address.

regards,
D.Bunyan

d.bunyan1@btinternet.com

www.ingramcontent.com/pod-product-compliance
Lightning Source LLC
Chambersburg PA
CBHW030409180626
46812CB00005B/1983